W9-AEM-981

PRAISE FOR *ON THE COME UP*

Entertainment Weekly Best YA Book of 2019

Time's Best Young Adult and Children's Books of 2019

NPR Best Books of 2019

Variety Best YA Books of 2019

Boston Globe–Horn Book Award Honor Book for Fiction

Washington Post's Best Books of 2019

Booklist Editors' Choice Books for Youth 2019

Paste Magazine Best Young Adult Novels of 2019

Dallas Morning News Best Books of 2019

YALSA 2020 Best Fiction for Young Adults Nominee

Junior Library Guild Selection

Horn Book Best Children's & YA Books of 2019

Kirkus Best Books of 2019

Shelf Awareness Best Children's & Teen Books of 2019

Multnomah County Library Best Books of 2019

"For all the struggle in this book, Thomas rarely misses a step as a writer. Thomas continues to hold up that mirror with grace and confidence. We are lucky to have her, and lucky to know a girl like Bri."—*NEW YORK TIMES BOOK REVIEW*

"This book beckons young readers and music lovers alike with an homage to the forefathers of hip-hop that also assures the feminine voice is never dismissed from the cypher."
—*THE WASHINGTON POST*

"*On the Come Up* offers a complicated, imperfect heroine who lives and breathes her truth on every page."
—*ENTERTAINMENT WEEKLY*

"*On the Come Up* is earnest and warm-hearted, a careful examination of social issues that's built around an immensely endearing main character. It's likely to assure Thomas's continued and well-deserved dominance on the bestseller lists."—VOX

"Bri's story is utterly compelling from first to last."
—*USA TODAY*

★ "This follow-up to Thomas's landmark *The Hate U Give*, set in the same fictional city after the events of that book, demonstrates again Thomas's gift for crackling dialogue, complex characterization, and impactful emotion. Readers already lining up for this title won't be disappointed."
—*BCCB* (starred review)

★ "While acknowledging that society is quick to slap labels onto black teens, the author allows her heroine to stumble and fall before finding her footing and her voice. Thomas once again fearlessly speaks truth to power; a compelling coming-of-age story for all teens."—*SLJ* (starred review)

★ "*On the Come Up* truly shines in its exploration of Bri's resilience, determination, and pursuit of her dreams. In this splendid novel, showing many facets of the black identity and the black experience, Thomas gives readers another dynamic protagonist to root for."
—ALA *BOOKLIST* (starred review)

★ "This honest and unflinching story of toil, tears, and triumph is a musical love letter that proves literary lightning does indeed strike twice. The rawness of Bri's narrative demonstrates Thomas's undeniable storytelling prowess. A joyous experience awaits. Read it. Learn it. Love it."
—*KIRKUS REVIEWS* (starred review)

★ "With sharp, even piercing, characterization, this indelible and intricate story of a young girl who is brilliant and sometimes reckless, who is deeply loved and rightfully angry at a world that reduces her to less than her big dreams call her to be, provides many pathways for readers."
—*THE HORN BOOK* (starred review)

★ "Thomas introduces readers to an unforgettable cast of characters who seek to thrive in close-knit neighborhoods also shaped by violence and systemic racism. Bri is a fully realized character who is both sympathetic and, occasionally, maddeningly impulsive, and the well-crafted dialogue, with some laugh-out-loud shade throwing, propels the dramatic plot."
—*PUBLISHERS WEEKLY* (starred review)

★ "Thomas's work is multifaceted and unusual. This young adult novel breathes life into the art and struggle of 'starting from the bottom.'"
—SHELF AWARENESS (starred review)

ON THE COME UP

ANGIE THOMAS

BALZER + BRAY
An Imprint of Harper Collins*Publishers*

Balzer + Bray is an imprint of HarperCollins Publishers.

Emojis by Premium Vector / Shutterstock,
Denis Gorelkin / Shutterstock, and Anas Mannaa / Shutterstock

Lettering by Jay Roeder / Good Illustration (pages 459, 477, 479, 484, 487)

On the Come Up
 For information address
HarperCollins Children's Books, a division of
HarperCollins Publishers, 195 Broadway, New York, NY 10007.
www.epicreads.com

Library of Congress Control Number: 2018933132
ISBN 978-0-06-299934-4

Typography by Jenna Stempel-Lobell
20 21 22 23 24 PC/LSCH 10 9 8 7 6 5 4 3 2 1
❖
Collector's Edition, 2020

For the kids with the SoundCloud accounts
and the big dreams. I see you.
And for my mom, who saw it in me first.

PART ONE

OLD SCHOOL

ONE

I might have to kill somebody tonight.

It could be somebody I know. It could be a stranger. It could be somebody who's never battled before. It could be somebody who's a pro at it. It doesn't matter how many punch lines they spit or how nice their flow is. I'll have to kill them.

First, I gotta get the call. To get the call, I gotta get the hell out of Mrs. Murray's class.

Some multiple-choice questions take up most of my laptop, but the clock though. The clock is everything. According to it, there are ten minutes until four thirty, and according to Aunt Pooh, who knows somebody who knows somebody, DJ Hype calls between four thirty and five thirty. I swear if I miss him, I . . .

Won't do shit 'cause Mrs. Murray has my phone, and Mrs. Murray's not one to play with.

I only see the top of her Sisterlocks. The rest of her is hidden behind her Nikki Giovanni book. Occasionally she goes "Mmm" at some line the same way my grandma does during a sermon. Poetry's Mrs. Murray's religion.

Everyone else cleared out of Midtown School of the Arts almost an hour ago, except for us juniors whose parents or guardians signed us up for ACT prep. It's not guaranteed to get you a thirty-six, but Jay said I better get close since she "paid these folks a light bill" for this class. Every Tuesday and Thursday afternoon, I drag myself into this classroom and hand my phone over to Mrs. Murray.

Usually I'm cool with an entire hour of not knowing what the president tweeted. Or getting texts from Sonny and Malik (sometimes about shit the president tweeted). But today, I wanna go up to that desk, snatch my phone from the pile, and run out of here.

"Psst! Brianna," someone whispers. Malik's behind me, and behind him Sonny mouths, *Anything yet?*

I tilt my head with a *How am I supposed to know, I don't have my phone* eyebrow raise. Yeah, that's a lot to expect him to get, but me, Sonny, and Malik have been tight since womb days. Our moms are best friends, and the three of them were pregnant with us at the same time. They call us the "Unholy Trinity" because they claim we kicked in their bellies whenever they were together. So nonverbal communication? Not new.

Sonny shrugs with an *I don't know, I'm just checking*, mixed in with *Damn, you ain't gotta catch an attitude.*

I narrow my eyes at his little light-skinned Hobbit-looking behind—he's got the curly hair and the big ears. *I don't have an attitude. You asked a dumb question.*

I turn around. Mrs. Murray eyes us over the top of her book with a little nonverbal communication of her own. *I know y'all not talking in my class.*

Technically we're not *talking*, but what I look like telling her that, verbally or nonverbally?

4:27.

Three minutes and that phone will be in my hand.

4:28.

Two minutes.

4:29.

One.

Mrs. Murray closes her book. "Time's up. Submit your practice test as is."

Shit. The test.

For me, "as is" means not a single question is answered. Thankfully, it's multiple choice. Since there are four choices per question, there's a 25 percent chance that I'll randomly choose the right one. I click answers while everyone else collects their phones.

Everyone except Malik. He towers over me as he slips his jean jacket over his hoodie. In the past two years, he went from being shorter than me to so-tall-he-has-to-bend-to-hug-me. His high-top fade makes him even taller.

"Damn, Bri," Malik says. "Did you do any of the—"

"Shhh!" I submit my answers and sling my backpack over my shoulder. "I did the test."

"Long as you're prepared to take an L, Breezy."

"An L on a practice test isn't really an L." I throw my snap-back on, pulling the front down enough so it can cover my edges. They're a little jacked at the moment and will stay jacked until Jay braids my hair.

Sonny beat me getting to Mrs. Murray's desk. He goes for my phone like the true ride-or-die he is, but Mrs. Murray grabs it first.

"That's okay, Jackson." She uses his real name, which happens to be my last name. His momma named him in honor of my grandparents, her godparents. "I need to talk to Brianna for a second."

Sonny and Malik both look at me. *What the hell did you do?*

My eyes are probably as wide as theirs. *Do I look like I know?*

Mrs. Murray nods toward the door. "You and Malik can go. It'll only take a moment."

Sonny turns to me. *You're fucked.*

Possibly. Don't get me wrong; Mrs. Murray is sweet, but she does not play. One time, I half-assed my way through an essay about Langston Hughes's use of dreams. Mrs. Murray went in on me so bad, I wished Jay would've gone in on me instead. That's saying something.

Sonny and Malik leave. Mrs. Murray sits on the edge of the desk and sets my phone beside her. The screen is dim. No call yet.

"What's going on, Brianna?" she asks.

I look from her to the phone and back. "What you mean?"

"You were extremely distracted today," she says. "You didn't even do your practice test."

"Yes, I did!" Kinda. A little. Sorta. Not really. Nah.

"Girl, you didn't submit any answers until a minute ago. Honestly? You haven't been focused for a while now. Trust me, when you get your report card next week, you'll see proof. Bs don't turn to Cs and Ds for nothing."

Shit. "Ds?"

"I gave you what you earned. So what's going on? It's not like you've been missing class lately."

Lately. It's been exactly a month since my last suspension, and I haven't been sent to the principal's office in two weeks. That's a new record.

"Is everything okay at home?" Mrs. Murray asks.

"You sound like Ms. Collins." That's the young, blond counselor who's nice but tries too hard. Every single time I get sent to her, she asks me questions that sound like they came from some "How to Talk to Statistical Black Children Who Come to Your Office Often" handbook.

How is your home life? (None of your business.)

Have you witnessed any traumatic events lately, such as shootings? (Just because I live in the "ghetto" doesn't mean I dodge bullets every day.)

Are you struggling to come to terms with your father's murder? (It was twelve years ago. I barely remember him or it.)

Are you struggling to come to terms with your mother's addiction? (She's been clean for eight years. She's only addicted to soap operas these days.)

What's good with you, homegirl, nah'mean? (Okay, she hasn't said that, but give her time.)

Mrs. Murray smirks. "I'm just trying to figure out what's up with you. So what's got you so distracted today that you wasted my time and your momma's hard-earned money?"

I sigh. She's not giving me that phone until I talk. So fine. I'll talk. "I'm waiting on DJ Hype to tell me I can battle in the Ring tonight."

"The Ring?"

"Yeah. Jimmy's Boxing Ring. He has freestyle battles every Thursday. I submitted my name for a chance to battle tonight."

"Oh, I know what the Ring is. I'm just surprised *you're* going in it."

The way she says "you're" makes my stomach drop, as if it makes more sense that anyone else in the world would go in the Ring except for me. "Why are you surprised?"

She puts her hands up. "I don't mean anything by it. I know

you've got skills. I've read your poetry. I just didn't know you wanted to be a rapper."

"A lot of people don't know." And that's the problem. I've been rapping since I was ten, but I've never really put myself out there with it. I mean yeah, Sonny and Malik know, my family knows. But let's be real: Your mom saying you're a good rapper is like your mom saying you're cute when you look a hot mess. Compliments like that are part of the parental responsibilities she took on when she evicted me from her womb.

Maybe I'm good, I don't know. I've been waiting for the right moment.

Tonight may be the perfect time, and the Ring is the perfect place. It's one of the most sacred spots in Garden Heights, second only to Christ Temple. You can't call yourself a rapper until you've battled in the Ring.

That's why I gotta kill it. I win tonight, I'll get a spot in the Ring's lineup, and if I get a spot in the lineup, I can do more battles, and if I do more battles, I'll make a name for myself. Who knows what could happen then?

Mrs. Murray's expression softens. "Following your dad's footsteps, huh?"

It's weird. Whenever other people mention him, it's like they're confirming that he's not some imaginary person I only remember bits and pieces of. And when they call him my dad and not Lawless, the underground rap legend, it's like they're reminding me that I'm his and he's mine.

"I guess. I've been preparing for the Ring for a minute now. I mean, it's hard to prepare for a *battle*, but a win could jump-start my career, you know?"

"Let me get this straight," she says, sitting up.

Imaginary alarms go off in my head. Warning: Your teacher is about to gather you, boo.

"You've been so focused on rapping that your grades have dropped drastically this semester. Forget that junior-year grades are vital for college admissions. Forget that you once told me you want to get into Markham or Howard."

"Mrs. Murray—"

"No, you think about this for a second. College is your goal, right?"

"I guess."

"You guess?"

I shrug. "College isn't for everyone, you know?"

"Maybe not. But a high school education? Critical. It's a D now, but that D will turn to an F if you keep this up. I had a similar conversation with your brother once."

I try not to roll my eyes. It's nothing against Trey or Mrs. Murray, but when you have an older brother who did great before you, if you don't at least match his greatness, people have something to say.

I've never been able to match Trey here at Midtown. They still have the programs and newspaper clippings on display from when he starred in *A Raisin in the Sun*. I'm surprised they haven't renamed Midtown "The Trey Jackson School of the Arts Because We Love His Ass That Much."

Anyway.

"He once went from As to Cs," Mrs. Murray says, "but he turned it around. Now look at him. Graduated from Markham with honors."

He also moved back home this summer. He couldn't find a decent job, and as of three weeks ago, he makes pizzas for minimum wage. It doesn't give me much to look forward to.

I'm not knocking him. At all. It's dope that he graduated. Nobody in our mom's family has a college degree, and Grandma, our dad's mom, loves to tell everyone that her grandson was "magnum cum laude." (That is so not how you say it, but good luck telling Grandma that.)

Mrs. Murray won't hear that though.

"I'm gonna improve my grades, I swear," I tell her. "I just gotta do this battle first and see what happens."

She nods. "I understand. I'm sure your mom will too."

She tosses me my phone.

Fuuuuuck.

I head to the hallway. Sonny and Malik lean against the lockers. Sonny types away on his phone. Malik fiddles with his camera. He's always in filmmaker mode. A few feet away, the school security guards, Long and Tate, keep an eye on them. Those two are always on some mess. Nobody wants to say it, but if you're black or brown, you're more likely to end up on their radar, even though Long himself is black.

Malik glances up from his phone. "You okay, Bri?"

"Go on now," Long calls. "Don't be lollygagging around here."

"Goddamn, can't we talk for a second?" I ask.

"You heard him," says Tate, thumbing toward the doors. He's got stringy blond hair. "Get outta here."

I open my mouth, but Sonny goes, "Let's just go, Bri."

Fine. I follow Sonny and Malik toward the doors and glance at my phone.

It's 4:45, and Hype still hasn't called.

A city bus ride and a walk home later, nothing.

I get to my house at exactly 5:09.

Jay's Jeep Cherokee is in our driveway. Gospel music blares in the house. It's one of those upbeat songs that leads to a praise break at church and Grandma running around the sanctuary, shouting. It's embarrassing as hell.

Anyway, Jay only plays those kinda songs on Saturdays when it's cleaning day to make me and Trey get up and help. It's hard to cuss as somebody sings about Jesus, so I get up and clean without a word.

Wonder why she's playing that music now.

A chill hits me soon as I step in the house. It's not as cold as outside—I can take my coat off—but my hoodie's gonna stay on. Our gas got cut off last week, and with no gas, we don't have heat. Jay put an electric heater in the hallway, but it only takes a bit of the chill out of the air. We have to heat water in pots on the electric stove if we wanna take hot baths and we sleep with extra covers on our beds. Some bills caught up with my mom and Trey, and she had to ask the gas company for an extension. Then another one. And another one. They got tired of waiting for their money and just cut it off.

It happens.

"I'm home," I call from the living room.

I'm about to toss my backpack and my coat onto the couch, but Jay snaps from wherever she is, "Hang that coat up and put that backpack in your room!"

Goddamn, how does she do that? I do what she said and follow the music to the kitchen.

Jay takes two plates out of a cabinet—one for me, one for her. Trey won't be home for a while. Jay's still in her "Church Jay" look that's required as the church secretary—the ponytail, the knee-length skirt, and the long-sleeved blouse that covers her tattoos and the scars from her habit. It's Thursday, so she's got classes tonight as she goes after that social work degree—she wants to make sure other people get the help she didn't back when she was on drugs. For the past few months, she's been in school part-time, taking classes several nights a week. She usually only has time to either eat or change, not both. Guess she chose to eat tonight.

"Hey, Li'l Bit," she says all sweet, like she didn't just snap on me. Typical. "How was your day?"

It's 5:13. I sit at the table. "He hasn't called yet."

Jay sets one plate in front of me and one beside me. "Who?"

"DJ Hype. I submitted my name for a spot in the Ring, remember?"

"Oh, that."

That, like it's no big deal. Jay knows I like to rap, but I don't think she realizes that I *want* to rap. She acts like it's the latest video game I'm into.

"Give him time," she says. "How was ACT prep? Y'all did practice tests today, right?"

"Yep." That's all she cares about these days, that damn test.

"Well?" she says, like she's waiting for more. "How'd you do?"

"All right, I guess."

"Was it hard? Easy? Were there any parts you struggled through?"

Here we go with the interrogation. "It's just a practice test."

"That will give us a good idea of how you'll do on the real test," Jay says. "Bri, this is serious."

"I know." She's told me a million times.

Jay puts pieces of chicken on the plates. Popeyes. It's the fifteenth. She just got paid, so we're eating good. Jay swears though that Popeyes isn't as good here as it is in New Orleans. That's where she and Aunt Pooh were born. I can still hear New Orleans in Jay's voice sometimes. Like when she says "baby," it's as if molasses seeped into the word and breaks it down into more syllables than it needs.

"If we want you to get into a good school, you gotta take this more seriously," she says.

If *we* want? More like if *she* wants.

It's not that I don't wanna go to college. I honestly don't know. The main thing I want is to make rapping happen. I do that, it'll be better than any good job a college degree could give me.

I pick up my phone. It's 5:20. No call.

Jay sucks her teeth. "Uh-huh."

"What?"

"I see where your head is. Probably couldn't focus on that test for thinking about that Ring mess."

Yes. "No."

"Mm-hmm. What time was Hype supposed to call, Bri?"

"Aunt Pooh said between four thirty and five thirty."

"*Pooh?* You can't take anything she says as law. She's the same one who claimed that somebody in the Garden captured an alien and hid it in their basement."

True.

"Even if he does call between four thirty and five thirty, you've still got time," she says.

"I know, I'm just—"

"Impatient. Like your daddy."

Let Jay tell it, I'm stubborn like my daddy, smart-mouthed

like my daddy, and hotheaded like my daddy. As if she's not all those things and then some. She says Trey and I look like him too. Same smile, without the gold grill. Same dimpled cheeks, same light complexions that make folks call us "red bones" and "light brights," same dark, wide eyes. I don't have Jay's high cheekbones or her lighter eyes, and I only get her complexion when I stay out in the summer sun all day. Sometimes I catch her staring at me, like she's looking for herself. Or like she sees Dad and can't look away.

Kinda how she stares at me now. "What's wrong?" I ask.

She smiles, but it's weak. "Nothing. Be patient, Bri. If he does call, go to the gym, do your li'l battle—"

Li'l battle?

"—and come straight home. Don't be hanging out with Pooh's rough behind."

Aunt Pooh's been taking me to the Ring for weeks to get a feel for things. I watched plenty of YouTube videos before that, but there's something about being there. Jay was cool with me going—Dad battled there, and Mr. Jimmy doesn't tolerate any nonsense—but she wasn't crazy about me going with Aunt Pooh. She definitely wasn't crazy about Aunt Pooh calling herself my manager. According to her, "That fool ain't no manager!"

"How you gon' shade your sister like that?" I ask her.

She scoops Cajun rice onto the plates. "I know what she's into. *You* know what she's into."

"Yeah, but she won't let anything happen—"

Pause.

Jay puts fried okra on the plates. Then corn on the cob. She finishes them off with soft, fluffy biscuits. Say what you want about Popeyes' biscuits, but they're neither soft nor fluffy.

This is Popkenchurch.

Popkenchurch is when you buy fried chicken and Cajun rice from Popeyes, biscuits from KFC, and fried okra and corn on the cob from Church's. Trey calls it "pre–cardiac arrest."

But see, Popkenchurch is problematic, and not because of digestive drama that may ensue. Jay only gets it when something bad happens. When she broke the news that her aunt Norma had terminal cancer a couple of years ago, she bought Popkenchurch. When she realized she couldn't get me a new laptop last Christmas, Popkenchurch. When Grandma decided *not* to move out of state to help her sister recover from her stroke, Jay bought Popkenchurch. I've never seen anybody take their aggression out on a chicken thigh quite like she did that day.

This isn't good. "What's wrong?"

"Bri, it's nothing for you to worry a—"

My phone buzzes on the table, and we both jump.

The screen lights up with a number I don't recognize.

It's five thirty.

Jay smiles. "There's your call."

My hands shake down to my fingertips, but I tap the screen and put the phone to my ear. I force out the "Hello?"

"Is this Bri?" an all-too-familiar voice asks.

My throat is dry all of a sudden. "Yeah. This is she . . . her . . . me." Screw grammar.

"What's up? It's DJ Hype! You ready, baby girl?"

This is the absolute worst time to forget how to speak. I clear my throat. "Ready for what?"

"Are you ready to kill it? Congratulations, you got a spot in the Ring tonight!"

TWO

I texted Aunt Pooh three words: I got in.

She shows up in fifteen minutes, tops.

I hear her before I see her. "Flash Light," by Parliament, blasts out front. She's beside her Cutlass, getting it in. Milly Rocking, Disciple Walking, all of that, like she's a one-woman *Soul Train* line.

I go outside and throw my hoodie over my snapback—it's colder than a polar bear's butt crack out here. My hands are freezing as I lock the front door. Jay left for class a few minutes ago.

Something's happened, I know it. Plus, she didn't say it was nothing. She said it's nothing *for me to worry about*. Difference.

"There she go!" Aunt Pooh points at me. "The Ring legend-in-the-making!"

The ponytail holders on her braids clink as she dances.

They're green like her sneakers. According to Garden Heights Gang Culture 101, a Garden Disciple's always gotta wear green.

Yeah, she's 'bout that life. Her arms and neck are covered in tattoos that only GDs can decipher, except for those red lips tatted on her neck. Those are her girlfriend's, Lena's.

"What I tell you?" She flashes her white-gold grill in a grin and slaps my palm with each word. "Told. You. You'd. Get. In!"

I barely smile. "Yeah."

"You got in the Ring, Bri! *The Ring!* You know how many folks around here wish they had a shot like this? What's up with you?"

A whole lot. "Something's happened, but Jay won't tell me what."

"What makes you think that?"

"She bought Popkenchurch."

"Damn, for real?" she says, and you'd think that would set off alarms for her, too, but she goes, "Why you ain't bring me a plate?"

I narrow my eyes. "Greedy ass. She only gets Popkenchurch when something's wrong, Aunt Pooh."

"Nah, man. You reading too much into this. This battle got you all jittery."

I bite my lip. "Maybe."

"*Definitely.* Let's get you to the Ring so you can show these fools how it's done." She holds her palm to me. "Sky's the limit?"

That's our motto, taken from a Biggie song older than me

and almost as old as Aunt Pooh. I slap her palm. "Sky's the limit."

"We'll see them chumps on top." She semi-quotes the song and pecks my forehead. "Even if you are wearing that nerdy-ass hoodie."

It's got Darth Vader on the front. Jay found it at the swap meet a few weeks ago. "What? Vader's that dude!"

"I don't care, it's nerd shit!"

I roll my eyes. When you have an aunt who was only ten when you were born, sometimes she acts like an aunt and sometimes she acts like an annoying older sister. Especially since Jay helped raise her—their mom was killed when Aunt Pooh was one and their dad died when she was nine. Jay's always treated Pooh like her third kid.

"Um, nerd shit?" I say to her. "More like dope shit. You need to expand your horizons."

"And you need to stop shopping off the Syfy channel."

Star Wars technically isn't sci—never mind. The top's down on the Cutlass, so I climb over the door to get in. Aunt Pooh pulls her sagging pants up before she hops in. What's the point of letting them sag if you're just gonna pull them up all the time? Yet she wants to criticize *my* fashion choices.

She reclines her seat back and turns the heat all the way up. Yeah, she could put the top up, but that combination of cold night air and warmth from the heater is A1.

"Let me get one of my shits." She reaches into the glove

compartment. Aunt Pooh gave up weed and turned to Blow Pops instead. Guess she'd rather get diabetes than get high all the time.

My phone buzzes in my hoodie pocket. I texted Sonny and Malik the same three words I texted Aunt Pooh, and they're geeking out.

I should be geeking out too, or at least getting in the zone, but I can't shake the feeling that the world has turned upside down.

At any second, it may turn me upside down with it.

Jimmy's parking lot is almost filled up, but not everybody is trying to get in the building. The "let out" has already started. That's the party outside that happens every Thursday night after the final battle in the Ring. For almost a year now, folks have been using Jimmy's as a party spot, kinda like they do Magnolia Ave on Friday nights. See, last year a kid was murdered by a cop just a few streets away from my grandparents' house. He was unarmed, but the grand jury decided not to charge the officer. There were riots and protests for weeks. Half the businesses in the Garden were either intentionally burned down by rioters or were casualties of the war. Club Envy, the usual Thursday nightspot, was a casualty.

The parking lot club's not really my thing (partying in the freezing cold? I think not), but it's cool to see people showing off their new rims or their hydraulics, cars bouncing up and down like they don't know a thing about gravity. The cops constantly drive by, but that's the new normal in the Garden. It's supposed to be on some "Hi, I'm your friendly neighborhood cop who won't shoot you" type shit, but it comes off as some "We're keeping an eye on your black asses" type shit.

I follow Aunt Pooh to the entrance. Music drifts from in the gym, and the bouncers pat people down and wave metal-detector wands around. If somebody's got a piece, security puts it in a bucket nearby and returns it once the Ring lets out.

"The champ is here!" Aunt Pooh calls as we approach the line. "Might as well crown her now!"

It's enough to get me and Aunt Pooh palm slaps and nods. "What's up, Li'l Law," a couple of people say. Even though we're technically cutting the line, it's all good. I'm royalty thanks to my dad.

I get a couple of smirks too though. Guess it's funny that a sixteen-year-old girl in a Darth Vader hoodie thinks she's got a shot in the Ring.

The bouncers slap palms with Aunt Pooh. "What's up, Bri?" the stocky one, Reggie, says. "You finally getting on tonight?"

"Yep! She gon' kill it too," Aunt Pooh says.

"A'ight," the taller one, Frank, says, waving the wand around us. "Carrying the torch for Law, huh?"

Not really. More like making my own torch and carrying it. I say, "Yeah," though, because that's what I'm supposed to say. It's part of being royalty.

Reggie motions us through. "May the force beam you up, Scotty." He points at my hoodie, then does the Vulcan salute.

How the hell do you confuse *Star Trek* and *Star Wars*? *How?* Unfortunately to some people in the Garden it's "nerd shit," or as some fool at the swap meet said, "white shit."

Folks need to get their space opera life right.

We go inside. As usual it's mostly guys in here, but I see a few girls too (which is reflective of the small ratio of women to men in hip-hop, which is total misogynistic fuckery, but anyway . . .). There are kids who look like they came straight from Garden Heights High, folks who look like they were alive when Biggie and Tupac were around, and old heads who look like they've been coming to the Ring since the Kangol hats and shell-toe Adidas days. Weed and cigarette smoke linger in the air, and everybody crowds around the boxing ring in the center.

Aunt Pooh finds us a spot beside the Ring. "Kick in the Door," by Notorious B.I.G., plays above all of the chatter. The bass pounds the floor like an earthquake, and B.I.G.'s voice seems to fill up the entire gym.

A few seconds of Biggie makes me forget everything else. "That flow though!"

"That shit is fire," Aunt Pooh says.

"*Fire?* That shit is legendary! Biggie single-handedly proves that delivery is key. Everything isn't an exact rhyme, but it works. He made 'Jesus' and 'penis' rhyme! C'mon! 'Jesus' and 'penis.'" Okay, it's probably offensive if you're Jesus, but still. Legendary.

"A'ight, a'ight." Aunt Pooh laughs. "I hear you."

I nod along, soaking up every line. Aunt Pooh watches me with a smile, making that scar on her cheek from that time she got stabbed look like a dimple. Hip-hop's addictive, and Aunt Pooh first got me hooked. When I was eight, she played Nas's *Illmatic* for me and said, "This dude will change your life with a few lines."

He did. Nothing's been the same since Nas told me the world was mine. Old as that album was back then, it was like waking up after being asleep my whole life. It was damn near spiritual.

I fiend for that feeling. It's the reason I rap.

There's a commotion near the doors. This guy with short dreadlocks makes his way through the crowd, and people give him dap along the way. Dee-Nice, aka one of the best-known rappers from the Ring. All of his battles went viral. He recently retired from battle rapping. Funny he'd retire from anything, young as he is. He graduated from Midtown last year.

"Yo, did you hear?" Aunt Pooh asks. "Ol' boy just got a record deal."

"For real?"

"Yep. Seven figures, up front."

Goddamn. No wonder he retired. A million-dollar deal? Not just that, but someone from *the Garden* got a million-dollar deal?

The music fades out, and the lights dim. A spotlight shines directly on Hype, and the cheers start.

"Let's get ready to battle!" Hype says, like this really is a boxing match. "For our first battle, in this corner we got M-Dot!"

This short, tatted guy climbs into the Ring to a mix of cheers and boos.

"And in this corner, we got Ms. Tique!" Hype says.

I scream loud as this dark-skinned girl with hoop earrings and a short curly cut climbs into the Ring. Ms. Tique is around Trey's age, but she spits like an old soul, as if she's lived a couple of lifetimes and didn't like either one of them shits.

She's goals to the highest degree.

Hype introduces the judges. There's Mr. Jimmy himself, Dee-Nice, and CZ, an undefeated Ring champion.

Hype flips a coin, and Ms. Tique wins it. She lets M-Dot go first. The beat starts up. "A Tale of Two Citiez," by J. Cole.

The gym goes nuts, but me? I watch the Ring. M-Dot paces, and Ms. Tique keeps her eyes on him like a predator watching prey. Even when M-Dot goes at her, she doesn't flinch, doesn't react, just stares at him like she knows she's gonna destroy him.

It's a thing of beauty.

He has some good lines. His flow is okay. But when it's Ms. Tique's turn, she hits him with punch lines that give me goose bumps. Every line gets a reaction out of the crowd.

She wins the first two battles, hands down, and it's over.

"A'ight, y'all," Hype says. "It's time for Rookie Royale! Two rookies will battle it out for the first time in the Ring."

Aunt Pooh bounces on her heels. "Yeeeeah!"

All of a sudden, my knees feel weak.

"Two names have been drawn," Hype says, "so without further ado, our first MC is—"

He plays a drumroll. People stomp their feet along with it, rattling the floor, so I'm not completely sure if my legs shake as much as I think.

"Milez!" Hype says.

Cheers go up on the other side of the gym. The crowd parts, and this brown-skinned boy with zigzags cut into his hair makes his way toward the Ring. He looks around my age. A big cross pendant hangs from a chain on his neck.

I know him, but I don't, if that makes sense. I've seen him somewhere.

A slim guy in a black-and-white tracksuit follows him. Dark shades hide his eyes, although the sun's down. He says something to the boy, and two gold fangs glisten in his mouth.

I nudge Aunt Pooh. "That's Supreme."

"Who?" she says around her Blow Pop.

"Supreme!" I say, like she's supposed to know. She should. "My dad's old manager."

"Oh yeah. I remember him."

I don't remember him. I was a toddler when he was around, but I've memorized my dad's story like a song. He recorded his first mixtape at sixteen. People still used CDs back then, so he made copies and passed them out around the neighborhood. Supreme got one and was so blown away that he begged Dad to let him manage his career. Dad agreed. From there, my dad became an underground legend, and Supreme became a legendary manager.

Dad fired Supreme right before he died. Jay claims they had "creative differences."

The boy with Supreme climbs into the Ring. Soon as Hype hands him a mic, he says, "It's your boy Milez with a *z*, the Swagerific prince!"

The cheers are loud.

"Ooh, he the one with that stupid-ass song," Aunt Pooh says.

That's how I know him. It's called "Swagerific," and I swear to God, it's the dumbest song ever. I can't go around the neighborhood without hearing his voice go, "Swagerific, so call me terrific. Swag-erific. Swag-erific. Swag, swag, swag . . ."

There's a dance that goes with it called the "Wipe Me Down." Little kids love it. The video's got like a million views online.

"Shout-out to my pops, Supreme!" Milez says, pointing at him.

Supreme nods as people cheer.

"Well, shit," Aunt Pooh says. "You going up against your pops's manager's son."

Damn, I guess so. Not just that, but I gotta go up against a somebody. Stupid as that song is, everybody knows Milez and they're already cheering for him. I'm a nobody in comparison.

But I'm a nobody who can rap. "Swagerific" has lines like, "Life ain't fair, but why should I care? Why should I care? I got dollars in the air. I got dollars, I got dollars, I got dollars . . ."

Um. Yeah. This won't be hard. But it also means that losing isn't an option. I'd never live that down.

Hype plays a drumroll again. "Our next MC is . . . ," he says, and a couple of people shout out their own names, as if that'll make him call them. "Bri!"

Aunt Pooh raises my arm high and leads me to the Ring. "The champ is here!" she shouts, like I'm Muhammad Ali. I'm definitely not Ali. I'm scared as hell.

I climb into the Ring anyway. The spotlight beams in my face. Hundreds of faces stare at me and phones point in my direction.

Hype hands me a mic.

"Introduce yourself," he says.

I'm supposed to hype myself up, but all I get out is, "I'm Bri."

Some of the crowd snicker.

Hype chuckles. "Okay, Bri. Ain't you Law's daughter?"

What's that got to do with it? "Yeah."

"Aw, damn! If baby girl is anything like her pops, we 'bout to hear some heat."

The crowd roars.

Can't lie, I'm a tad bit annoyed that he mentioned my dad. I get why, but damn. Whether I'm good or not shouldn't have a thing to do with him. He didn't teach me to rap. I taught myself. So why does he get the credit?

"Time to flip the coin," Hype says. "Bri, you get to call it."

"Tails," I mutter.

Hype tosses the coin and slaps it onto the back of his hand. "Tails it is. Who's first?"

I nod toward Milez. I can hardly speak. No way I can go first.

"A'ight. Y'all ready out there?"

For the crowd, it's basically a hell yes. For me? A hell no.

But I don't have a choice.

THREE

The beat starts—"Niggas in Paris" by Jay-Z and Kanye.

My heart pounds harder than the bass in the song. Milez comes up to me, waaay too close. It gives me a chance to size him up. He talks a lot of shit, but damn, there's fear in his eyes.

He starts rapping.

I ball so hard, you wish you was like me.
I'm fresh down to my Nikes.
Spend one hundred K in a day,
The boy don't play,
Going broke ain't likely.
I ball hard, this hood life crazy.
But I'm a G, it don't faze me.
Ferrari gassed, Glock in back,
Ready to pop if paparazzi chase me.

Okay, I'll give props. Those lines are better than anything in "Swagerific," but this boy can't be serious. He's not an uppercase G, a lowercase g, or any kind of G, so why is he claiming that life? He doesn't even live in the hood. Everybody knows Supreme lives in the suburbs now. Yet his son is 'bout that life?

Nah.

I gotta call him out. Maybe something like, "Your career? I end it. Your G status as authentic as them gems in your pendant."

Ha! That's a good one.

He's still rapping about being such a gangster. I smirk, waiting for my turn. Until—

I ball hard, so why bother?
This ain't a battle, more like slaughter.
I murder this chick in cold blood,
Like someone did her whack-ass father.

The.

Fuck?

I advance on Milez. "What the hell you say?"

Hype cuts off the music and I hear, "Whoa, whoa, whoa," as a couple of people rush into the Ring. Aunt Pooh pulls me back.

"You li'l asshole!" I shout. "Say it again!"

Aunt Pooh drags me to the corner. "The hell is wrong with you?"

"You heard that shit?"

"Yeah, but you handle him with your bars, not your fists! You trying to get disqualified before you start?"

I breathe extra hard. "That line—"

"Got you like he wanted it to!"

She's right. Damn, she's right.

The crowd boos. You don't make digs about my dad to them either.

"Ay! Y'all know the rules. No holds barred," Hype says. "Even Law is fair game in the Ring."

More boos.

"A'ight, a'ight!" Hype tries to calm everyone down. "Milez, that was a low blow, fam. C'mon, now."

"My bad," Milez says into the mic, but he smirks.

I'm shaking, that's how much I wanna hit him. Just makes it worse that my throat is all tight, and now I'm almost as pissed at myself as I am at Milez.

"Bri, you ready?" Hype asks.

Aunt Pooh pushes me back to the center of the Ring.

"Yeah," I bite out.

"A'ight then," Hype says. "Let's get it!"

The beat starts again, but all the lines in my head suddenly don't exist.

"I . . ."

Murder this chick in cold blood.

I can still hear the gunshots that took him from us.

"He . . ."

Like someone did her whack-ass father.

I can still hear Jay wailing.

"I . . ."

Murder . . . Whack-ass father.

I can still see him in the coffin, all cold and stiff.

"Choked!" someone shouts.

Shit.

It becomes contagious and turns into a chant. Milez's smirk becomes a grin. His dad chuckles.

Hype stops the beat.

"Damn," he says. "Round one automatically goes to Milez."

I stumble over to my corner.

I blanked.

I fucking *blanked*.

Aunt Pooh climbs up on the ropes. "What the hell? You let him get to you?"

"Aunty—"

"You know how much you got on the line right now?" she says. "This is *it*. Your chance to blow up, and you gon' hand this battle over to him?"

"No, but . . ."

She pushes me back into the Ring. "Shake that shit off!"

Milez gets palm slaps and fist bumps over in his corner. His dad laughs proudly.

I wish I had that. Not an asshole for a dad, but my dad. At

this point I'd settle for good memories. Not just from the night he was murdered.

It happened in front of our old house. He and Jay were going out for date night. Aunt Pooh lived with us back then and agreed to babysit me and Trey while they were gone.

Dad kissed us goodbye as we started a game of *Mario Kart*, and he and Jay walked out the front door. The car cranked up outside. Just as my Princess Peach gained on Trey's Bowser and Aunt Pooh's Toad, five shots went off. I was only four, but the sound hasn't left my ears. Then Jay screaming, wailing really, in a way that didn't sound human.

Word is, a Crown pulled the trigger. The Crowns are the largest King Lord set here on the east side. They may as well be their own gang, big as they are. Dad wasn't a gangbanger, but he was so close to so many Garden Disciples that he got caught up in their drama. The Crowns took him out.

From everything I've heard, he wouldn't have let anybody make him blank like this. I can't either.

"Round two!" Hype announces. "Milez, since you won round one, you decide who goes first."

He cheeses. "I got this."

"Let's take it old school then!" says Hype.

He scratches the records and the beat starts. "Deep Cover," by Snoop and Dre. He wasn't kidding about the old school. That was the first song Snoop ever did.

The old heads in the gym go crazy. Some of the young ones

seem confused. Milez doesn't look at me when he raps, like I'm no longer relevant.

Yo, they call me the prince,
I ain't new to this game.
Been plotting for years
And I can't be tamed.
You can call me a G,
Your son wish he was me,
And every girl with a pulse
Falls inevitably.
I get money,
Like it's going out of style.
All my whips brand new.
I got Jordan on the dial.

Rule numero uno of battling? Know your opponent's weakness. Nothing he's spit this round is directed at me. That may not seem like a red flag, but right now it's a huge one. I blanked. A real MC would go for the kill because of that. Hell, *I'd* go for it. He's not even mentioning it. That means there's a 98 percent chance this is prewritten.

Prewritten is a no-no in the Ring. A bigger no-no? Prewritten by someone else.

I don't know if he wrote those lines, maybe he did, but I can make everyone think he didn't. Dirty as hell? Absolutely.

But since my dad isn't off-limits, not a damn thing is off-limits.

Rule number two of battling—use the circumstances to your advantage. Supreme doesn't look too worried, but trust: He should be.

That goes in my arsenal.

Rule number three—if there's a beat, make sure your flow fits it like a glove. Flow is the rhythm of the rhymes, and every word, every syllable, affects it. Even the way a word is pronounced can change the flow. While most people know Snoop and Dre for "Deep Cover," one time I found a remake of it by this rapper named Big Pun on YouTube. His flow on this song was one of the best I've ever heard in my life.

Maybe I can mimic it.

Maybe I can wipe that dumb smirk off Milez's face.

Maybe I can actually win.

Milez stops, and the beat fades off. He gets a couple of cheers, but not many. The Ring loves punch lines, not weak lines about yourself.

"Okay, I hear you," Hype says. "Bri, your go!"

My ideas are spread out like puzzle pieces. Now I gotta put them all together into something that makes sense.

The beat starts again. I nod along. There's nothing but me, the music, and Milez.

The words have strung themselves together into rhymes and into a flow, and I let it all come tumbling out.

Ready for war, Milez? Nah, you fucked up this time.
Should address this cipher to the writer,
The biter, who really wrote them rhymes.
Come at Brianna, you wanna get buried?
Spit like a legend, feminine weapon,
I reckon your own father's worried.
Bow down, baby, get down on your knees.
You got paper, but I'm greater.
Ask your clique, and while you at it ask Supreme.
Straight from the Garden where people dearly departin'.
Screw a pardon, I'm hardened,
And Milez's heart is on back of milk cartons.
It's MIA, and this is judgment—

I stop. The crowd is going bananas. B-a-n-a-n-a-s.

"What?" Hype shouts. "What?"

Even the rough-and-tough-looking dudes bounce up and down with their fists at their mouths going, "Ohhhh!"

"What?" Hype shouts again, and he plays a siren. *The* siren. The one he uses when an MC spits something dope.

I, Brianna Marie Jackson, got the siren.

Holy shit.

"She came with the pun flow!" Hype says. "Somebody get a water hose! We can't handle the heat! We can't handle it!"

This is magical. I thought the reactions I'd get when I

freestyled for Aunt Pooh's friends were something. This is a new level, like when Luke went from being just Luke to Jedi-ass Luke.

"Milez, I'm sorry, but she murdered you in a couple of bars," Hype says. "Call the DA! This is a homicide scene! Judges, what y'all think?"

All of them lift signs with my name on it.

The crowd goes wilder.

"Bri wins it!" Hype says.

Milez nervously rubs the peach fuzz on his chin.

I grin. Got him.

"Let's get to the final round," Hype says. "We're at a tie, and whoever wins this one wins it all. Bri, who goes first?"

"Him," I say. "Let him get his garbage out the way."

A bunch of oohs echo around us. Yeah, I said it.

"Milez, you better come correct," Hype says. "Let's get it!"

The beat starts—"Shook Ones," by Mobb Deep. It's slower than "Deep Cover," but it's perfect for freestyling. In every YouTube battle I watched, shit got real whenever that beat dropped.

Milez glares at me as he raps. Something about how much money he has, how many girls like him, his clothes, his jewelry, the gangster life he's living. Repetitive. Stale. Prewritten.

I gotta go for the kill.

Here I am, going at him as if I don't have any manners. Manners. A lot of words rhyme with that if I deliver them right. Cameras. Rappers. Pamper. Hammer—MC Hammer. Vanilla

Ice. Hip-hop heads consider them pop stars, not real rappers. I can compare him to them.

I gotta get my signature line in there—you can only spell "brilliant" by first spelling Bri. Aunt Pooh once pointed that out right before teasing me about being such a perfectionist.

Perfection. I can use that. Perfection, protection, election. Election—presidents. Presidents are leaders. Leader. Either. Ether, like that song where Nas went in on Jay-Z.

I need to get something in there about his name too. Milez. Miles per hour. Speed. Light speed. Then I need to end with something about myself.

Milez lowers the mic. There are a couple of cheers. Supreme claps, yet his face is hard.

"Okay, I see you, Milez!" Hype says. "Bri, you better bring the heat!"

The instrumental starts up again. Aunt Pooh said I only get one chance to let everybody and their momma know who I am.

So I take it.

My apologies, see, I forgot my manners.
I get on the mic 'cause it's my life. You show off for girls and cameras.
You a pop star, not a rapper. A Vanilla Ice or a Hammer.
Y'all hear this crap he dumping out? Somebody get him a Pamper.

And a crown for me. The best have heard about me.
You can only spell "brilliant" by first spelling Bri.
You see, naturally, I do my shit with perfection.
Better call a bodyguard 'cause you gon' need some protection,
And on this here election, the people crown a new leader.
You didn't see this coming, and your ghostwriters didn't either.
I came here to ether. I'm sorry to do this to you.
This is no longer a battle, it's your funeral, boo. I'm murdering you.
On my corner they call me coroner, I'm warning ya.
Tell the truth, this dude is borin' ya.
You confused like a foreigner. I'll explain with ease:
You're just a casualty in the reality of the madness of Bri.
No fallacies, I spit maladies, causin' fatalities,
And do it casually, damaging rappers without bandaging.
Imagining managing my own label, my own salary.
And actually, factually, there's no MC that's as bad as me.
Milez? That's cute. But it don't make me cower.
I move at light speed, you stuck at per hour.
You spit like a lisp. I spit like a high power.

Bri's the future, and you Today *like Matt Lauer.*
You coward. But you're a G? It ain't convincing to me.
You talk about your clothes, about your shopping sprees.
You talk about your Glock, about your i-c-e.
But in this here ring, they all talking 'bout me,
Bri!

The crowd goes nuts.

"I told y'all!" Aunt Pooh shouts as she stands on the ropes. "I told y'all!"

Milez can't look at me or his dad, who seems to glare at him. He could be glaring at me, too. Hard to tell behind those shades.

"A'ight, y'all." Hype tries to calm everyone down as he comes from behind the turntables. "It's down to this vote. Whoever takes this one is the winner. Judges, who y'all got?"

Mr. Jimmy raises his sign. It says Bri.

Dee-Nice raises his sign. Bri.

CZ raises his sign. Li'l Law.

Holy shit.

"We have a winner!" Hype says to thunderous cheers. He raises my arm into the air. "Ladies and gentlemen, the winner of tonight's Rookie Royale, Bri!"

FOUR

Hours after my battle, I dream my nightmare.

I'm five years old, climbing into my mom's old Lexus. Daddy went to heaven almost a year ago. Aunt Pooh's been gone a couple of months. She went to live with her and Mommy's aunty in the projects.

I lock my seat belt in place, and Mommy holds my overstuffed backpack toward me. Her arm has all these dark marks on it. She once told me she got them because she wasn't feeling well.

"You're still sick, Mommy?" I ask.

She follows my eyes and rolls her sleeve down. "Yeah, baby," she whispers.

My brother gets in the car beside me, and Mommy

says we're going on a trip to somewhere special. We end up in our grandparents' driveway.

Suddenly, Trey's eyes widen. He begs her not to do this. Seeing him cry makes me cry.

Mommy tells him to take me inside, but he won't. She gets out, goes around to his side, unlocks his seat belt, and tries to pull him out the car, but he digs his feet into the seat.

She grabs his shoulders. "Trey! I need you to be my little man," she says, her voice shaky. "For your sister's sake. Okay?"

He looks over at me and quickly wipes his face. "I'm . . . I'm . . . I'm okay, Li'l Bit," he claims, but the cry-hiccups break up his words. "It's okay."

He unlocks my seat belt, takes my hand, and helps me out the car.

Mommy hands us our backpacks. "Be good, okay?" she says. "Do what your grandparents tell you to do."

"When are you coming back?" I ask.

She kneels in front of me. Her shaky fingers brush through my hair, then cup my cheek. "I'll be back later. I promise."

"Later when?"

"Later. I love you, okay?"

She presses her lips to my forehead and keeps them

there for the longest. She does the same to Trey, then straightens up.

"Mommy, when are you coming back?" I ask again.

She gets in the car without answering me and cranks it up. Tears stream down her cheeks. Even at five, I know she won't be back for a long time.

I drop my backpack and chase the car down the driveway. "Mommy, don't leave me!"

But she goes into the street, and I'm not supposed to go into the street.

"Mommy!" I cry. Her car goes, goes, and soon, it's gone. "Mommy! Mom—"

"Brianna!"

I jolt awake.

Jay's sitting on the side of my bed. "Baby, are you okay?"

I try to catch my breath as I wipe the dampness from my eyes. "Yeah."

"Were you having a nightmare?"

A nightmare that's a memory. Jay really did leave me and Trey at our grandparents' house. She couldn't take care of us and her drug habit, too. That's when I learned that when people die, they sometimes take the living with them.

I saw her in the park a few months later, looking more like a red-eyed, scaly-skinned dragon than my mommy. I started calling her Jay after that—there was no way she was my mom anymore. It became my own habit that was hard to break. Still is.

It took three years and a rehab stint for her to come back. Even though she was clean, some judge decided that she could only have me and Trey every other weekend and on some holidays. She didn't get us back full-time until five years ago, after she got her job and started renting this place.

Five years back with her, and yet I still dream about her leaving us. It hits me out of nowhere sometimes. But Jay can't know I dream about it. It'll make her feel guilty, and then I'll feel guilty for making her feel guilty.

"It was nothing," I tell her.

She sighs and pushes up off the bed. "Okay. Go ahead and get up. We need to have a little talk before you head to school."

"About what?"

"How you could tell me you won in the Ring, but you couldn't tell me your grades are dropping faster than Pooh's sagging-ass pants."

"Huh?"

"Huh?" she mocks, and shows me her phone. "I got an email from your poetry teacher."

Mrs. Murray.

The conversation in ACT prep.

Aw, hell.

Honestly? I forgot. I was floating after my battle, for real. That feeling when the crowd cheered for me is probably what getting high is like, and I'm addicted.

I don't know what to say to my mom. "I'm sorry?"

"Sorry nothing! What's your main responsibility, Bri?"

"Education over everything," I mumble.

"Exactly. Education over everything, *including rapping*. I thought I made that clear?"

"It's not that big of a deal though, dang!"

Jay raises her eyebrows. "Girl," she says in that slow way that sends a warning. "You better check yourself."

"I'm just saying, some parents wouldn't make a big deal out of this."

"Well gosh golly darn, I'm not some parents! You can do better, you've done better, so do better. Only Cs I wanna see are pictures of *seas*, the only Ds I better see are *deez* grades improving. We clear?"

I swear she's so hard on me. "Yes, ma'am."

"Thank you. Get ready for school."

She leaves.

"Goddamn," I mutter under my breath. "Killing my vibe, first thing in the morning."

"You ain't *got* no vibe!" she hollers from the hall.

I can't ever say *shit* in this house.

I get up, and almost immediately I wanna get back under my covers. That first feel of the chill in the air is always the hardest. Moving around helps.

The ladies of hip-hop watch from the wall beside my bed. I've got some of everybody, from MC Lyte to Missy Elliott to Nicki Minaj to Rapsody . . . the list goes on and on. I figure if I wanna be a queen, queens should watch over me when I sleep.

I throw my Vader hoodie back on and slip on my Not-Timbs. Nah, they're not the real deal. The real deal costs a water bill. These cost twenty bucks at the swap meet. I try to pull them off like they are Timbs except—

"Shit," I hiss. Some of the black "leather" on one has rubbed off, revealing white cloth. This happened to the other last week. I take a black Sharpie and go to work. Ratchet, but I gotta do what I gotta do.

Soon I'm getting some real Timbs though. I've been saving the money I make from my snack dealing. Aunt Pooh buys my stock and lets me keep the profits. It's the closest Jay will let her get to giving me money. Thanks to the kids at Midtown, I'm about halfway to a pair of brand-new Timbs. Technically, we're not supposed to sell stuff on school campus, but I've gotten away with it so far. Shout-out to Michelle Obama. That health kick of hers made the school take the good stuff from the vending machines and made my business very lucrative.

A horn blows outside. It's seven fifteen, so it's gotta be Mr. Watson, the bus driver. He claims that even when he's dead, he'll be on time. If his zombie ass pulls up in the bus one day, I am *not* climbing on board.

"I'm gone," I call to Jay. Trey's bedroom door is closed. He's probably knocked out. He gets home from work when I'm almost gone to bed, and he leaves for work when I'm at school.

A short yellow bus waits out front. Midtown-the-school is in Midtown-the-neighborhood, where people live in nice condos and expensive historic houses. I live in Garden High's zone, but Jay says there's too much bullshit and not enough people who care there. Private school's not in our budget, so Midtown School of the Arts is the next best thing. A few years ago, they started busing students in from all over the city. They called it their "diversity initiative." Jay calls it their "they needed grant money and wouldn't nobody give it to them for just a bunch of white kids initiative." You've got rich kids from the north side, middle-class kids from downtown and Midtown, and hood kids like me. There's only fifteen of us from the Garden at Midtown. So they send a short bus for us.

Mr. Watson wears his Santa hat and hums along with the Temptations' version of "Silent Night" that plays on his phone. Christmas is less than two weeks away, but Mr. Watson has been in the holiday spirit for months.

"Hey, Mr. Watson," I say.

"Hey, Brianna! Cold enough for you?"

"*Too* cold."

"Aw, ain't no such thing. This the perfect weather!"

For what, freezing your ass off? "If you say so," I mumble, and head toward the back. I'm his third pickup. Shana's dozing up front, her head just barely touching the window. She's not about to mess up her bun, nap or not. All the eleventh-grade dancers look exhausted these days.

Deon nods at me from his seat in the very back, his saxophone case propped up beside him. Deon's a junior too, but since he's in the music program, I only ever see him on the bus. "Hey, Bri. Let me get a Snickers."

I sit a couple of rows ahead of him. "You got Snickers money?"

He tosses me a balled-up dollar. I toss the candy bar back to him.

"Thanks. You killed it in the Ring."

"You know about that?"

"Yeah. Saw the battle on YouTube. My cousin texted it to me. He said you got next."

Dang, I got folks talking like that? I definitely had the Ring talking. I could barely get out of there last night without somebody telling me how dope I was. It was the first time I realized I can do this.

I mean, it's one thing to wanna do something. It's another to think it's possible. Rapping has been my dream forever, but dreams aren't real. You wake up from them or reality makes them seem stupid. Trust, every time my fridge is almost empty, all of my dreams seem stupid. But between my win and Dee-Nice's deal, anything feels possible right now. Or I'm that desperate for things to change.

The Garden passes by my window. Older folks water their flowers or bring out their trash cans. A couple of cars blast music on high. Seems normal, but things haven't been the same since the riots. The neighborhood doesn't feel nearly as safe. Not that the Garden was ever a utopia, hell no, but before I only worried about GDs and Crowns. Now I gotta worry about the cops too? Yeah, people get killed around here, and nah, it's not always by the police, but Jay says this was like having a stranger come in your house, steal one of your kids, and blame you for it because your family was dysfunctional, while the whole world judges you for being upset.

Zane, a senior with a nose ring, gets on the bus. He's stuck-up as hell. Sonny says Zane thinks he's fine, but Sonny and I also agree that he *is* fine. It's an internal struggle, being annoyed by his ass and being mesmerized by his face.

And if I'm real, being mesmerized by his ass. Boy's got a donk.

He never speaks to me, but today he goes, "Your battle was fire, ma!"

Well, goddamn. "Thanks."

How many people have seen it?

Aja the freshman saw it. She gives me props soon as she gets on. So do Keyona, Nevaeh, and Jabari, the sophomores. Before I know it, I'm the talk of the short bus.

"You got skills, Bri!"

"I was geeking the whole time!"

"Bet she couldn't beat me in a battle. On God, bruh."

That little dig is from Curtis Brinkley, this short, wavy-haired, brown-skinned boy who puts a lot of lies *on God, bruh*. In fifth grade, he claimed that Rihanna was his cousin and that his mom was on the road with her, working as her hairstylist. In sixth grade, he said his mom was on tour with Beyoncé as her hairstylist. Really, his mom was in prison. She still is.

Mr. Watson pulls up at Sonny's and Malik's houses. They live next door to each other, but they both come out of Malik's front door.

I take off my snapback. My edges still need help, but I laid them as best as I could earlier. I put on some lip gloss, too. It's stupid as hell, but I'm hoping Malik notices.

I notice way too much about him. Like the way his eyes sometimes get this glint about them that makes me think he knows every secret there is about me, and he's cool with them all. Like the fact that he's fine, and the fact that he doesn't realize he's fine, which somehow makes him even finer. Like the way my heart speeds up every time he says "Breezy." He's the only one who calls me that, and when he says it, he stretches it slightly, in a way that nobody else can really imitate. Like he wants the name to only belong to him.

All these feelings started when we were ten. I have this real clear memory of us wrestling in Malik's front yard. I was the Rock and he was John Cena. We were obsessed with wrestling videos on YouTube. I pinned Malik down, and while sitting on top of him in his front yard, I suddenly wanted to kiss him.

It. Freaked. Me. Out.

So I punched him and said in my best *the Rock* voice, "I'm laying the smackdown on your candy ass!"

Basically, I tried to ignore my sexual awakening by imitating the Rock.

I was so weirded out by the whole thing. Those feelings didn't go away either. But I told myself over and over again that he's Malik. Best friend extraordinaire, Luke to my Leia.

Yet here I am, using my phone to check my Pink Pursuit lip gloss (who comes up with these names?), hoping he'll see me some kinda way, too. Pathetic.

"Why won't you admit I whooped that ass?" Sonny asks him as they climb on board.

"Like I said, my controller was acting funny," Malik claims. "We gotta rematch."

"Fine. I'll still whoop your—Briiii!"

Sonny dances down the aisle to a beat nobody hears. When he gets close, he bows like he's worshipping me. "All hail the Ring queen."

I laugh. "Queen I am not."

"Well, you killed it, Yoda." We slap palms and end with the Wakanda salute. Wakanda forever.

Malik shrugs. "I won't say I told you so. But I won't *won't* say I didn't tell you so, either."

"That doesn't make sense," I tell him.

Sonny sits on the seat in front of me. "Nope!"

Malik plops down beside me. "It's a double negative."

"Um, no, Mr. Film Major," I say. "As a literary arts major, I can assure that's just a mess. You basically said that you won't say you told me so."

His eyebrows meet and his mouth drops slightly open. Confused Malik is so damn cute. "What?"

"Exactly. Stick with filmmaking, boo."

"Agreed," says Sonny. "Anyway, that battle was ridiculous, Bri. Except when you just stood there that first round. I was about to pull a Mariah Carey 'I don't know her' on you."

I punch his arm. Troll.

"But seriously, you killed it," Sonny says. "Milez, on the other hand, needs to stop rapping."

Malik nods. "He Jar Jar Binksed that."

Malik insists that Jar Jar Binks should be a verb, adjective, and an adverb to describe whack stuff because Jar Jar Binks is the worst character in the Star Wars universe.

"Bruh, you know that's never gonna catch on, right?" Sonny asks him.

"But it makes sense! Wanna say something is whack? Call it a Jar Jar Binks."

"Okay. *You're* a Jar Jar Binks," Sonny says. "Got it."

Malik thumps Sonny's forehead. Sonny punches Malik's shoulder. They go back and forth, punching and swatting at each other.

Totally normal. In fact, a Sonny and Malik fight is one of the few things guaranteed in life, right up there with death, taxes, and Kanye West rants.

Sonny's phone buzzes, and suddenly Malik no longer exists. His face lights up almost as bright as the screen.

I sit up a little and stretch my neck. "Who you texting?"

"Dang, bish. Nosy ass."

I stretch some more to try and see the name on the screen, but Sonny dims it so I can't. I only catch the heart-eyes emoji next to the name. I raise my eyebrows. "Is there someone you'd like to tell me about, sir?"

Sonny glances around, almost like he's afraid somebody heard me. Everybody's having their own conversations though. Still he says, "Later, Bri."

Considering how he's on edge, there must be a guy. When we were eleven, Sonny came out to me. We were watching Justin Bieber perform at some awards show. I thought he was cute, but I wasn't obsessed with him like Sonny was. Sonny turned to me and blurted out, "I think I only like boys."

It was out of nowhere. Sorta. There were little things here and there that made me wonder. Like, how he'd print out pictures of Bieber and secretly carry them around. How he acted around my brother—if Trey liked something, Sonny suddenly loved it; if Trey spoke to him, Sonny blushed; and if Trey got a girlfriend, Sonny acted like it was the end of the world.

But I can't lie; I didn't really know what to say at the time. So I just told him, "Okay," and left it at that.

He told Malik not long after and asked if they could still be friends. Apparently, Malik was like, "Long as we can still play PlayStation." Sonny told his parents, too, and they've always been cool with it. But I guess sometimes he's afraid of how other people will act if they know.

The bus pulls up at an intersection, beside a cluster of bleary-eyed kids. Their breath turns to smoke around them as they wait for the bus to Garden High.

Curtis lets his window down. "Ay, Basics! Talk that shit you were saying yesterday!"

School pride turns us into gangs. We call the kids from Garden Heights Basics 'cause we say they're "basic as hell." They call us short-bus nerds.

"Man, fuck your li'l lollipop-head-looking ass," a boy in a bubble vest says. "Bet you won't get off that bus and say shit to my face."

I smirk. Keandre tells no lies.

He looks at me. "Ay, Bri! You did your thing in the Ring, baby girl!"

I let my window down. Some of the other kids nod or say, "Whaddup, Bri?"

If school pride makes us gangs, I'm neutral thanks to my dad. "You saw the battle?" I ask Keandre.

"Hell yeah! Props, queen."

See? Around the neighborhood, I'm royalty. Everybody shows love.

But when the bus pulls up at Midtown, I'm nothing.

At Midtown you have to be great for anyone to notice you. Brilliant, actually. And it's like everybody's trying to outdo everyone else. It's all about who got the lead in this play or that recital. Who won that award for their writing or their art. Whose vocal range is the best. It's a popularity contest on steroids. If you're not exceptional, you're a nobody.

I'm the exact opposite of exceptional. My grades are so-so. I don't win awards. Nothing I do is enough. *I'm* not enough. Except for when I'm too much for my teachers to handle and they send me to the principal's office.

On the school steps, a couple of boys do the "Wipe Me Down" dance as Milez goes "Swag, swag, swag" on one of their phones. Don't know why they're torturing themselves with that garbage.

"So . . ." I grip my backpack straps. "What are y'all doing at lunch?"

"I've got SAT prep," Sonny says.

"Damn, you're doing both?" I ask. Sonny's more obsessed with this college stuff than Jay is.

He shrugs. "Gotta do what I gotta do."

"What about you?" I ask Malik, and suddenly, my heart beats super fast at the idea of lunch alone with him.

But he frowns. "Sorry, Bri. Gotta go to the lab and work on this documentary." He holds up his camera.

Welp, so much for my idea. I probably won't see either of them until we get back on the bus. See, Sonny and Malik have their groups at Midtown. Unfortunately for me, Sonny and Malik *are* my group. When they're with their groups, I have nothing on top of being nobody. They're both pretty damn brilliant, too. Everybody in visual arts loves Sonny's graffiti pieces. Malik's won a couple of awards for his short films.

I just gotta get through one more year in this place. One more year of being quiet, unassuming Bri who stays to herself as her friends get their glow-ups.

Yeah.

We get in line for security. "Think Long and Tate have calmed down since yesterday?" Sonny asks.

"Probably not." They're always power tripping. Last week, they put Curtis through an extra security screening, even though the metal detector didn't beep when he went through. They claimed they wanted to be "sure."

"I'm telling y'all, the way they do security is not normal," Malik says. "My mom doesn't do people like this, and she deals with criminals."

Malik's mom, Aunt 'Chelle, is one of the security guards at the courthouse.

"Y'all do realize they've gotten worse since last year, right?" says Malik. "Seeing that cop get away with murder probably made them think they're invincible too."

"You might be on to something, Malik X," says Sonny.

That's been our nickname for Malik since the riots. The whole situation shook him up. It shook me up too, can't lie, but Malik's been on another level, always talking about social justice and reading up on stuff like the Black Panthers. Before the riots, the only Black Panther he cared about was T'Challa.

"We need to do something," he says. "This isn't okay."

"Just ignore them," says Sonny. "They're more talk than anything."

Curtis goes through the metal detector with no problems. Then Shana, Deon, the three sophomores, Zane. Next it's Sonny, followed by Malik. I stroll through after him.

The metal detector doesn't beep, but Long puts his arm out in front of me. "Go back."

"Why?" I ask.

"Because he said so," says Tate.

"But it didn't beep!" I say.

"I don't care," Long says. "I told you to go back through."

Fine. I go through the metal detector again. No beep.

"Hand over the bag," Long says.

Oh, shit. My candy stash. If they find it, I could get suspended for selling on campus. Considering how much I've been suspended over other stuff, shit, I may get expelled.

"Hand. Over. The. Bag," Long says.

I swallow. "I don't have to—"

"Oh, you got something to hide?" Long says.

"No!"

"Put that camera away!" Tate tells Malik.

He's got it out and pointed at us. "I can record if I want!"

"Hand over the bag!" Long tells me.

"No!"

"You know what—"

He reaches for my backpack strap, but I snatch it away. By the look that flashes across his eyes, I shouldn't have done that.

He grabs my arm. "Give me that backpack!"

I yank away. "Get your hands off me!"

Everything happens in a blur.

He grabs my arm again and pulls it behind me. The other one goes behind me too. I try to yank and tug away, which only makes his grip tighter. Before I know it, my chest hits the ground first, then my face is pressed against the cold floor. Long's knee goes onto my back as Tate removes my backpack.

"Yo! What the fuck!" Sonny shouts.

"Get off of her!" Malik says, camera pointed at us.

"You brought something in here, huh?" Long says. He wraps plastic around my wrists and pulls it tight. "That's why you didn't want us to see it, huh? You li'l hoodlum! Where's all that mouth you had yesterday?"

I can't say a word.

He's not a cop.

He doesn't have a gun.

But I don't wanna end up like that boy.

I want my mom.

I want my dad.

I wanna go home.

FIVE

I end up in Principal Rhodes's office.

My arms are tied behind me. Long dragged me in here and made me sit down a few minutes ago. He's in Dr. Rhodes's office now. She told her secretary, Ms. Clark, to call my mom and keep an eye on me, like I'm the one who needs to be watched.

Ms. Clark looks through my files on her computer for Jay's work number. Surprised she doesn't know it by heart by now.

I stare straight ahead. The office has inspirational posters on every wall. One is a complete lie: "You can't control what other people do. You can only control the way that you react."

No, you can't. Not when your arm is jerked behind you, or you're lying on the floor with a knee in your back. You can't control shit then.

Ms. Clark picks up her phone and dials. After a couple of

seconds, she goes, "Hi, this is Midtown School of the Arts. May I speak to Mrs. Jayda Jackson, please?"

Jay answers the phones at Christ Temple, so I expect Ms. Clark to go right into explaining the situation to her. But she frowns. "Oh. I see. Thank you."

She hangs up.

Weird. "What did my mom say?"

"I was told that your mother doesn't work there anymore. Is there another way to reach her?"

I sit up as best as I can. "What?"

"Should I try her cell phone or her home phone?"

"Are you sure you called Christ Temple Church?"

"Positive," Ms. Clark says. "Cell phone or home phone?"

My heart stops.

The Popkenchurch.

Jay only gets it when something bad happens.

Did she . . . did she lose her job?

She couldn't have. Ms. Clark's got it wrong somehow. She probably called the wrong place and just doesn't realize it.

Yeah. That's it.

I tell Ms. Clark to try Jay's cell phone. About fifteen minutes later, the office door flies open, and Jay storms in. She's in her work clothes, so she must've left the church.

"Brianna, what in the world happened?"

She kneels in front of me and looks me over, almost like she did when she came back from rehab. Her eyes couldn't get enough of me. Now they examine every inch of me . . . except my hands. She whirls around on the secretary. "Why the hell is my daughter handcuffed?"

Dr. Rhodes appears in her doorway. Her glasses take up most of her face, and her curly red hair is in a bun. She was the principal back when Trey went here, too. I met her at his Freshman Welcome Night. She gave me this sugary-sweet smile and said, "Hopefully in a few years, you'll join us too."

She didn't say there would be a security guard ranting in her office about "those kids" bringing "that stuff" into "this school." The door was closed, but I heard him.

Those kids. *This* school. Like one doesn't belong with the other.

"Mrs. Jackson," Dr. Rhodes says, "may we please have a word in my office?"

"Not until my daughter is released."

Dr. Rhodes looks back over her shoulder. "Mr. Long, would you please release Brianna?"

He lumbers out and removes the little scissors hanging from a clip on his waist. He grumbles, "Stand up."

I do, and with one little snip my hands are uncuffed.

Jay immediately cups my cheeks. "Are you okay, baby?"

"Mrs. Jackson, my office, please?" Dr. Rhodes says. "You too, Brianna."

We follow her in. The look she gives Long tells him to stay outside.

My backpack sits on top of her desk. It's unzipped, revealing every pack of candy I had.

Dr. Rhodes points at the two chairs in front of her. "Please, have a seat."

We do. "Are you going to tell me why my daughter was handcuffed?" Jay asks.

"There was an incident—"

"Obviously."

"I will be the first to admit that the guards used excessive force. They put Brianna on the floor."

"Threw," I mumble. "They *threw* me on the floor."

Jay's eyes widen. "Excuse me?"

"We've had issues with students bringing illegal drugs—"

"That doesn't explain why they manhandled my child!" says Jay.

"Brianna was not cooperative at first."

"It still doesn't explain it!" Jay says.

Dr. Rhodes takes a deep breath. "It will not happen again, Mrs. Jackson. I assure you that there will be an investigation and disciplinary action will take place if the administration sees fit. However, Brianna may have to face disciplinary action as well." She turns to me. "Brianna, have you been selling candy on campus?"

I fold my arms. I'm not answering that shit. And let her turn this around on me? Hell no.

"Answer her," Jay tells me.

"It's only candy," I mumble.

"Maybe so," says Dr. Rhodes, "but it's against school policy to sell contraband on campus."

Contraband? "The only reason y'all found out about it is because Long and Tate like to go after the black and Latinx kids!"

"Brianna," Jay says. It's not a warning. It's an "I got this." She turns to Rhodes. "Since when is *candy* contraband? Why did they come after my daughter in the first place?"

"The security guards have the right to conduct random searches. I can assure you that Brianna was not 'targeted.'"

"Bullshit!" I don't even bite my tongue. "They always harass us."

"It may seem that way—"

"It is that way!"

"Brianna," Jay says. That's a warning. She turns to the principal. "Dr. Rhodes, my son told me that the guards picked on certain kids more than others when he was here. I don't think my children are making this up. I'd *hate* to think you're saying that."

"There will be an investigation," Dr. Rhodes says so calmly, it pisses me off. "But I stand by what I said, Mrs. Jackson. The guards treat all of the students the same."

"Oh," says Jay. "They throw them all on the floor, huh?"

Silence.

Dr. Rhodes clears her throat. "Again, Brianna was not

cooperative. I was told she was argumentative and aggressive. This is not the first time we've had behavioral issues with her."

Here we go.

"What are you trying to say?" Jay asks.

"Today's behavior follows a pattern—"

"Yes, a pattern of my daughter being targeted—"

"Again, no one is targeting—"

"Do the white girls who make slick comments get sent to your office every other week too?" Jay asks.

"Mrs. Jackson, Brianna is frequently aggressive—"

Aggressive. One word, three syllables. Rhymes with excessive.

I'm so excessive,
that I'm aggressive.

"Aggressive" is used to describe me a lot. It's supposed to mean threatening, but I've never threatened anybody. I just say stuff that my teachers don't like. All of them except Mrs. Murray, who happens to be my only black teacher. There was the time in history class during Black History Month. I asked Mr. Kincaid why we don't ever talk about black people before slavery. His pale cheeks reddened.

"Because we're following a lesson plan, Brianna," he said.

"Yeah, but don't you come up with the lesson plans?" I asked.

"I will not tolerate outbursts in class."

"I'm just saying, don't act like black people didn't exist before—"

He told me to go to the office. Wrote me up as being "aggressive."

Fiction class. Mrs. Burns was talking about the literary canon, and I rolled my eyes because all the books sounded boring as shit. She asked if there was a problem, and I told her exactly that, just without saying "as shit." She sent me to the office. I mumbled something under my breath on the way out, and she wrote me up for aggressive behavior.

Can't forget the incident in my theater elective. We'd done the same scene one hundred times. Mr. Ito told us to start from the top yet again. I sucked my teeth and went, "Oh my God," throwing my hands at my sides. My script flew from my grasp and hit him. He swore I intentionally threw it. That got me a two-day suspension.

That's all from this year. Freshman year and sophomore year were full of incidents, too. Now I've got another under my belt.

"Per school policy, Brianna will have to serve a three-day suspension for selling banned items on school property without permission," Dr. Rhodes says. She zips up my backpack and hands it to me.

We go into the hallway just as the bell for second period rings. Classroom doors open, and it seems like everybody and their momma pour into the halls. I get second glances I've never gotten before, and stares and whispers.

I'm no longer invisible, but now I wish I was.

I'm quiet on the ride home.

Hoodlum. One word, two syllables. Can be made to rhyme with a lot of things. Synonyms: thug, delinquent, hooligan, low-life, gangster, and, according to Long, Brianna.

Can't no good come,
From this hoodlum.

Nah. Fuck that word.

Fuck that school.

Fuck all of this.

I stare at what's left of the Garden. We're on Clover Street, which used to be one of the busiest streets in Garden Heights, but ever since the riots, there's a bunch of charred rubble and boarded-up buildings. The Mega Dollar Store was one of the first to get hit. Cellular Express got looted first and then burned down. Shop 'n Save burned down to the frame, and now we have to go to the Walmart on the edge of the Garden or the little store over on the west if we wanna get groceries.

I'm a hoodlum from a bunch of nothing.

"Doubt they'll ever fix this mess," Jay says. "It's like they want us to remember what happens when we step out of line."

She glances over at me. "You okay, Bookie?"

According to my granddaddy, Jacksons don't cry—we suck it up and deal with it. Doesn't matter how much my eyes burn. "I didn't do anything wrong."

"No, you didn't," Jay says. "You had every right to keep your backpack. But Bri . . . Promise me, if that ever happens again, you'll do what they tell you to do."

"What?"

"Bad things can happen, baby. People like that sometimes abuse their power."

"So I don't have any power?"

"You have more than you know. But in moments like that, I—" She swallows. "I need you to act as if you don't have any. Once you're safely out of the situation, *then* we'll handle it. But I need you *safely* out of the situation. Okay?"

This is like that talk she gave me about the cops. Do whatever they tell you to do, she said. Don't make them think you're a threat. Basically, weaken myself and take whatever's thrown at me so I can survive that moment.

I'm starting to think it doesn't matter what I do. I'll still be whatever people think I am. "They're always on my case at that school."

"I know," Jay says. "And it's not fair. But you only have to get through two more years, baby. All these incidents . . . we can't risk you getting expelled, Bri. If that means keeping your mouth shut, I need you to do it."

"I can't speak up for myself?"

"You pick your battles," she says. "Not everything deserves a comment or an eye roll or an attitude—"

"I'm not the only one who does that stuff!"

"No, but girls like you are the only ones getting hits on their permanent record!"

The car goes quiet.

Jay sighs out of her nose. "Sometimes the rules are different for black folks, baby," she says. "Hell, sometimes they're playing checkers while we're in a complicated-ass chess game. It's an awful fact of life, but it's a fact. Midtown is unfortunately one of those places where you not only gotta play chess, but you gotta play it by a different set of rules."

I hate this shit. "I don't wanna go back there."

"I understand, but we don't have any other options."

"Why can't I go to Garden High?"

"Because your daddy and I swore that you and Trey would never step foot in that school," she says. "You think the guards are bad at Midtown? They have actual cops at Garden High, Bri. The damn school is treated like a prison. They don't set anybody up to succeed. Say what you want about Midtown, but you've got a better chance there."

"A better chance at what? Getting tossed around like a rag doll?"

"A better chance at making it!" She's louder than me. She takes a deep breath. "You're gonna face a whole lot of Longs and Tates in your life, baby. More than I'd like. But you never let their actions determine what you do. The moment you do, you've given them the power. You hear me?"

Yeah, but does she hear me? Neither of us speaks for the longest.

"I wish . . . I wish I could give you more options, baby. I do. We don't have any. Especially right now."

Especially right now. I look over at her. "Did something happen?"

She shifts in her seat a little. "Why you say that?"

"Ms. Clark called the church. They said you don't work there anymore."

"Brianna, let's not talk about—"

Oh, God. "You lost your job?"

"This is temporary, okay?"

"You lost your job?"

She swallows. "Yes, I did."

Oh no.

No.

No.

No.

"The church daycare got damaged during the riots, and the insurance company isn't covering the damages," she says. "Pastor and the elders board had to adjust the budget in order to pay for repairs, so they let me go."

Shit.

I'm not stupid. Jay tries to act like everything's all good, but we're struggling. We already don't have gas. Last month, we got an eviction notice. Jay used most of her check to cover the rent, and we ate sandwiches until her next payday.

But if she lost her job, she won't have a payday.

If she doesn't have a payday, we might not ever have gas again.

Or food.

Or a house.

What if—

"Don't worry, Bri," Jay says. "God's got us, baby."

The same God who let her get laid off from a *church*?

"I've been going on interviews," she says. "Left one to pick you up, actually. Plus, I've already filed for unemployment. It's not a lot, but it's something."

She's *already* filed? "How long have you been away from the church?"

"That's not important."

"Yes, it is."

"No, it's not," she says. "Trey and I are taking care of things."

"Trey knew?"

She opens and closes her mouth a couple of times. "Yes."

Figures. When the gas got cut off, Trey knew it was gonna happen. I found out when I woke up in a cold house. The eviction notice? Trey knew. I found out when I overheard them talking about it. I wish it didn't bother me, but it does. It's like

Jay doesn't trust me enough to tell me the important stuff. Like she thinks I'm too young to handle it.

I handled her being gone for years. I can handle more than she thinks.

She parks in our driveway behind Trey's old Honda Civic, then turns toward me, but I look out my window.

Okay, maybe I am a little bit immature. Whatever.

"I know you're worried," she says. "Things have been tough for a while. But it's gonna get better. Somehow, someway. We gotta believe that, baby."

She reaches for my cheek.

I move away and open my door. "I'm going for a walk."

Jay grabs my arm. "Brianna, wait."

I'm shaking. Here I am, worried about real problems, and she wants me to "believe"? "Please, let me go."

"No. I'm not letting you run instead of talk to me. Today's been a lot, baby."

"I'm fine."

She runs her thumb along my arm, like she's trying to coax the tears out of me. "No, you're not. It's okay if you're not. You do know you don't have to be strong all the time, right?"

Maybe not all the time, but I have to be right now. I tug away from her. "I'm fine."

"Brianna—"

I throw my hoodie over my head and march down the sidewalk.

Sometimes I dream that I'm drowning. It's always in a big, blue ocean that's too deep for me to see the bottom. But I tell myself I'm not going to die no matter how much water gets in my lungs or how deep I sink, I am not going to die. Because I say so.

Suddenly, I can breathe underwater. I can swim. The ocean isn't so scary anymore. It's actually kinda cool. I even learn how to control it.

But I'm awake, I'm drowning, and I don't know how to control any of this.

SIX

The Maple Grove projects are a whole different world.

I live on the east side of the Garden, where the houses are nicer, the homeowners are older, and the gunshots aren't as frequent. The Maple Grove projects are a fifteen-minute walk away on the west side, or as Grandma calls it, "that ol' rough side." It's on the news more, and so many of the houses look like nobody should live in them. But it's kinda like saying one side of the Death Star is safer than the other. It's still the goddamn Death Star.

At Maple Grove, six three-story buildings sit close enough to the freeway that Aunt Pooh says they used to go on the rooftops and throw rocks at the cars. Badasses. There was a seventh building, but it burned down a few years ago and instead of rebuilding it, the state tore it down. Now there's a grassy field in its place where kids go play. The playground is for junkies.

"Whaddup, Li'l Law," a guy shouts from inside a raggedy car as I cross the parking lot. Never seen him in my life, but I wave. I'll always be my dad's daughter if nothing else.

He should be here. Maybe if he was, I wouldn't be wondering how we're gonna make it since Jay doesn't have a job.

I swear, we can never just be "good." Something always happens. Either we barely got food or this thing got shut off. It's. Always. Something.

We can't have any power, either. I mean, think about it. All these people I've never met have way more control over my life than I've ever had. If some Crown hadn't killed my dad, he'd be a big rap star and money wouldn't be an issue. If some drug dealer hadn't sold my mom her first hit, she could've gotten her degree already and would have a good job. If that cop hadn't murdered that boy, people wouldn't have rioted, the daycare wouldn't have burned down, and the church wouldn't have let Jay go.

All these folks I've never met became gods over my life. Now I gotta take the power back.

I'm hoping Aunt Pooh knows how.

A boy zooms toward me on a dirt bike wearing a Celtics jersey with a hoodie underneath, clear beads on his braids. He hits the brakes just inches away from me. Inches.

"Boy, I swear if you would've hit me," I say.

Jojo snickers. "I wasn't gon' hit you."

Jojo can't be any more than ten. He lives with his momma in the apartment right above Aunt Pooh's. He makes it his business to speak to me every time I'm over here. Aunt Pooh thinks he has a crush on me, but nah. I think he just wants somebody to talk to. He'll hit me up for candy, too. Like today.

"You got some king-size Skittles, Bri?" he asks.

"Yep. Two dollars."

"Two dollars? That's expensive as hell!"

This li'l boy's got a whole bunch of money pinned to the front of his jersey—it must be his birthday—and he's got the nerve to complain about my prices?

"One, watch your mouth," I tell him. "Two, that's the same price they are at the store. Three, why you not in school?"

He pops a wheelie. "Why *you* not in school?"

Fair enough. I slide off my backpack. "You know what? Since it's your birthday, I'm gonna go against my own rules and let you have a pack for free."

The second I hand them over, he rips them open and pours a bunch into his mouth.

I tilt my head. "Well?"

"Thank you," he says with a mouthful.

"We gotta work on your manners. For real."

Jojo follows me to the courtyard. It's mostly dirt now thanks to the cars that people have parked there, like the one Aunt Pooh and her homeboy, Scrap, sit on. Scrap's hair is half braided, half Afro, like he got up in the middle of getting it braided to go do something else. Knowing Scrap, he did. His socks poke out of his flip-flops, and he shoves huge spoonfuls of cereal into his mouth from a mixing bowl. He and Aunt Pooh talk to the other GDs standing around them.

Aunt Pooh sees me and hops off the car. "Why the hell you ain't in school?"

Scrap and the GDs nod at me, like I'm one of the guys. I get that a lot. "I got suspended," I tell Aunt Pooh.

"*Again?* For what?"

I hop up on the car beside Scrap. "Some BS."

I tell them everything, from how security loves to target black and brown kids to how they pinned me to the ground. The GDs shake their heads. Aunt Pooh looks like she wants blood. Jojo claims he would've "whooped them guards' ass," which makes everybody but me laugh.

"You wouldn't have done nothing, boy," I say.

"On my momma." Aunt Pooh claps her hands with each word. "On my momma they messed with the wrong one. Point them out and I'll handle them fools."

Aunt Pooh doesn't go from zero to one hundred—she goes from chill to ready to kill. But I don't want to have her in prison over Long and Tate. "They're not worth it, Aunty."

"How much time you get, Bri?" Scrap asks.

Damn. He makes it sound like I'm going to prison. "Three days."

"That ain't bad," he says. "They take your candy?"

"Nah, why?"

"Let me get some Starbursts then."

"That'll be a dollar," I tell him.

"I ain't got cash. I can pay you tomorrow though."

This fool did not. "Then you can get the Starbursts tomorrow."

"Goddamn, it's just a dollar," Scrap says.

"Goddamn, it's just twenty-four hours," I say in my best Scrap voice. Aunt Pooh and the others crack up. "I don't do credit. That's against the Ten Snack Commandments, bruh."

"The what?" he says.

"Yo! That shit!" Aunt Pooh backhands my arm. "Y'all, she redid Big's 'Ten Crack Commandments.' It's dope as hell, too. Bri, spit that shit."

This is how it goes. I let Aunt Pooh hear some rhymes I wrote, she gets so hype over them that she tells me to rap them for her friends. Trust, if you're whack, a gangbanger will be the first to let you know.

"All right." I throw my hoodie on. Aunt Pooh pounds out a rhythm on the hood of the car. More people in the courtyard drift over.

I nod along. Just like that I'm in my zone.

I been at this game for months, and the money's been gradual,
So I made some rules, using Big's manual

A couple of steps unique, for me to keep
My game on track while I sell these snacks.
Rule numero uno, never let no one know,
how much cash I stack, 'cause it's fact
that cheddar breeds jealousy 'specially
when it comes to Basics. They'll be quick to take it.
Number two, never tell folks my next move.
Don't you know competition got a mission and
ambition
to make exactly what I'm getting?
They'll be at my spots where it's hot with plans to
open up shop.
Number three, I only trust Sonny and Leek.
Li'l kids will set my ass up, properly gassed up,
hoodied and masked up. Huh, for a couple bucks
Stick me up on playgrounds when no one's around.
Number four is actually important the more:
No eating the stash while I'm making the cash.
Number five, never sell no junk where I bunk.
I don't care if they want some chips, tell them dip.
Number six—them things called refunds? See none.
Make the sale, take the bills, let them bail, and be done.
Seven, this rule gets people up in arms,
but no credit or discounts, not even for my mom.
Family and biz don't gel, like bubble guts and Taco
Bell

Find myself saying, "What the hell?"
Number eight, never keep no profits in my pockets
and wallets. Deposit. Or buy a safe and lock it.
Number nine is just as bad as number one to me:
No matter where I'm at, keep an eye for police.
If they thinkin' I'm suspicious, they ain't trying to
listen.
They'll unload them mags, make me a hashtag.
Number ten, two words—perfect timin'.
I want some lines then? Do early grinding,
missing out on clientele, that's a hell no.
If they don't see me out, they going straight to the
store.
Using these steps, I'll have cash out the anus,
to get what I need, and help out with bill payments,
and sell more cookies, than that famous named Amos.
On my mom and on my dad, and word to Big, one of
the greatest.

"What?" I finish.

A collective "Ohhhhh!" goes up. Jojo's mouth is wide open. One or two GDs bow to me.

There's absolutely nothing like this. Yeah, they're gangbangers, and they've done all kinds of foul shit that I don't even wanna know about. But I'm enough to them, so frankly, they're enough to me.

"A'ight, a'ight," Aunt Pooh calls over to them. "I need to talk to the superstar in private. Y'all gotta go."

Everybody but Scrap and Jojo leave.

Aunt Pooh lightly pushes Jojo's head. "Go on, li'l badass."

"Dang, Pooh! When you gon' let me claim?"

He means claim colors, as in become a Garden Disciple. This little boy's always trying to join, like it's the Maple Grove basketball team. He's been throwing up GD signs for as long as I've known him.

"Forever never," Aunt Pooh says. "Now go."

Jojo makes this sound like a tire pump spitting air. "Man," he groans, but he pedals away.

Aunt Pooh turns to Scrap, who still hasn't left. She tilts her head like, *Well?*

"What?" he says. "This my car. I stay if I wanna."

"Man, whatever," Aunt Pooh says. "You good, Bri?"

I shrug. It's weird. Ever since Long called me a "hoodlum," it's like the word's branded on my forehead, and I can't get it off me. Hate that this is bothering me so much.

"You sure you don't want me to handle them guards?" Aunt Pooh asks.

She's so serious it's almost scary. "Positive."

"A'ight. I got you, just give the word." She unwraps a Blow Pop and sticks it in her mouth. "What Jay gon' do about this?"

"She's not letting me leave that school, so it doesn't matter."

"What, you wanna go to Garden High?"

I pull my knees closer. "At least I wouldn't be invisible there."

"You ain't invisible," Aunt Pooh says.

I snort. "Trust, I basically walk around with an invisibility cloak on."

"A what?" Scrap asks.

I stare at him. "Please tell me you're joking."

"It's some nerd shit, Scrap," Aunt Pooh says.

"Um, excuse you, but Harry Potter is a cultural phenomenon."

Scrap goes, "Ohhhh. That's the one with the li'l dude with the ring, right? 'My precioussss,'" he says in his best Gollum voice.

I give up.

"Like I said, nerd shit," says Aunt Pooh. "Anyway, stop worrying about whether them fools notice you at Midtown, Bri. Listen." She props her foot on the car bumper. "High school ain't the end or the beginning. It ain't even in the middle. You 'bout to do big things, whether they see it or not. I see it. Everybody last night saw it. Long as *you* see it, that's all that matters."

Sometimes she's my personal Yoda. If Yoda was a woman and had a gold grill. Unfortunately, she doesn't know who Yoda is. "Yeah. You're right."

"I'm what?" She puts her hand to her ear. "I ain't hear that good. I'm what?"

I laugh. "You're right, dang!"

She tugs my hoodie so it covers my eyes. "Thought so. How you get over here anyway? Your momma drop you off on her way back to work? Should've told me I was gon' be babysitting your hardheaded ass."

Oh.

I forgot the reason I came over here in the first place. I stare at my Not-Timbs. "Jay got laid off."

"Oh, shit," Aunt Pooh says. "For real?"

"Yep. The church let her go so they could pay for repairs to the daycare."

"Shit, man." Aunt Pooh wipes her face. "You a'ight?"

Jacksons can't cry, but we can tell the truth. "No."

Aunt Pooh pulls me into her arms. As much of a hard-ass as my aunt is, her hugs are the best. They somehow say "I love you" and "I'll do whatever for you" all at once.

"It'll be a'ight," Aunt Pooh murmurs. "I'm gon' help y'all out, okay?"

"You know Jay won't let you." Jay never takes money from Aunt Pooh, since she knows where she gets it from. I understand. If drugs almost destroyed me, I wouldn't take money that's made from them either.

"Her stubborn ass," Aunt Pooh mumbles. "I know this shit is probably scary as hell right now, but one day you gon' look back, and this gon' feel like a lifetime ago. This a temporary setback for a major comeback. We ain't letting it stop the come up."

That's what we call our goal, the come up. It's when we finally make it with this rap stuff. I'm talking get-out-the-Garden-and-have-enough-money-to-never-worry-again make it.

"I gotta do something, Aunty," I say. "I know Jay's looking for a job, and Trey's working, but I don't wanna be deadweight."

"What you talking 'bout? You ain't deadweight."

Yeah, I am. My mom and my brother bust their butts so I can eat and have somewhere to lay my head, and what do I do? Absolutely nothing. Jay doesn't want me to get a job—she wants me fully focused on school. I picked up candy dealing. I figured if I handled some stuff for myself, that would help.

I need to do more, and the only thing I know to do is rap.

Now, let me be real: I know not every rapper out there is rich. A whole lot of them fake for the cameras, but even the fakers have more money than me. Then you got folks like Dee-Nice who don't have to fake thanks to that million-dollar deal. He played his cards right and got his come up.

"We gotta make this rap stuff happen," I tell Aunt Pooh. "Like now."

"I got you, okay? I was gon' call you anyway. I've had all kinds of folks hitting me up because of the battle. I made some stuff happen for you a li'l while ago."

"For real?"

"Uh-huh. For one, we getting you back in the Ring. That'll help make a name for you."

A name? "Yeah, but it won't make me any money."

"Just trust me, a'ight?" she says. "Besides, that ain't the only thing I arranged."

"What else then?"

She rubs her chin. "I don't know if you can handle this one yet."

Oh my God. This is not the time to drag me along. "Just tell me, dang!"

Aunt Pooh laughs. "A'ight, a'ight. Last night, a producer came up to me after the battle and gave me his card. I called him earlier, and we arranged for him to make a beat and for you to go into his studio tomorrow."

I blink. "I . . . I'm going in a studio?"

Aunt Pooh grins. "Yep."

"And I'm making a song?"

"You damn right."

"Yooooooo!" I put my fist at my mouth. "For real? For real?"

"Hell yeah! Told you I was gon' make something happen!"

Damn. I've dreamed of going into a studio since I was like ten. I would stand in front of my bathroom mirror with my headphones on my ears and a brush in my hand like it was a mic, as I rapped along with Nicki Minaj. Now I'm gonna make my own song.

"Shit." There's a slight problem. "Which song will I do though?"

I've got tons in my notebook. Plus, a hell of a lot more ideas that I haven't written down. But this is my first real song. It's gotta be the right one.

"Look, whatever you do is gon' be a banger," Aunt Pooh says. "Don't sweat it."

Scrap shoves a spoonful of cereal into his mouth. "You need to do something like that song ol' boy you battled got."

"That 'Swagerific' trash?" Aunt Pooh asks. "Man, get outta here! That shit ain't got no substance."

"It ain't gotta have substance," Scrap says. "Milez lost last night, yet that song so catchy, he got even more folks talking 'bout it. Shit was trending this morning."

"Hold up," I say. "You mean to tell me that I won the battle, am *clearly* the better rapper, and yet he's getting all the buzz?"

"So basically," Scrap says, "you won the popular vote 'cause everybody loved you in the Ring, but you still lost the election since he the one getting fame?"

I shake my head. "Too soon."

"Touché," he says, because he's Scrap, and sometimes he says *touché*.

"Look, don't worry 'bout that, Bri," Aunt Pooh says. "If that fool can blow up 'cause of some garbage, I know you can—"

"Pooh!" This skinny older man zigzags across the courtyard. "Lemme holla at you!"

"Goddamn, Tony!" Aunt Pooh groans. "I'm in the middle of an important conversation."

It's not *that* important. She goes over to him.

I bite my lip. I don't know how she does it. I don't mean the actual selling drugs part. She hands them the product, they hand her the money. Simple. I mean I don't know how she can do it, knowing that at one time somebody else was the dealer and my mom, *her sister*, was the junkie.

But if I make this rap stuff happen, hopefully she'll give all that up.

"Real talk, Bri," Scrap says. "Although Milez getting all the attention, you oughta be proud. You got skills. I mean, he blowing up, and I don't know what the hell gon' happen for you, but yeah, you got skills."

What kinda shady-ass compliment is this? "Thanks?"

"The Garden need you, for real," he says. "I remember when your pops was on the come up. Every time he made a music video around the neighborhood, my li'l ass tried to get in it. Just wanted to be in his presence. He gave us hope. Hardly anything good ever come from around here, you know?"

I watch Aunt Pooh slip something into Tony's shaky hand. "Yeah, I know."

"But *you* could be the something good," says Scrap.

I hadn't thought about it like that. Or the fact that so many people looked up to my dad. Enjoyed his music? Yeah. But he gave them hope? It's not like he was the "cleanest" rapper.

But in the Garden, we make our own heroes. The kids in the projects love Aunt Pooh because she gives them money. They don't care how she gets it. My dad talked about foul shit, yeah, but it's shit that happens around here. That makes him a hero.

Maybe I can be one, too.

Scrap slurps the rest of the milk from his bowl. "'Swag-erific, so call me terrific,'" he raps with a little shoulder bounce. "'Swag-erific. Swag-erific . . . Swag, swag, swag . . .'"

SEVEN

Here's the thing about my brother's car: You hear it before you see it.

Scrap's still rapping "Swagerific" to himself when I notice that all-too-familiar grumble getting closer. Granddaddy says Trey needs a new tailpipe. Trey says he needs money for a new tailpipe.

That old Honda Civic pulls into the Maple Grove parking lot, and heads turn in its direction like they always do. Trey parks, gets out, and seems to look straight at me.

Welp. This isn't good.

He crosses the parking lot. His hair and his beard have grown out since he moved back home. Granddaddy says he looks like he's in a midlife crisis.

Grandma says our dad spit Trey out. They look exactly

alike, right down to their dimples. Jay claims he even walks like Dad, with this swagger about him as if he's got everything figured out already. He's in his Sal's uniform—a green polo with a pizza-slice logo on the chest and a matching hat. He's supposed to be heading to work.

A GD in the courtyard notices him and nudges one of his friends. Soon all of them watch Trey. With smirks.

When he's close to me, Trey goes, "I guess phones are useless now, huh?"

"Good morning to you too."

"You know how long I been driving around looking for you, Bri? You had us worried sick."

"I told Jay I was going for a walk."

"You need to tell folks *where* you're going," he says. "Why couldn't you answer your phone?"

"What are you talking—" I take it out of my hoodie pocket. Damn. I've got a ton of texts and missed calls from him and Jay. Sonny and Malik have texted me too. That little half-moon in the top corner explains why I didn't know. "Sorry. I put it on Do Not Disturb for school and forgot to turn it back on."

Trey tiredly wipes his face. "You can't be—"

Loud laughs erupt across the courtyard from those GDs. They're all looking at Trey.

Trey looks right back at them, like, *We got a problem?*

Aunt Pooh comes over, smirking too. "My dude," she says as she slips money in her pocket. "What you doing?"

"I'm getting my little sister, that's what."

"Nah, bruh." She eyes him from head to toe. "I mean this shit! You the pizza boy? C'mon, Trey. Really?"

Scrap busts out laughing.

I don't see a damn thing funny though. It took my brother forever to find something, and nah, making pizzas ain't "goals," but he's trying.

"I mean, damn," Aunt Pooh says. "You spent all that time in college, being Mr. Big Man on Campus with the good grades and shit, and *this* the result?"

Trey's jaw ticks. It's nothing for these two to get into it. Trey usually doesn't hold back, either. Aunt Pooh's not that much older than him, so that whole "respect your elders" thing is a no-go.

But today, he says, "You know what? I don't have time for immature, insecure folks. C'mon, Bri."

"'Immature'? 'Insecure'?" Aunt Pooh says the words like they're nasty. "The hell you talking 'bout?"

Trey pulls me toward the parking lot.

We pass the GDs. "How he gon' be the big homie's son and making pizzas?" one says.

"Law probably rolling in his grave at this weak shit," another says, shaking his head. "Good thing li'l momma keeping it going for him."

Trey doesn't respond to them, either. He's always been "too nerdy to be Law's son." Too soft, not street enough, not hood enough. I don't think he cares though.

We get in his car. There are candy wrappers, receipts, fast food bags, and papers all over. Trey is messy as hell. Once I lock my seat belt, Trey pulls out.

He sighs. "Sorry if it seemed like I was coming at you, Li'l Bit."

Trey was the first person in the family to call me that. Word is he didn't get why everybody was obsessed with me when our parents brought me home because I was just a "li'l bit cute, not a lot." It stuck.

For the record, I was a whole lot cute.

"You had us worried," he goes on. "Ma was about to ask Grandma and Granddaddy to look for you. You *know* it's bad if she was about to do that."

"Really?" Grandma would've never let her live that down, either. Seriously, I could be grown with kids of my own and Grandma would be one cough away from death, telling Jay, "Remember that time you couldn't find my grandbaby and called me for help?"

The petty is strong in that one.

"Yeah, really," Trey says. "Besides, you don't need to be hanging out in the projects."

"It's not that bad over there."

"Listen to yourself. Not *that* bad. It's bad enough. Doesn't help that you're hanging around Pooh, considering all that she's into."

"She wouldn't let anything happen to me."

"Bri, she can't stop something from happening to herself," he says.

"I'm sorry for that stuff she said back there."

"I'm not bothered," he says. "She's insecure about her predicament and picks on me to make herself feel better."

Thanks to that psychology degree, my brother can read folks like a pro. "Still doesn't make it right."

"It is what it is. But I wanna talk about you, not me. Ma told me what happened at school. How are you feeling?"

If I close my eyes tight enough, I can still see Long and Tate pinning me to the ground. I can still hear that word. "Hoodlum."

One damn word and it feels like it's got all the power over me. But I tell Trey, "I'm fine."

"Yeah, and Denzel Washington is my daddy."

"Damn, for real? The good genes skipped you, huh?"

He side-eyes me. I grin. Trolling him is a hobby.

"Asshole," he says. "But for real, talk to me, Bri. How are you feeling?"

I rest my head back. There are a couple of reasons my brother majored in psychology. One, he says he wants to keep somebody from ending up like our mom did. Trey swears that if Jay had gotten counseling after seeing Dad die, she wouldn't have run to drugs to deal with the trauma. Two, he's always in somebody's business about their feelings. Always. Now he has a degree to certify his nosiness.

"I'm sick of that school," I say. "They always single me out, Trey."

"Ever thought that maybe you should stop giving them a reason to single you out?"

"Hold up, you're supposed to be on my side!"

"I am, Bri. It's bullshit that they're always sending you to the office. But you also gotta chill a little bit. You're a classic case of oppositional defiant disorder."

Dr. Trey is in the building. "Stop trying to diagnose me."

"I'm simply stating facts," he says. "You tend to be argumentative, defiant, you speak impulsively, you get irritable easily—"

"I do not! Take that shit back!"

His lips thin. "Like I said, ODD."

I sit back and fold my arms. "Whatever."

Trey busts out laughing. "You're predictable at this point. Sounds like that ODD helped you out last night though. Congrats on the Ring win." He holds his fist to me.

I bump it. "You watch the battle yet?"

"Haven't had time. Kayla texted me about it."

"Who?"

He rolls his eyes. "Ms. Tique."

"Ohhhh." I forgot she has a real name. "It's so damn cool that you work with her." Even though it's kinda sad that somebody as dope as Ms. Tique has to make pizzas for a living. "I'd be starstruck around her."

Trey chuckles. "You act like she's Beyoncé."

"She is! She's the Beyoncé of the Ring."

"She's something, all right."

He probably doesn't realize he's all dimples at the moment. I pull my head back a little with my eyebrows raised.

Trey notices me staring. "What?"

"Are you trying to be her Jay-Z?"

He laughs. "Shut up. We're supposed to be talking about *you*." He pokes my arm. "Ma told me she broke the news about her job before you ran off. How are you feeling about that?"

Dr. Trey is still on duty. "I'm scared," I admit. "We were already struggling. Now it'll only be harder."

"It will be," he says. "I can't lie—between my student loans and my car note, feels like most of my check's already gone. Things are gonna be extra tight until Ma gets a job or I get a better one."

"How's your job search going?" He's been looking for something since his first day at Sal's.

Trey runs his fingers through his hair. He definitely needs a haircut. "It's okay. Just taking a while. Thought about going back to school to get my master's. That would open up a hell of a lot more doors, but . . ."

"But what?"

"That would take away hours I could be working. It's all good though."

No, it's not.

"But I promise you this," he says, "no matter what happens, it's gonna be okay. Your almighty, all-knowing big brother will make sure of that."

"I didn't know I had another big brother."

"You're such a hater!" He laughs. "But it'll be fine. Okay?" He holds his fist to me again.

I bump it. Things can never go wrong on Dr. Trey's watch.

He shouldn't have to fix this though. He shouldn't have had to come back to Garden Heights. At Markham State, he was king. Literally, he was the homecoming king. Everybody knew him from starring in campus productions and from leading the drum majors. He graduated with honors. Worked his ass off to get there in the first place, only to have to come back to the hood and work in a pizza shop.

It's bullshit, and it scares me, because if Trey can't make it by doing everything "right," who can?

"All right, so this ODD of yours," he says. "We need to get to the root of it, then work—"

"I do not have ODD," I say. "End of discussion."

"End of discussion," he mocks.

"Don't repeat what I say."

"Don't repeat what I say."

"You're an asshole."

"*You're* an asshole."

"Bri is right."

"Bri is ri—" He looks at me.

I grin. Got him.

He pushes my shoulder. "Smartass."

I bust out laughing. As awful as the situation is and as big of a pain in the butt as he can be, I'm glad I have my big brother to go through it with me.

EIGHT

When I wake up the next morning, my headphones hang lopsided off my head as my dad raps in them. I fell asleep listening to him. His voice is as deep as Granddaddy's, a bit raspy at times, and as hard as the stuff he raps about. To me it's as warm as a hug. It always puts me to sleep.

According to my phone, it's eight a.m. Aunt Pooh will be here in about an hour to take me to the studio. I flipped through my notebook most of last night, trying to figure out what song to record. There's "Unarmed and Dangerous." I wrote that after that kid got killed, but I don't know if I wanna be political from jump. There's "State the Facts," which reveals too much personal shit—I'm not ready for that yet. There's "Hustle and Grind," which has potential. Especially that hook.

I don't know though. I don't freaking know.

Laughs come from somewhere in the house, quickly followed

by a "Shhh! Don't be waking my babies up."

I lift my headphones off. It's Saturday morning, so I know who those laughs belong to.

I slide into my Tweety Bird slippers. They match my pajamas. I will always be a fool for that little yellow bird. I follow the voices toward the kitchen.

Jay's at the table, surrounded by recovering drug addicts. One Saturday per month, she has meetings with people she knew from when she lived on the streets. She calls the meetings check-ins. The community center used to hold them, but they ran out of funds and had to stop. Jay decided to keep the program going herself. Some of these folks have come a long way, like Mr. Daryl, who's been clean for six years and works in construction now. There's Ms. Pat, who just recently got her GED. Others, like Ms. Sonja, show up once in a while. Jay says the shame of falling off the wagon makes her stay away.

Sonny's and Malik's moms are here, too. Aunt Gina sits on the counter with a plate of pancakes in her lap. Aunt 'Chelle's already starting dishes at the sink. They were never on drugs, but they like to help Jay cook breakfast and even make bagged lunches for folks like Ms. Sonja, who may not get a good meal otherwise.

Sometimes we barely have food, yet Jay finds a way to feed us and other people, too.

I don't know if it impresses me or annoys me. Maybe it's both.

"I'm telling you, Pat," Jay says, "your momma will come

around and let you see your kids. Keep working on gaining her trust. I understand the frustration though. Lord, do I understand. After I finished rehab, my in-laws put me through it when it came to my babies."

I'm not sure I'm supposed to hear this.

"I'm talking court cases, supervised visits—how you gon' have some stranger supervise me as I spend time with *my* babies? All these stretch marks I got from bringing them big heads into the world, and you don't trust me around them?"

The others chuckle. Um, my head is normal-size, thank you very much.

"I was pissed," Jay says. "Felt like everybody held my mistakes against me. Still feels like that sometimes. Especially now as I go on this job hunt."

"They giving you a hard time?" Mr. Daryl asks.

"The interviews start out fine," says Jay. "Until they ask about my gap of unemployment. I tell them the truth, and suddenly I become another junkie in their eyes. I don't hear back."

"That's such bull," Aunt 'Chelle says, picking up Ms. Pat's empty plate. Malik looks nothing like his momma. She's short and plump, he's tall and lanky. She says he's his daddy's clone. "You know how many rich white folks come to the courthouse on drug possession?"

"A whole lot," says Jay.

"Too many," Aunt 'Chelle says. "Every single one gets a little slap on the wrist and goes right back into society, like it's all good. Black folks or poor folks get on drugs?"

"We're ruined for life," Jay says. "Sounds about right."

"You mean sounds about *white*," says Aunt Gina, pointing her fork. Sonny is his momma's twin, right down to their short, curly cuts.

"Mm-hmm. But what can I do?" Jay says. "I just hate that I don't know what's gonna happen nex—"

She spots me in the doorway. She clears her throat. "See? Y'all woke my baby up."

I inch into the kitchen. "No, they didn't."

"Hey, Li'l Bit," Aunt Gina says in that careful way that people only use if they feel bad for you. "How you doing?"

She must know what happened. "I'm fine."

That's not enough for Jay. She tugs at my hand. "C'mere."

I sit on her lap. I should be too big for this, but somehow, I always fit perfectly in her arms. She snuggles me close, smelling like baby powder and cocoa butter.

"My Bookie," she murmurs.

Sometimes she babies me, like it's her way of making up for when she wasn't around. I let her do it, too. I wonder though if she only sees me as her baby girl who used to snuggle up with her until I fell asleep. I don't know if the snuggles are for who I am now.

This time, I think the snuggles are for her.

Aunt Pooh picks me up as planned. I tell Jay that we're just hanging out. If I told her I'm going to a studio, she'd say I can't go because my grades dropped.

The studio is in an old house with peeling paint over on the west side. When Aunt Pooh knocks on the front door, some older woman talks to us through the screen and sends me, Aunt Pooh, and Scrap to the garage in the back.

Yeah, Scrap's here. Aunt Pooh must've brought him for backup, because this house . . .

This house is a mess.

Hard to believe anybody lives here. A couple of the windows are boarded up, and weeds and vines grow up the walls. Beer cans litter the grass. I think I spot some needles, too.

Hold up. "Is this a trap house?" I ask Aunt Pooh.

"That ain't your business," she says.

A pit bull lying in the backyard suddenly perks his head up and barks at us. He charges our way, but a chain keeps him near the fence.

Guess who almost peed herself? That'd be me. "Who's this guy again?" I ask Aunt Pooh.

"His name is Doc," she says, her thumbs tucked into the waist of her pants, either to hold them up or so she can easily get to her piece. "He ain't big-time or nothing like that, but he's talented. I got you a dope beat for a good price. He gon' mix it and everything. Have you sounding professional." She looks me up and down with a grin. "I see you rocking the Juicy special."

"Huh?"

"'Way back, when I had the red and black lumberjack.'"

She tugs at the plaid shirt under my bubble vest as she quotes Biggie. "'With the hat to match.'" She tugs at my trapper hat, too. "Finally learned some style from your aunty, huh?"

Any good I do, she finds a way to take credit. "Learn to keep your pants on your butt and we'll talk."

The garage has graffiti all over it. Aunt Pooh knocks on the side door. Feet shuffle and someone hollers out, "Who is it?"

"P" is all Aunt Pooh says.

Several locks click, and when the door opens, it's like that moment in *Black Panther* when they go through the hologram and enter the real Wakanda. It's like we just stepped through a hologram that showed everyone else a trap house and into a studio.

It's not the fanciest, but it's better than I expected. The walls are covered in those cardboard cup holders that restaurants give when you have multiple drinks to carry. Soundproofing. There are several computer monitors at a table, with drum pads, keyboards, and speakers nearby. A mic sits on a stand over in a corner.

A potbellied bearded guy in a wife beater sits at the table. "Whaddup, P?" he says with a mouthful of gold. His words come out slow, like somebody turned down the tempo on his voice.

"Whaddup, Doc?" Aunt Pooh slaps palms with him and the other guys. There are about six or seven of them. "Bri, this is

Doc, the producer," Aunt Pooh says. Doc nods at me. "Doc, this is Bri, my niece. She 'bout to murder this beat you got for her."

"Hold up, you made that for this li'l girl?" some guy on the couch asks. "What she gon' do, spit some nursery rhymes?"

There go the smirks and snickers.

This is that stale and predictable shit Aunt Pooh warned me about when I first told her I wanted to be a rapper. She said I'd have to do double the work to get half the respect. On top of that, I gotta be just as cutthroat, and I better not show weakness. Basically, I gotta be one of the guys and then some in order to survive.

I look dude on the couch dead in his eyes. "Nah. I'll leave the nursery rhymes to you, Father Goose."

"Ooh," a couple of the guys say, and one or two give me dap as they crack up. Just like that, I'm one of them.

Doc chuckles. "He wish this beat was for him, that's all. Check it out."

He clicks some stuff on one of the computers and a bass-heavy up-tempo beat blasts through the speakers.

Well, damn. It's nice as hell. Reminds me of soldiers marching for some reason.

Or the hands of a school security guard patting me down for drugs I didn't have.

Rat-tat-tat-tat ta-ta-tat-tat.

Rat-tat-tat-tat ta-ta-tat-tat.

I get my notebook out and flip through. Shit. Nothing I've

got seems to go with this beat. It needs something new. Something tailored to it.

Aunt Pooh bounces on her heels. "Oooh-weee! We really gon' be on the come up once this drops."

On the come up.

"Dun-dun-dun-dun, on the come up," I mumble. "Dun-dun-dun-dun, on the come up."

I close my eyes. The words are there, I swear. They're just waiting for me to find them.

I see Long throwing me to the ground. One false move would've stopped any chances of a come up.

"But you can't stop me on the come up," I mutter. "You can't stop me on the come up."

I open my eyes. Every single person in here watches me.

"You can't stop me on the come up," I say, louder. "You can't stop me on the come up. You can't stop me on the come up. You can't stop me, nope, nope."

Smiles slowly form and heads nod and bob.

"You can't stop me on the come up," Doc echoes. "You can't stop me on the come up."

One by one, they join in. Slowly, heads nod harder, and those few words become a chant.

"Yo! That's it!" Aunt Pooh shakes my shoulder. "That's that shit we—"

Her phone goes off. She glances at the screen and slips it back in her pocket. "I gotta go."

Hold up, what? "I thought you were staying with me?"

"I got some business to take care of. Scrap will be here."

He nods at her, like this is an agreement they made already.

So *that's* why he's here. What the hell? "*This* is supposed to be our business," I say.

"I said I'll be back later, Bri. A'ight?"

She walks out, as if that's that.

"Excuse me," I tell the others, and rush out. I have to jog to catch up with Aunt Pooh. She opens her car door, but I grab it and shut it before she can get in. "Where you going?"

"Like I said, I got some business to take care of."

"Business" has been her code word for drug dealing since I was seven years old and asked her how she made enough money to buy expensive sneakers.

"You're my manager," I say. "You can't leave now."

"Bri. Move," she says through her teeth.

"You're supposed to stay with me! You're supposed—"

To put that all aside. But truth is she never said she would. I assumed.

"Bri, move," she repeats.

I step aside.

Moments later, her Cutlass disappears down the street, and I'm left in the dark, without a manager. Worse, without my aunt.

Curious eyes wait for me back in the studio. But I can't show weakness. Period. I clear my throat. "We're good."

"All right," Doc says. "You gotta come hard on this one. This your introduction to the world, know what I'm saying? What you want the world to know?"

I shrug.

He wheels his chair closer to me, leans forward, and asks, "What's the world done to you lately?"

It put my family in a messed-up situation.

It pinned me to the ground.

It called me a hoodlum.

"It's done a hell of a lot," I say.

Doc sits back with a smile. "Let 'em know how you feeling then."

I sit in a corner with my notebook and my pen. Doc's got the beat on repeat. It gives the floor a pulse, making it thump slightly beneath me.

I close my eyes and try to soak it in, but every time I do, Long and Tate sneer back at me.

If I was Aunt Pooh, I would've whooped their asses, no lie. Anything just to make those cowards regret even looking at me twice.

I'm not Aunt Pooh though. I'm weak, powerless Bri who had no choice but to lie there on the ground. But if I was Aunt Pooh, I'd tell them . . .

"Run up on me and get done up," I mutter, and write it. Done up. The good news? A lot rhymes with "done up." The bad news? A lot rhymes with "done up." I tap my pen against my palm.

Across the garage, Scrap shows Doc and his boys his two pieces. One's got a silencer, and the guys damn near drool over it. Aunt Pooh says Scrap's got more heat than a furnace—

Wait.

"Run up on me and get done up. My squad got more heat than a furnace," I mumble as I write. "Silencer is a must, they ain't heard us."

Heard us.

Nobody hears us around here. Like Dr. Rhodes. Or all those politicians who flooded the neighborhood after the riots. They did all these "stop the gun violence" talks, like we were to blame for that boy's death. They didn't care that it wasn't our fault.

"We don't bust, yet they blame us for murder," I say under my breath.

Scrap points his Glock at the door to show it off. He even cocks it. If I had one, I would've aimed it and cocked it yesterday.

"This Glock, yeah, I cock it, and aim it," I write. Wait, no, something should come before that. Aim it. Ain't it. Frame it . . . Claim it.

Truth is, if I would've had that Glock, that would've just given Tate and Long another reason to call me a thug. Well, you know what?

"You think I'm a thug, well I claim it," I mutter. "This Glock, yeah, I cock it and aim it. That's what you expect, bitch, ain't it? The picture you painted, I frame it."

I've got this.

Half an hour later, I step up to the mic and put the headphones over my ears.

"You ready?" Doc says in the headphones.

"I'm ready."

The music starts. I close my eyes again.

They wanna call me a hoodlum?

Fine.

I'll be a goddamn hoodlum.

You can't stop me on the come up.
You can't stop me on the come up.
You can't stop me on the come up.
You can't stop me, nope, nope.
You can't stop me on the come up.
You can't stop me on the come up.
You can't stop me on the come up.
You can't stop me, nope, nope.

Run up on me and get done up.
Whole squad got more heat than a furnace.
Silencer is a must, they ain't heard us.
We don't bust, yet they blame us for murder.
You think I'm a thug? Well, I claim it.

This Glock, yeah, I cock it and aim it.
That's what you expect, bitch, ain't it?
The picture you painted, I frame it.
I approach, you watch close, I'm a threat.
Think I bang, think I slang, claim a set.
Cops can draw, break the law, 'cause you fret.
Yet I bet you won't even regret.

But you can't stop me on the come up.
You can't stop me on the come up.
You can't stop me on the come up.
You can't stop me, nope, nope.
You can't stop me on the come up.
You can't stop me on the come up.
You can't stop me on the come up.
You can't stop me, nope, nope.

Pin me to the ground, boy, you fucked up.
Wrote me off, called your squad, but you lucked up.
If I did what I wanted and bucked up,
You'd be bound for the ground, grave dug up.
Boys in blue rolling all through my neighborhood,
'Cause I guess that they think that we ain't no good.
We fight back, we've attacked, then they say they should
Send in troops wearing boots for the greater good.

But let me be honest, I promise,
If a cop come at me, I'll be lawless.
Like my poppa, fear nada. Take solace
In my hood going hard in my honor.

'Cause you can't stop me on the come up.
You can't stop me on the come up.
You can't stop me on the come up.
You can't stop me, nope, nope.

I'm a queen, don't need gray just to prove it.
Rock a crown, and you ain't gon' remove it.
Royalty in my blood, didn't choose it,
'Cause my daddy still king and the truest.
Strapped like backpacks, I pull triggers.
All the clips on my hips change my figure.
'Cause I figure they think I'm a killer,
May as well bust them thangs, go gorilla.
I hate that my momma got struggles.
Bills and food, she be trying to juggle,
But I swear, I'm gon' pop like a bubble
And make sure she don't have no more troubles.

So you can't stop me on the come up.
You can't stop me on the come up.
You can't stop me on the come up.
You can't stop me, nope, nope.

NINE

Aunt Pooh never came back. Scrap walked me home.

I left her voice mails, texted her, everything. That was yesterday, and I still haven't heard back. Her girlfriend Lena hasn't heard from her either. Aunt Pooh does this sometimes though. Will ghost for a bit, then pop back up out of nowhere, acting as if everything's all good. If you ask her what she's been up to, she'll be like, "Don't worry 'bout it," and move on to something else.

Honestly, it's best that way. Look, I know my aunt does foul stuff, okay? But I'd rather see her as my hero than as somebody else's villain. Can't lie though, I'm pissed that she left me like she did.

I got the song done, Doc polished it up, put it on a USB for me, and that was that. No problems at all. But Aunt Pooh should've been there. She was supposed to tell me if a line was off or hype me up when a verse was good. She's supposed to tell me what to do with it.

I haven't uploaded it online. One, I don't know what to do with it. How do I promote it? I do *not* wanna be that random person on Twitter, going into threads and dropping Dat Cloud links that nobody asked for.

Two, as dumb as this will sound, I'm scared. To me it's like putting nudes online. Okay, maybe that's a stretch, but it's like putting part of me out there that I can't hide again.

There's already a part of me out there that I can't hide. Somebody at school uploaded a video of Long and Tate pinning me to the ground. It doesn't show them throwing me down or anything that happened before that. Whoever recorded it called it, "Drug dealer caught at MSOA."

Drug dealer. Two words.

Since they think I'm a drug dealer,
Nobody could really give a
Fuck.

The video's barely got views. It's messed up, but I'm glad nobody's watching it.

Trey peeks into the bathroom. "Dang, you ain't ready yet?"

"Treeey!" I groan. I'm just standing here, putting gel on my edges, but who wants their older brother sticking his nose in the bathroom while they're getting ready? "Do you know what privacy is?"

"Do you know what timeliness is?" He looks at his watch. "Church starts in twenty minutes, Bri. Ma's ready to go."

I comb my baby hairs into a swoop. "Don't know why we're going in the first place." Straight up, it would take Jesus himself to make me go back to the same church that let me go. For real, for real. Even then, I'd tell him, "Let me think about it."

"I don't know why Ma wants to go either," Trey says. "But she does. So hurry up."

This makes no sense, I swear. Trey heads outside, and I'm not far behind. Jay's already in her Jeep.

"All right, y'all," she says. "You know folks will be talking about me losing my job. Try to ignore it and don't get smart, okay?"

She looks dead at me in her rearview mirror.

"Why are you looking at me?"

"Oh, you know why." She puts the truck in reverse. "Got a mouth like your daddy."

Also like her. But anyway.

Christ Temple is only a five-minute drive away. The parking lot is so full, cars are parked in the gravel lot next door that the church owns. That's where we end up, instead of in the church secretary spot that Jay used to have. They've taken the sign down.

Jay greets people inside with a smile like nothing's happened. She even hugs Pastor Eldridge. He opens his arms toward me. I give him a *S'up* nod and keep it moving. Trey does, too. Our petty doesn't discriminate.

We have a pew near the back that may as well have our names on it. From here we can see some of everything. Service hasn't started yet, but there are people all around the sanctuary, talking in little clusters. There are the older "mothers," as they're called, up in the front row with their big hats on.

Some of the deacons are over to the side, including Deacon Turner with the Jheri curl. My stank-eye is strong for that one. A few months ago, he got up in front of the congregation and ranted about how parents don't need to hug and kiss their sons because it makes them gay. Sonny's parents said that rant was a "bunch of bullshit." They haven't brought Sonny and his sisters back to church since. I've flipped Deacon Turner off every chance I get since.

Like now. He's not wearing his glasses though, which explains why he just waves at me. So I give him the double-middle-finger special.

Trey pushes my hands down. His shoulders shake from fighting a laugh.

Grandma's up front with her group from the decorating committee. Her hat's the biggest of them all. She says something to her friends, and they glance back at us.

"Heffa bet' not be talking about me," Jay says. "With that synthetic mess on her head. Wig looking like roadkill."

"Ma!" Trey says. I snort.

Granddaddy comes up the center aisle. He can't take a step without somebody saying, "Morning, Deacon Jackson!"

This is the only place where people don't call him "Senior." His round belly looks like it'll pop out of his vest. His purple tie and handkerchief match Grandma's dress and hat. My grandparents always match. Not just on Sundays, either. They'd show up to Markham's football games in identical tracksuits to watch Trey. He didn't play—he was a drum major—but the band is just as important as the football team at HBCUs. Shoot, more important.

"All right now, y'all," Granddaddy says to us.

That's his way of saying good morning. He leans across the pew and kisses Jay's cheek. "Glad to see y'all made it today."

"Of course, Mr. Jackson," Jay says. "Nothing could keep me from the house of the Lord. Glory!"

I side-eye her. Not that Jay doesn't love the Lord, but she gets extra-Christian when we're in church. Like her, Aunt Gina, and Aunt 'Chelle weren't just twerking to bounce music last night in our living room. Less than twenty-four hours later, and every other word out of Jay's mouth is "glory" or "hallelujah." I doubt even Jesus talks like that.

Granddaddy leans toward me and points to his cheek. I kiss it. It's fat and dimpled, like my dad's was.

"Always gotta get my sugar from my Li'l Bit," he says with a smile. He eyes Trey, and the smile is gone. "Boy, you know you need to go to a barbershop. Got more hair than a white man who done got lost on a hike."

I smirk. Only Granddaddy.

"You really gotta start this morning?" Trey says.

"You the one gon' have wildlife running out your head. Y'all making it, Jayda?"

He knows. Not surprised. As the head deacon, Granddaddy finds out everything.

"Yes, sir," Jay claims. "We'll be all right."

"I ain't ask if you will be, I asked how you doing *now*."

"I'm handling it," says Trey.

"With that li'l mess you call a job?" Granddaddy asks.

Granddaddy thinks Trey should get a "real job." Last week, he went into this whole thing about how "this new generation don't wanna work hard," and that making pizzas "ain't a man's job." See, Granddaddy was a city maintenance worker for forty years. Was one of the first black men to hold a job there, too. Let him tell it, if Trey isn't coming home sweaty and grimy, he's not working hard enough.

"I said I'm handling it," Trey says.

"Mr. Jackson, we're fine," Jay says. "Thank you for asking."

Granddaddy takes out his wallet. "Least let me give you something."

"I can't take—"

He counts out a couple of twenties and puts them in Jay's hand. "Stop all that foolishness. Junior would want me to."

Junior's my dad and the key to ending any argument with my mom.

"No," Jay says. "If he were here, he'd be giving *you* money."

Granddaddy chuckles. "That boy was generous, wasn't he? The other day, I was looking at this watch he bought me and got to thinking 'bout it." He taps the gold piece that stays on his wrist. "It's the last thing he gave me, and I almost didn't take it. I would've regretted that, had I known . . ."

Granddaddy goes quiet. Grief hasn't left my grandparents. It hides in the shadows and waits for moments to hit.

"Keep that money, Jayda," Granddaddy says. "I don't wanna hear another word about it, you hear me?"

Grandma comes over. "Just don't go wasting it."

Jay rolls her eyes. "Hi to you too, Mrs. Jackson."

Grandma looks at her from head to toe and purses her lips. "Mm-hmm."

I'll be the first to say my grandma's stuck-up. I'm sorry, but she is. Main reason she doesn't like Jay is 'cause she's from Maple Grove. She's called Jay that "ol' hood rat from the projects" plenty of times. Then again, Jay has called her "that ol' bougie heffa" just as much.

"I hope you use that money for my grandbabies and not some of the other mess you probably into," Grandma says.

"Excuse me?" says Jay. "What other mess?"

"Louise, c'mon now," Granddaddy says.

Grandma kisses her teeth and looks at me. "Brianna, baby, don't you wanna sit with us?"

It's the same question every Sunday. Thankfully, I've got a system for this. Every other Sunday, I sit with my grandparents.

That way, Grandma isn't disappointed that I've chosen Jay over her more and Jay isn't disappointed that I've chosen my grandparents over her. Basically, it's joint custody: church pew edition.

It's tricky, but it's my life. So, since I was with Jay last Sunday, this Sunday goes to my grandparents. "Yes, ma'am."

"That's my girl," Grandma says all smugly. She clearly hasn't caught on to my scheme. "What about you, Lawrence?"

She means Trey. He's Lawrence Marshall Jackson III. Grandma rarely uses his nickname.

Trey puts his arm around our mom. "I'm good."

That's his answer every week.

Grandma purses her lips. "All right. C'mon, Brianna."

Jay gives my hand a slight squeeze as I slide past her. "See you later, baby."

She knows I split my Sundays between them. Told me that I don't have to. But I'll do anything to keep the peace.

I follow Grandma toward the front of the sanctuary. She and Granddaddy have a spot on the second row that's theirs. See, the first row is for folks who wanna show off. The second row is for folks who wanna show off but wanna act like they're subtler about it.

Grandma squints as she eyes me up and down. "You look tired. Bags under your eyes and everything. That woman been letting you stay up all kinds of hours, hasn't she?"

First of all, dang, the shade. Second of all, "I go to bed at a decent hour." Sometimes. That's not Jay's fault. Blame my PlayStation.

Grandma goes, "T'uh! I'm sure you do. You looking kinda po', too."

Not poor, but *po'*, as in skinny, which I'm not. That's the country way of saying it. As bougie as Grandma wants to act, according to Granddaddy she's just "one foot out the backwoods and one toe from ignorant."

"I'm eating fine, Grandma," I tell her.

"Mm-hmm. Don't look like it to me. She probably don't cook, do she? These young mothers live in drive-thrus. Probably giving you hamburgers every night. A mess!"

I didn't even say anything but go off.

Grandma picks at my hair. "And why she always putting your hair in these ol' braids? You got good hair! It don't need to be in this mess."

What the hell is "good" hair? Hell, what's "bad" hair?

"Lord, that woman don't know how to take care of you," she goes on. "You know you can come back home, right?"

As far as she's concerned, her and Granddaddy's house will always be my "home." Seriously, she acts like I'm just visiting Jay. I can't lie, I used to wanna go back to them too. When your mom is only your mom on weekends and holidays, she's just one step up from being a stranger. Living with her was brand new.

But now, I know how hard she fought to get us in the first place and how much it would hurt her if we left. That's why I tell Grandma, "I know. But I wanna stay with my mom."

Grandma goes, "Hm!" like she doubts it.

Sister Daniels switches her way over. She's another member of the "saved and bougie" crew. Wanna act like she doesn't lay her head down in the Maple Grove projects every night. Grandma hugs her and smiles all in her face, knowing she badmouths Sister Daniels every chance she gets. In fact, Grandma started the rumor that she has roaches. That's why the food committee never asks Sister Daniels to cook for events anymore and now they ask Grandma.

"Girl, you know you looking sharp today!" Sister Daniels claims.

I can practically see Grandma's head swell. You gotta be careful with church compliments though. The person's probably thinking the exact opposite of what they're saying but says something nice in case Jesus is listening in.

"Thank you, girl," Grandma says. "My niece bought this at one of them outlet malls she likes."

"I can tell."

Oh, that was shade. By the quick glare that crosses Grandma's face, she knows it, too.

She straightens out her skirt. "What you doing over here, girl?" Which is church speak for "You better get up out my face."

"Oh, I wanted to check on Brianna," Sister Daniels says. "Curtis told me what happened at school. You all right, baby?"

I look across the aisle. Curtis waves at me with the biggest grin.

Curtis is Sister Daniels's only grandson. With his mom in prison, he lives with his grandma, and he's always yapping to her. Like in fifth grade, he said something that pissed me off, so I popped him in his mouth. He ran and told his grandma. His grandma told my grandma and I got a whooping. Snitch.

Grandma whips around at me. "What happened at school, Brianna?"

I didn't wanna tell her. It's gonna lead to a million questions I don't wanna deal with. "Nothing, Grandma."

"Oh, it was something," says Sister Daniels. "Curtis said security threw her on the ground."

Grandma gasps. Sister Daniels lives for gasps like that.

"Threw you?" Grandma says. "What in the world they do that for?"

"They thought she had drugs on her," Sister Daniels says before I can say a word.

Another gasp. I close my eyes and hold my forehead at this point.

"Brianna, what you doing with drugs?" says Grandma.

"I didn't have drugs, Grandma," I mumble.

"Sure didn't," Sister Daniels says. "She been selling candy. Curtis claims them guards love to start mess. They're at fault, but Brianna still got suspended."

Welp, no need to tell my own story. I'll just let Sister Daniels take over at this point. In fact, why don't I just let her write my autobiography since she knows so damn much?

"They gave you three days, right, baby?" she asks.

"Three days?" Grandma shrieks.

The dramatics. I rest my chin in my hand. "Yes."

"What you selling candy for anyway?" says Grandma.

"Probably to help her momma out," says the expert in all things Bri. Surprise! It's apparently not me.

"Lord, I knew you wasn't looking right," Grandma says. "You didn't act like this when you lived with us."

"Carol and I were talking"—Sister Daniels lowers her voice—"and this whole thing odd, ain't it? Pastor would pay a salary out his own pocket before he let somebody be without. He don't easily let folks go. Unless . . ."

She raises her eyebrows as if there's a message hidden in them.

Grandma goes, "Hm!"

"Mm-hmm."

Um, huh? "Unless what?" I say.

"I wouldn't be surprised," Grandma says as they glance at Jay. "You know what they say, folks ain't ever truly clean once they been on that mess."

Wait, what?

"Chiiile," Sister Daniels says. "You better keep your eyes and ears open, Louise. For your grandbaby's sake."

I'm sitting right here. "My mom's not on drugs."

Sister Daniels sets her hand on her hip. "You sure 'bout that?"

The "yes" is on the tip of my tongue, but it sits there a second.

I mean . . . I don't think she is.

For one, eight years is a hell of a long time to be clean. Two, Jay wouldn't go back to all of that. She knows how much it messed us up. She wouldn't put me and Trey through that again.

But.

She put us through it in the first place.

The choir fills in the stands and the band starts an upbeat song. People clap along around the sanctuary.

Sister Daniels pats Grandma's knee. "Be watchful, Louise. That's all I'm saying."

Four hours later, church is over.

The spirit forgot the concept of time—I mean, the spirit hit Pastor Eldridge hard. He huffed and puffed until a praise break broke out. Grandma took off running, as always, and that wig went flying, as always. Granddaddy tucked it under his arm, looking like he had overgrown armpit hair.

After service is over, everyone files into the church basement for "fellowship." I can't help but shiver a little bit every time I come down here. It's like this place is haunted. They have portraits of all the old, dead pastors on the walls. None of them smile, like they're judging us for not tithing enough. Doesn't help that the place is decorated like a funeral home. I'm convinced that one day, Jesus is gonna jump out from a corner and scare the bejesus out of me.

Question: If Jesus scares you, do you call on Jesus? Do you even say, "Oh my God?"

Stuff to ponder.

Anyway, fellowship at Christ Temple really means snack time, and snack time really means fried or baked chicken, potato salad, green beans, pound cake, and soda. I don't think church folks know how to just "snack."

Grandma and a couple of her girlfriends serve the food, including Sister Daniels. They wear plastic gloves and plastic hairnets that seem a bit too thin for my germaphobe liking. Granddaddy and some of the deacons chat over in a corner. Granddaddy sips on a diet soda. Anything other than diet and Grandma will go off about him not watching his sugar. Trey's gotten cornered by a couple of the other deacons not far away. He looks like he'd rather be invisible. Jay's talking to Pastor Eldridge and laughs and smiles like nothing's wrong.

I'm still in line to get food. There's an unspoken rule that when your grandparent is serving, you have to get in the back of the line. I'm not complaining. Grandma's over the chicken, and she'll save a big piece for me. She'll tell Sister Grant to give me the corner edge of the peach cobbler, too. Peach cobbler is the love of my life, and the corner edge is perfection.

Somebody comes up behind me. Their breath brushes against my ear as they say, "You didn't get into too much trouble with your grandma, did you, Princess?"

Without any hesitation, I ram my elbow back, straight into his gut. The "ow!" makes me smile.

Curtis has called me "Princess" since we were seven. He said it was because people call my daddy the "King of the Garden." It's always irked me, too. Not so much being called a princess—trust, I'd make a badass one—but the way he says it. *Princess*, like it's an inside joke but he's the only one who gets it.

Hope he "gets" that elbow.

"Dang," he says. I turn around, and he's bent over. "Violent butt."

"Snitching butt," I say through my teeth. "Just had to go and tell your grandma what happened, huh? You *knew* she was gon' blab."

"Ay, I just told her what happened at school, like a good grandson's supposed to do. Ain't my fault she's telling everybody and their momma you got thrown onto the ground."

"Wow. You think what they did to me is funny?"

The smirk disappears. "Nah. Actually, I don't."

"Sure you don't."

"Seriously, Bri, I don't. It's messed up. I'm sick of them making assumptions about us."

I feel that in my soul. There are more people with an idea

of who they think I am than there are people who really know who I am.

"On God, bruh," Curtis says, "them guards gon' get what's coming one day. On God."

This is one time I don't think he's lying on God. "Don't do anything stupid, Curtis."

"Look at this. The princess is worried about li'l ol' *me*?"

"Ha! Hell no. But if you think they're bad now? Let something happen. We'll be lucky if they let us back through the doors."

Let's be real: We're black kids from one of the worst neighborhoods in the city. All it takes is one of us messing up, and suddenly all of us messed up. I've probably made things worse already.

"You right," Curtis admits. "I would ask how you're doing after all of that, but that's a stupid question. The rumors at school probably ain't helping, huh?"

"What rumors?"

"That you sell drugs, and that's why Long and Tate went after you."

So that person who uploaded the video isn't the only one. "What the hell? How they figure that?"

"You know how it goes. It somehow went from you slipping folks candy in the halls to you slipping folks weed in the halls."

"Woooow."

"Look, ignore all that nonsense," Curtis says. "Just remember you didn't do anything wrong."

Now *I'm* amused. "Look at this. You're acting like you actually care about me."

He bites his lip and stares at me for one long, awkward moment, in a way he hasn't stared at me before. Finally, he says, "I do care about you, Bri."

What?

Curtis reaches around me, his arm brushing against my arm, as he gets a Styrofoam plate from the table. His eyes meet mine.

"Brianna, baby," Sister Daniels says. It's my turn in line. "What you want, green salad or potato salad?"

My eyes are still locked with Curtis's though.

He straightens up with a smirk. "You gon' stare or you gon' get some food?"

TEN

"Is Curtis cute?"

Sonny looks at me like I grew an extra head. "Which Curtis?"

I nod ahead. "That Curtis."

It's Wednesday, my first day back from suspension. Curtis is in one of the front rows of the bus. A "diamond" earring glistens in one of his ears, and his snapback matches his sneakers. He brags about his rating in some basketball video game to Zane-with-the-nose-ring. Loud as always and putting it "on God, bruh" that he'd beat Zane in a game, as always.

Sonny squints his eyes. He tilts his head one way and then the other. "I guess? He's no Michael Bae Jordan."

Lord. Ever since *Black Panther*, Sonny has sworn that Michael B. Jordan is the standard for fineness. I can see why though. When he took his shirt off in the movie, Sonny and I looked at each other and went, "Goddamn!" During that whole scene, Sonny squeezed my hand, going, "Bri . . . Bri!"

It was a moment.

"Nobody is Michael B. Jordan, Sonny," I remind him.

"You're right. That is some one-of-a-kind fine," he says. "But I guess Curtis is cute in the same way rodents are weirdly adorable? You know how you'll see a baby mouse and will be like, 'Aw, cute!' Until that bitch is raiding your cabinet, eating the Halloween candy you hid from your little sisters."

"That's oddly specific."

"Um, *you* asked *me* if Curtis is cute. The only odd one is you, Bri."

Touché. That question has been bugging me since Sunday. I mean, maybe he is a little bit cute? He's short and kinda thick, which I like, can't lie, and he's got these really full lips that he bites a lot, especially when he's smiling. His eyes are softer than you'd expect, like even though he talks a lot of shit, he's really a teddy bear. He's not a pretty boy, but I can't stand pretty boys anyway. They usually act like they know they're pretty. He's just the right amount of cute that can be considered fine.

But it's Curtis.

Curtis.

Sonny glances at his phone and slips it back in his jacket pocket. He got on the bus alone this morning. Malik wanted to work on his documentary in the lab before school.

"What's got you wondering about Curtis's looks or lack thereof?" Sonny asks. "Being on lockdown made you *that* desperate?"

I push him so hard, he tips over, laughing all the way down.

Sonny sits up. "Vi-o-lent. Seriously, where's this coming from?"

"We talked at church about me getting suspended, and he was actually decent."

"Damn, Bri. He talked to you like a human being, now all of a sudden you're thirsty for him? What kind of heterosexual bullshit is that?"

I tuck in my lips. "That's not what I mean, Sonny. I'm just saying . . . that conversation made me look at him a little different, that's all."

"Like I said, are your standards *that* low that you're suddenly falling for him?"

"I have not fallen, thank you very much."

"You see that troll as more than a troll. That's bad enough," Sonny says. "Whew, chile. The ghetto."

I roll my eyes. Sonny only watches *Real Housewives of Atlanta* to get NeNe quotes, just like he watches *Empire* for Cookie quotes, and he lives for moments to use them.

"Anyway, you never told me how the studio went," he says. "Did you record a song?"

"Yep."

Sonny raises his eyebrows. "Can I hear it or nah?"

"Umm . . ."

It takes everything in me not to tell him, "No!" I became a whole new person when I stepped up to that mic—it happens whenever I rap. But when Sonny hears "On the Come Up," he won't hear Bri the rapper. He'll hear Bri his best friend.

I should be used to this, as much as I let him and Malik hear rhymes that I wrote, but I'm always afraid to show people who know me that other side of me. What if they don't like it?

"Please, Bri?" Sonny says, his hands together. "Pleeeeease?"

You know what? Fine. Otherwise he'll bug me all day. "Okay."

For some reason my hands shake, but I manage to pull up "On the Come Up" on my phone. I hit Play, and I wish I could jump off this bus.

I don't know how rappers do this. When I got on that mic, it was just me and the mic. I didn't care about what Sonny would think or anybody, really. I just said what Bri the rapper wanted to say.

Fuck. Why'd I do that?

But the good news? Sonny nods to the beat with a wide grin. "Briiii!" He shakes my shoulder. "This is dooope!"

"As hell," Deon adds behind us. He nods along. "That's you, Bri?"

My heart's about to jump out of my chest. "Yeah."

He lets out a slow whistle. "That's fire right there."

"Turn this shit up!" Sonny says. This boy takes my phone and raises the volume, loud enough for errybody, yes, *errybody*, on the bus to hear.

Conversations stop, heads turn back, and people nod along.

"Yo, whose song is that?" Zane asks.

"Bri's!" says Deon.

"Damn, what's that called?" Aja the freshman asks.

I'm sweating. Seriously. "'On the Come Up.'"

"'You can't stop me on the come up.'" Sonny dances as best as he can on the seat. "'You can't stop me, nope, nope.'"

There's something about hearing it from him that makes it sound different, like a real song and not just some shit I did.

Pin me to the ground, boy, you fucked up.
Wrote me off, called your squad, but you lucked up.
If I did what I wanted and bucked up,
You'd be bound for the ground, grave dug up.

"Oh, shiiiit," Curtis says, fist to his mouth. "Princess, you went at Long and Tate?"

"Hell yeah. Had to let 'em know."

You'd think everybody just found out they're getting a thousand dollars, the way they react. Deon lays out on his seat, acting like I just killed him.

"You. Did. That!" Sonny says. "Oh my God, you did that!"

I'm cheesing super hard. They have me play the song twice, and I'm pretty sure I'm floating.

Until the bus pulls up in front of Midtown.

Everybody else gets off without hesitation. Christmas break starts tomorrow, so I guess they're ready to get the day over with. I stay in my seat and stare out at the building. I wish the last time I was here was the last time I was here, but Jay told me this morning to "walk in there with your head held high."

She didn't say how to do that though.

"You good?" Sonny asks.

I shrug.

"Don't worry about those two," he says. "Like I told you, they haven't been here all week."

Long and Tate. Sonny and Malik texted me Monday and let me know they were MIA. I'm not really worried about them anyway. There's no way they're coming back. It's the whispers, the glances, and the rumors that bother me.

"I've got your back," Sonny says. He holds his arm out to me. "Shall we, my lady?"

I smile. "We shall."

I hook my arm in Sonny's, and we get off the bus together.

Half the school's out front, as usual. The glances and whispers start the moment we step off the bus. One person will nudge another and look at me, and soon they're both looking at me until everybody is looking at me.

This isn't what I meant when I said I wanted to be visible.

"So," Sonny begins. "There's this guy I've been talking to—"

I whip my head toward him so fast. "Full name, date of birth, and social security number."

"Goddamn, Bri. Can I finish?"

"Nope." If his plan was to distract me from being the talk of the school, he succeeded. "Where'd you meet?" I ask.

"We haven't met. Only talked online."

"What's his name?"

"I only know his screen name."

"How old is he?"

"Sixteen like me."

"What does he look like?"

"I haven't seen pictures of him."

I raise my eyebrows. "You're sure there's a guy?"

"Positive. We've been talking for weeks—"

I seriously grab my chest. "Jackson Emmanuel Taylor, there is a guy you've been talking to for *weeks*, and I'm *just* hearing about it?"

He rolls his eyes. "You're so damn dramatic. And nosy. And can't keep shit to yourself. So yeah, you're *just* hearing about it."

I punch his arm.

He grins. "I love you too. The problem is, I only know this guy's screen name, Rapid_One, and—what are you doing?"

I scroll through my phone. "Cyberstalking. Go on."

"Creep. Anyway, he messaged me a few weeks ago. He does

photography and sent me a picture of my rainbow fist in Oak Park."

Sonny does graffiti around the Garden and posts it on Instagram under the alias "Sonn_Shine." Malik and I are the only people who know it's him. "Ooh! He lives here. What's his address?"

"I'm sure you'll find it, Olivia Nope."

Sonny and I were obsessed with *Scandal*. Kerry Washington is goals. "You know, I'm actually flattered by that."

"Of course you are. Anyway, he said he connected with it and came out to me. We've been DM'ing every day since."

He gets this shy, un-Sonny-like smile as we climb the steps.

"Oh my God, you like him!" I say.

"Obviously. I think he likes me too, but we technically don't *know* each other, Bri. We haven't even exchanged pics. Who does that?"

"Two people born in the social media generation who, despite being labeled as shallow and vain, are actually super self-conscious and would rather hide behind avatars than reveal themselves."

Sonny just stares at me.

I shrug. "Saw it on Instagram."

Sonny tilts his head. "I'm not sure if you just came at me or not. Anyway, I recently read this book about these two guys who fall for each other over email. Reading that made me go, 'Damn. Maybe this could work out for us too.'"

"But?" I ask. There is obviously a but.

"I can't get distracted. I've got too much at stake."

"If you mean all that college prep stuff—"

"*Life* prep stuff, Bri. My ACT and SAT scores will get me into a good art school, help me get scholarships. Get me out of the Garden. I know, nothing is guaranteed, but damn, for at least four years, maybe I can live somewhere other than that neighborhood with all its bullshit. Somewhere I don't have to worry about colors, stray bullets. Homophobes."

I get that . . . and I don't. I've caught glimpses of things Sonny and Aunt Pooh both deal with in the neighborhood, but I won't ever *know*-know because I don't live it.

"Plus, I gotta set the example for my little sisters," Sonny says. "They have to see me make it or they won't think they can make it."

"People go to college *and* have relationships, Sonny."

"Yeah, but I can't risk it, Bri. Luckily, Rapid understands. We're taking our time or whatever. I guess I haven't told you and Malik about him because it's been nice to not have to explain shit and just . . . exist, you know?"

Meaning he doesn't feel like he can "just exist" with me and Malik. I think I get it though. It's kinda like the rap side of me. I don't wanna have to explain shit. I just wanna be.

I kiss his cheek. "Well, I'm glad you have him."

Sonny cuts me a side-eye. "You're not getting mushy on me, are you?"

"Never."

"You sure? Because that felt extra mushy."

"It was not mushy."

"Actually, I think it was," he says.

"Is this mushy?" I give him a middle finger.

"Ah. There's my Bri."

Troll.

We get in line for security. There's a woman and a man I've never seen before, directing people through the metal detectors, one at a time.

I suddenly feel sick.

I didn't have anything on me that day. I don't have anything on me today. Not even candy. I'm done selling that shit, since it makes people think I'm a drug dealer.

Yet I'm shaking as if I really am a drug dealer. It's like how when I go in a store in Midtown-the-neighborhood, and the clerks watch me extra close or follow me around. I know I'm not stealing, but I get scared that they think I'm stealing.

I don't want these new guards to assume, too. Especially when I can see the very spot where Long and Tate pinned me down. There's no blood there or anything, but it's one of those things I'll never forget. I could lay my face on the exact same spot without a second thought.

It's harder to breathe.

Sonny touches my back. "You're good."

The woman motions me through the metal detector. It

doesn't beep, and I'm free to go on my way. Same with Sonny.

"Poetry's your first class, right?" he asks, like I didn't almost have a panic attack just now.

I swallow hard. "Yep. You got history?"

"Nah. Precalculus. Like I need to know that shit to—"

"Free Long and Tate!"

We both turn around. This red-haired white guy pumps his fist while looking at us. His friends crack up.

There's always that one white boy who says stupid shit in the name of making his friends laugh. You can usually find them trolling on Twitter. We just spotted one in the wild.

"How 'bout you free these nuts for you and your klan-cestors?" Sonny asks, holding his crotch.

I grab his arm. "Ignore them."

I drag him down the hall, toward our lockers. Malik stuffs his books into his already-full locker. He miraculously makes it work every time. He and Sonny slap palms and end with the Wakanda salute.

"Y'all good?" Malik asks, but he looks at me when he says it.

"We're good," I say.

"More than good," says Sonny. "Bri let everybody on the bus hear her song. Shit. Is. Dope."

"It's all right," I say.

"*All right?* Understatement," says Sonny. "It's way better than that 'Swagerific' garbage Milez has."

I smirk. "That's not saying much."

Malik looks at me with bright eyes. "I'm not surprised."

His smile . . . good Lord, it scrambles my brain all the way up.

But this is Malik.

This is Malik.

Goddammit, this is Malik. "Thanks."

"When can I hear it?" he asks.

Around all these people who are already looking at me? Definitely not now. "Later."

He tilts his head, eyebrows cocked. "How later?"

I tilt my head too. "Later-when-I-feel-like-it later."

"Not specific enough. How about later at lunch?"

"Lunch?" I say.

"Yeah. Wanna hit up Sal's?"

I think I have a couple of dollars to go in on a pizza. "Sure. Meet y'all here at twelve?"

"Not me," Sonny says. "I've got SAT prep."

"Yeah," says Malik, like he already knew. "I thought we could hang out, Bri."

Wait. Is this . . .

Is he asking me out?

Like out-on-a-date out?

"Um, yeah." Don't know how I managed to form a word. "Sure."

"Cool, cool." Malik smiles without showing his teeth. "Meet here at twelve?"

"Yep. At twelve."

"All right, bet."

The bell rings. Sonny gives us dap and goes off to the visual arts wing. Malik and I hug and go our separate ways. Halfway down the hall, he turns around.

"Oh, and for the record, Breezy?" he calls as he walks backward. "I've got no doubt that song is dope."

ELEVEN

My head's everywhere except where it needs to be.

Malik asked me out.

I think.

Okay, confession: According to Granddaddy, I "jump to conclusions faster than lice jump between white kids' heads." That's something only my granddaddy would say, but he may have a point. The first time he said that I was nine, and he'd just told me and Trey that he had diabetes. I burst into tears and cried, "They're gonna cut your legs off and you're gonna die!"

I was a dramatic child. Plus, I'd just watched *Soul Food* for the first time. RIP Big Mama.

Anyway, I could be jumping to conclusions, but it felt like Malik was asking me out without asking me out, you know? That casual "Hey, we're friends, it's normal for friends to have lunch together, but I'm glad it'll just be the two of us" kinda thing.

I think that's a thing. Or I'm reaching. I'm gonna say it's a thing. That way I can ignore the way people look at me in the hall.

There's pity. There's surprise, like I'm supposed to be in prison or something. Some look like they wanna speak to me, but they don't know what to say so they stare instead. One or two whisper. Some idiot coughs to cover the "drug dealer" he says as I pass.

I don't walk with my head high like my mom said. I actually wish I was invisible again.

When I walk into poetry, my classmates suddenly go silent. Five bucks says they were talking about me.

Mrs. Murray looks at me from over the top of a book at her desk. She closes it and sets it down with a smile that has so much sympathy it's almost a frown. "Hey, Bri. Glad to see you back."

"Thanks."

Even she looks unsure of what to say next, and now I know this is a mess—Mrs. Murray always knows what to say.

Every eye in the room follows me to my desk.

I'm over this already.

At noon, I head straight for my locker.

I use my phone to check my hair. Monday I sat between

Jay's legs for hours as she braided my hair into fishbone cornrows that end in French braids. Are they cute? Yeah. Is it a process? Unfortunately. They're so tight I can feel my thoughts.

Malik's tall enough that I spot him towering over several people as he makes his way down the hall. He's laughing and talking to someone. Sonny, maybe?

But Sonny's not a short, dark-skinned girl with a bun.

"Sorry I'm late," Malik says. "Had to get Shana."

Shana from the bus slips her coat on. Malik helps her with it part of the way. "Oh my God, I'm so looking forward to this. I haven't been to Sal's in for-ev-er."

I think I know what a balloon feels like when it's deflated. "Um . . . I didn't know Shana was coming."

"Wow. Really, Malik?" Shana punches his arm. "Forgetful butt."

She punched him. *I* usually punch him.

He grabs his arm, laughing. "Dang, woman. It slipped my mind, okay? You ready, Bri?"

What the hell is going on? "Yeah. Sure."

I walk ahead of them. I knew those two were cool with each other—the dancers have rehearsals after school, and Malik's been staying late to work on his documentary, so he and Shana end up taking the city bus back to the Garden together sometimes—but I didn't know they were *this* cool with each other.

They laugh and talk behind me as we head down the

sidewalk. I grip my backpack straps. Sal's is only a couple of blocks away. Usually when we go somewhere in Midtown-the-neighborhood we gotta abide by the rules. They're unspoken but understood:

1. If you go in a store, keep your hands out of your pockets and out of your backpack. Don't give them a reason to think you're stealing.

2. Always use "ma'am" and "sir" and always keep your cool. Don't give them a reason to think you're aggressive.

3. Don't go in a store, a coffee shop, or anything unless you plan on buying something. Don't give them a reason to think you're gonna hold them up.

4. If they follow you around the store, keep your cool. Don't give them a reason to think you're up to something.

5. Basically, don't give them a reason. Period.

Thing is, sometimes I follow the rules and still deal with crap. Sonny, Malik, and I went into a comic shop a few months back, and the clerk followed us around until we left the store. Malik recorded the whole thing on his camera.

Sal's is one of the only places where the rules don't apply. The walls are dingy and tan, and all the booths have tears in the leather. The healthiest things on the menu are the peppers and onions you can add to a pie.

Big Sal takes orders at the counter and yells them to the folks in the back. If they take too long to get an order done, she'll say, "Do I need to come back there and make it myself?"

She's as tiny as they come, yet everybody in Midtown and the Garden knows you don't mess with her. This is one of the few places that never gets hit up.

"Hey, Bri and Malik," she says when it's our turn. When Trey started working here back in high school, Sal became the Italian aunt we never had. "Who's this lovely young lady with you?"

"Shana," says Malik. "She hasn't been here in a minute, so please forgive her."

Shana lightly elbows him. "Why you gotta snitch?"

Um, she is super comfortable with him.

"Ah, it's okay. No hard feelings," Sal says. "Once you have a slice though, you'll be back soon. What will it be?"

"Medium pepperoni with extra cheese?" I ask Malik. That's our usual.

"Ooh, can we add Canadian bacon?" Shana says.

"Sounds good to me," says Malik.

One: Who adds Canadian bacon to a pizza?

Two: That shit isn't even bacon. No offense, Canada. It's skinny ham.

Sal puts our order in, takes Malik's money (he insists on paying), gives us cups, and tells us to find a booth. She also says that Trey's not here. He's gone to lunch. Apparently it's possible to get tired of eating pizza.

We fill our cups at the soda fountain, and Malik and I lead Shana to our little corner booth that we usually share with Sonny. Somehow, it's always available. I honestly couldn't imagine sitting anywhere else. We treat it the same way old ladies at Christ Temple treat their seats—if somebody ever beat us to our booth, we'd give them a stank-eye powerful enough to smite them on the spot.

Malik stretches his arm across the back of the booth, technically around Shana. I'm gonna act like it's only across the booth though. "Can I hear the song now, Bri?" he asks.

Shana sips her soda. "What song?"

"Bri recorded her first song the other day. She played it for everyone on the bus this morning."

"Ooh, I wanna hear it," says Shana.

Had she been on the bus this morning, I would've had no problem letting her hear it. Now? Now is different. "Maybe another time."

"Aww, come on, Bri," says Malik. "Everybody heard it but me. You're gonna have me feeling some kinda way."

I'm already feeling some kinda way. "It's not that good."

"Considering how you've written some of the best rhymes I've ever heard in my life, I bet it is," he says. "Like, 'There's a beast that roams my streets—'"

"'—and he goes by the name of crack cocaine—'" I say my own lyrics.

"'It's kinda strange how he gets in the veins and turns mothers into strangers who only share the same name.'" Malik finishes. "Can't forget my ultimate favorite, 'Unarmed and dangerous, but America, you made us, only time we famous—'"

"'Is when we die and you blame us,'" I finish for him.

"That's deep," says Shana.

"Bri's got skills," says Malik. "So, I know this song is probably amazing. Just promise that you won't act brand new when you blow up. I knew you when you were afraid of Big Bird."

Shana snorts. "Big Bird?"

"Yes." Malik chuckles. "She'd close her eyes every time he came on *Sesame Street*. One time, Sonny's dad put on a Big Bird costume for Sonny's birthday party. Bri ran away screaming."

Shana busts out laughing.

I clench my jaw. That was not his business to tell, and especially not for a joke about me. "It's not logical for a bird to be that big," I bite out.

Really, it's not. Tweety Bird? The love of my life. Big Bird? I don't trust that ho. Plus, have they *seen* his nest? He probably hides bodies in it.

Malik's laugh fades. There's not a damn thing funny to me. "Chill, Bri. I'm joking."

"Fine," I mumble. "Whatever."

I take out my phone, pull up the song, and hit Play.

Shana shimmies a little in her seat. "O-kaay. That beat is nice."

My first verse starts, and Malik's eyebrows meet. They stay together through the rest of the song. When it gets to the lines about the incident, he and Shana both look at me.

Once the song's over, Shana says, "You did your thing, Bri."

Malik bites his lip. "Yeah. Dope."

That look on his face says more than he's saying. "What's wrong?" I ask.

"It's just . . . you talked about doing stuff you've never actually done, Bri."

"I think you're missing the point, Maliky," Shana says.

Maliky?

"She's not saying she actually does that stuff. She's saying this is what they expect her to do."

"Exactly," I say.

"I get that, but I don't think a lot of other people will," says Malik. "What's with all the talk about guns?"

Oh my God. Seriously? "Does it matter, Malik?"

He puts his hands up. "Forget I said anything."

He's this close to pissing me off. "What's up with you?"

He looks at me. "I should be asking you that."

A waitress sets our piping-hot pizza on the table. We're pretty quiet as we dig in.

After a little while, Shana sets her slice down and wipes her hands with her napkin. "I actually wanted to talk to you, Bri."

"Oh?"

"Yeah. About the other day."

"Oh."

"Yeah . . ." She trails off and looks at Malik. He kinda nods, as if he's giving her the go-ahead. "A bunch of us have been talking about how Long and Tate seem to target certain students more than others."

She may as well say it. "You mean the black and brown kids."

"Right," she says. "It's ridiculous, you know? Of course you know now . . ." She closes her eyes. "God, that came out wrong. I'm the worst at this."

Malik puts his hand on hers. "You're good. Promise."

I zero straight in on their hands, and my whole world stops.

He . . . they . . .

There's something between them.

I should've known better. He's the Luke to my Leia. Nothing more.

Shana smiles at him as he rubs his thumb along her hand, then she looks at me. I've somehow kept tears out of my eyes. "A bunch of us were talking, and we've decided that we're gonna do something about this."

I'm trying to remember how to speak. My heart's trying to remember how to beat. "Something like what?"

"We don't know yet," she says. "Ever since the riots and protests last year, I've been inspired to do something. I can't just sit around and let things happen anymore. We were hoping you'd feel the same way."

"We've formed an unofficial black and Latinx student coalition," says Malik.

This is my first time hearing about it.

"We plan to demand changes from the administration. Fact is, they need us at that school. They only started busing kids in from other neighborhoods so they could get grants. If word gets out that the black and brown kids are being harassed—"

"It would mean problems for Midtown," Shana says.

"Right," says Malik. "And if word got out about what happened to you specifically—"

Whoa, whoa, whoa. "Who said I wanna be the poster child for this?"

"Hear me out, Bri," Malik says. "A couple of people recorded what happened, but only after you were already on the ground. I recorded the entire incident. I could post it online."

"What?"

"It shows that you didn't do anything to deserve what they did," he continues. "All these rumors that are spreading are just a way to try to justify what happened."

"Yeah," Shana says. "I've already heard that some of the parents are okay with it because they heard you were a drug dealer. They want Long and Tate back."

That's a slap to my face if there ever was one. "Are you serious?"

That explains why that boy yelled out "Free Long and Tate." Well, he's an asshole too, but still, that gives some insight.

"It's ridiculous," says Malik. "Who knows what could happen though once I post the video?"

Oh, I know what could happen. It could end up all over the news and social media. People all over the world will watch me get thrown onto the ground. Eventually, it'll be forgotten, because guess what? Something similar will happen to another black person at a Waffle House or Starbucks or some shit, and everybody will move on to that.

I'd rather forget that it happened at all. Besides, I don't have time to worry about that stuff. My family doesn't have heat.

Malik leans forward. "You have a chance to do something here, Bri. This video gets out and you speak up? It could actually change things at our school."

"Then you speak up," I say.

He sits back. "Wow. Let me get this straight: You'd rather rap about guns and stuff you don't do instead of speak up in a positive way about something that actually happened to you? That's some sellout shit, Bri."

I look him up and down. "Excuse you?"

"Let's be real," he says. "Only reason you rapped like that is 'cause that's how everybody raps, right? You thought it would be an easy way to a hit song and make money."

"Nah, 'cause not everybody has lines about getting pinned to the goddamn ground!"

I'm so loud, several heads turn our way.

"It's none of your business why I rapped what I rapped," I say through my teeth. "But I said what I wanted to say, including about the incident. That's all I'm gonna ever say about it. But if I did rap that way just to get a 'hit' and make money, then good for me, considering all the bullshit my family's dealing with. Until you wake up in a cold house, then come at me, bruh."

It seems to hit him over the span of a few seconds—his eyes widen as he probably remembers that Jay lost her job, he looks horrified that he forgot that we don't have gas, and he opens and closes his mouth like he regrets what he said. "Bri, I'm sorry—"

"Screw you, Malik," I say, for multiple reasons.

I slide out of the booth, throw my hoodie over my head, and storm out of the shop.

TWELVE

I didn't talk to Malik for the rest of the day. We passed each other in the halls, and as far as I was concerned, he was a stranger. He got on the bus that afternoon, and I guess the fact I wouldn't speak to him made him sit up front with Shana.

Sonny hates it.

"When you two fight, it's like Captain America versus Iron Man, and my ass is Peter Parker, in awe of both of you," he said. "I can't pick sides, dammit."

"I don't want you to. But you do know Peter was technically on Iron Man's side, right?"

"Not the point, Bri!"

I hate he's in this position, but it is what it is. I'm not talking to Malik until he apologizes. I mean, come on, sellout? I was already pissed at him for making Shana laugh at my expense.

Okay, and a little pissed that he brought her in the first place. Can you blame me though? I had no clue there was something between them, and then all of a sudden I'm the third wheel on what I thought was lunch with my best friend.

And what I stupidly assumed was a date. But I'm madder at myself about that. I always get feelings for boys who will never have feelings for me. I'm just destined to be that person.

Anyway, I can't worry about Malik. At the moment I'm more worried about this almost empty refrigerator I'm standing in front of.

It's the second day of break, and I've been here a minute now. Long enough that I've counted how many items there are. Eighteen, to be exact. Eight eggs, four apples, two sticks of butter, one jar of strawberry jelly (to go with the one jar of peanut butter in the cabinet), one gallon of milk, one gallon of orange juice, one loaf of bread. The freezer isn't much better—a ten-pound bag of chicken, a bag of peas, and a bag of corn. That'll be dinner tonight and tomorrow night, too. Don't know what we'll have for dinner after that. Christmas is a giant question mark.

Trey reaches past me. "Stop letting the cold air out of the refrigerator, Bri."

Make that seven eggs. He grabs one and the bread.

"You sound like Grandma." I could have the refrigerator open ten seconds and here she comes talking about, "Close that door before you spoil the food!"

"Hey, she had a point," Trey says. "You run up the light bill like that, too."

"Whatever." I close the refrigerator. The door is covered in new bills. The gas bill got paid, which is why the house is warm and the fridge is almost empty. When it came down to more food or heat, the cold weather made Jay choose heat—we're supposed to get snow flurries next week. She said we can "stretch" the food we have.

I can't wait for the day we don't have to stretch or choose. "What am I supposed to do for breakfast?"

Trey cracks the egg into a sizzling skillet. "Scramble an egg like I'm doing."

"I hate eggs though." He knows this. They're too . . . eggy.

"Make a PB and J then," Trey says.

"For breakfast?"

"It's better than nothing."

Jay comes in, pulling her hair into a ponytail. "What y'all going on about?"

"There's hardly anything to eat," I say.

"I know. I'm heading over to the community center. Gina said there's a food giveaway. We can get some stuff to hold us over until the first."

Trey slides his egg onto a slice of bread. "Ma, maybe you should go downtown soon."

Downtown is code for "the welfare office." That's what folks around the Garden call it. Saying "downtown" keeps people out of your business. But everybody knows what it really means. I'm not sure what the point is.

"I will absolutely not go down there," Jay says. "I refuse to let those folks in that office demean me because I have the audacity to ask for help."

"But if it'll help—"

"No, Brianna. Trust me, baby, Uncle Sam ain't giving anything for free. He's gonna strip you of your dignity to give you pennies. Besides, I couldn't get anything anyway. They don't allow college students to get food stamps if they don't have a job, and I'm not dropping out."

What the hell? I swear, this shit is like quicksand—the harder we try to get out, the harder it is to get out.

"I'm just saying it would help, Ma," says Trey. "We need all the help we can get."

"I'm gonna make sure we have food," she says. "Stop worrying about that, okay?"

Trey sighs out of his nose. "Okay."

"Thank you." Jay kisses his cheek, then wipes away the lipstick mark. "Bri, I want you to come with me to the giveaway."

"Why?"

"Because I said so."

Dear black parents everywhere,
That's not a good enough answer.

Signed, Brianna Jackson on behalf of the black kids of the world.

P.S. We aren't brave enough to say that to your face, so we head to our rooms to get dressed while mumbling everything we want to say.

"What was that?" Jay calls.

"Nothing!"

Goddamn. She even picks up on mumbling.

The community center is a couple of streets over on Ash. It's not eight o'clock yet, but there's a parking lot full of cars, an eighteen-wheeler full of boxes, and a line stretched out the door.

There's also a news van.

Aw, hell. "I'm not trying to be on the news!" I say as Jay parks.

"Girl, you not gonna be on the news."

"The camera may pan to me or something."

"And?"

She doesn't get it. "What if people at school see me?"

"Why you so worried about what they think?"

I chew on my lip. Anybody notices me, I'll suddenly be the piss-poor girl in the Not-Timbs who not only got pinned to the ground but also has to get food from a giveaway.

"Look, you can't be worried about what folks think, baby,"

Jay says. "There will always be someone with something to say, but it doesn't mean you gotta listen."

I stare at the news van. She acts like it's easy *not* to listen. "Can't we—"

"No. We're gonna go in here, get this food, and be thankful for it. Otherwise, it won't be that there's *hardly* food to eat. There won't be *any* food to eat. Okay?"

I sigh. "Okay."

"Good. C'mon."

The line moves pretty quickly, but it also doesn't seem like it's gonna shorten anytime soon. We get in line, and not a minute later four more people are behind us. There are all kinds of folks in line, too, like moms with their kids and elderly people on walkers. Some of them are wrapped up in coats, others have on clothes and shoes that look like they belong in the trash. Christmas music plays loudly in the building, and volunteers in Santa hats unload the truck.

A man in the parking lot pans a news camera along the line. I guess somebody somewhere loves to see poor folks in the hood begging for food.

I look at my shoes. Jay nudges my chin and mouths, *Head. Up.*

For what? This isn't shit to be proud of.

"That's your baby?" the woman behind us asks. She's in a zipped-up coat, house shoes, and hair rollers, like she got straight out of bed to come here.

Jay runs her fingers through my hair. "Yep. My baby girl. *Only* girl."

"That's sweet of her to come help you. I couldn't get mine away from the TV."

"Oh, trust. I had to make her come."

"These kids don't know a blessing when they see it. But they wanna eat everything we bring back."

"Ain't that the truth?" Jay says. "How many you got?"

I swear, we can't go anywhere without her striking up a conversation with a complete stranger. Jay's a people person. I'm more of a "yes, people exist, but that doesn't mean I need to talk to them" person.

By the time we get into the building, I've heard this lady's life story. She also tells Jay about the churches and organizations that distribute food. Jay takes note of every single one. Guess this is our life now.

There are tables around the gymnasium covered in clothes, toys, books, and packaged foods. One of the volunteers takes some information from Jay, gives her a box, tells us to make our way around. Other volunteers pass stuff out. Over near the basketball hoops, a black Santa gives kids candy from his bag. A boy with zigzags cut into his hair helps him and poses for selfies. The front of his sweatshirt says "Mr. Swagerific."

I've always had this theory that God is a sitcom writer who loves to put me in ridiculous situations. Like, "Hahahaha, not only does she have to beg for food, but she has to do it in front of Milez. Hilarious!"

This show needs to go in a new direction.

Jay follows my eyes over to Milez. "That's that boy you battled, isn't it? The one with that dumb song?"

How does she know? "Yeah."

"Ignore him."

If only. As dumb as "Swagerific" is, I can't go around the neighborhood without hearing it.

I'm waiting for Aunt Pooh to tell me what to do with "On the Come Up." She's still MIA though. I'm not worried. Like I said, she does this sometimes.

"C'mon." Jay tugs at my arm. "We're only getting food. That's all we need. Some of these other folks aren't so lucky."

The first table is covered in canned goods. These two elderly ladies—one black and one white—staff the table. They wear matching Christmas sweaters.

"How many in your household, dear?" the black one asks Jay.

Her table partner watches me with the smallest smile, and the look in her eyes makes me wanna scream.

Pity.

I wanna tell her that this isn't how it normally is for us. We don't usually get in long lines at community centers and beg for food. We sometimes have an empty fridge, yeah, but it used to be guaranteed to fill back up.

I wanna tell her to stop looking at me like that.

That I'm gonna fix this one day.

That I wanna get the hell up out of here.

"I'm gonna walk around," I mumble to Jay.

The food's on one side of the gym, and clothes, toys, and books are on the other side. Near the toys and books, little kids circle Milez and do his dance. A camerawoman catches that action.

I get as far away from them as I can and go to the shoe table. It's about as long as the tables in Midtown's cafeteria and sectioned off by sizes. All the shoes are secondhand, at least. I glance around the women's size six section for the heck of it.

Then, I see them.

They're taller than most of the other shoes. There's a small scuff on the toe of the left one, but they're new enough that the little leather tag hangs from the chain.

Timbs.

I pick them up. These aren't the knockoffs like I got at the swap meet either. The little tree carved into the side is proof.

Real Timbs that could easily be mine.

My eyes drift to my own shoes. Jay said to only get food. These Timbs should go to someone who might not have any shoes at all. I don't need them.

But I do. My insoles have almost rubbed out. It started days ago. I haven't told Jay. I can deal with a little discomfort, and she doesn't need to worry about getting me shoes right now.

I bite the inside of my cheek. I could take these, but the

moment I walk out of here with them, I'm fucked. *We're* fucked. It means we've gotten to the point that we need shoes that someone decided to give away.

I don't wanna be that person. Yet I think I *am* that person.

I cover my mouth to hold back the sob. Jacksons don't cry, especially not in community centers with eyes full of pity and news cameras looking for pitiful moments. I suck it up, literally suck it up by taking a deep breath, and put the boots on the table.

"Why don't you try them on, Li'l Law?" someone behind me asks.

I turn around. Santa wears dark shades that hide his eyes, has two gold fangs in his mouth, and rocks a couple of gold chains. Unless the traditional Santa look changed and nobody told me, that's Supreme, my dad's old manager.

"Ain't nothing like some real Timbs," he says. "Go 'head. Try 'em on."

I fold my arms. "Nah, I'm good."

There are rules for battling, and there are rules for after the battle. Rule numero uno? Stay on guard. Last time I saw Supreme, I whooped his son's butt in the Ring. Doubt he was happy about that. How I know he's not about to come at me sideways?

Rule number two? Don't forget anything. I haven't forgotten how he laughed at that garbage Milez said about my dad. I can't let that slide.

Supreme chuckles to himself. "Boy oh boy. You *just* like your daddy. Ready to fight, and I ain't hardly said anything to you."

"Do I need to be ready to fight?" I mean, hey, knuck if you buck.

"Nah, I ain't mad. You made Milez look like a damn fool up in the Ring, yeah, but I can't hold that against you. His head was somewhere else."

"It wasn't somewhere else that much. He said that disrespectful line about my daddy."

"Yep, you definitely Law. Mad over a line."

"It wasn't just a line."

"Yeah, but that was *just* a battle. Milez only wanted to get under your skin. Nothing personal."

"Well, personally, screw him and you." I turn back around.

We're silent until Supreme says, "You need them boots, don't you?"

The lie comes out easily. "No."

"Nothing to be ashamed of if you do. I been there myself. My momma dragged me to all kinds of giveaways like this when I was a shorty."

"My mom hasn't 'dragged me' to a bunch of giveaways."

"Ah, a first-timer," he says. "First time always the hardest. Especially with them sympathetic looks folks give you. You learn to ignore them eventually."

Impossible.

"Listen, I ain't come over to get in your business," he claims. "I saw you and Jayda come in and figured I'd give props. You did the damn thing in the Ring."

"I know." No, I don't, but I have to act like I do.

"I saw something in you that I ain't seen in a long time," he says. "We folks in the industry call it 'It.' Nobody can explain what 'It' is, but we know It when we see It. You got It." He laughs. "Damn, you got It."

I turn around. "Really?"

"Oh, yeah. Law would be proud as hell, no doubt."

I get a twinge in my chest. Can't tell if it hurts or if it feels good. Maybe it's both. "Thanks."

He sticks a toothpick in his mouth. "Shame you ain't doing nothing with It."

"What you mean?"

"I looked you up. You ain't got no music out there or anything. You missed out on an opportunity. Shit, Milez lost the battle and it still gave him buzz. If you had the right management, you'd be even bigger than him right now."

"My aunt's my manager."

"Who? That li'l girl who used to follow Law around?"

Aunt Pooh idolized my dad. Says she stayed with him like a shadow. "Yeah, her."

"Ah. Let me guess: She saw that Dee-Nice got a million-dollar deal and now she wanna keep throwing you in the Ring and hope it gets you one, too."

Yeah, but that's none of his business.

Supreme puts his hands up. "Hey, I don't mean no harm. Hell, that's what half the neighborhood's trying to do now. But I'll be honest, baby girl. If you wanna make it, you'll need more than the Ring. You gotta make music. That's what I told Dee-Nice. Now look at him."

"Wait, *you're* his manager?"

"Yep. He brought me on a year ago," Supreme says. "The Ring didn't get him a deal. It just got him some attention. His music got him a deal. Same thing with your daddy. All it took was the right buzz, the right song at the right time, then bam! He blew up."

The right song. "How do you know if something is the 'right song'?"

"I know hits when I hear 'em. Got yet to be wrong. Look at 'Swagerific.' I'll admit, it's a simple-ass song, but it's a hit. One song is sometimes all it takes."

I've got one song.

"Anyway," Supreme says, "just thought I'd give props. I probably wouldn't be where I am now if it wasn't for your daddy, so if you ever need help"—he hands me a business card—"hit me up."

He starts to walk away.

He knows hits when he hears them, and I need one. Maybe then I won't be back at this giveaway next year. "Wait," I say.

Supreme turns around.

I take my phone from my pocket. "I have a song."

"Okay?"

There's a pregnant pause as he waits for the rest.

"I, um . . ." Suddenly words are hard. "I . . . I don't know if it's good or not . . . My classmates like it, but I . . ."

He smirks. "You wanna know what I think about it?"

I do and I don't. What if he says it's garbage? Then again, why do I suddenly care what he thinks? My dad fired him. His son dissed me.

But he made my dad a legend. He got Dee-Nice a million-dollar deal. Plus, Milez may be trash, but Supreme's doing something right for him. "Yeah," I say. "I'd like your opinion."

"All right." He takes some earbuds from his pocket. "Let me hear it."

I pull up the song and hand him my phone. Supreme sticks his earbuds into the plug, puts them in his ears, and hits Play.

I fold my arms to keep them still. Usually I can read people, but his face is as blank as a brand-new notebook. He doesn't nod along or anything.

I could puke.

After the longest three minutes of my life, Supreme takes his earbuds from his ears, unplugs them from my phone, and hands my phone back to me.

I swallow. "That bad?"

The edges of his lips turn up and slowly form a full smile. "That's a hit, baby girl."

"For real?"

"For real! Goddamn. That song right there? Could jump-start your career."

Holy shit. "Please don't play with me."

"I'm not. The hook's catchy, the verses are good. You ain't put that online yet?"

"No."

"I tell you what," he says. "Upload it and text me the link. I'll make a couple of calls and see what I can do to get you some buzz. Everybody's on vacation now, so it'll have to be after the holidays. But damn, if I talk to the right people, you could be on your way."

"Just like that?"

He flashes those gold fangs in a smile. "Just like that."

Jay comes over with a box. "Bri, let's—"

She squints at Santa. It takes a second, but she says, "Supreme?"

"Long time no see, Jayda."

She doesn't return his smile, but she doesn't give him a stank-face either. "What you doing here?"

Supreme slings the Santa bag over his shoulder. "I was just telling Bri that I used to come to giveaways like this when I was a shorty. I figured my son and I may as well give back now that we're in a better position. Plus, it's good for him to remember how blessed he is."

I almost roll my eyes. How would these people feel if they

knew Milez was here to see how messed up we are to remind him how good he's got it? He's gonna go to his nice house in the suburbs and forget this in a week, tops, while we're still struggling.

My situation shouldn't be his after-school special.

"You look good," Supreme tells Jay. Not in a flirty way, but the way people do when somebody's gotten clean. "Y'all hanging in there?"

"Yep," Jay says. "Don't have any other choice."

"You know, you can always hit me up if you need help," Supreme says. "Law was like a little brother to me. No matter what went down with us, he'd want me to—"

"Brianna and I should get going," Jay says.

Dad's what I call a "depends on the day" topic. Some days Jay will tell me stories that make up for the memories I don't have. Other days, it's like his name is a bad word that we shouldn't say. Today, he must be a bad word.

Jay turns to me. "C'mon."

I follow her across the gym and glance back at Supreme. He gives me the saddest smile.

The line for the giveaway's been shut down. A couple of volunteers tell all these people on the sidewalk to leave. No cameras around to catch the cuss words that fly or to see the mom with the baby on her hip who begs them for food.

The worst part is walking past them as your mom carries a

box of food, knowing you can't give a single thing away because you need it all.

I help Jay load the box into her Jeep. It's packed full of canned goods, boxed goods, and a frozen turkey.

"We should be okay for a while," she says. "I'll be like Bubba from *Forrest Gump* with that turkey."

Forrest Gump is my favorite movie. (Wait, no, second favorite. Wakanda forever.) I don't know, there's something about the idea that this simple-ass dude witnessed so much history. Makes me think that anything is possible. I mean, if Forrest Gump can meet three presidents, I can make it out of the Garden one day.

We leave as more cars pull into the parking lot. The news camera may have to come back. At this rate, somebody's gonna cause a scene.

"We're lucky we got there when we did," Jay says.

It's scary that luck decided whether we got food or not. That's what happened in *Forrest Gump* though. Luck put him in the right places at the right times.

What if I just had a Forrest Gump moment with Supreme?

Jay glances over at me. "What were you and Supreme talking about?"

I shift in my seat. I haven't told her about the song. Thing is, if I jump to conclusions fast, Jay teleports to them. Doesn't matter what the song is actually about, she'd hear one line about Glocks and bury me eight feet deep. Six feet wouldn't be enough.

I wanna see what I can do with the song first. I mean, it'll be hard for her to be pissed if it gets me a million-dollar deal like Dee-Nice got, right?

"We were just talking about the battle and stuff," I tell her. "Supreme thinks I have It. You know, that thing that makes stars *stars*."

"He's right about that. Shoot, I saw It myself on that battle video."

"You watched my battle?"

"Of course. Why wouldn't I?"

"You never mentioned it."

"I was pissed about your grades. That's more important. But I watched that video right after it went up on the Ring's YouTube page. You were incredible, Bri. I'm not surprised. When you were little, you turned everything into a microphone. If I couldn't find my hairbrush, I knew you were babbling into it somewhere. Your daddy would say"—she deepens her voice—"'Our li'l miracle gon' be a superstar.'"

"Miracle?"

"I had four miscarriages before I finally had you."

"Oh."

Miracle. One word. Kinda rhymes with mythical.

It seems kinda mythical,
That I'd be called a miracle.

Jay blinks fast but keeps her eyes on the road. Sometimes she stares at me like she's looking for herself, and sometimes

I stare at her when she's not looking. Not in a creepy way, but enough to get an idea of who she used to be and get a glimpse of what I could be.

She gives me hope and scares me at the same time.

"Our li'l miracle." She looks over at me. "I love you. You know that, right?"

I feel a slight twinge in my chest again. This one definitely feels good.

"I know," I say. "I love you too."

THIRTEEN

Christmas manages to be Christmas.

Even though it's Sunday and we kinda owe it to Jesus to go to church on his birthday, none of us wake up until around eleven so we miss service. I've never understood those movies that show families up at the crack of dawn, all cheerful because, "Yay, Christmas!" For us it's, "Yay, sleep!" Seriously though, sleeping in is the best part about Christmas. Wearing pajamas most of the day is the ultimate bonus. My Pikachu onesie feels like perfection.

It's noon before we start breakfast. Jay always makes apple cinnamon pancakes on Christmas, and today is no different thanks to the bag of flour from our community center box. We're supposed to have bacon, too, the thick kind that I would marry if it was legal, but there wasn't any bacon in the box.

We take plates to the den, and the three of us sit on the couch, slathering our pancakes in jelly and butter. After breakfast, it's usually time for presents, except this year there's absolutely nothing under the tree. Jay couldn't afford Christmas, and Trey obviously couldn't either. Besides, I'm used to it. If there are three gifts under our tree, it's a miracle. Zero isn't far from that.

It's fine.

Jay goes to her room to call elderly relatives who are surprisingly still alive, and Trey and I load up this Michael Jackson video game on the Wii Dad bought when we were younger. I swear to God, this game is one of the best things in existence. It teaches you how to dance like MJ. Technically you could move the Wii controllers in the right direction and win, but Trey and I get into it. The kicks, the crotch pops, all of it. Doesn't help that we're both competitive as hell.

"Look at that kick!" Trey says as he does one. It gets a "perfect" rating on the game. His kicks are always super high. It's a skill he carries from his drum major days. "Ooooh-weee! You can't keep up, girl!"

"Lie!" I hit a twirl that gets a "perfect." Of course. I know every move by heart. My love for Mike started when I saw a YouTube video of the first time he performed "Billie Jean." I was six, and Michael was magic. The way he moved effortlessly. The way the crowd responded to every kick, every step. It didn't hurt that he had my last name. I loved him like I knew him.

I watched that performance until I learned every move. My grandparents played "Billie Jean" at family gatherings, and I put on a show. Cookouts, Sunday dinners, funeral repasts, didn't matter. Everybody got a kick out of my performance, and I got a kick out of their reactions.

Yeah, dude had his problems—some stuff I won't try to figure out—but his talent remained. No matter what, he was always Michael Goddamn Jackson.

I wanna be like that. Wait, not exactly like that, no offense to Mike, but one day I want people to look at me and say, "Despite the fact this girl lost her father to gun violence, had a drug addict for a mom, and is technically a ghetto statistic, she's Brianna Goddamn Jackson, and she's done some amazing shit."

I push Trey's chest and moonwalk away from him, hit a spin, and land on my tiptoes while flipping him off with both middle fingers. Like a legend.

Trey cracks up. "That ain't an MJ move!"

"Nope, that's a BJ," I say.

"That don't sound right."

"I know, shut up."

He falls back on the couch. "All right, you win this round. I can't beat that."

"I know." I plop down beside him. "Since I win, you know what you gotta do."

"Hell no."

"It's the rule!"

"It's Jesus's birthday, therefore that rule does not apply since it's a clear violation of one of the Ten Commandments."

I tilt my head. "You're getting religious on me?"

"You didn't win! I conceded."

"That's. A. Win." I clap my hand with each word. "So do it."

"Man," he groans, but he gets down on his knees and worships me. "All hail, the most excellent Bri."

"Who's better at MJ than me," I add.

"Who's better at MJ than me."

"And who beautifully kicked my ass."

"And who beautifully . . ." He mumbles the rest to the point it sounds like gibberish.

I put my hand to my ear. "What was that?"

"Who beautifully kicked my ass!" he says louder. "There? Happy?"

I grin. "Yep!"

"Whatever," he mumbles as he gets back on the couch. "Be ready next time."

Jay comes back in the den, holding the phone with her cheek and shoulder. Her hands are occupied with a box. "Here they are. Y'all, say hey to Uncle Edward." She shifts the box to one hand and holds the phone out.

"He ain't dead?" Trey asks.

I elbow him. Rude ass. "Hey, Uncle Edward," we say. He's

Jay's mom's uncle, making him my great-great-uncle. I've never seen him in my life, yet Jay makes me speak to him whenever they chat.

She puts the phone back to her ear. "All right, you get back to your nap. Just wanted to say Merry Christmas . . . All right, now. Talk to you later." She ends the call. "Lord. The man fell asleep in the middle of talking to me."

"You lucky he didn't *die* in the middle of talking to you," Trey says. Jay shoots him a stank-eye. He nods toward the box. "What's that?"

"Some Christmas surprises for y'all."

"Ma, we said we weren't buying gifts—"

"I didn't buy anything, boy. I was looking through the garage to see if there was anything worth selling. Found some of your daddy's things."

"This is his stuff?" I ask.

Jay sits cross-legged on the floor. "Yep. I had to hide it from your grandma. Woman wants everything that belonged to him. Even had to hide it from myself." Her eyes cast down. "I probably would've sold some of it back when I was sick."

That's what she calls her addiction.

I stare at the box. There's stuff inside that belonged to my dad. Stuff he actually touched at some point, that may have been a part of his everyday life. Stuff that made him *him*.

I pull back the flaps of the box. An army-green bucket hat sits on top. It's dope, and it's me. It was obviously him, too.

"Law acted like he couldn't be seen without a hat," Jay says. "That man would get on my nerves. Didn't matter where we were going, he needed some kind of hat. He thought his head was shaped funny."

I'm the same way. I lower the hood of my Pikachu onesie and put the bucket hat on instead. It's kinda big and a bit floppy, but it's perfect.

I scoot to the end of the couch and dig some more. There's a sweatshirt that still has the scent of his cologne lingering on it. There's a composition notebook. Every page has something written on it in a sloppy handwriting that shouldn't really be called handwriting. I can read it though. It's a lot like mine.

There are more notebooks, a worn leather wallet with his driver's license inside, more shirts and jackets, CDs or DVDs, hard to tell which. At the very bottom of the box, there's gold.

I lift it out. A glistening crown pendant dangles from a gold rope chain. Diamonds spell out "Law" at the bottom, like the crown sits on top of his name.

Holy. Shit. "Is this real?"

"Yep," Jay says. "He bought it with his first big check. Wore it all the time."

This thing has to be worth thousands of dollars. That's probably why Trey says, "We need to sell that."

"No, hell no." Jay shakes her head. "I want Bri to have it."

"Really?" I say.

"And I want Bri to have food and shelter," Trey says. "Come

on, Ma. Sell it! Hell, it's worth more than he was."

"Watch. Your. Mouth," Jay growls.

When it comes to Dad, Trey's not a fan. I don't mean he doesn't listen to Dad's music—he doesn't do that either—but let Trey tell it, Dad died over stupid stuff he could've avoided. Trey never talks about him because of it.

Trey tiredly wipes his face. "I . . . yeah."

He pushes off the couch and goes to his room.

Jay stares at the spot where he sat. "You can have everything in the box, Bri. Your brother obviously doesn't want any of it. I'm gonna go start dinner."

Yeah, she's starting dinner already. Christmas is for eating in Jesus's honor.

I sit across the couch. The chain's draped over my hand, and the hat's on my head. I hold the pendant up against the living room light, and the diamonds glisten like a lake on a sunny day.

The doorbell rings. I pull the curtain back and peek out. Aunt Pooh's got on a Santa hat and a dabbing-Santa sweater. Her arm is hooked through Lena's.

I open the door for them. "Where you been?"

Aunt Pooh slides past me into the house. "Merry Christmas to you, too."

"Don't even bother, Bri," Lena says. "It's the same as usual."

Considering half the stuff Lena puts up with from Aunt Pooh, she's a saint. They've been together since they were seventeen. Just like Aunt Pooh has Lena's lips tatted on her neck, Lena has "Pooh" on her chest.

"I'm grown," Aunt Pooh says, sitting on the couch. "That's all Bri need to know."

Lena plops down extra hard on her lap.

"Ow! Get your big butt off of me!"

"You gon' tell *me* you grown, too?" Lena says. She pinches Aunt Pooh, who laughs and winces at once. "Huh?"

"You lucky I love your annoying ass." Aunt Pooh kisses her.

"Nope. *You* lucky," Lena says.

Fact.

Jay comes in, wiping her hands on a towel. "I thought that was y'all."

"Merry Christmas, Jay," Lena says. Aunt Pooh just throws up a peace sign.

"I figured Pooh would show up soon as I started on dinner. Where you been anyway?"

"Dang, can y'all get up out my business?" Aunt Pooh asks.

Jay sets her hand on her hip and gives her the *say that again if you're bold* look.

Aunt Pooh glances away. It doesn't matter how old she gets—Jay will always be her big sister.

Jay kisses her teeth. "Thought so. Now get your shoes off my couch." She swats at Aunt Pooh's feet.

"You gon' stop treating me like a kid one day."

"Well, today ain't that day!"

Lena covers her mouth to hold back a laugh. "Jay, you need help with dinner?"

"Yeah, girl," Jay says, but her glare is set on Pooh. "C'mon."

The two of them go into the kitchen.

Aunt Pooh starts to put her feet up again but Jay hollers, "I said keep your big-ass shoes off my furniture!"

"Goddamn!" Aunt Pooh looks at me. "How she do that?"

I shrug. "It's like a sixth sense."

"For re—" My dad's chain catches her eye. "Oh, shit! Where'd you get that?"

"Jay gave it to me. It was in a box of his stuff."

"Damn." Aunt Pooh takes it between her fingers. "That thing still clean as hell. You don't need to wear it though."

I frown. "Why not?"

"Just trust me, a'ight?"

I'm so sick of these answers that don't answer anything. "Was I supposed to 'just trust you' when you left me at the studio?"

"Scrap was there, wasn't he?"

"But *you* were supposed to be there."

"I told you, I had something to take care of. Scrap said you got the song done and that it's fire. That's all that matters."

She doesn't get it.

Aunt Pooh slides her Jordans off and throws her legs across the couch. She eagerly rubs her hands. "Let me hear it. Been waiting for this since the other week."

"You've definitely made it a priority." Yeah, I said it.

"Bri, I'm sorry, a'ight? Now c'mon. Let me hear the song."

I pull it up and toss her my phone.

She takes out her own earbuds. I can tell when it starts—she dances while lying there on the couch.

"That hook," she says loudly. She must not be able to hear herself. "Love that shit!"

Suddenly she stops dancing. She points at my phone. "What's this?"

"What's what?"

She tugs the earbuds out and looks toward the kitchen. Jay and Lena are busy talking as some old R&B Christmas song plays. "What's this shit you saying on the song?" Aunt Pooh asks in a low voice. "You not 'bout that life!"

She can't be serious. Malik is one thing, but Aunt Pooh, who walks around with a piece all the time? Who disappears for days to do her drug-dealing shit? "Nah, but you are."

"This ain't got shit to do with me, Bri. This about you portraying yourself as somebody you not."

"I never said it's me! The whole point is about playing into the stereotype."

She sits up. "You think these fools in the streets gon' listen for 'deeper meaning'? Bri, you can't go around talking street and not expect somebody to test you. And what's that shit about the Crowns? You *trying* to have problems?"

"Wait, what?"

"You said you don't need gray to be a queen."

"Because I don't!" Damn, do I really have to explain it to her? "That was my way of saying I don't claim any set."

"But they gon' take it some kinda way!" she says.

"That's not my problem if they do! It's only a song."

"No, it's a statement!" Aunt Pooh says. "*This* is what you want folks to think of you? That you pull triggers and stay strapped? That's the kinda reputation you want?"

"Is it the kind you want?"

Silence. Absolute silence.

She crosses the room and gets all in my face. "Delete that shit," she says through her teeth.

"What?"

"Delete it," she says. "We'll make another song."

"Oh, so you're staying around this time?"

"You can point fingers at me all you want, but *you* fucked up." She pokes my chest. "You gon' record new verses. Plain and simple."

I fold my arms. "What you plan to do with the new version?"

"What?"

Supreme's on my mind. "If you think it's good, what's your plan for it?"

"We'll upload it and see what happens," she says.

"That's it?"

"Once you do a song that's actually you, you gon' blow up," she says. "I don't need to know how."

I stare at her. She *cannot* be for real. That wouldn't fly on a good day. When your family's one missed check away from rock bottom? That shit wouldn't fly if it had wings.

"It's not enough for me," I say. "Do you know how important this is?"

"Bri, I understand, okay?"

"No, you don't!" Jay and Lena laugh about something in the kitchen. I lower my voice. "My mom had to go to a fucking food drive, Aunt Pooh. You know how much I got on the line right now?"

"I got a lot on the line, too!" she says. "You think I wanna be stuck in the projects? You think I wanna be selling that shit for the rest of my life? Hell no! Every single day, I know there's a chance it could be my last day."

"Then stop doing it!" Goddamn, it's that simple.

"Look, I'm doing what I gotta do."

Bullshit. Bull. Shit.

"Getting our come up with this rap shit?" she says. "That's all I got."

"Then act like it! I can't wait around for 'something to happen.' I need guarantees."

"I got guarantees. We putting you back in the Ring after the holidays and we gon' make you big."

"How?"

"Just trust me!" she says.

"That's not enough!"

"Hey," Jay calls. "Y'all okay up there?"

"Yeah," Aunt Pooh says. She looks at me. "Delete that shit."

She goes off to the kitchen, joking to Jay and Lena as if everything's all good.

Hell no, it's not. Supreme said I have a hit. Aunt Pooh thinks I'm just gonna let that slip through my fingers?

I can show her better than I can tell her.

I go to my room, close the door, and get my laptop. It takes ten minutes for "On the Come Up" to upload on Dat Cloud, and twenty seconds to text Supreme the link.

He responds in less than a minute.

I got you, baby girl.

Get ready.

You about to blow up.

PART TWO

GOLDEN AGE

FOURTEEN

On the morning of the first day after Christmas break, loud banging on our front door wakes me up.

"Who in their right mind!" Jay snaps from somewhere in the house.

"It's probably Jehovah's Witnesses," Trey calls groggily from his room.

"On a Monday?" Jay says. "Hell no. If it is them, they're about to witness something, how 'bout that?"

Welp. This should be fun.

Her feet stomp toward the living room, and it's quiet enough that I hear the "Aw, hell" she mutters. The lock on the front door clicks, and it creaks open.

"Where's my money?"

Shit. That's Ms. Lewis, our landlord.

I get up, holey Spider-Man pajamas and all (they're comfortable, okay), and rush to the front. Trey dragged himself outta bed, too. He wipes crust from his eyes.

"Ms. Lewis, I need a little more time," Jay says.

Early as it is, Ms. Lewis takes a drag from a cigarette on our front porch. I'd lose track trying to count all of the beauty marks on her face. She has a black-and-gray 'fro that her brother, a barber, used to keep trimmed for her. He moved recently, and now her 'fro is all over the place.

"More time? T'uh!" She sounds like a laugh got stuck in her throat. "You know what day it is?"

The ninth. Rent was due on New Year's Day.

"I gave you a couple of weeks for the rest of last month's rent, and I'm still waiting on that," she says. "Now I need this month's too, and your begging ass got the nerve to—"

"'Begging ass'?" I echo.

"Now wait," Trey says. "Don't be talking to my momma like—"

"Y'all!" Jay says.

For the record, I've never liked Ms. Lewis. Yeah, my house is technically her house, but she can choke on her spit for all I care. She's always got her nose in the air, acting as if she's better than us because we rent from her. Like she doesn't live two streets over in the hood, too.

"Ms. Lewis," Jay says calmly, "I'll get you your money. But please, do me a huge favor and give me a little more time."

Ms. Lewis points her cigarette in Jay's face. "See, that's

what's wrong with so many of y'all black asses. Think somebody *supposed* to do you a favor."

Um, she has a black ass too.

"What? You back on that stuff? Wasting my money on drugs?"

"Hold the hell up—"

"Brianna!" Jay snaps. "No, I'm not back on drugs, Ms. Lewis. I'm simply in a bad situation at the moment. I'm begging you, mother to mother, to give me more time."

Ms. Lewis drops her cigarette on the porch and puts it out with the toe of her shoe. "Fine. You lucky I'm saved."

"Are you really?" I ask.

Jay glares at me over her shoulder.

"This the last time I'm doing this," Ms. Lewis warns. "I don't get my money, y'all out."

Ms. Lewis storms off, mumbling the whole way down the steps.

Jay closes the door and rests her forehead against it. Her shoulders slump and she releases the deepest breath, as if she's letting go of everything she wanted to say. Not fighting is harder than fighting.

"Don't worry, Ma," Trey says. "I'll go to one of those check advance places on my lunch break."

Jay straightens up. "No, baby. Those places are traps. That kinda debt is impossible to get rid of. I'll figure something out."

"What if you don't?" I ask. "If we get evicted, then we'll be—"

I can't say it. Yet the word fills the room, like a foul odor. Homeless. One word, two syllables.

This whole mess
May make us homeless.

"Somehow, it's gonna work out," Jay says. "Somehow, someway, it will."

It sounds like she's telling herself that more than us.

The whole thing throws me off. When Mr. Watson blows the bus horn, I'm still getting dressed. Jay takes me to school instead.

She holds my headrest as she backs out of the driveway. "Don't let this rent situation distract you, Bri. I meant what I said, it's gonna work out."

"How?"

"I don't have to know how."

I'm so sick of folks saying that. First, Aunt Pooh and now Jay. They really don't know how it will work out and they're hoping it miraculously will. "What if I get a job?" I say. "It would help."

"No. School is your job," she says. "I got my first job when I was thirteen, after my momma died, so I could help my daddy out. I didn't get to be a teenager because I was so focused on bills. Thought I was grown. That's partially why I ended up with Trey at sixteen."

Yeah, my mom and dad were those stereotypical teen parents. They were grown when I came along, but Trey made them grow up way before that. Granddaddy says my dad had two jobs at sixteen and still pursued rapping. He was determined that . . .

Well, that we wouldn't end up like this.

"I don't want you to grow up too fast, baby," Jay says. "I did, and it's not something I can ever get back. I want you to enjoy your childhood as much as possible."

"I'd rather grow up than be homeless."

"Hate that you even have to think like that," she murmurs. She clears her throat. "But this is on me. Not you and not Trey. I'm gonna figure something out."

I stare down at my dad's old chain, hanging from my neck. I probably shouldn't wear it around the Garden—that's like asking to get robbed—but school should be fine. Besides, everybody will be showing off the new clothes and shoes they got for Christmas. I wanna show off something, too. But if we need rent . . . "Maybe we could pawn—"

"We're not getting rid of that chain." Damn. She read my mind.

"But—"

"Some things are worth more than money, baby. Your daddy would want you to have it."

He probably would. But he wouldn't want us to be homeless, either.

We pull up at Midtown-the-school. It's too cold for a lot

of people to hang around outside. Sonny's out here though. He waves at me from the steps. He sent me a text earlier and said he needs to talk to me.

"Later," I tell Jay, and start to hop out.

"Hey," she says. "Can I get a kiss or something?"

We don't usually do all of that, but I guess this is one of those days she needs it more than I do. I kiss her cheek.

"I love you," she says.

"I love you, too."

She gives a quick peck to my temple. I'm halfway up the steps when she rolls down the window and goes, "Have a good day, Bookie!"

I freeze.

Oh, God. She didn't.

I don't know what the hell it means, but "Bookie" has been Jay's exclusive nickname for me for as long as I can remember. It's a miracle I didn't think my actual name was "Bookie" when I was little, considering how much she used it.

The few people who are out here definitely heard her. I throw my hood over my head and hurry up the stairs.

Sonny smirks. "You do know you'll always be Bookie, right?"

"Zip it, Sonny Bunny." That's his mom's nickname for him.

"Screw you." He picks at my pendant. "Damn. That was Uncle Law's, huh?"

"Yep. My mom gave it to me. What's up? You said we needed to talk."

We climb the steps. "I should be asking what's up with you. You didn't text Malik back all break."

I didn't. I actually haven't talked to him since he called me a sellout and made me the butt of his jokes to Shana. "What, he's got you playing middleman now?" I ask Sonny.

"Unfortunately, I'm the middleman by default. You're still pissed about what he said at Sal's, huh?"

I should be madder at myself, but yeah, I am still pissed. And hurt. But admit that? Hell nah. I may as well admit that I stupidly had feelings for him and thought we had a chance.

We definitely don't have one now. According to the text Sonny sent me on New Year's Day, Shana and Malik are officially a couple.

Whatever.

"I'm fine." I tell Sonny what I've been telling myself. "You really waited out here in the freezing cold to talk to me about Malik?"

"Ha! Hell no. I don't care about y'all that much."

I side-eye him. He cheeses. Such. A. Troll.

"But for real, this is what I wanted to talk to you about," he says.

Sonny shows me his phone. It's a text message from Rapid, sent this morning, and it consists of one simple-but-not-so-simple question:

Wanna meet up?

My mouth drops. "Seriously?"

"Seriously," Sonny says.

"Holy shit." There's one problem though. "Why haven't you responded?"

"I don't know," he says. "Part of me is like, hell yeah. The other part feels like this shit is too good to be true. What if he's really a fifty-year-old man who lives in his mom's basement and has a malicious plot to murder me and leave my body parts spread out across his backyard, unknown to anyone, until twenty years from now when a stray dog sniffs me out?"

I stare at him. "The specifics in your examples are disturbing sometimes."

"It could happen. Then what do I do?"

"Um, I'd hope you'd run like hell before he could murder you."

Sonny's lips thin. "After that."

"Call the cops."

"Bri!" he says as I laugh. "Serious. He could be a fraud."

"Yeah, he could," I gotta admit. I mean, the internet is full of lying creeps. And I don't know if it would be exactly like Sonny's example, but it could be dangerous.

"Plus, once again, this is a—"

"Distraction," I say for him.

"Right. Malik's trying to find out who Rapid really is. I gave him some info and he's already running with it. We did a bunch of research the other day."

"Oh. That's cool."

My stomach drops. Sonny's told Malik stuff about Rapid

that he hasn't told me. And they researched him together. Without me.

It's stupid but it stings.

Sonny bites on his already-raggedy nail. "I'll tell Rapid let's wait to meet up. In the meantime, Malik and I will keep researching."

He and Malik. Like the Unholy Trinity is now a duo.

Fuck. Why am I in my feelings so much?

"This could be some dumbass's attempt to embarrass me, for all I know," Sonny goes on. "Considering all the stuff I've shared with him . . . I'll look like a fool."

That shame in his eyes makes my feelings irrelevant.

I lightly elbow him. "You're not a fool. He's the fool if he's Catfishing you. Because I promise you, I'll whoop his butt."

"Even if it's a fifty-year-old in a basement?"

"Even if it's a fifty-year-old in a basement. I'll personally rip his fingers off and shove them down his throat."

Sonny kisses my cheek. "Thank you for being violent on my behalf."

"Aww, anytime. You know I've got your little disturbing-ass back."

"It's only disturbing because you know it could happen."

Security is a breeze. The new guards are still here. Everybody moves slower through the halls than usual. I think Christmas break makes us long for summer even more.

Sonny nudges me. Up ahead, Malik waits at my locker.

"Will you two be okay?" Sonny asks.

"Yep." I lie. I really don't know.

Sonny has to talk to one of his teachers before class, so he goes off toward the visual arts wing. I go up to my locker.

I pop it open and slip off my backpack. "Hey."

Malik's eyes slightly widen. "You're not mad at me anymore?"

I grab my (white) American History book and stuff it in my backpack. "Nope. We're good."

"I don't believe you. You hold grudges like cheapskates hold money."

Has he been going to Granddaddy's School of One-Liners? "I told you we're fine."

"No, we're not. Breezy, look." Malik takes my arm. "I really am sorry, okay? It's been hell not talking to you."

Actually, this is hell. The way he's holding my arm, running his thumb along my skin. Every single part of me is aware that he's touching me.

No. Scratch that. *Shana's boyfriend* is touching me.

I tug out of his grasp. "We're fine, Malik. Drop it."

Because I'm making myself drop him.

He sighs. "Will you at least tell me what's really going—"

"Ay! Princess!"

Curtis makes his way toward us, most likely to make some stupid joke that only Curtis can come up with.

"What, Curtis?" I ask.

His snapback and Jordans match as usual and look brand new. Probably Christmas presents. "You think you big shit now, huh? I ain't even mad."

"What are you talking about?"

"You ain't seen *Blackout* yet?" he asks.

"*Blackout*?" Malik says.

Blackout is this gossip blog that loves to "throw shade and pour tea" (their words) on black celebs for all of the thirsty people to consume. It's ridiculous . . . and addictive. How else am I supposed to know which Kardashian is knocked up by a black celebrity this week?

"Yeah. They posted Bri's song a little while ago," Curtis says.

I must've heard him wrong. There is no way. "Come again?"

Curtis opens the site on his phone. "See?"

There I am, on the front page of *Blackout*. They posted a picture from when I was in the Ring. The headline? "Teen Daughter of Murdered Underground Rap Legend Lawless Just Killed Us Her Damn Self with This New Heat!"

Side note: Do I have a name or nah? It's short enough that it could've fit, too.

I'm willing to overlook that sexist BS for now. Right below the picture is an embedded player for "On the Come Up," straight from my Dat Cloud page. According to the listeners count . . .

Ho.

Ly.

Shit.

"Twenty thousand streams!" I shout. "I got twenty thousand streams!"

Every eye in the hall lands on me. Dr. Rhodes is a few feet away, and she looks at me over her glasses.

Yeah, I'm loud. I don't care.

"Twenty thousand and counting," Curtis says. "You trending, too."

"But . . . how . . . who . . ."

Supreme. He kept his word.

Malik's lips turn up slightly. "That's cool, Bri."

"*Cool?*" Curtis says. "My dude, how many folks from the Garden you know are getting attention like this? This is major, Princess. Props."

I don't know what's more shocking—the fact my song is going viral or the fact Curtis gave me props.

Curtis waves his hand in front of me. He knocks on my forehead. "Anybody in there—"

I swat his hand away. "Boy, if you don't—"

He laughs. "I thought you died on us for a second."

"No." But I'm wondering if I'm having an out-of-body experience. I hold my forehead. "This is insane."

"Yeah . . ." Malik trails off. "I better head to class. Congrats, Bri."

He disappears down the hall.

"Your boy is weird, yo," Curtis says.

"Why you say that?"

"Ay, if I was as close to somebody as he's supposed to be to you, I would be geeking out for them right now. He could barely tell you congrats."

I bite my lip. I noticed that, too. "He doesn't like the stuff I say in the song, that's all."

"What's wrong with what you say?"

"I talk about guns and stuff, Curtis. He doesn't want people to think that's me."

"They're gonna think it anyway. If you can get something from this, forget the nonsense and go for it."

I stare at him. "Wow."

"What?"

"You're actually more decent than I thought."

"You love to hate, huh? Anyway." He lightly taps my arm with his knuckle. "Don't let this make your head big. It's big enough already."

"Funny. I bet the same can't be said about a certain part on you."

"Ouch!" His forehead wrinkles. "Wait, you been thinking 'bout it, Princess?"

Remind me why I considered him cute. "That would be a hell no for five hundred, Alex."

"Testy. I am happy for you though. For real, not even lying."

I twist my mouth. "Yeah right."

"I am!" he says. "'Bout time we had something good come from the Garden. Although"—he shrugs—"I'd still whoop that ass in a battle."

I bust out laughing. "I think not."

"I think so."

"All right," I say. "Prove it."

"All right," he says.

He gets in my face, super close.

Why do I just stare at him at first?

Why does he just stare at me?

"You go," I say.

"Nah," he says. "Ladies first."

"That's a cop-out."

"Or that's me being a gentleman."

I can almost feel his words, that's how little space there is between us. My eyes drift down to his lips. He wets them, and they practically beg for me to k—

The bell rings.

I back away from Curtis. What the hell?

He smirks and walks off. "Next time, Princess."

"You won't beat me," I call after him.

He turns around. "Sure, Jan."

Did he just meme me?

I flip him off.

* * *

To semiquote Biggie, this is all a dream.

I can't walk around the school without somebody noticing me or pointing me out, and it has zero to do with the incident or the drug dealer rumors. People who have never spoken to me suddenly say what's up. My dad's chain gets me more glances and stares. In Long Fiction, somebody plays my song before class starts. Mrs. Burns tells them to "turn off that nonsense," and I'm on such a high that I bite my tongue. I *internally* say that her wig is the only nonsense in this room.

Brianna Jackson will not be going to the office today.

Mrs. Murray's heard the song, too. When I walk into Poetry class, she goes, "There's the MC of the hour!" But she adds, "Since hip-hop is poetry, your grades should never drop again."

Anyway.

Seeing my streams go up and my classmates geek out has me thinking that, damn, all this stuff I've dreamed of could actually happen. I could really make it as a rapper. It's not some wild shit my imagination came up with. It's . . .

It's possible.

FIFTEEN

It's been a little over two weeks since *Blackout* posted my song. My numbers keep going up. I'm talking followers, streams, all of that. Yesterday, I walked over to my grandparents' house to have dinner with them (Grandma insisted), and a car passed me blasting it.

But the car that pulls up in front of my house tonight isn't playing it. Aunt Pooh waits in her Cutlass. I've got another battle in the Ring tonight. No clue who I'm going up against, but that's what makes the Ring what it is—you gotta be ready for whatever.

Jay's at class and Trey's at work, so I lock up the house. As much online attention as I've gotten, I don't think either one of them knows about the song. Plus, Jay doesn't do the internet, unless it's to watch YouTube or stalk friends and family on Facebook. Trey thinks social media promotes insecurity and doesn't use it much. For now, I'm good.

Scrap's reclined in Aunt Pooh's passenger seat. He pulls it forward so I can hop in the back. "'You can't stop me on the come up. Ayyyyyyy!'" he says. "Can't get that shit out my head, Li'l Law. It's too fire."

"Thanks. Hey, Aunty."

"S'up," she mumbles, looking straight ahead.

The day *Blackout* posted "On the Come Up," I told her all about it. I didn't hear back from her until yesterday when she texted to tell me she was picking me up for the Ring tonight.

I guess she's all in her feelings because I didn't delete the song like she told me. Does it matter though if it means we're on our way? I mean, damn. That's the goal, right?

Scrap looks back at me. "Okay, okay, I see you with your daddy's chain."

I look down at the crown pendant hanging from the gold necklace. I've worn it every day since I got it. Slipping it on is a habit, like brushing my teeth. "Guess I like having a part of him with me."

"Ooooh-wee!" Scrap says into his fist. "I remember when Law first got that thing. Had the whole neighborhood talking. We knew he made it then."

Aunt Pooh glares at me in the rearview mirror. "Didn't I tell you not to wear that shit?"

What's she worried about, somebody robbing me? That's

why I usually tuck it under my shirt around the neighborhood. But at the Ring? "Nobody's gonna snatch it, Aunt Pooh. You know how security is."

She shakes her head. "Don't know why I bother with your hardheaded ass sometimes."

We pull up at the gym. Some of the most ridiculous-looking cars are being shown off in the parking lot. There's a lowrider that's painted to look like a box of Froot Loops, and a truck on some of the biggest rims I've ever seen in my life. We pass a car that looks purple at first, but when the streetlights hit it, it's neon green.

Aunt Pooh finds an empty spot and the three of us get out. Music plays all around. Folks love to show off their sound systems just as much as their rides. Maybe more. One car has my voice blasting out of it.

You can't stop me on the come up.

"Ayyyyyyy!" a guy inside the car shouts, and points at me. "Do it for the Garden, Bri!"

More people notice me and shout all kinds of love and props.

Scrap nudges me. "See? You got the whole neighborhood talking."

Aunt Pooh silently sticks a Blow Pop in her mouth.

The line to get into the boxing gym is stretched out to the sidewalk, but as always we head straight for the doors. It's usually all good, but some guy goes, "Y'all better take y'all asses to the back!"

The three of us turn around.

"Who you think you talking to?" Aunt Pooh asks.

"Your bitch ass," the guy says. He's got a mouth full of silver teeth and wears a gray baseball jersey. All the dudes around him wear gray somewhere. Crowns.

"You better rethink that shit, partna," Scrap warns.

"What it is then, nig—" The Crown's eyes go straight to my dad's chain. "Aww, shit." His lips curl up. "Look what we got here."

His friends notice it too. Their eyes light up, and I'm suddenly a steak thrown into a den of hungry lions.

"You that punk-ass Lawless's daughter, ain't you?" the instigator says.

Aunt Pooh advances, but Scrap grabs her shirt. "What you say 'bout my brother?"

In-law. But let Aunt Pooh tell it, that's just fine print.

"Aunty." My voice trembles. "Let's go inside, okay?"

"Yeah, Aunty, go inside," the Crown mocks. He looks at me again. "You the one that's got that song, too, ain't you?"

I suddenly can't speak.

"What if she is?" Aunt Pooh asks.

The Crown rubs his chin. "She said some real street shit on there. There's a line that tripped us up a bit. Something about not needing gray to be a queen. The fuck's that supposed to mean?"

"It meant whatever the hell she want it to," says Aunt Pooh. "She don't claim nothing, so what's the problem?"

"It made us feel some kinda way," the Crown says. "She better watch herself. Wouldn't want her to end up like her pops."

"The fuck you say?" Aunt Pooh starts toward him.

He starts toward her.

There are shouts of, "Oh, shit!" and screams. Phones point in our direction.

Aunt Pooh reaches for the back of her waist.

The Crown reaches for his.

I'm frozen.

"Hey! Cut it out!" Frank the bouncer yells.

He and Reggie rush over. Reggie pushes Aunt Pooh back and Frank pushes the Crown.

"Nah, man, nah," Frank says. "This shit ain't going down here. Y'all gotta go."

"These fools started it with us!" Aunt Pooh says. "We was just trying to get in so my niece could battle."

"I don't care," says Reggie. "We don't tolerate that street shit, Pooh. You know it. Y'all gotta go."

Whoa, hold up. All? "I'm battling tonight though."

"Not anymore," says Frank. "You know the rules, Bri. If you *or your crew*"—he motions to Scrap and my aunt—"bring any of that gang nonsense over here, you gotta go. Plain and simple."

"But I didn't do anything!"

"It's the rules," says Reggie. "All of y'all, off the property. Now."

The Crowns cuss, but they leave. There are whispers along the line.

"C'mon, y'all," I say to Frank and Reggie. "Please? Let me in."

"I'm sorry, Bri," says Frank. "Y'all have to go."

"The rules are the rules," says Reggie.

"But I haven't done shit! Yet y'all kicking me out because of what *my crew* did? That's some bullshit!"

"It's the rules!" Frank claims.

"Fuck your rules!" Do I speak without thinking? All the time. Does my temper go from zero to one hundred in seconds? For sure. But the way the crowd murmurs, they seem to agree.

"Nah, Bri. You gotta go." Reggie thumbs toward the street. "Now."

"For what?" I yell as the crowd gets louder. This time, Scrap grabs *my* shirt. "For what?"

"'Cause we said so!" Frank tells me and the crowd.

They're not hearing that though. Somebody starts playing "On the Come Up" from their car and everybody loses their minds.

You know what? Fuck it.

"Run up on me and get done up," I say loudly.

"Whole squad got more heat than a furnace," the crowd finishes.

"Silencer is a must, they ain't heard us," I say.

"We don't bust, yet they blame us for murder!" the crowd says.

When that hook hits? Oh my God. Just about everybody gets into it. People bounce around and yell it out with me. It's a mini concert, right here in the parking lot.

Frank and Reggie shake their heads and go back to the doors. I flip them both off. Somebody yells out, "Y'all some bitches!"

I get props from every direction. If my dad is the king of the Garden, I really am the princess.

But Aunt Pooh glares hard at me. She marches toward the parking lot.

What the hell? I catch her arm. "What's your problem?"

"You my goddamn problem!"

I step back. "What?"

"I told you not to release that damn song!" she screams, spit flying from her mouth. "Now we can't come back here!"

"Hold up, you're blaming my *song*? I ain't tell you to get into it with those Crowns!"

"Oh, so this my fault?" she bellows.

"You were the one about to pull your gun on them!"

"Yeah, to protect you!" Aunt Pooh yells. "Man, forget it. Bring your dumb ass on."

I watch as she marches off. Did she not see how much everyone loves the song? Yet she's pissed at me because some Crowns got in their feelings over a line?

How am *I* the dumbass in this?

Aunt Pooh looks back at me. "Come on!"

With her snapping on me like that? "Nah. I'm good. What I look like, riding with somebody who calls me a dumbass when I didn't do anything wrong?"

Aunt Pooh glares at the sky. She throws her hands up. "Fine! Do what you want."

"I don't think that's a good idea—" Scrap starts.

Aunt Pooh stomps toward her car. "Let her dumb ass stay! Shit done gone to her head."

Scrap looks from her to me but follows her. They hop in the car, and Aunt Pooh peels off.

Honestly? I probably shouldn't be out here alone. I wasn't the one who almost got into it with those Crowns, but you never know what a gangbanger will do when they're in a mood. Just gotta keep my head down, my eyes peeled, and my ears open. Just gotta get home.

I head for the sidewalk.

"Ay! Li'l Law!"

I turn around. Supreme strolls over to me. He's wearing his shades, even though it's pitch black out.

"You need a ride?" he asks.

Supreme drives a black Hummer with a gold grille on the front. Milez sits in the passenger seat. Supreme opens the driver's side door and snaps his fingers at his son.

"Ay, get in the back. I want Bri up front."

"Why can't she—"

"Boy, I said get in the back!"

Milez unlocks his seat belt and climbs in the back, mumbling under his breath.

"Say it with your chest if you got something to say!" Supreme says.

Welp. This is awkward. Like when Aunt 'Chelle or Aunt Gina go off on Malik and Sonny about stuff when I'm at their houses. Not sure if I should leave, stay, or act as if nothing's happening.

I act like nothing happened. This is the most expensive ride I've ever been in. Supreme's dashboard looks like something from the *Millennium Falcon* with all the screens and buttons. The seats are white leather, and seconds after he cranks up, mine feels all toasty.

Supreme seems to look at his son in the rearview mirror. "You could at least speak to folks."

Milez sighs and holds his hand to me. "Miles, without a *z*. My apologies for the stuff I said about your dad in our battle."

He sounds . . . different. It's like how when I go with my grandma to one of the nice grocery stores out in the suburbs and she tells me to "talk like you got some sense." She doesn't want people to think we're "some of those hood rats who frequent their establishments." Trey calls it code-switching.

Miles sounds like it's not code-switching for him. It sounds like how he naturally talks, like he belongs in the suburbs. I mean, he *is* from the suburbs, but in the Ring a few weeks back, he sounded extremely hood.

I shake his hand. "It's fine. No more hard feelings."

"No *more*?"

"Hey, you had to know there were some. That's why you apologized, right?"

"Accurate," he says. "It wasn't personal. I wasn't prepared for you to come back as hard as you did though."

"What? Surprised that a girl beat you?"

"No, it had nothing to do with you being a girl," he says. "Trust me, my playlists are full of Nicki and Cardi."

"Wow, you're one of the rare people who love both?" I am too. They may have beef, but just because they don't like each other doesn't mean I can't like them both. Besides, I refuse to ever "choose" between two women. It's so few of us in hip-hop as it is.

"Hell yeah." Miles sits forward a little. "But let's be real: Lil' Kim is the ultimate queen bee."

"Um, of course." Jay's a fool for Lil' Kim. I grew up on her. Hearing Kim told me that not only can girls rap, but they can hold their own with the boys.

"The *Hard Core* cover alone is iconic," says Miles. "From a visual standpoint, the aesthetic—"

"Boy," Supreme says. Even though it's all he says, Miles slinks back and quietly messes around with his phone, as if we weren't just having a conversation. Weird.

"Where we going, Bri?" Supreme asks.

I give him my address, and he puts it in his GPS. He pulls off. "What happened with you and your aunt back there?" he asks.

"You saw that?"

"Yep. Saw that mini show you put on, too. You know how to work a crowd. That viral life treating you well, huh?"

I rest my head back. Damn. Even the headrest is warm. "It's surreal. I can't thank you enough for what you did."

"Don't even mention it," he says. "If it wasn't for your pops, I wouldn't have a career. It's the least I could do. So what's the plan now? You gotta take advantage of the moment."

"I know. That's why I was at the Ring."

"Aw, that? Ain't big enough," Supreme says. "Although what happened tonight *is* gonna have people talking. Every phone in the parking lot was pointed at y'all. I can see the headlines now. 'Ghetto Rapper Has Ghetto Encounter.'" He laughs.

"Hold on. I was just speaking up for—"

"Calm down, baby girl. I know you were," Supreme says. "They're still gonna run with it though. It's what they do. The key for you is to play the role, whatever that role is."

I'm confused. "Play the role?"

"Play the role," he repeats. "Look at me. I show up to meetings with these execs, right? In expensive suits that I get tailored, designer shoes that cost what my momma used to make in a year. They *still* think I'm a hood nigga. But guess what? I don't walk outta there a *broke* nigga, I bet you that. 'Cause I play the role that they think I am. That's how we make this game work for us. Use whatever they think of us to our advantage. You know who the biggest consumers of hip-hop are?"

"White kids in the suburbs," Miles answers dryly, as if he's heard this before.

"Exactly! White kids in the suburbs," Supreme says. "You know what white kids in the suburbs love? Listening to shit that scares their parents. You scare the hell outta their folks, they'll flock to you like birds. The videos from tonight? Gonna scare the hell outta them. Watch your numbers shoot up."

It actually makes sense that white kids in the suburbs will love the videos. But Long and Tate called me a "hoodlum," and I can't seem to shake that word. Now people are gonna call me ghetto? One word. Two syllables.

Just 'cause I wasn't mellow,
They're gonna think I'm ghetto.

"I don't want people thinking that's who I am," I say to Supreme.

"Like I said, it doesn't matter," he says. "Let them call you whatever the hell they want, baby girl. Just make sure you getting paid when they do it. You getting paid, right?"

Paid? "From what?" I ask.

"Somebody should be booking performances for you," he says. "Getting you verses on other artists' songs. Your aunt ain't handling that?"

I don't know. Aunt Pooh's never talked about stuff like that.

"Now look, I ain't trying to get in the middle of family business," Supreme says, "but you sure she the best person to be your manager?"

"She's been there from jump," I tell him and myself. "When nobody else cared that I wanted to rap, Aunt Pooh did."

"Ah, you loyal. I can respect that. She a GD, ain't she?"

It wasn't long after my dad died that Aunt Pooh started wearing green all the time. "Yeah. Been one for most of my life."

"That mess is a distraction of the worst kind," he says. "I know so many folks who'd go far if they left the streets alone. But it's like my pops used to say—'Never let yourself drown while trying to save somebody that don't wanna be saved.'"

No, see, he's got it wrong. Aunt Pooh's not a lost cause. Yeah, she has her moments and she gets too caught up in the streets, but once I make it, she'll give all that up.

I think.

I hope.

SIXTEEN

Supreme was right. Tons of people posted videos of what happened at the Ring last night, and tons more listened to my song. My streams keep going up.

Lots of people think that I'm somebody I'm not, too. I've been called ghetto, ratchet, a hood rat with no home training. All of that. I don't know if I'm more pissed or hurt. I can't speak up for myself and even lose my cool without somebody writing me off.

So yeah, Supreme was right. I wonder if he was right about Aunt Pooh, too.

I shouldn't even think like that. She's my aunt. My A1 since day one. But she also doesn't know what the hell she's doing. She hasn't said anything about booking shows or putting me on other people's songs. Absolutely nothing about how to get me paid. She's still in her feelings that I uploaded the song to begin with.

But she's my aunt. I can't drop her. At least that's what I tell myself as I poke at this sausage on my plate.

Jay slides a pancake beside it. "That was the last of the flour. Pooh's talking about bringing some groceries over later this week. I almost said no, but . . ."

Our fridge and cabinets are just about empty. That's another reason I can't drop Aunt Pooh. She always makes sure I have food.

Trey stirs cream in his coffee. He's got on a dress shirt and there's a tie draped around his neck. He has a job interview this morning. "Pooh and her drug-dealing money, saving the day."

It is kinda messed up. Here my brother is, doing everything right, and nothing's coming from it. Meanwhile, Aunt Pooh's doing everything we've been told not to do, and she's giving us food when we need it.

That's how it goes though. The drug dealers in my neighborhood aren't struggling. Everybody else is.

Jay squeezes Trey's shoulder. "Baby, you're trying. You do so much around here. More than you should have to do."

She goes quiet and almost zones out, then tries to recover with a smile. "I've got a feeling today's interview will be the one. I also was looking online at grad school programs for you."

"Ma, I told you, I'm not going to grad school right now."

"Baby, you should at least apply to some programs. See what happens."

"I already did," he says. "I got in."

I glance up from poking at my sausage. "For real?"

"Yeah. Applied before I started at Sal's. Just recently got a couple of acceptance letters, but the closest school is three hours away. I gotta stay around here and—"

He doesn't finish, but he doesn't have to. He's gotta stay and help us.

Jay blinks several times. "You didn't tell me you got in."

"It's not a big deal, Ma. I'm where I wanna be. Promise."

Trey sipping his coffee is the only sound for a long while.

Jay sets the platter of pancakes on the table. "Y'all go ahead and finish up."

"Ma—"

"Good luck with your interview, baby."

She goes to her room and closes the door.

My heart's in my throat. I don't remember a whole lot from when she first got sick, but I do remember that she'd always go off to her room. She'd stay in there for hours, leaving me and Trey to ourselves just like . . .

"She not using," Trey says.

Some days, it's like my thoughts are his own. "Are you sure?"

"She won't do that to herself again, Bri. She just needs . . .

space. Parents never wanna break in front of their kids."

"Oh."

Trey holds his forehead. "Damn, I shouldn't have said anything."

It's hard to know what to tell him. "Congrats on getting in?"

"Thanks. It was stupid to apply, frankly. Guess I was just curious."

"Or you really wanna go."

"Eventually, I do," he admits. "But not right now."

If I have my way, he'll go soon. "Don't worry. You'll get to go before you know it."

"Because you're about to get your come up, right?"

"Um, what?"

"I know about your song, Bri," he says. "I also know you got kicked out of the Ring last night."

"I . . . how'd you . . ."

"I'm not on social media, but I don't live under a rock," Trey says. "About half of my coworkers sent me links, asking if that was my little sister rolling with the GDs at Jimmy's. Kayla texted me right after it happened."

"Who—oh, Ms. Tique." Damn, I gotta respect sis a li'l more and remember her actual name. "Trey, I can explain."

"I told you not to hang around Pooh's rough behind," he says. "Didn't I tell you? You're lucky nothing happened."

"She was only protecting me."

"No, she was being the hothead she always is. Shoot first, ask questions later behind bars. Doesn't help that you showed your ass."

He sure knows how to make me feel like shit. "I was only defending myself."

"There's a way to do it, Bri. You know this," he says. "Now, I listened to your song, and I'll admit, you got some dope-ass lines in there."

My lips turn up a little.

"But," he says, in a way that tells me to wipe the smile off my face, "although I get the song, now people are gonna take your words at face value. And let's be real: You're clueless about half the shit you rapped about. Clips on your hips?" Trey twists his mouth. "You know damn well you don't know what a clip is, Bri."

"Yes I do!" It's the thingy that goes on the thingy on a gun.

"Sure you do. All that aside, this is a distraction on so many levels," he says. "If you put this much energy into school, you know how far you'd go?"

Not as far as this song could take me. "This is our way out, Trey."

He rolls his eyes. "Bri, that's a long shot. Look, if you wanna be a rapper, fine. I personally think you can do something even better, but it's your dream. I won't get in the way of that. However, even if your song does blow up, it's not the lotto. It doesn't mean you'll be rich all of a sudden."

"But I could be on my way."

"Yeah, but at what cost?" he asks.

Trey pushes away from the table and kisses the top of my head before he leaves.

There are only two people on the bus when I get on—Deon and Curtis.

"Bri, you really got kicked out of the Ring?" Deon asks, soon as I step on.

"Why, good morning to you as well, Deon," I say, fake smile and all. "I'm just dandy; how about yourself?"

Curtis busts out laughing.

"For real though," Deon says as I take my usual seat. Curtis happens to be in front of it today. "Did you really get banned?"

It's like I said nothing at all.

"D, you saw the video, you know the answer," says Curtis. "Ease up."

"Dawg, some people think that was staged," Deon says. "It wasn't though, was it, Bri? You really be hanging with GDs like that, huh? You claim it or you just affiliated?"

"You know what? Here." Curtis tosses a water bottle all the way to the back of the bus. "For your thirsty ass."

I snort. Ever since he talked to me like a decent human being at church, my tolerance levels for Curtis have been much higher. I even laugh at some of his jokes. It's weird. And I never thought I'd say this, but—"Thank you, Curtis."

"No problem. I'll invoice you for my bodyguard work."

I roll my eyes. "Bye, Curtis."

He laughs. "Cheapskate. It's all good."

"Whatever," I say. "What are you doing on the bus this early anyway? You're usually one of the last pickups."

"Spent the night at my dad's."

I'm pretty sure my face says what I don't. I had no idea he had a dad. Wait, I mean, of course he has a dad. I didn't know he had a dad who's around.

"He's a truck driver," Curtis explains. "He's always on the road, so I live with my grandma."

"Oh, my bad."

"It's cool. At least he's not around for a good reason."

I've always wanted to ask him something, but frankly, it's not my business. Curtis kinda brought it up, so maybe it's okay? "You don't have to answer this," I say. "For real, you don't, but do you get to see your mom?"

"I used to go every couple of weeks. I haven't been in months. My grandma goes every weekend though."

"Oh. What did she do?"

"Stabbed an ex-boyfriend who used to beat her up. She snapped one night and stabbed him in his sleep. But since he wasn't doing anything to her at that moment, it wasn't self-defense or whatever. She got locked up. Meanwhile, he's still around the Garden, probably beating somebody else's momma."

"Damn. That's messed up."

"It is what it is."

I'm being super nosy. "Why don't you go see her?"

"Would you wanna see your momma as a shell of herself?"

"I already have."

Curtis tilts his head.

"Back when my mom was on drugs. I saw her strung out in the park one day. She came up and tried to hug me. I ran off screaming."

"Damn."

"Yeah." That memory is still fresh. "It was weird though. As scared as I was, part of me was happy to see her. I used to look for her, like she was some mythical creature I wanted to spot or something. I guess even when she wasn't herself, she was my mom. If that makes sense?"

Curtis rests his head back against his window. "It does. Don't get me wrong, I love seeing my mom, but I hate that I can't save her. Shit's the worst feeling in the world."

I can practically hear Jay's bedroom door closing. "I get it. I'm sure your mom will, too."

"I don't know," he says. "I been away so long, I'm hesitant to go back. I'd have to tell her why I've been away, and that shit wouldn't help her at all."

"I doubt she'd care why, Curtis. She'd just care that you're there."

"Maybe," he mutters as Zane climbs on the bus. Curtis

nods at him. "Since you got all in my business, now it's my turn to get into yours."

Here we go. People love to ask me what it's like to have Lawless as my dad. They don't realize the question should really be, "What's it like having a dad that everyone seems to remember but you?" I always lie and tell them how great he was, even though I barely know.

"All right, be honest with me here." Curtis sits up a little more. "Who are your top five rappers, dead or alive?"

That's a new one. I appreciate it, too. It's nothing against my dad, I'm just not in the mood to fake about a stranger. "That's a hard-ass question."

"C'mon, it can't be that hard."

"Yes it is. I have two top five lists." I hold up two fingers. "One for goats, aka the greatest of all time, and one for what I call could-be goats."

"Damn, you're a serious hip-hop head. All right. Who are your top five could-be goats?"

"Easy," I say. "In no order, Remy Ma, Rapsody, Kendrick Lamar, J. Cole, and Joyner Lucas."

"Solid. Who are your top five goats then?"

"Okay, disclaimer: I actually have ten, but I'm gonna keep it to five," I say, and Curtis chuckles. "Again, in no particular order, Biggie, 'Pac, Jean Grae, Lauryn Hill, and Rakim."

He frowns. "Who?"

"Oh my God! You don't know who Rakim is?"

"Jean Grae either," he says, and I nearly have a heart attack. "The Rakim name's familiar though . . ."

"He's one of the greatest to ever touch a mic!" I'm probably a little too loud. "How in the living hell can you call yourself a hip-hop head and not know Rakim? That's like a Christian not knowing John the Baptist. Or a Trekkie not knowing Spock. Or an HP head not knowing Dumbledore. Dumbledore, Curtis."

"Okay, okay. Why is he in your top five?"

"He invented flow as we know it," I say. "My aunt put me on to him. I swear listening to him is like listening to water—he never sounds forced or choppy. Plus, he's a master at internal rhymes, which is like a rhyme in the middle of the line instead of at the end. Every single rapper with skills is his offspring. Period."

"Damn, you're really into this stuff," Curtis says.

"Have to be. I wanna be one of the goats one day."

He smiles. "You will be." He eyes me from head to toe over the seat, and if I didn't know any better, I'd say he was checking me out. "You look cute today, by the way."

Well, damn. He was checking me out. "Thanks."

"You look cute every day, honestly."

I raise my eyebrows.

Curtis laughs. "What?"

"You pay attention to me like that?"

"Yeah. I do. For instance, you always wear dope hoodies, but it's not like you're trying to hide or something. You're just being you. You've also got this one dimple, right here." He touches my cheek, right near the corner of my mouth. "That shows when you're laughing, but not when you're smiling, like it only wants to appear for special occasions. It's real cute."

Why are my cheeks suddenly warm? What do I say? Do I compliment him back? *How* do I compliment him back? "Your hair looks nice."

Wow, Bri. Are you saying the rest of him doesn't look nice? Okay, but his hair is on point. He clearly got a line up within the last day or so.

He runs a hand over the top. His waves are gone, and it looks like someone twisted the ends by hand. "Thanks. Thinking 'bout growing it out this summer for some locs or cornrows. Just gotta find somebody who can do them."

"I can do them," I say. "The cornrows, I mean. I don't know how to do locs."

"I don't know if I could trust you in my hair like that."

"Boy, bye. I know my stuff. Sonny's momma is a beautician. She taught me ages ago. I used to hook my baby dolls up."

"Okay, okay. I believe you," Curtis says. He leans a little closer over the seat. "So, what? I'll sit between your legs and let you do your thing?"

The corners of my mouth turn up. "Yeah. But you gotta let me do them however I want."

"However you want?"

"However I want."

"All right. So, what do you want?"

I try not to smile too much. "You'll have to wait and see."

Is this flirting? I think this is flirting.

Wait. I'm flirting with Curtis? And I'm okay with the fact that I'm flirting with Curtis?

At some point, Mr. Watson pulled up at Sonny's and Malik's houses, and they climbed on board. Sonny's in the aisle, his eyebrows raised about as high as they can go. Malik's near one of the front seats. Shana's already sitting down and seems to be talking to him, but he's looking straight at me. And Curtis.

He turns forward and slinks into the seat.

Sonny slowly lowers himself into a seat ahead of us, staring at me the whole way down. He wiggles his eyebrows just before he disappears.

I won't hear the end of this. I won't.

Eventually, the bus pulls up at our school. I let Curtis get off before I do because Sonny is waiting for me at his seat. He just looks at me with those raised eyebrows.

"Zip it," I tell him as I climb off the bus.

"I didn't say anything."

"You didn't have to. Your face says it all."

"Nah, *your face* says it all." He pokes my cheeks. "Aww, look at you, blushing and shit. Over Curtis though? Really, Bri?"

"I said zip it!"

"Hey, I'm not judging. I simply ask that you name your son and daughter after me. Sonny and Sonnita."

This boy didn't. "How *the hell* did we go from talking on the bus to having two kids, Sonny?"

"Two kids *and a dog*. A pug you'll name Sonningham."

"What goes on in that head of yours?"

"It's better than whatever has you flirting with Curtis."

I punch his arm. "You know what? I'll let you and Rapid name your kids those ridiculous names instead. How about that?"

Sonny's eyes cast down. "Uhh . . . I kinda ghosted on Rapid."

"What? Why?"

"I did my SAT practice test the other day and couldn't focus on that shit for thinking about him. I can't fuck this up, Bri."

Nobody's harder on Sonny than Sonny. I've witnessed him have straight-up panic attacks over his grades and even his art pieces. "It was only a practice test, Son'."

"That reflects how I'll do on the real test," he croaks. "Bri, if I get a low score on that shit—"

I cup his cheek. "Hey, look at me."

He does. My eyes won't let his look away. I've witnessed him have so many panic attacks that I can spot them before they fully form. "Breathe," I tell him.

Sonny takes in a long, deep breath and lets it out. "I can't mess this up."

"You won't. That's why you ghosted on him?"

"That's not all. Malik and I were hanging out the other day

and did more research. We found out Rapid's IP address doesn't trace to the Garden."

He and Malik hung out without me. That still gets me in my feelings a bit. But I gotta shake it off. "What's wrong with that?"

"Rapid had me thinking he lived in the neighborhood. That's where all of his photography is from."

"Wait. Did he actually *say* he lived in the Garden or did you *assume* he lived in the Garden?"

"Okay, I assumed. But it shows me how much I don't know about him." Sonny stuffs his hands in his pockets. "It's not worth the distraction."

Yet the way his voice dips says otherwise.

There are more people outside the school than usual. Mainly near the front doors. There's lots of chatter. We have to push through the crowd to try to get a glimpse of what's happening.

"This is some bullshit!" somebody shouts up ahead.

Sonny and I find Malik and Shana. Malik's height helps him see over the crowd.

"What's going on?" Sonny asks.

Malik's jaw ticks as he looks straight into the school. "They're back."

"Who?" I ask.

"Long and Tate."

SEVENTEEN

"What the hell?" Sonny says.

There is no way.

I stand on my tiptoes. Long ushers a student through the metal detectors, as if he never left, and Tate checks a backpack nearby.

My whole body tenses up.

Dr. Rhodes said there would be an investigation and that disciplinary action would take place if the administration *saw fit*. Long and Tate throwing me to the ground must not have "fit" their idea of bad behavior.

Dr. Rhodes is near the doors, telling everybody to come inside in an orderly fashion.

"How the hell can they be back?" Sonny asks.

"There wasn't enough noise made about what they did," Malik says. He looks at me.

No, hell no. "This is not on me."

"I didn't say it was."

"You may as well have!"

"Y'all!" Sonny says. "Not now, okay?"

"We need to do something," says Shana.

I glance around. Half the school's out here, and most of them eye me.

Am I pissed? Doubt that's even the word for it. But whatever they want me to do, I don't have it in me to do. Hell, I don't know what to do.

Malik watches me for the longest. When I don't say or do anything, he shakes his head. He opens his mouth and starts to shout, "Hell no, we won't—"

"'Pin me to the ground, boy, you fucked up,'" Curtis yells over him. "'Pin me to the ground, boy, you fucked up!'"

Malik tries to start his own chant over him, but Curtis is loud and angry, and it becomes contagious. A second person yells out my lyrics. A third. Fourth. Before I know it, I'm hearing my words from everybody but me.

And Malik.

"We will not tolerate that type of language," Dr. Rhodes calls over them. "All students must stop at—"

"'You can't stop me, nope, nope!'" Curtis yells. "'You can't stop me, nope, nope!'"

The chant shifts to that.

I have a moment. Of all the places and times to have one,

I do. See, those words started in my head. Mine. Conceived from my thoughts and my feelings. Birthed through my pencil and onto my notepad. Somehow, they've found their way to my classmates' tongues. I think they're saying them for themselves, yeah, but I know they're saying them for me.

That's enough to make me say them, too.

"'You can't stop me, nope, nope,'" I yell. "'You can't stop me, nope, nope!'"

It's hard to say this is a protest. So many of my classmates who look like me are rocking to a beat that's not even playing. They're jumping around, bouncing, dancing. Locs and braids shake, feet won't stay still. There are ayes and yahs mixed in, upping the hype. It's different from what happened in the Ring parking lot. That was a mini concert. This is a call to war.

"'You can't stop me, nope, nope! You can't stop me, nope, nope!'"

Long and Tate appear in the doors. Long has a bullhorn.

"All students must report to class," he says. "If you do not, you risk suspension."

"'Run up on me and get done up!'" someone yells out.

That becomes the new chant, and it's definitely a warning.

"'Run up on me and get done up! Run up on me and get done up! Run up on me and get done up!'"

"This is your final warning," Long says. "If you do not disperse, you will—"

It happens so fast.

A fist connects with Long's jaw. The bullhorn flies from his hand.

Suddenly, it's as if that punch was the green light some students were waiting for. A cluster of boys charge Long and Tate, taking them to the ground. Curtis is one of them. Fists fly and feet kick.

"Oh, shit!" Sonny says.

"We need to go!" says Malik.

He grabs my hand, but I tug away and rush forward.

"Curtis!"

He stops kicking and whirls around toward me.

"Cops!" I say.

That one word is enough. I bet everything that the police are en route. Curtis hurries over to me, and we run with Sonny, Malik, and Shana. Sirens wail nearby, and the chants behind us are replaced with screams and shouts.

We run until we can't hear them. When we do stop, it's so we can catch our breath.

"This is bad," Sonny says, bent over. "Holy shit, this is bad."

Malik marches up to Curtis and shoves him so hard, Curtis's hat flies off. "What the hell were you thinking?"

Curtis catches himself midstumble and shoves Malik right back. "Man, get your hands off me!"

"You started a riot!" Malik screams in his face. "You realize what you've done?"

"Hey!" I push Malik away from Curtis. "Stop it!"

"Oh, you're on his side now?" Malik yells.

"Side? What the hell are you talking about?"

"I guess it's fine 'cause he was chanting your song! Forget the fact he incited a riot!"

"It's not his fault somebody threw a punch!"

"Why the fuck are you sticking up for him?"

"Malik!" Shana says.

Sonny snatches him back. "Bruh, what the hell? Chill!"

A patrol car zooms by.

"If we don't get outta here, the next cop might stop and question us," Sonny says.

Malik's glare is set on Curtis. "We can go to my house. My mom should be at work by now."

Another patrol car races toward the school, lights flashing.

"C'mon," Sonny says.

Shana tugs at Malik's hand. That's the only thing that makes him stop glaring at Curtis. He lets her pull him down the sidewalk.

In less than an hour, almost every black and Latinx student from Midtown shows up at Malik's.

He and Shana got word out to their coalition to come over for an emergency meeting. One after another, they bring details of what happened after we ran off. At least ten cop cars arrived, a news van showed up, and the boys who jumped Long and Tate were arrested. One of them was Zane.

Curtis glances at me when we're told that. I just mouth, *You're welcome.*

Long and Tate were both loaded into ambulances. Nobody knows how bad either of them are.

Parents and guardians received a recorded message from the school saying that there was an emergency and that they must come get their children. Jay thought there was a shooting and immediately called me. She calmed down once I told her I'm fine. I gave her a quick rundown of what really happened, specifically the part about Long and Tate being back. She was pissed but not surprised.

Everyone sits and stands around Malik's living room, eating sandwiches and chips and drinking just about every soda Aunt 'Chelle has. Sonny, Curtis, and I made room on the couch for three other people. Shana's on Aunt 'Chelle's recliner with a girl sitting on each arm.

Malik won't stay still. He paces the living room, the way he used to do when a mission on a video game wasn't going his way.

"This will not help us with any of the concerns we had," he says. "In fact, this is gonna make shit worse."

He eyes Curtis. Curtis eats his sandwich as if Malik said nothing.

"You don't know that," says Sonny.

"No, he's right," says Shana. "They're probably about to go the Garden High route. Have actual cops acting as security."

"What?" I say, and other people in the room basically say the same thing.

"I guarantee those two are back because so many parents bought that 'drug dealer' narrative about Bri," Malik says. "They've got reason to believe we're all threats now. I bet there will be armed cops at the doors."

Ever since that boy got killed, my heart races whenever I see a cop. I could've been him, he could've been me. Luck's the only thing that separated us.

Now my heart may be racing for most of the day.

Curtis sits forward, his arms folded on his knees. "Look, all I know is we were tired of Long and Tate treating us like shit and getting away with it, so we whooped their asses. Plain and simple."

Malik pounds his fist into his palm. "There's a way to go about it! You think you're the only one tired? You think I *wanted* to see my best friend thrown onto the ground?"

Wow. Malik and I haven't been great lately. Hell, that's an understatement, honestly. But he basically just told me all that doesn't matter—he still cares about me.

I catch Shana staring at me. She quickly looks away.

"We finally got Dr. Rhodes to agree to a meeting with us and this happens?" Malik says. "She won't hear *shit* we have to say. Nah. We gotta go above her now."

"The superintendent?" Sonny asks.

"Yep. Or the school board."

"No, we need even bigger," Shana says. She focuses on me again. "We need that video to get in the news."

She means Malik's video of Long and Tate throwing me like a trash bag. I shake my head. "Nah, not happening."

"Bri, c'mon," Deon from the bus says. One or two people echo him.

"It's the only way things will change," Shana says. "We have to show people why everyone was upset today, Bri."

"I already told y'all, I'm not gonna be the poster child for this."

Shana folds her arms. "Why not?"

"Because she said so," Curtis says. "Goddamn, get off her back."

"I'm just saying, if it was me, and I knew it would change things at our school, I would release the video in a heartbeat."

I raise my eyebrows. "*Clearly*, I'm not you."

"What's that supposed to mean?"

I'm starting to think that this isn't just about the school incident. "It means what I said. I'm not you."

"Yeah, because if you were me, you'd prefer that that video was released instead of videos of you acting ratchet at the Ring," Shana says. "But those videos are okay, right?"

She didn't. Please tell me she didn't.

She did though, because several mouths around the room have suddenly dropped. I'm well aware that Malik is silent during all of this.

I sit up. "First of all," I say with a clap.

"Aww, shit," Sonny mutters. He knows what that clap means. "Calm down, Bri."

"Nah, let me answer this. First of all, I had no control over those videos from the Ring being released, *sweetie*."

I am totally my mom's child, because when she says "sweetie," she means the exact opposite. She does the clap thing, too. I don't know when I became her.

"Second," I say with another clap, "how is speaking up for myself being ratchet? If you saw those videos, you'd know that's all I did."

"I'm only saying what people are already saying about—"

"Third!" I clap over her. I'm gon' finish, dammit. "If I don't want the video released, I don't want the video released. I frankly don't owe you or anybody else an explanation."

"Yes, you do, because this affects us too!" she says.

"Oh. My. God!" I clap with each word. That's the only thing keeping me in my seat. "Bruh, for real. For real!"

Translation: Somebody get this girl.

Sonny immediately understands. "Bri, chill, okay? Look, maybe she has a point though. If the video was released—"

Him too? I push up from the couch. "You know what? Y'all can continue your li'l meeting without me. I'm gone."

Sonny tries to grab my hand, but I move it away. "Bri, c'mon. Don't be like that."

I sling my backpack over my shoulder and step over people

sitting on the floor. "I'm good. I'd rather not stay around for the 'jump down Bri's throat' part of the meeting."

"Nobody's jumping down your throat," Malik says.

Oh, *now* he speaks. He couldn't say shit when his girlfriend was going in on me.

"We just don't get why you don't wanna help us," Shana says. "This is your chance to—"

"I don't wanna be that person!" I scream so that every single one of them hears me. "They're just gonna explain the shit away! Don't you get that?"

"Bri—"

"Sonny, you know they will! That's what they do. Hell, they're already doing it with the 'drug dealer' rumors. This gets in the news? They'll mention every time I've been sent to the office, every goddamn suspension. Hell, they'll use those Ring videos. Anything to make it seem like what happened was okay 'cause I'm not from shit! You think I wanna deal with that?"

I fight to breathe. They don't get it. That video can't be released. Because all of a sudden, even more people will try to justify what happened to me, and it'll get so loud that I may start thinking that I deserved it to begin with.

I didn't. I know I didn't. I wanna keep knowing that I didn't.

The room is blurry, but I blink it into focus. "Screw y'all," I mumble, and throw my hoodie over my head.

I leave and don't look back.

* * *

When I get home, Jay's lying across the living room sofa. The remote's in her hand, and the theme music for *As We Are* fades off. She's addicted to that soap opera.

"Hey, Bookie," she says as she sits up. She stretches and yawns, revealing the big hole under the arm of her T-shirt. She says it's too comfortable to get rid of. Plus, it's got Dad's first album cover on it. "How was Malik's?"

The shortest answer is the best answer. "Fine. How was *As We Are*?"

"It was too good today! Jamie finally found out that baby ain't his."

She's super upbeat. I think she fakes for me though.

"Whoa, for real?" I ask.

"Yep! It's about damn time."

When I was younger, Granddaddy would let me watch soap operas with him every afternoon in the summer. He loves his "stories." *As We Are* was our favorite. I would sit on his lap, the air conditioner in the window blowing on us and my head resting back against his chest as Theresa Brady pulled off her latest scheme like a boss. Now it's me and Jay's thing.

She tilts her head and stares at me long and hard. "You okay?"

"Yeah." I can fake, too.

"Don't worry, I'm calling the superintendent's office about this," she says, and goes toward the kitchen. "Those bastards should not be back on the job. You hungry? We have some sausages left over from breakfast. I can make you a sandwich."

"No thanks. I ate at Malik's." I plop down on the sofa. Now that *As We Are* is off, the afternoon news is starting.

"Our top story: A student rally turned violent earlier today at Midtown School of the Arts," the newscaster says. "Megan Sullivan has more."

"Turn that up, Bri," Jay calls from the kitchen.

I do. The reporter stands in front of my now-deserted school.

"The day had only begun at Midtown School of the Arts," says Megan Sullivan, "when students took to the steps and rallied."

They show cell-phone footage from this morning of everybody in front of the building, chanting, "'You can't stop me, nope, nope!'"

"School officials say there were concerns among students regarding recent security measures," Sullivan says.

Jay comes to the doorway with the loaf of bread in her hand, untwisting the tie. "Security measures? You mean the fact those two were back on the job?"

"However, what started as a peaceful rally quickly turned violent," says Sullivan.

There go the screams as punches get thrown and Long and Tate are knocked out of view. The news bleeps the "Oh, shit" that the person recording yelps.

"Security officials were physically attacked by several

students," Sullivan says. "According to eyewitnesses, it didn't take long for the melee to begin."

"We were all standing around outside, trying to figure out what was going on," this white girl says. She's in the vocal music department. "Then people started chanting a song."

Oh. No.

Another cell-phone video is shown. In this one, my classmates say my lyrics.

"'Run up on me and get done up!'"

"The song, called 'On the Come Up,' is said to be by local rapper Bri," Megan Sullivan says. They show my Dat Cloud page. "The track, with its violent nature, includes attacks against law enforcement and is said to be a hit among young listeners."

Next thing I know, my voice comes through the TV, with bleeps where the curse words should be. But it's not the whole song. It's bits and pieces.

*Pin me to the ground, boy, you **** up . . .*
If I did what I wanted and bucked up,
You'd be bound for the ground, grave dug up . . .

Strapped like backpacks, I pull triggers.
All the clips on my hips change my figure.
But let me be honest, I promise,
If a cop come at me, I'll be lawless . . .

The loaf of bread falls from Jay's hands. She stares at the TV, frozen.

"Brianna." She says my name like it's her first time saying it. "Is that you?"

EIGHTEEN

Words won't come out of my mouth. But the words I wrote blare from the TV.

"'You can't stop me, nope, nope,'" my classmates chant. "'You can't stop me, nope, nope!'"

"As they used the song to taunt school officials," Sullivan says, "the lyrics seemed to have encouraged students to violently take matters into their own hands."

Wait, what?

It's not the fact that those two assholes harassed all the black and brown kids.

Not the fact that whoever threw that first punch made that decision themselves.

It's the fact that they were reciting a *song*?

"Several students were arrested," she goes on. "The security guards have reportedly been hospitalized but are expected to make a full recovery. Students were sent home for the day as school officials work to determine their next course of action. We'll have more tonight at six."

The picture goes black. Jay turned the TV off.

"You never answered my question," she says. "Was that you?"

"They didn't play the whole song! It's not about attacking law enforce—"

"Was. That. You?"

She's somehow loud and calm all at once.

I swallow. "Yes . . . yes, ma'am."

Jay puts her face in her hands. "Oh, God."

"Hear me out—"

"Brianna, what the hell were you thinking?" she yells. "Why would you say that stuff?"

"They didn't play the whole song!"

"They played enough!" she says. "Where's the gun you rapped about, huh? Show me. *Tell* me. I *need* to see how my sixteen-year-old is 'strapped like backpacks'!"

"I'm not! That's not what I meant! They took it outta context!"

"You said that stuff. There's no way to get around—"

"Would you listen to me for once?" I bellow.

Jay puts her hands to her mouth like she's praying. "One: Check. Your. Tone," she growls. "Two: I am listening. I listened enough to hear my child rapping like a thug!"

"It's not like that."

"Oh, it's not? Then why didn't you tell me a goddamn thing about this song before now? Huh, Brianna? According to the news, it's pretty well known. Why haven't you mentioned it?"

I open my mouth, but before I can even say a word, she goes, "Because you knew damn well you were saying stuff you had no business saying!"

"No, because I knew you'd jump to conclusions!"

"People only jump on what you give them!"

Did she just—did she of all people *really* say that? "So that's why everyone accuses you of being on drugs?" I ask. "They're jumping on what you give them?"

She can't say anything to that at first.

"You know what?" Jay eventually says. "You've got a point. You've absolutely got a point. People are gonna assume things about you, about me, no matter what we say or do. But here's the difference between me and you, Brianna." She closes the space between us. "I'm not giving people more reasons to make those assumptions about me. Do you see me walking around talking about drugs?"

"I—"

"Do. You. See. Me. Walking. Around. Talking. About. Drugs?" She claps with each word.

I stare at my shoes. "No, ma'am."

"Do you see me acting like I'm on drugs? Bragging about

drugs? No! But you made yourself out to be everything people were gonna assume about you! Did you think about what this will make *me* look like as your mother?"

She's still not listening to me. "If you would just listen to the song—it's not what they made it out to be, I swear. It's about playing into their assumptions about me."

"You don't get that luxury, Brianna! *We* don't! They never think we're just playing!"

The room goes quiet again.

Jay closes her eyes and holds her forehead. "Jesus," she mutters, like calling his name will calm her down. She looks at me. "I don't want you rapping anymore."

I step back as if she slapped me. It feels like it. "What—but—"

"I refuse to stand by and let you end up like your daddy, do you hear me? Look what 'rapping gangsta' got him. A bullet in his head!"

I've always heard that my dad got caught up in the streets because he rapped about the streets. "But that's not me!"

"And I won't let it be you." Jay shakes her head. "I won't. I *can't*. You're gonna focus on school and you're gonna leave that mess alone. Do I make myself clear?"

Only thing clear is that she doesn't get it. Or me. That stings worse than the news report.

But I suck it up like a Jackson's supposed to and look her dead in her eyes. "Yes, ma'am. We're clear."

* * *

We're so clear that when Supreme texts me that night asking to meet up in the morning, I don't hesitate to say yeah. He saw the news report and wants to talk to me about it.

He also saw that "On the Come Up" is the number one song on Dat Cloud. The news has everyone listening to it.

We meet up at the Fish Hut, this little run-down spot over on Clover. It's easy for me to get out of the house. It's Saturday, and Jay's having her monthly check-in meeting with the recovering addicts. We don't have enough food for her to feed them today, but everybody's talking so much it doesn't seem to matter. I tell Jay I'm going to my grandparents' house, and she's so caught up in their conversation, she only says, "Okay."

Soon I'm on my bike with my headphones, my backpack, and my dad's chain tucked under my hoodie, headed to Clover Street.

I pedal fast so I don't freeze. Granddaddy says that cold weather's the only thing that'll shut the Garden down. That explains why the streets are almost deserted.

Riding through Clover is like riding through an abandoned war zone. The Fish Hut is one of the only places still standing. Aunt Pooh says it's 'cause Mr. Barry, the owner, put "black owned" on the doors during the riots. Yeah, she was out during all of that. Even looted some stores and got a couple of TVs.

I haven't heard from her since the Ring. She hasn't ghosted, nah. Jay talked to her last night. Aunt Pooh just doesn't wanna talk to me.

Supreme's Hummer sits in a spot near the door of the Fish

Hut. I take my bike in with me. I'd be a damn fool to leave it outside. I'd never get it back. Plus, Mr. Barry, the owner, won't trip. In fact, he says, "Hey, Li'l Law!" soon as I walk in. I get away with a hell of a lot because of my dad.

The Fish Hut has wood-paneled walls like my grandparents' den, but there's this kinda dark, greasy film on them. Grandma would never let her walls look like that. A TV in the ceiling corner always plays a news station, and Mr. Barry always yells at it. Today he's at the counter talking about, "Can't believe a damn thing that come outta that fool's mouth!"

Supreme's got a table in the corner. I'm starting to think he never takes those dark sunglasses off. He stuffs his face with fried fish and eggs—that's the Fish Hut's breakfast special. When he sees me, he wipes his mouth. "The celebrity of the hour is here."

He points to the seat across from him. I prop my bike against the wall as he motions Mr. Barry over. "Mr. B! Make sure you get this young lady whatever she wants. It's on me."

Mr. Barry writes our orders on his pad. I used to think he looked like a young Santa Claus with his full black beard and mustache. It's grayer these days.

I go for the shrimp and grits with a Sunkist. It's never too early for Sunkist—it's fizzy orange juice. I'll stand by that until I die.

"Props on hitting number one on Dat Cloud," Supreme says after Mr. Barry walks away. "Got you a congratulatory gift."

He pulls a gift bag from under the table. It's not huge, but it's heavy enough that I have to grab it with both hands. Inside, there's a dark-gray shoe box with a tree logo on it.

I look up at Supreme. He flashes those gold fangs.

"Go 'head," he says. "Open it."

I slide the box out of the bag. I already know what's inside, but my heart still speeds up. I flip the lid on the box and can't even stop the "Oh, shit" that comes out of my mouth.

A pair of brand-new Timbs. Not the scuffed ones at the community center giveaway but brand-new, never-worn Timbs.

"Now, if the size is wrong, I can exchange them, no problem," Supreme says as I take one out.

I trace the tree carved into the side of the boot. My eyes are prickly as hell. I worked months to buy a pair. Months. Still hadn't made enough when Dr. Rhodes suspended me for selling candy. It was a finish line I could never reach. Yet Supreme's just handing me a pair like it's nothing.

I can't believe I'm about to say this though. "I can't take these."

"Why not?"

My granddaddy says you never take big gifts that seem to be for no reason, because there's a chance that there's a big reason you can't afford. "Why'd you get them for me?"

"I told you, to congratulate you on hitting number one," he says.

"Yeah, but these cost a ton—"

Supreme laughs. "A ton? They only one fifty. I spend more than that on sunglasses."

"Oh."

Damn. I wish one fifty was chump change for me. Shit, I probably look dumb as hell for saying that's a ton of money. Not to mention broke as hell.

Mr. B brings my shrimp and grits. I keep my eyes on them for the longest.

"It's all good," Supreme says. "I remember when that was a hell of a lot of money to me, too. Keep the shoes. I swear, ain't no strings attached."

I glance down at my faux pair. The bottom has slowly started to separate from the rest of the boot. Doubt they can last another month. Maybe not even a week.

I mumble, "Thank you" and stuff both boots into my backpack.

"You're welcome."

Supreme shakes hot pepper sauce onto his plate. "I thought that shit at the Ring was gonna have people talking. You really went and outdid yourself, huh, baby girl?"

Um, did he watch the same news report that I watched? "They're not exactly talking in a good way."

"Truthfully, this probably the best thing that could've happened to you. Publicity is publicity, I don't give a damn how bad it is. It made you number one on Dat Cloud, didn't it?"

"Yeah, but not everybody's listening because they like it."

Trust me, I messed up and read the comments. "What if people make a lot of noise because of what happened at my school?"

"Ah, so that's your school?"

That's one thing the news didn't tell. Probably can't for legal reasons. "Yeah. Part of the reason people were upset is because of something that happened to me."

He nods, as if that's all he needs to know. "Well, they probably will make a lot of noise about the song. Folks love to blame hip-hop. Guess that's easier than looking at the real problems, you know? Just think though, you in legendary company. They did it to N.W.A, they did it to Public Enemy. 'Pac. Kendrick. Shit, anybody who's ever had something to say on the mic, they've come at them 'bout how they said it."

"Really?"

"Hell yeah. You young'uns just don't know. N.W.A got letters from the FBI over 'Fuck tha Police.' Some boy shot a cop and had a 'Pac song playing in the car. Politicians blamed the song."

"What the hell?"

"Exactly," says Supreme. "This ain't new. They love to make us the villains for telling the truth." He sips his orange juice. "You need a real manager to make sure this doesn't get outta control and that it works to your advantage."

A *real* manager. The Aunt Pooh shade is obvious.

The bell on the restaurant door dings. Supreme raises his hand to catch the person's attention.

Dee-Nice makes his way over. His gold chains are almost as long as his locs. He and Supreme slap palms and end it in a one-armed hug.

Supreme stretches his neck to look outside. "Okay, I see you with the Beamer." He lightly elbows Dee-Nice, who laughs. "Already spending that money."

"Had to show these boys how it's done." He looks at me. "The princess of the Garden. We finally meet. Nothing but props, love." He gives me one of those palm slap/handshake things that guys sometimes do. "Between that first battle and the song? You killing it out here."

Confession: I'm a little tongue-tied. Starstruck even. Dee-Nice is a legend. What the hell do you say if you get a stamp of approval from a legend?

"I still think it's bullshit that you lost to Ef-X that time."

He and Supreme both laugh. "What?" Dee-Nice says.

I studied battles way before I ever stepped foot in the Ring. "Two years ago, you and Ef-X battled," I say. "Your flow was absolutely ridiculous. I'm still in awe that you came up with that rhyme scheme on the spot. You should've won, hands down."

"Wow. I see you been paying attention."

"An MC must be a student before they're ever a master," I say. "That's what my aunt always—"

The Timbs. Dee-Nice showing up. This is a setup to get me away from Aunt Pooh.

See, the shoes are bait, like I'm one of those fat bass fish Granddaddy likes to catch in the summer and Dee-Nice is Supreme's bobber. Having Dee-Nice talk to me will let Supreme know if I'm biting the bait or not.

But honestly? I swam into this water knowing I'd probably get caught. I knew what this meeting with Supreme was about the moment he texted me. Forget that even being here would hurt Aunt Pooh. Forget the fact that if I take his offer, it'll mean I have to get rid of her. Forget that if she's not my manager, she'll probably stay in the streets. I came here anyway.

What kinda niece does that make me?

"Listen, your aunt sounds like cool people," Supreme says. "But you need more."

I bite my lip. "Supreme—"

"Hear me out," he says. "Truth is, you've got a unique opportunity here, Bri. Situations like this, *publicity* like this, don't come around often. You gotta take advantage of it. Dee didn't have the buzz you're getting. Look what I did for him. I also got a big deal in the works for my son . . . if he can keep his act straight."

Dee-Nice laughs. There's a joke I'm clearly missing here. "He still giving you problems?"

Supreme chugs back some orange juice. "He can't focus worth a damn lately. But that's a whole 'nother discussion for another day."

Dee-Nice nods. "Straight up though, Bri? This guy here?"

He points at Supreme. "Changed my life. I'm able to take care of my whole family now."

"For real?"

"Oh yeah," he says. "I was doing battles in the Ring, hoping it would lead to something someday, but my family was struggling. Supreme came along, set up a game plan, now my family ain't gotta worry about a damn thing. We good."

Good. One word, one syllable.

If I could, I'd give everything I should,
To make my family good.

I swallow the tightness in my throat and look at Supreme. "If I work with you, can you make sure my family is okay?"

"I'll make sure you and your family are good," he says. "You got my word."

He holds his hand out to me.

It's a betrayal to Aunt Pooh, but it's a way for my mom and Trey. I shake his hand.

"We 'bout to get paid!" Supreme practically shouts. "You won't regret this, baby girl, I swear you won't. But first things first, I gotta come over and talk to your mom. The three of us gotta sit down and—"

If my life really was a sitcom, this is the moment where the record would scratch. "You, uhhh . . . you gotta talk to Jay?"

Supreme gives this kinda unsure laugh, as if he thinks he's

missing a joke. "Of course. Is there a problem?"

Too many problems to name. I scratch the back of my head. "That may not be a good idea right now."

"O-kay," he says slowly, waiting for the rest. That's all I'm giving him. "I'll have to talk to her eventually. You know that, right?"

Unfortunately. And she would shut all of this down, though, in a heartbeat.

But it's like how when she does stuff I don't like and says it's "for my own good." This is for hers. I'm willing to do anything to keep that sadness in her eyes from becoming permanent.

"Let me talk to her first," I lie to Supreme.

"All right." He grins. "Let's work on getting this money then."

NINETEEN

When I get home, all of the recovering addicts are gone, and Jay is putting cans in the kitchen cabinet. Grocery bags cover the table.

I slide my backpack off and set it on the kitchen floor. "How did you get all of—"

"Girl, if you don't put that backpack in your room, I swear!" Jay snaps.

Goddamn, she's not even looking at me! Peripheral vision is the devil.

I toss my backpack in my room. Probably should've done that anyway. Those Timbs Supreme gave me are stuffed inside. Nobody's got time for the interrogation that'll come once Jay sees them things.

Supreme went on for hours about all of the plans he has for

me. He wants me to do some interviews to address the drama, he wants me to do a song with Dee-Nice and a song with Miles. He wants me to do a mixtape of my own. Said he's gonna pay for the studio time and the beats.

It's hard to be excited, knowing I gotta tell Aunt Pooh that I'm basically dropping her, and knowing I can't tell my mom yet. I gotta wait for some things to fall in place first. You know, have a seven-figure contract in my hands and be like, "Look what I got!" There's no way she'll say no to that.

Okay, there's a hundred ways she'll say no, but I'm gonna try for a yes.

She's moved on to the freezer by the time I return to the kitchen. She slides a pack of chicken in, next to the frozen vegetables that are already in there.

I peek in one of the bags. There are crackers, bread, chips, juice. "Did Aunt Pooh bring all of this?"

"No, I got it," Jay says.

"How?"

She keeps her head in the freezer as she stuffs another pack of frozen meat inside. "I got my EBT card in the mail today."

EBT? "You got food stamps? But you said we weren't gonna—"

"You can say a whole lot before things happen," she says. "You never truly know what you will or won't do until you're going through it. We needed food. Welfare could help us get food."

"But I thought you said they don't give college students food stamps unless they have a job."

"I withdrew from school."

She says it as casually as if I asked her about the weather.

"You what?" I'm so loud, nosy Ms. Gladys next door probably heard me. "But you were so close to finishing! You can't quit school for some food stamps!"

Jay moves around me and gets a box of cereal from a bag. "I can quit to make sure you and your brother don't starve."

This . . .

This hurts.

This physically fucking hurts. I feel it in my chest, I swear. It burns and aches all at once. "You shouldn't have to do that."

She crosses over to me, but I watch the glimmer of sunlight that's shining through the window and lighting up the tile on the floor. Granddaddy used to say, look for the bright spots. I know he didn't mean literally, but that's all I've got.

"Hey, look at me," Jay says. She takes my chin to make sure that I do. "I'm fine. This is temporary, okay?"

"But becoming a social worker is your dream. You need a degree for that."

"You and your brother are my first dream. That other one can wait to make sure you two are okay. That's what parents do sometimes."

"You shouldn't have to," I say.

"But I want to."

That makes this harder. Having to is a responsibility. Wanting to is love.

She holds my cheek. "I listened to your song."

"You did?"

"Mm-hmm. I've gotta admit it's catchy. It's pretty damn brilliant, too, Ms. Brilliant Bri." She smiles and runs her thumb along my cheek. "I get it."

Three words, yet they somehow feel as good as a hug. "Really?"

"I do. But you get where I was coming from, don't you?"

"Yeah. You don't want people to make assumptions about me."

"Exactly. We have to prepare ourselves, baby. That local news story may only be the start. I need you to stay low during all of this."

"What? I can't go outside? Or go to school?" I'm totally fine with that.

"Girl!" She lightly smacks my arm. I laugh. "I don't mean *that* low. Your butt is still going to school, so don't even try. I mean . . ." She pauses, searching for the words. "I mean don't provoke them. Don't respond to anything, don't do anything. Just . . . act like they're talking about somebody else. Don't be getting all on Tweeter or whatever, making comments."

She's gotta step up her social media game. "I can't even troll people who come at me?"

I'm a pro at trolling gamer boys online. In fact, I may put

it on my future résumé as a skill, alongside rapping and laying edges. Honestly, trolling is easy. All you gotta do is find multiple ways to call a gamer boy's penis little and he'll rage.

"You better not say anything, period," Jay says. "Matter of fact, hand me your phone."

She holds her palm out.

My eyes widen. "You're kidding."

"I'm not. Give me your phone."

"I promise I won't—"

"Phone, Bri."

Craaap. I take it out of my pocket and set it in her hand.

"Thank you," she says, and slips it into her own pocket. "Go study for that ACT."

I groan. "Really?"

"Really. The test will be here before you know it. *That* needs to be your priority. Gina says that Sonny's been studying for two hours a day. You could learn something from him."

Dammit, Sonny. His overachieving ass. Got me looking like I'm slacking. Okay, I am, but that's not the point.

Jay turns me toward the hallway. "Go. Only thing I better hear is you studying."

"Um, how do you hear somebody—"

"Just go study, girl!"

She doesn't make me study for two hours. No, that's too short for my mom apparently. It's four hours before she brings me my phone. *Four.* I don't know what words are anymore.

Jay steps over my dirty clothes and junk on my bedroom floor.

"I oughta make you clean this nasty-ass room before I give you this phone," she says. "Bet' not be bringing roaches up in my house."

Grandma used to say the same thing. They make it sound like people smuggle them into houses. Do I look like I wanna be anywhere near a roach? They're right below Big Bird on my "Things I Don't Mess With" list.

Jay sets my phone on my desk and maneuvers around clothes and junk again. "Just trifling!" she says.

"I love you, too," I call after her. I've got texts from Sonny and Malik that I delete. Yes, I'm still in my feelings about how things went down at Malik's house.

I've got tons of notifications from Dat Cloud, too. It's been like that for a minute now though. I usually open the app to make that annoying red-circled number go away and close it. But when I open it today, there are a lot of unread messages waiting for me.

Probably trolls. I mean, I dish it, so I should be able to take it, right? Trust, as many times as I've been called "nigger" and "bitch" by gamer boys, I can take a hell of a lot. Just need a moment to prepare myself.

The first one is from a user called "RudeBoi09." Great sign. I open it. There's a link and below that he wrote:

This is bullshit! Don't let them censor you, Bri!

Huh?

I don't click the link. What I look like, trusting somebody named RudeBoi? It could be a virus or porn. But the next message from another user has the same link with a comment:

You got them big mad hahahaha!

The third message has the link, too. The fourth and fifth. New texts from Sonny pop up on my screen.

U okay?

Call me.

Love u.

He sent me the link, too. I click it. It takes me to an article on the website of the *Clarion*, the local newspaper. The title stops my heart.

"On the Come Up" Should Come Down: Local Teen Rapper's Violent Song Leads to Violence

"What the—" I mutter.

It's an entire page of some chick named Emily Taylor complaining about my song. Her thirteen-year-old son loves it, she says, but according to her, I "spend the entire track rapping about things that would make any parent hit the Stop button immediately, including boasts about guns and antipolice sentiment."

The hell is she talking about? There's not shit in that song that says anything against police. Just 'cause I'm tired of them patrolling my neighborhood like we're all criminals, *I'm* in the wrong?

In the middle of the article, she embedded a video from the incident in the Ring parking lot. Emily uses it to describe me as a "gang-affiliated, unruly teen who was recently kicked out of a local establishment."

Give me five seconds with her and I'll show her unruly.

She goes on to mention the uprising at Midtown and actually says, "It only makes sense that a song that encourages violence encouraged them to act violently."

But the end though. The end of the article is the real kicker, because that's when Emily earns a permanent spot on my shit list.

"I respectfully ask the website Dat Cloud to remove 'On the Come Up' from their catalog. It has already caused damage. We cannot allow it to continue. You can add your voice by signing the petition at the link below. We must do more to protect our children."

Protect *our* children. I'm definitely not included in that.

Fuck Emily. Yeah, I said it. Fuck her. She doesn't know a thing about me, yet she wants to use one song to make me into the big bad villain who is influencing her precious son. God forbid he *hear* about what people like me have to deal with on the daily. It must be nice to panic over some goddamn words, because that's all they are. Words.

I can't help it, but I click her profile. I wanna lay eyes on this idiot.

She has several highlight pictures that are supposed to reveal more about her. One is of her, her husband, and her son.

A dead deer hangs behind them, and the three of them wear camouflage and hold rifles. And yeah, they're white.

What really gets me though? The title of her article before this one.

Why You Won't Take My Guns:
Gun Control Has No Place Here

But it's different when I rap about guns?

I wonder why.

It's like that crap at Midtown, I swear. White girls don't get sent to the office for making snide remarks. Hell, I've seen it happen with my own eyes. They get a warning. But anytime I open my mouth and say something my teachers don't like, to the office I go.

Apparently words are different when they come out of my mouth. They somehow sound more aggressive, more threatening.

Well, you know what? I've got plenty of words for Emily.

I close my door, pull up Instagram on my phone, and immediately go live. Usually only Sonny and Malik will show up. Tonight, about a hundred people are watching me in seconds.

"What's up, y'all? It's Bri."

The comments start immediately.

Your song is 🔥🔥🔥

Fuck what they say!

You my new favorite rapper 💯

"Thanks for the support," I tell them, and a hundred more people are suddenly watching. "As you may know, there's a petition to get my song taken off Dat Cloud. Besides the fact it's censorship, it's stupid as hell."

Hell yeah, somebody writes.

Fuck censorship!

"That's right, fuck censorship," I say, to three hundred viewers. "They don't get it because it ain't for them to get. Besides, if I am strapped like backpacks, maybe it's 'cause I gotta be, bitch. Ain't my fault if it makes you uncomfortable. I'm uncomfortable every goddamn day of my life."

Four hundred viewers. People respond with 💯 or high-five emojis.

"But check this," I say. "I got something for everybody who wanna come at me 'bout my song."

I lift my middle finger without hesitation.

Five hundred viewers. More comments.

Preach!

Fuck em all!

We with you, Bri!

"So, Ms. Reporter," I say, "and anybody else who wanna call 'On the Come Up' this, that, or whatever the hell else. Do it. Hell, get the song taken down if you want. But you'll never silence me. I got too goddamn much to say."

TWENTY

I've only been drunk once in my life. The summer before sophomore year, Sonny, Malik, and I decided to try the Hennessy Sonny's dad keeps in his cabinet to see what the big deal was. Biggest. Mistake. Of. My. Life. The next morning, I severely regretted touching that bottle. I also regretted it once Jay released her wrath.

I think I have an Instagram hangover. I went to bed pissed at Emily and all the Emilys of the world. But when I woke up, I was like, "Oh, shit. Did I say that?"

Too late to do anything. I may not have saved it on my page, but somebody saved it and now it's spreading. I'm praying that my "you better stay low and not respond to anything" mom doesn't see it.

I'm not sure she'd care, though, considering how she's acting today.

She came to my room as I was getting ready for church. But Jay told me, "You can go back to bed, baby. We're staying home."

Any other day, I would've ironically shouted, "Hallelujah!" It's nothing against Jesus. It's his people I've got a problem with. But I couldn't celebrate—Jay gave me this smile that couldn't really be called one because it was so sad. She went to her room and hasn't come out since.

I couldn't go back to bed. Too worried about her. Trey couldn't either, so we've been watching Netflix for a couple of hours now. We got rid of cable a while back. It was either that or our phones, and Jay and Trey both need those for potential jobs. I prop my feet on the back of the couch, inches from my brother's head.

He pushes them away. "Move them ol' stanky, crusty feet out of my face, girl."

"Trey, stop!" I whine, and put them back up. I always have to have my feet up high on the couch.

He throws back some dry knockoff Cheerios. Trey rarely eats cereal with milk. "Ol' Bruce Banner Hulk–looking feet."

Just for that, I stick my big toe in his ear. He hops up so fast, his cereal bowl almost falls from his lap, but he manages to catch it. I die laughing.

Trey points at me. "You play too much!"

He sits down and I'm still cracking up. I rub my foot all on his cheek. "Aww, I'm sorry, big bro."

Trey moves his face away. "All right, keep playing."

The floorboards in the hall creak, and I peek around the

doorway. It's not Jay though. Granddaddy says that houses this old sometimes tend to stretch. That's why they make sounds on their own. "You think she's okay?"

"Who? Ma?" Trey says. "Yeah, she's fine. Just needs a day away from all the church gossip."

I get it. Church is full of people with plenty to say and nothing to do. You'd think some of them would help us instead of talk about us, but I guess it's easy to say you love Jesus and harder to act like him.

Anyway.

"Soooo . . . ," Trey says as I get some of his cereal. "You no longer give a fuck, huh?"

I come this close to choking on a knockoff Cheerio. This close. I cough to clear my throat. "Hold up. You have an Instagram?"

He laughs. "Wooow. You online, showing your ass, and the first thing you wanna know is if I got an Instagram profile?"

"Um, yeah."

"You need to get your priorities straight. For the record, Kayla convinced me to get one."

There go the dimples. They appear whenever he talks about her. "Is she gonna be my future sister-in-law?"

He pushes the side of my head. "Don't worry about me, worry about yourself. What's going on with you, Bri? For real. Because that? That video was not my little sister."

I pick at a thread on the couch. "I was mad."

"And? How many times I gotta tell you—the internet is

forever. You want a future employer seeing that?"

I'm not as worried about them as I am a certain person. "Are you gonna tell Jay?"

"No, I'm not gonna tell *Ma*." He always corrects me when I call her by her name. "She's got enough on her as it is. You gotta learn to ignore people, Bri. Not everything deserves your energy."

"I know," I mumble.

He pinches my cheek. "Then act like it."

"Wait. That's it?"

"What?" he asks.

"You're not gonna go off on me?"

He throws back some cereal. "Nope. I'll let Ma do that when she finds out, because believe me, she's gonna find out. I'll have my popcorn ready too."

I hit his face with a pillow.

The doorbell rings. Trey pulls back the window curtain to look out. "It's the other parts of the Unholy Trinity."

I roll my eyes. "Tell them I'm not here."

Trey answers the door, and of course he says, "Hey, y'all. Bri's right here."

He looks back at me with a trollish grin that doesn't show his teeth. Jerk.

Trey gives them dap as they come in. "Haven't seen y'all in a minute. How's it going?"

Malik tells him everything is fine, but you'd think he was telling me since he's staring at me. I purposely watch the TV.

"ACT and SAT prep are kicking my butt," Sonny says. I'm so proud of him. He actually managed to get words out to Trey. There was a time he could only stutter around my brother, that's how big of a crush he had. Sometimes I think he's *still* got a crush on Trey. Trey's always known that Sonny likes him. He just laughs it off. Back when Sonny and I were in fifth grade though, one of Trey's friends said something about Sonny, using a word I refuse to repeat. After that he was no longer Trey's friend. At sixteen, my brother was calling toxic masculinity "one hell of a drug." He's dope like that.

Trey sits on the arm of the couch. "Ah, don't sweat it too much, Son'. You can take the tests more than once."

"Yeah, but it looks good if I nail it the first time."

"Nah. It looks good if you nail it, period," says Trey. "Smart as you are, you'll be all right."

Sonny's cheeks get a rosy tint to them. He is so not over his crush.

The TV does all of the talking for a while. *The Get Down*, to be exact. I watch it, but I can feel Sonny, Malik, and Trey watching me.

"Well?" Trey says. "You're gonna act like they're not here?"

I throw back some cereal. "Yep."

Trey snatches the bowl out of my hands. Then he has the audacity, *the audacity*, to pull my legs off the couch and make me sit up.

"Um, excuse you?" I say.

"You're excused. Your friends are here to talk to *you*, not me."

"We wanted to hang out with you today," Malik says. "You know, play video games, chill out."

"Yeah, like we used to do," Sonny adds.

I crunch extra hard on my cereal.

"C'mon, Bri, really?" Malik says. "Will you at least talk to us?"

Cruuunch.

"Sorry, fellas," Trey says. "Looks like she's made up her mind."

My brother is evil. Why do I say that? Because he starts to sit next to me, and while his butt is midair, he lets out the loudest, hardest fart I've ever heard in my life. Near. My. Face.

"Oh my God!" I scream, and hop up. "I'm going, damn!"

Trey gives an evil laugh and throws his legs across the couch. "That's what you get for putting them crusty feet in my face."

Just because I leave with Sonny and Malik doesn't mean I have to talk to them. We make our way down the sidewalk. There's silence between us, except for the thump of my dad's chain knocking against my sweatshirt.

Malik tugs at the strings of his hoodie. "Nice Timbs."

First time I've worn them. Jay was still in her room when I left, and Trey doesn't pay enough attention to stuff like that to notice. I mean, he's worn the same Nikes for seven years and counting. "Thanks," I mumble.

"Where'd you get them?" Malik asks.

"*How'd* you get them?" says Sonny.

"I'm sorry, I didn't know that was your business."

"Bri, c'mon," Sonny says. "You know we didn't mean anything by the other day, right?"

"Wooow. That is a half-assed attempt at an apology."

"We're sorry," Malik says. "Better?"

"Depends. Sorry for what?"

"For not having your back," Sonny says.

"And for things being so different," Malik adds.

"Different how?" Oh, I absolutely know how, but I wanna hear it from them.

"We don't hang out as much lately," Malik admits. "But don't act like this is all on us. You've changed on folks, too."

I stop. Mrs. Carson passes us in her beat-up Cadillac that's older than my grandparents. She blows her horn and throws her hand up. We wave back. Typical for the Garden.

"How have *I* changed up on *y'all*?" I ask.

"This whole rap persona of yours? I don't know that person," Malik says. "Especially not the one who said that stuff on Instagram."

Oh. "Y'all saw that?"

Sonny nods. "Yep. Along with half the internet. I can't lie, I probably would've been pissed too. So . . ." He shrugs.

"Pissed is one thing, that was another," says Malik. "Then at school—"

"Hold up, I haven't changed at school," I say. "Y'all are the ones with little time for me because you've got other people. For the record, I'm okay with that, but I won't act like it doesn't sting. Plus, y'all been hanging out together without me, researching Rapid."

"I figured you had too much other shit going on to worry about that," says Sonny. "We know your family's struggling right now."

"Is that all? Or do—" I can't believe I'm actually about to say this. "Or do y'all not wanna be associated with me?"

Fuck, my eyes sting. See, there's this teeny, tiny voice that's made my thoughts its home for a while now. It says that Sonny and Malik are too brilliant at Midtown to be linked to somebody who's not. They're going places, so why should they hang out with somebody who's only going to the principal's office?

It's believable. In fact, it's so believable that it could be true.

"What *the hell* are you talking about?" Sonny says loudly. "Bri, you're my sis, okay? I knew you when you were afraid of Big Bird."

"Oh my God, it is not logical for a bird to be that big! Why can't y'all get that?"

"We knew Malik when he wore the same denim jacket for a year straight."

"That jacket was comfortable as hell though," Malik points out.

"And y'all knew me when I was a Justin Bieber fanboy," Sonny adds.

Whew, that was a phase. He's recently switched over to Shawn Mendes. "If you ever play 'Baby' again, I'll murder you," I say.

"See? We've been through the worst together," Sonny says. "We even survived the great Killmonger debate."

I bite my lip. The three of us exchange looks.

"He. Was. Not. An. Antivillain," I clap with each word. "He was a straight-up villain!"

"Wow, really?" Malik says. "He wanted to liberate black people!"

"Nakia did too! You didn't see her killing women to do it!" I say.

"How can you watch that flashback scene and not feel something for his fine ass though?" says Sonny. "C'mon!"

I kiss my teeth. "I feel more for the Dora Milaje whose throat he slit."

"My point is," Sonny says over me, "screw all that other stuff. Nothing can change what we've got."

He holds his fist to me and Malik. We knock ours against it, give each other dap, and chunk the deuces like we used to do in middle school.

"Bam!" we say.

Just like that, we're good.

* * *

Temporarily. You see, one day, I'll be an old, gray-haired woman (without wrinkles because black don't crack), and my grandchildren will ask me about my best friends. I'll tell them how Sonny, Malik, and I were cool since womb days, that they were my ride-or-dies, my brothers from other mothers.

I'll also tell them how a simple game of *Mario Kart* ended our friendship, because I'm about to chuck this damn controller across Malik's living room.

"You did not throw a shell at me!" I screech.

Malik laughs as his Mario speeds by my Toad. Sonny's Yoshi is ahead of both of us. This is our third race. I won the first one, and Sonny won the second, hence why Malik's salty butt is resorting to dirty tactics.

Okay, yes, he's using the shells like they're supposed to be used, but this is me, dammit. Hit that ol' trick known as CPU Bowser if you wanna throw a shell.

"Hey, you were in my way," Malik says. "Mario's gotta do what Mario's gotta do."

"All right, bet." I'm gonna get him back, watch. Not just on the game either. He's gonna need something from me. Could be tomorrow, could be ten years from now, and I'm gonna be like, "Remember that time you threw a shell at me in *Mario Kart*?"

I was born petty.

Toad's a G though. Even though that knocked my little dude down for a bit, he gets up and gains on Sonny's Yoshi.

"The superintendent is apparently meeting with parents at

Midtown this coming Friday," Sonny says.

I look at him. "For real?"

"Yes!" Sonny jumps up with his arms in the air. "In. Yo. Face!"

I turn to the screen. "What? Noooooo!"

I took my eyes away for one second, and that was enough for Sonny's Yoshi to cross the finish line first.

Malik falls across the couch, screaming laughing.

I can't believe this. "You little asshole!"

Malik gives Sonny dap. "Perfect, bruh. Absolutely perfect."

Sonny takes a bow. "Thank you, but seriously." He sits next to me. "The superintendent really is holding a meeting."

I scoot away from him, but no, that puts me closer to Malik. I move to the love seat instead. "I don't wanna hear a word your cheating butt has to say."

"Wow, Bri. All these flavors out here, and you choose to be salty," Sonny says. "This is serious."

Malik dusts cat hair off of his high-top fade. Aunt 'Chelle's other baby, 2Paw, lurks around here somewhere. Malik named him that. "Yeah. The school is hiring cops to work as security at Midtown. My mom got an email about it and about the PTA meeting."

I unfold my arms. "For real?"

Sonny disappears into the kitchen. "Yep! They want students, parents, and guardians to come to the meeting and voice their opinions."

"It probably won't change anything," I say. "They're gonna do what they want."

"Unfortunately," says Malik. "It'll take something big to change their minds, and no, I don't mean releasing that video of you, Bri."

"You don't?" I ask as Sonny returns with a bag of Doritos, a pack of Chips Ahoy! and Sprite cans.

"No. They probably would villainize you to justify it." Malik bites his thumbnail. "Just wish we could use it some—Sonny, why are you eating up my food?"

Sonny stuffs an entire cookie in his mouth. "Sharing is caring."

"I don't care that much."

"Aww, thanks, Malik," Sonny says. "Why yes, yes I will go back and help myself to that Chunky Monkey in your freezer, too."

I snort. Malik's lips thin. Sonny goes back to the kitchen, grinning.

Malik scoots to the end of the couch. "Bri, let me ask you something. Promise not to fly off the handle, okay?"

"Fly off the handle? You act like I'm quick to—"

"You are," he and Sonny say together. Sonny's not even in here.

"Forget y'all. What is it?"

"If there was a way to release that video on your own terms, would you?" Malik asks.

"My own terms how?"

"You said you've talked about what Long and Tate did to you already, in your song. Well, what if we use your song to show people what happened?"

Sonny returns with the pint of ice cream and three spoons. I don't have to hold my hand out for him to pass me one. "What? Like an artistic music video?" he asks.

Malik snaps his fingers. "That's it. We could go through every line, right? Show people what you mean, using footage I've shot for my documentary. Then when you talk about getting pinned to the ground—"

"Show the video of when it happened," I finish for him.

Holy shit. That may actually work.

"Exactly," Malik says. "This way it explains the song to all of these idiots who come at you *and* it shows what happened at school."

I could hug him. Seriously, I could. Without saying he understands the song, he's saying he understands the song, and really, he's saying he understands me. That's all I wanted from him. Okay, that and some less-than-PG-13 things at one time, but that's not the point.

Do I hug Malik? Ha! No. I punch him. "That's for all the crap you said about my song!"

"Ow!" He grabs his arm. "Damn, woman! I understood the song all along. I just didn't want people to make assumptions about you. I won't say I told you so, but—nah, forget it, I'm saying I told you so!"

I tuck in my lips. Knew that was coming.

"After thinking about how everyone reacted to it at school though, I realized you were right," he says. "You already spoke up for us, Breezy. Not your fault if other people don't get it. So"—he shrugs—"why don't we use the song to stir some shit up?"

TWENTY-ONE

So, stir shit up we do. It takes several hours, but Malik, Sonny, and I put together a music video for "On the Come Up," using footage that Malik recorded for his documentary. Like when I say, "Whole squad got more heat than a furnace," it's a video of guns on some GDs' waists. Malik blurred their faces out.

"We don't bust, yet they blame us for murder" brings on news clips from when that boy was killed last year.

"I approach, you watch close, I'm a threat," I rap, and there's Malik's secret footage of the clerk who followed us around the Midtown comic shop a few months ago.

And just like we said, when I rap, "Pin me to the ground, boy, you fucked up," Malik puts in a clip of the incident.

Will it change the minds of the Emilys though? Probably not. Honestly, nothing will. They'll never truly understand because they don't wanna understand someone like me.

Regardless, I hope my video gives them heart palpitations.

We're uploading it to YouTube when Sonny's phone buzzes. He takes it out and practically has a temper tantrum on the couch. "Dammit! My pops wants me to come home and babysit the gremlins."

I hit his face with a pillow. "Stop talking about your little sisters like that!"

Sonny has three little sisters: Kennedy is ten, Paris is seven, and Skye is four. They are the absolute cutest, and if it was possible to adopt siblings, I would. Sonny loves them to death . . . except when he has to babysit them.

"They are gremlins!" he claims. "I was talking to Rapid the other day and they—"

"Whoa, whoa, whoa. Time out." I make a T with my hands. "You can't just slip something like that in *casually*! You're talking to Rapid again?"

Sonny's cheeks get super rosy. "Yeah. I actually talked to him on the phone. This guy here convinced me to explain to him why I ghosted." He points at Malik.

Malik pretends to bow. "Happy to help."

"So, I messaged Rapid and told him that we found his IP address, and that I knew he didn't live in the Garden," Sonny goes on. "He asked if we could talk on the phone. I agreed. He reminded me that he never said he lived here, I just assumed. He understood why I was thrown off by it though. We talked a long time."

Um, I need more than that. "What else did he say? What's

his name? What does he sound like?"

"Goddamn, I swear you're nosy," Sonny says. "I ain't telling you all of our business."

I raise my eyebrows. "So y'all have business?"

Malik wiggles his. "Sounds like they do."

"And you two clearly have none since you're all in ours," Sonny says. "We talked about everything and nothing. But it's weird. We were so caught up in talking that I never got his real name. He didn't get mine, either. We didn't need them though. I knew him without knowing his name."

Am I grinning? Yes. I poke his cheek, the same way he did when it came to Curtis. "Look at you, blushing and shit."

He dodges my finger. "Whatever. What's even weirder? I think I've heard his voice before. Just can't figure out *where* I've heard it."

"At school?" Malik asks.

Sonny pinches his top lip. "Nah. I don't think so."

"Are y'all gonna meet up?" I ask.

He slowly nods. "Yeah. I want y'all to come along when we do. You know, just in case his ass is a serial killer."

"What? So we can all end up dead?" Malik asks.

"That's what ride-or-die means, ain't it?"

I roll my eyes. "You're lucky we love you."

"I am. And since you do love me"—he cheeses at Malik—"can I bring the gremlins over here? That way we can start another round of *Mario*—"

"Hell no," Malik says. "*Your* sisters need to stay at *your* house. I'm an only child for a reason."

"Dammit!" Sonny groans. He steps over Malik's outstretched legs. "Rude ass." He punches Malik's thigh.

"Ow! Hobbit-looking ass!"

Sonny gives him a middle finger and leaves.

Malik rubs his thigh. I smirk. "You okay?"

Malik sits up, straightening out his basketball shorts. "Yeah. I'll get revenge. The Punching Game is back on."

Not again. The last one was in seventh grade and lasted for months. Just out of nowhere, one of them would punch the crap out of the other. Whoever got the best reaction was the winner. Sonny won after punching Malik in the middle of prayer at church.

"You hungry?" Malik asks me. "I can fix us something."

"Nah. I should probably head home, too. Besides, you can't cook."

"Says who? Girl, I can hook you up with the best Chef Boyardee you ever had in your life! Quote me on that. But for real." He gently elbows me. "You can stay as long as you want."

I pull my knees up to my chest. I took my shoes off ages ago. I'm not dumb enough to mess up Aunt 'Chelle's sofa like that. "Nah. I should probably go check on my mom."

"What's wrong with Aunt Jay?"

"I think everything's getting to her. We didn't go to church, and then she went in her room and stayed in there. I mean, that's not a big deal, but that's what she used to do back when . . ."

"Oh," Malik says.

"Right."

We're quiet for a while.

"It's gonna get better one day, Breezy," Malik says.

"Will it?" I murmur.

"You know what? I got something for this. I bet that I can make you smile in less than two minutes." He gets up and scrolls through his phone. "Actually, I bet I can do it in a minute."

He taps his screen. "P.Y.T." by Michael Jackson starts playing. It's no secret that MJ is the key to making me smile. So are Malik's attempts at dancing. He lip-synchs, "'You're such a P.Y.T., a pretty young thing,'" and does some kinda move that looks more like he's itching.

I bust out laughing. "Really?"

He goes, "Uh-huh," and dances over to me. He stands me up and somehow gets me to lip-synch and dance with him. I gotta admit, I am smiling.

He does a moonwalk that's worse than anything Trey's ever attempted. I lose it laughing.

"What?" he says.

"You can't dance, boo."

"The shade."

"The truth."

He wraps me up in a tight hug, resting his chin on the top of my head. "If it'll cheer you up, Breezy, I'm game for whatever."

I wrap my arms around him too. I look up at him, and he stares down at me.

When he inches his lips toward mine, I don't move away. I simply close my eyes and wait for the fireworks.

Yes, fireworks. Like in all those cheesy romance movies that I low-key love. This kiss is supposed to sweep me off my feet, make my heart leap from my chest, and give me all the tingles.

But, um, this kiss? This kiss ain't none of that.

It's wet, awkward, and tastes like all those Cheetos Puffs Malik ate a little while ago. We can't even get our noses in the right places. My heart isn't racing—there's no boom. Hell, no bam. It's weird. Not that me or Malik are bad kissers; nah, we know what we're doing. It's just not . . .

Right.

We step away from each other.

"Umm . . . ," Malik says. "I, um . . ."

"Yeah."

"That wasn't . . ."

"No."

It gets uncomfortably quiet.

"Umm . . ." Malik holds the back of his head. "Want me to walk you home?"

We haven't said a word for three blocks now. Dogs bark back and forth in the distance. It's completely dark out and cold enough that most folks are inside. We pass one house that has voices coming from the porch, but the people are sitting in the dark. The only sign of them is the orange flicker coming from the end of a cigarette. Wait, no, that smells like weed.

"Bri, what happened back there?" Malik asks.

"You tell me. You're the one who kissed me. You're also the one with a girlfriend."

"Shit," he hisses, like that part just crossed his mind. "Shana."

"Yeah." She may have caught an attitude with me, but this is foul, regardless. "You seem to really be into her, so why'd you kiss me?"

"I don't know! It just happened."

I stop walking. We're far away from the voices on the porch, and it's so quiet, I sound louder than I am. "It *just* happened? Nobody just kisses anyone, Malik."

"Whoa, hold up. You kissed me back."

No point denying it. "I did."

"Why?"

"The same reason you kissed me in the first place."

Truth is, there's something between us, even if we're not sure what it is. But I'm starting to wonder if it's like a bad puzzle. The pieces are all there to create what could be a perfect picture, but after that kiss, what if they don't fit together?

A gray Camaro passes us.

"All right, yeah. I've got feelings for you," Malik says. "I have for a while. I kinda figured you felt something for me, too, but I wasn't sure."

"Yeah . . ." I trail off. No point denying that either.

"Look, I know you're upset that I'm with Shana," he says. "But Bri, you don't have to flirt with Curtis to make me jealous."

I squawk. Actually, I don't know if the sound I make can be called a squawk. "Are you freaking kidding me?"

"On the bus, you were all in his face," Malik says. "Then you defended him after the riot. You were trying to make me jealous."

I look him up and down. "Wasn't nobody thinking 'bout you!"

"I'm supposed to believe that?"

"Bruuuh," I say, slapping the back of my hand into my palm. "Oh my God, that had nothing to do with you. Straight up."

"Being all in his face had nothing to do with me?"

"Hell nah! I didn't even notice you were on the bus! You got some nerve, Malik. For real. This is such a fuckboy move."

"*Fuckboy?*" he says.

"Yes! Here you go with all this talk of feelings and kissing me, but you never once even *hinted* that you liked me before. But now, because I like somebody else, you suddenly have feelings? Get outta here, bruh. For real."

Malik's forehead wrinkles. "Wait. You like *Curtis*?"

Oh.

Damn.

I like Curtis?

Tires screech. That gray Camaro makes a U-turn. It races back up the street and skids to a stop beside us.

"What the hell?" Malik says.

The door on the driver's side flies open, and a guy hops out. He grins at us with a mouth full of silver teeth. He's got a gun in his hand.

It's the Crown from the Ring.

"Well, well, well," he says. "Look what we got here."

I can't watch him for watching the gun. My heart pounds in my ears.

Malik stretches his arm out in front of me. "We don't want any problems."

"I don't want any either. I just want baby girl here to hand over her shit."

I don't know whether to focus on him or his piece. "What?"

He motions his gun toward my chest. "I want that chain."

Shit. I forgot to tuck it.

"See, your daddy was real disrespectful, walking around with that crown on his chain and calling himself the King of the Garden while rolling with them Disciple bitches," the Crown says. "So, you gon' right his wrong and hand that shit over."

"I can't—" I'm shaking like I've got chills. "It's my—"

He points his gun at me. "I said hand it over!"

Some people say that your life flashes before your eyes in moments like this. But for me, all the stuff I haven't done flashes before mine. Making it big, getting out of the Garden, living past sixteen. Going home.

"I . . . I can't . . ." My teeth chatter. "I can't give this up."

"Bitch, did I stutter? Hand that shit over!"

"Man, chill—"

The Crown rams his fist into Malik's face. Malik hits the ground.

"Malik!" I start for him.

Click click. The gun cocks.

"Please?" I blubber. "Please don't take it."

I can't lose this thing. My mom could've pawned it by now and taken care of bills, filled our fridge, but she entrusted it to me. Me. I know she said she wouldn't get rid of it, but I always figured if things got really hard, we could sell it.

Losing it will be like losing a safety net.

"Oh, look who crying," the Crown mocks. "What about all that disrespectful shit you talked on your song, huh?"

"It's just a song!"

"I don't give a fuck!" He points the gun directly between my eyes. "Now you gon' make this easy or make it hard?"

Malik groans near my feet. He holds his eye.

I can't risk his life or mine. Not even to make sure my family is okay.

I straighten up and look the Crown dead in his eyes. I want this coward to look in mine and see no fear.

"The chain," he says through his teeth.

I lift it from around my neck. The pendant glistens, even in the dark.

The Crown snatches it out of my hands. "That's what I thought."

He keeps his eyes on me, and I keep mine on him as he backs up to his car. He doesn't lower his gun until he's in his Camaro. He speeds off down the street, taking my family's safety net with him.

PART THREE

NEW SCHOOL

TWENTY-TWO

I almost got killed by a Crown. So I call my aunt, the Garden Disciple.

Soon as she hears "robbed," she's on her way.

Malik and I wait on the curb. His eye is starting to bruise and swell. He claims he's okay, but that's all he's said since the Camaro sped off.

I wrap my arms around myself. There's a tight knot in my stomach that won't go away. Not sure I want it to. It's like it's holding every inch of me together and the moment it comes undone, I'm screwed.

Aunt Pooh's Cutlass races down the street. It barely stops beside us when she and Scrap hop out. They both have their guns.

"What the hell?" she says. "Who did this shit?"

"That Crown who messed with us at Jimmy's," I bite out.

Malik whips his head at me. "Wait, you've dealt with him before?"

It sounds like an accusation more than a question.

"We had a li'l run-in" is all Aunt Pooh says. "What he take, Bri?"

My jaw aches from clenching it so hard. "The chain."

Aunt Pooh folds her hands on her head. "Shit!"

"The Crown's been wanting that chain since they killed Law," Scrap says.

For what? So they could have a trophy for taking my daddy from me?

"I didn't wanna give it up." Dammit, my voice cracks. "He had a gun and—"

"Whoa, whoa, whoa," Aunt Pooh says. "He held y'all at gunpoint?"

There's fury in her eyes waiting to spark. I know six words that will light it up.

My own fury makes me say them with ease. "He pointed it in my face."

Aunt Pooh slowly straightens up. Her face is blank, calm almost. "This ain't over."

She marches for the car, her way of telling us to come on. Malik hangs back on the sidewalk.

"You coming?" I ask him.

"No. I'll walk home. It's only a couple of blocks."

Home. Where Aunt 'Chelle's probably waiting by now. "Hey, um . . . Maybe don't tell Aunt 'Chelle about this, all right?"

"Are you serious?" Malik says. "You got robbed, Bri! I got a black eye!"

I'm as serious as a heart attack. He tells her, she'll tell my mom, and my mom will bring a halt to anything Aunt Pooh and I plan to do. "Just don't, okay?"

"Wait, are you thinking of going after that guy?"

I don't respond.

"Bri, are you nuts?" Malik says. "You can't go after him! You're asking for trouble."

"Look, I didn't ask you to help us!" I yell. "I simply said don't tell her! All right?"

Malik stands as straight as a board. "Yeah," he says. "Whatever you want. *Bri*."

He says my name like it's a foreign word.

I don't have time for whatever his problem is. I don't. I need to get that chain back. I hop in the car. He's still standing on the sidewalk when we peel off.

Aunt Pooh and Scrap go back and forth about the Crown. Apparently, he's known as Kane and he likes to race his Camaro on Magnolia. I figure that's where we're headed, but Aunt Pooh pulls up in front of my house.

She puts the car in park. "C'mon, Bri."

She gets out herself and holds her seat forward. I climb out, too. "What are we doing here?" I ask.

Aunt Pooh suddenly hugs me extra tight. She kisses my cheek, then whispers in my ear, "Lay low."

I push away from her. "No! I wanna go, too!"

"I don't give a damn what you want. You staying here."

"But I gotta get that—"

"You wanna die or go to prison, Bri? Either a Crown will kill you in retaliation, or somebody will snitch and the cops will take you down. That's all that can come from this."

Shit. She's right. But suddenly it hits me—

She could get killed. *She* could get arrested.

Forget a spark. I've lit a bomb that will explode any second.

No, no, no. "Aunty, forget about it. He's not worth—"

"Fuck that! Don't nobody come at my family!" she says. "They took my brother, and then one points a gun at you, and I'm supposed to let that shit go? Hell nah!"

"You can't kill him!"

"What the hell you call me for then?"

"I . . . I didn't . . ."

"You could've called your momma, you could've called Trey, hell, you could've called the cops. Instead, you called me. Why?"

Deep down, I know why. "Because—"

"Because you knew I'd handle him," she says through her teeth. "So, let me do what I do."

She heads for her car.

"Aunt Pooh," I croak. "Please?"

"Go inside, Bri."

That's the last thing she says before she speeds off.

Now I know why I called her. Not because I wanted her to handle him. But because I needed her.

I drag myself up the walkway and unlock the front door. Jay and Trey's voices drift from the kitchen as some nineties R&B plays on the stereo. A creaky floorboard announces me.

"Bri, is that you?" my mom calls.

Thank God she doesn't peer around the kitchen doorway. I don't think my face can hide what just happened. I clear my throat. "Y-yes, ma'am."

"Okay. Dinner's almost ready."

"I, um . . ." My voice weakens. I clear my throat again. "I ate at Malik's."

"Probably a bunch of junk food, knowing you three," she says. "I'll put a plate up for you."

I manage to get out an "Okay" before I make it to my bedroom.

I close the door. I just wanna hide under my covers, but my bed feels miles away. I lower myself in the corner and pull my knees up to my chest, which feels like it's gonna cave in.

I wanted that guy dead, I swear I did. Now all I can think about is how a gunshot's gonna take him like one took Dad.

If he has a wife, his death will mess her up like it messed Jay up.

If he has a momma, she'll cry like Grandma cried.

If he has a dad, his voice will dip when he talks about him like Granddaddy.

If he has a son, he'll be angry at him for dying, like Trey is.

If he has a little girl, she'll never get a response when she says, "Daddy." Like me.

They'll bury him and make him into everything he wasn't. The best husband, the best son, the best dad. There will be T-shirts worn around the neighborhood with his face on them and murals in his honor. His name will get tatted on somebody's arm. He'll forever be a hero who lost his life too soon, not the villain who ruined my life. Because of my aunt.

They'll only show her mug shot on the news. Not the pictures of us smiling together on her Cutlass or her cheesing with that GED Jay thought she'd never get. She'll be called a ruthless murderer for about a week, until somebody else does something fucked up. Then I'll be the only one mourning her.

She'll become the monster for handling the monster I couldn't handle myself. Or somebody's gonna kill her. Either way, I'm gonna lose Aunt Pooh.

Just like I lost my daddy.

Every tear I've held back rushes out, bringing sobs with them. I cover my mouth. Jay and Trey cannot hear me. They can't. But the sobs come out of me so hard that it's almost impossible to breathe.

I hold my mouth and fight for air all at once. Tears fall over my fingers.

Jacksons can cry. Even when we have blood on our hands.

* * *

Nas once called sleep the cousin of death, and I suddenly get that. I could barely sleep for thinking about death. I said six words that may have summoned it.

He pointed it in my face.

They felt heavy when I said them, like I was taking a weight off of my tongue, but somehow, it's as if they're still lingering there. I practically see them and all seven of their syllables.

Since he pointed it in my face,
My aunt may be gone to waste.

Because those six words told Aunt Pooh something else: *Handle him for me. Ruin your life for me. Let everyone pin one word—"murderer"—on you. For me.*

I hear those six words in my ears all night. They make me text her three: Are you okay?

She doesn't respond.

I drift off to sleep at some point. When I open my eyes, my mom is sitting on my bed.

"Hey," she says gently. "You okay?"

From the looks of things, it's morning. "Yeah. Why you ask?"

"Every time I came to check on you, you were tossing and turning."

"Oh." All of my limbs feel heavy as I sit up. "Why were you checking on me?"

"I always check on you and Trey." She strokes my cheek. "What's going on, Bookie?"

"Nothing." She can't know that I ordered Aunt Pooh to kill somebody. She can't know the chain is gone, either. It would break her heart.

At this rate, I'm piling up secrets.

"It's not that petition, is it?" Jay asks.

Oh. Ironic that a gun made me forget that someone hates that I rapped about guns. "You know about it?"

"Mm-hmm. Gina and 'Chelle texted it to me. You know how your godmothers are. They'll go hood in a minute over you." She chuckles. "They're ready to whoop that woman's behind. But I told them to ignore it, just like I'm telling you."

It's easy to ignore now, but I'm wondering if Emily may have been right. Maybe my words are dangerous. "Okay."

Jay kisses my forehead. "That's my girl. Come on." She pats my leg. "Let's get you some breakfast before you head to school."

I glance at my phone. It's been eleven hours. No word from Aunt Pooh.

I follow Jay to the kitchen. Trey's still asleep. He's taking off from Sal's today just for a mini vacation.

Something's . . . off. There's an odd stillness, like the house is quieter than it should be.

Jay opens a cabinet. "I think I've got time to make you some French toast before the bus comes. The kind my momma used to do. She called it *pain perdu*."

I love it when Jay pulls out those recipes her momma used to make in New Orleans. I've never been there, but they taste like home. "I'll get the eggs."

I open the refrigerator door and stale warmth hits me. All of the food is blanketed in darkness. "Umm . . . the fridge isn't working."

"What?" Jay says. She closes the door and opens it, as if that'll fix the issue. It doesn't. "What in the world?"

Something over near the oven catches her eye and her face falls. "Shit!"

The numbers are usually lit on the oven's clock. They aren't.

Jay flips the kitchen light switch. Nothing happens. She hurries to the hall and flips that switch. Nothing. She goes in my room, the bathroom, the living room. Nothing.

The commotion is enough to wake Trey up. He comes in the hall, rubbing his eyes. "What's wrong?"

"They shut the power off," Jay says.

"What? I thought we had more time."

"We were supposed to! That man told me—he said—I asked for another week." Jay buries her face in her hands. "Not now, God. Please, not now. I just bought all that food."

That'll probably spoil in less than a week.

Fuck. We could've pawned the chain and paid the light bill. Fuck. Fuck. Fuck.

Jay uncovers her face, straightens up, and looks at us. "No. We're not doing this. We're not about feeling sorry for ourselves."

"But Ma—" Even Trey's voice is rough.

"I said no, Trey. We're down, but we're not out. You hear me? This is only a setback."

Yet it feels like a major blow.

But the final blow may be around the corner.

Eleven hours, twenty minutes. Still no word from Aunt Pooh.

TWENTY-THREE

Since the stove is electric, we can't have pain perdu. I eat some cereal instead.

I'm quiet on the bus. It's just me and Sonny today. Sonny says he stopped by Malik's house, and Aunt 'Chelle told him that Malik had some sort of freak accident that left him with a black eye. He's staying home to recover. He obviously didn't tell her what really happened, just like I asked.

I should be relieved, but somehow I feel worse. Malik never stays home from school. So either his eye is really bad or he's so shaken up that he needs a day.

Either way, it's my fault.

But maybe it's a good thing Malik took today off. That way he doesn't have to see the four armed cops acting as security just yet.

He and Shana were right. Midtown considers all of us black and brown kids threats now. We go through metal detectors as usual, but it's hard to focus on anything but the guns on the cops' waists. Feels like I'm entering a prison instead of my school.

I'm happy to go home at the end of the day, even if that means entering a dark house.

It's as if my brain's got a playlist of all the shitty things happening in my life on repeat. That gun pointed in my face. That article on the newspaper's website. Long and Tate pinning me down. The cops at school. The lights going out. Aunt Pooh.

Twenty hours and no response.

Only thing that distracts me a little bit are the Uno cards Jay pulls out after dinner. With no TV and no internet, there's nothing else to do, so she suggested we have a family game tournament. She and Trey are so not acting like family though.

"Bam!" Trey slaps a card onto the kitchen table. The sun's still out, giving us all the light we need to play. "Wild card, baby! We making this thing as green as y'all gon' be when I whoop them behinds."

"That's a lie," I say, and put a green card down.

"Boy, sit your li'l narrow behind down somewhere," Jay says. "You ain't did nothing, 'cause, bam!" She slaps a card down, too. "I got a wild card, and I say we're going back to mellow yellow, baby."

"Okay, okay. I'll let you have that one," Trey says. "You gon' regret it though."

They're both gonna regret it. See, I'm letting them do all the trash talk. They don't know I got two draw fours, a wild card, a yellow skip, and a red reverse. I'm ready for whatever.

This is our third game, and miraculously we're still on speaking terms. The first game got so heated that Jay walked away from the table and disowned both of us. She's the definition of a sore loser.

Exhibit A? I put down that yellow skip and Jay flashes me the glare of death.

"You're really gonna skip your own momma?" she asks.

"Um, you're not my momma. Right now, you're simply some chick I gotta beat."

Trey goes, "Ha!"

"You mean nothing to me as well, sir."

"Ha!" Jay mimics him.

"Well, since I mean nothing." Trey slowly lifts a card, going, "Ahhhhhh," like a heavenly choir, then, "Bam! Draw two, boo."

Ooh, I can't wait to pull that draw four on his ass.

I draw my two, and there is a God. I got another wild card plus a skip. In the words of the late, great philosopher Tupac Shakur: "I ain't a killer, but don't push me."

It's kinda messed up that I'm enjoying this. We don't have lights, and Aunt Pooh could be—

Several loud knocks at the front door startle me.

Trey gets up to answer. "Chill, Bri. It's just the door."

Time slows, and my heart slams against my chest.

"Shit," Trey hisses.

I'm gonna puke.

"Who is it?" Jay asks.

"Grandma and Granddaddy," he says.

Thank God.

But my mom goes, "Dammit!" She holds her brow. "Let them in, Trey."

The door has barely creaked open when Grandma says, "Where in the world y'all been?"

She lets herself in the house, peeking in every room like she's looking for something. Sniffing. Knowing Grandma, she's searching for drugs.

Granddaddy lumbers into the kitchen behind Trey. He and Grandma wear matching Adidas tracksuits. "We happened to be over this way and wanted to check on y'all," he says. "Y'all wasn't at church yesterday."

"Don't lie!" Grandma says as she joins us in the kitchen. "We purposely stopped by! I had to check on my grandbabies."

Figures.

"We're fine, Mr. Jackson," Jay says, to Granddaddy and Granddaddy alone. "We just decided to stay home yesterday, that's all."

"We barely in the house and you already lying," Grandma says. "Y'all ain't fine. What's this about Brianna making vulgar songs?"

God, not now.

"First Lady came to me yesterday after service, said her and Pastor's grandchildren been listening to some ol' garbage that Brianna recorded," Grandma says. "Said it's so bad that it was on the news. Liked to embarrass the hell out of me!"

"Can't nothing get the hell out of you," Jay mumbles.

Grandma narrows her eyes and sets her hand on her hip. "If you got something to say to me, say it."

"You know what? Actually, I do—"

"We already know about the song," Trey says before World War III can break out. "Ma addressed it with Bri. It's fine."

"No, it ain't," Grandma says. "Now, I done bit my tongue when it comes to a lot of stuff with you and your sister—"

Um, she hasn't bit her tongue about anything.

"But this? This the final straw. Brianna wasn't acting like that when y'all lived with us. Making vulgar songs and getting suspended. Got everybody in the church talking 'bout her. Some mess!"

Granddaddy fiddles with the button on the oven clock, as if Grandma hasn't said a word. He's a pro at tuning her out. "Jayda, when this here clock stop working?"

If Granddaddy sees a problem, he's gonna try to fix it. Once, we were at my pediatrician when I was younger, and a light in the waiting room kept flickering. True story, Granddaddy asked the nurse if they had a ladder. He got up there and fixed it.

Jay closes her eyes. If she's about to tell them what I think she's about to tell them, we're about to have a blowup. "The lights are off, Mr. Jackson."

"What?" Grandma shrieks.

"What your lights doing off?" says Granddaddy. "It's that box, ain't it? I been saying it need to be replaced."

"No, no," Jay says. "They were turned off by the electric company. We're behind on a payment."

There's a moment of calm before the storm.

"I *knew* something was going on," Grandma insists. "Geraldine said her daughter thought she saw you come into the welfare office where she works. That was you, wasn't it?"

Lord, Ms. Geraldine. Grandma's best friend and partner-in-gossip. Grandma says "Geraldine said" almost as much as she breathes.

"Yes, it was me," Jay admits. "I applied for food stamps."

"Now Jayda, you could've asked us for help," Granddaddy says. "How many times I gotta tell you that?"

"I've got it under control," Trey says.

"Boy, you ain't got nothing under control," says Granddaddy. "You ain't got lights."

Grandma puts her hands up. "That's it. I done had enough. Brianna and Trey coming home with us."

Trey raises his eyebrows. "Um, hi, I'm twenty-two, how are you?"

"I don't care how old you are. You and Bri don't need to be suffering like this."

"*Suffering?*" Jay says. "They have shelter, clothes, I made sure they have food—"

"But they ain't got lights!" Grandma says. "What kinda mother are—"

"The worst thing I've done is become poor, Mrs. Jackson!"

Jay's loud, rough. Seems like her voice is using every inch of her body.

"The worst thing!" she says. "That's it! Excuse me because I have the *audacity* to be poor!"

Trey touches her shoulder. "Ma—"

"You think I *want* my babies sitting in the dark? I'm trying, Mrs. Jackson! I go on interviews. I withdrew from school so these kids could have food! I begged the church not to let me go. I'm sorry if it's not enough for you, but good Lord, I'm trying!"

Grandma straightens up. "I just think they deserve better."

"Well, that's one thing we actually agree on," says Jay.

"Then they oughta come live with us," Grandma says.

Trey puts his hands up. "No, Grandma. I'm staying here. I'm not gonna be the rope in this tug-of-war of yours anymore."

"I ain't *ever* gon' apologize for fighting for my son's babies!" Grandma says. "If you wanna stay here, that's on you. I ain't gon' force you, Lawrence. But Brianna coming with us."

"Hold on now, Louise," Granddaddy says. "This girl old enough to decide for herself, too. Li'l Bit, what you want?"

I want food. I want lights. I want guarantees.

There's this look in my mom's eyes that I've seen before. It's the one she had the day she came back from rehab. But that day there were tears in her eyes, too. She brushed my hair from my face and asked me one question: "Brianna, do you know who I am?"

That look was fear. Back then, I didn't understand it. Now I do. She had been gone so long that she was afraid I forgot her.

Fast-forward to now, and she's terrified that I'm gonna leave her.

I may not know if we'll have lights again or if we'll have enough food, but I do know that I don't wanna be away from my mom again.

I look at her as I say it. "I wanna stay here."

"Well, there you go," Trey says. "You got your answer."

"You sure, Li'l Bit?" Granddaddy asks.

I don't look away from my mom. I want her to know that I mean it. "Yeah. I'm sure."

"All right then." Granddaddy takes out his wallet. "'Bout how much is this light bill, Jayda?"

"I can't pay you back anytime soon, Mr. Jackson."

"Hush. I ain't said nothing 'bout paying nobody back. You know good and well Junior would have a fit if I didn't—"

Grandma's lips tremble. She turns on her heel and hurries out. The front door slams shut behind her.

Granddaddy sighs. "Grief one hell of a thing. I think Louise holds on to these kids 'cause it's like holding on to him."

Granddaddy looks through his wallet and places some

money in my mom's hand. "Call me if you need me."

He kisses her cheek and kisses mine. Then he pats Trey on the back and leaves.

Jay stares at the money for the longest. "Wow," she says thickly.

Trey rubs her shoulder. "Hey, Li'l Bit. Why don't you get my keys and take our phones out to my car? Charge them up."

That's code for "Jay needs some space." I think she'll cry in front of Trey before she'll cry in front of me. That comes with him being the oldest.

I make myself nod. "All right."

I go out and crank his Honda up. Trey's got one of those chargers that'll handle multiple phones at once. I hook his and Jay's up. Just as I pick up mine, it rings.

Damn. It's not Aunt Pooh. Instead, Supreme's name appears on the screen.

I try not to sound too disappointed as I answer on the speaker. "Hey, Supreme."

"Whaddup, baby girl?" he says. "I got big news."

"Oh yeah?" I may not sound disappointed, but I can't make myself sound upbeat either. Unless Supreme is about to tell me he's got a deal for me, nothing can amp me up. And even that can't save Aunt Pooh.

"Hell yeah. Hype wants you to come on his show next Saturday," Supreme says. "He saw the petition and the news story and wants to give you a chance to speak."

"Oh, wow." See, DJ Hype is more than just the DJ at the Ring. He's a radio legend. I don't think there's a hip-hop head in the world who hasn't heard of *Hype's Hot Hour* on Hot 105. The show plays live around the country, and all the interviews end up on his YouTube channel. Some of them even go viral, but that's usually only if a rapper acts a fool. But Hype's known to push the right buttons to make folks act a fool.

"Yeah. Of course, he'll wanna talk about the Ring incident, the Instagram video. Even that li'l music video you put up yesterday." Supreme chuckles. "It's creative, I'll give you that."

Damn, I forgot about that, too.

Wait, why'd he call it a *li'l* music video though? As if there's not much to it. "That video is supposed to explain the song."

"Let the song speak for itself," he says.

"But people were saying—"

"Look, we'll get into all that later," he says. "This is a big opportunity, all right? I'm talking life-changing shit. It's gon' put you in front of an even bigger audience. Only thing I need is for you to be ready. All right?"

I stare at the last text I sent Aunt Pooh. How can I be ready for anything when I know nothing about her?

But I force the words out. "I'll be ready."

TWENTY-FOUR

It's been almost exactly five days to the hour, and Aunt Pooh hasn't gotten back to me yet.

I don't know what to do. Do I tell my mom or my brother? I could, but it may not be worth the drama if it turns out she didn't do anything. Do I call the cops? Both of those options are a hell no. I'd have to tell them Aunt Pooh may have committed murder, which is basically snitching. Not only that, but she committed murder on my order.

I'm out of options and full of fears.

Good thing is we aren't in the dark anymore. Granddaddy gave my mom enough to pay the light bill and to get us some groceries. Since the lights are back on, the stove is back on. I didn't know how much I missed hot dinners. Things are looking up.

School is another story though. For one, it still feels like a prison. Two, there's Malik. He got on the bus Tuesday morning and sat with Shana. His eye was only slightly bruised and the swelling had gone down. I guess he still hasn't told anyone what happened. It's our secret.

It's so secret that he not only won't speak to me about it, but he won't speak to me, period.

I get why. Honestly, I hate putting him in this position. Hell, I hate being in it myself. But he has to know that if anyone hears a word about this, it's just as bad as ratting on Aunt Pooh. And on me.

I'm gonna try to talk to him tonight, after this PTA meeting with the superintendent. The Midtown auditorium is packed. Dr. Rhodes talks to some man in a suit and tie. Not far away, Mrs. Murray chats with some of the other teachers.

Sonny and I follow our moms and Aunt 'Chelle down the middle aisle. Jay's still in the skirt and blouse that she wore for an interview today. She even brought the little briefcase that she carries her résumés in. Aunt 'Chelle came straight from the courthouse in her security uniform, and Aunt Gina left the beauty shop early. She says Wednesdays are slow anyway.

Malik's with Shana and some of the other kids from the coalition. They're standing on the side aisles, holding posters for the superintendent to see with stuff like, "Black or brown shouldn't mean suspicious," and, "Are grants more important than students?"

Sonny leans in to me. "You think we should be over there?"

Across the room, Malik laughs at something Shana says. He's in full Malik X mode, with a wooden black power fist hanging from a necklace. His sign says, "School or prison?" with a picture of an armed cop.

Last thing he probably wants is me over there. "No," I say. "Let him do his thing."

"I'll be glad when you two fix whatever's going on," Sonny says.

I lied and told him that Malik and I had an argument after he went to babysit his sisters. Technically, it's not a lie. There is an argument between us. It just hasn't been spoken. Yet.

Aunt Gina finds us some seats near the front. We've barely sat down when this balding Latino man goes up to the podium.

"Good evening, everyone. I'm David Rodriguez, president of the Midtown School of the Arts Parent-Teacher Association," he says. "Thank you all for coming out tonight. I think I can speak for everyone when I say there are concerns regarding recent events here at the school. I invite Superintendent Cook to the podium to discuss the next steps and answer any questions we may have. Please welcome him."

The older white man who was talking to Dr. Rhodes makes his way to the podium to polite applause.

He starts by saying how much of a "beacon of light" Midtown is for the school district—it's one of the highest performing schools, one of the most diverse schools, and boasts one of the highest graduation rates. He's a crowd pleaser, considering how much he tells us to applaud ourselves for our accomplishments.

"I think we're all saddened by what took place last week," he says, "and I personally want you to know that the school district is committed to ensuring that Midtown is a place of safety and of excellence. With that said, I invite you all to ask questions or make comments as you see fit."

Conversations break out all around us. Parents and students line up at the mics on each side of the room. My mom's one of them.

The first question comes from a parent—how did something like this happen?

"Due to an ongoing investigation, I am unable to go into a lot of details at the moment," Superintendent Cook says. "However, when that information can be shared, it will be."

Another parent asks about the metal detectors, random pat-downs, and the armed cops. "This is not a prison," he says. He's got an accent, like Spanish is his first language. "I do not understand why our children must be subjected to these sort of security measures."

"Due to recent crime spikes in the area, we felt it was best for the safety of the students if security was heightened," says Superintendent Cook.

He doesn't explain the cops. We all know why they're here now though.

Sonny backhands my arm and nods toward the other mic. Shana's up next.

She clears her throat. At first, she doesn't say anything. Someone yells out, "Speak, Shana!" and a couple of people clap, including Malik.

She looks straight at the superintendent. "My name is Shana Kincaid. I'm a junior here at Midtown. Unfortunately, it's different for me and students who look like me at this school, Dr. Cook. Both Officer Long and Officer Tate were known to target black and Latinx students far more than anyone. We were more likely to be subjected to pat-downs, to random locker checks, and to secondary screenings. Several of us have been in physical altercations with them. Now that armed police officers have been brought on, honestly, many of us fear for our lives. We shouldn't have that fear when we come to school."

There's an uproar of applause and cheers, especially from the kids from the coalition. I clap along with them.

"It's no secret that Midtown needs students like me in order to get grants," Shana says. "Yet students like me do not feel welcomed here, Dr. Cook. Are we just dollar signs to you all, or are we actual human beings?"

I clap at that, too. Most of the students do.

"The uprising last week was the result of frustration," Shana says. "Many of us have filed complaints against Officers Long and Tate. There is video showing them physically assaulting a black student. Yet they were allowed back on the job. Why, Dr. Cook?"

"Ms. Kincaid, I thank you for your insight," Dr. Cook says. "I agree that racism and racial profiling are unacceptable. However, due to the ongoing investigation, there is a lot I can't speak on regarding that specific incident."

"What?" I say as my classmates boo and shout.

"We should at least know why they were allowed back on the job!" Shana says.

"Settle down," Dr. Cook says over everyone. "Ms. Kincaid, I thank you for your time. Next question."

Shana starts to say something, but Mrs. Murray comes up behind her and whispers in her ear. Shana's clearly frustrated, but she lets Mrs. Murray lead her to a seat.

A middle-aged white woman steps to the other mic. "Hi, my name is Karen Pittman," she says. "This is not so much a question but a comment. I currently have a tenth grader here at Midtown. This is my third child to attend this wonderful school. My oldest son graduated seven years ago, before the various initiatives were put into place. During his four years here, there were no security guards. This will probably be an unpopular comment, but I think it must be pointed out that security measures were only heightened once students were brought in from certain communities, and rightfully so."

Aunt 'Chelle turns all the way around in her seat to look at this woman. "I wish she would. Ooh, I wish she would."

She basically did. Everybody knows what she means.

"There have been weapons brought on campus," Karen claims. "Gang activity. If I'm not mistaken, Officers Long and Tate recently apprehended a drug dealer on campus."

She is so mistaken it's funny. And gang activity? The closest thing we've had to a gang war was when the musical theater kids and the dance kids tried to out-flash-mob each other. Shit got real when they both did numbers from *Hamilton*.

"Her name just *had* to be Karen," Sonny says. "Bet she puts raisins in her potato salad." I smirk, and we cross our arms over our chests. Wakanda forever.

"Like everyone," Karen says, but there's so much noise from the audience. "Like everyone, I saw the videos from the incident, and I was appalled. There was no respect for authority from many of our students. They used a vulgar, violent song to taunt two gentlemen who were simply doing their jobs. A song that my son says was done by a student and specifically targets them. We cannot and should not allow our children to be exposed to such things. I personally signed a petition this morning to have that song taken offline. I encourage other parents to do the same."

Screw Karen and her son.

"Thank you, Mrs. Pittman," Superintendent Cook says. Karen gets a mix of applause and boos as she returns to her seat. "Next question, please."

Jay has made her way to the front of the line. From over

here, I can practically see the steam coming off of her.

"Go, Aunty Jay!" Sonny shouts. His momma and Aunt 'Chelle clap for her.

"Superintendent Cook," she says into the mic. "Jayda Jackson. It's a pleasure to finally speak to you."

"Thank you," he says with a small smile.

"It's a shame it has taken this long. For weeks, I have left you voice mails and have yet to receive a call back."

"My apologies. I'm extremely behind on—"

"My daughter was the one physically assaulted by Officers Long and Tate last month," Jay says, cutting him off. "Wanna know why? She sold candy, Dr. Cook. Not drugs. Candy."

Jay turns with the mic, looking at Karen. "While some of us are afraid of the impact *songs* will have on our children, there are parents who are absolutely terrified for the safety of our children at the hands of people who are supposed to protect them."

There's so much applause. Aunt 'Chelle shouts, "Preach!"

"A lot of these kids are afraid to roam this neighborhood because well-meaning people may get the wrong idea," she says. "At home, they're afraid because not-so-well-meaning people may put them in danger. You're telling me they have to come to school and deal with the same mess?"

We can barely hear her for the applause.

"The fact is, Superintendent," Jay says, "the uprising on Friday was in response to what happened to my daughter. Those two were back on the job after assaulting her, as if what they did was okay. Is this the kind of message you want to send to your students? That the safety of some of them is more important than the safety of others? If that's the case, there is no concern for the safety of *all* of them."

She gets a standing ovation from half the people in here. I clap harder than anyone.

Superintendent Cook has the most uncomfortable smile as he waits for the applause to die down. "Mrs. Jackson, I'm sorry that you feel that the school district has not been proactive regarding the incident with your daughter; however, an investigation is ongoing."

"You're sorry I feel—" She catches herself, like she's one second from going off. "That's not an apology, Superintendent. As far as this investigation goes, nobody's spoken to me or my child. That's not much of an investigation."

"It is ongoing. Again, I am sorry you feel we have not been proactive. However, at the moment, I am unable to . . ."

That's basically all he said the entire meeting. When it's over, so many parents and students swarm Dr. Cook that a police officer has to guide him through.

Malik's over to the side. Maybe now I can try to—

Jay grabs my hand. "C'mon."

She pushes through the crowd and gets us right on Dr. Cook's heels just as he reaches the hall.

"Dr. Cook!" she calls.

He looks back. The officer beckons him to come on, but Dr. Cook puts a hand up and comes over to us. "Mrs. Jackson, right?"

"Yes," Jay says. "This is my daughter, Brianna, the student who was assaulted. May we have a moment of your time now since you won't return my phone calls?"

Dr. Cook turns to the police officer. "Give us a few minutes."

The officer nods back, and Dr. Cook leads us into a room full of large, shadowed objects. He flicks a light switch, revealing drum sets and horns.

Dr. Cook closes the door behind us. "Mrs. Jackson, again, my sincerest apologies that we haven't spoken before today."

"It's a shame," Jay says. She's not the type to lie, even to be polite.

"It is. I take full responsibility for that." He holds his hand out to me. "Nice to meet you, Brianna."

I don't shake it at first. Jay nods at me and I do.

"I want you to look at her for a second, Dr. Cook," Jay says. "*Really* look at her."

She sets her hand on my back so I have no choice but to stand straight and look him in the eye, too.

"She's sixteen, Dr. Cook," Jay says. "Not a grown woman, not a threat. A child. Do you know how I felt when I was told that two grown men manhandled my *child*?"

Dr. Cook's eyes are full of pity. "I can only imagine."

"No, you can't," Jay says. "But this was not the first call I've received about my child, Dr. Cook. Now, Brianna can be argumentative, I'll be the first to admit that. She unfortunately got it from me."

Look at her, not putting something off on Dad for once.

"But she has been sent to the office for 'aggressive behavior' simply for rolling her eyes. You are more than welcome to pull her records. In fact, please do. Read the reports from when she was sent to the office or suspended, then tell me if any of those situations truly called for those consequences.

"I only have two options for my daughter, Dr. Cook," Jay says. "Two. It's either the school in our neighborhood or this school. At that school, they don't set students up to succeed, but here? It's starting to feel like they're setting my child up to fail. As a mother, what am I supposed to do? As the superintendent, what are you *going* to do?"

Dr. Cook is quiet at first. He sighs. "Hopefully much more than I've currently done. I'm sorry that we've failed you in any way, Brianna."

Two words, three syllables: I'm sorry.

Does he know how far we've
Come without hearing, "I'm sorry?"

I blink before too many tears build up. "Thank you."

"You've given me a lot to think and act on, Mrs. Jackson,"

Dr. Cook says. "Please feel free to reach out to me at any time with any concerns either of you may have. It may take me a while to get back to you, but I will."

"Because you currently don't have a secretary, right?" Jay says. "I saw the opening on the school district's website."

"Ah, yes. I almost need a secretary to schedule time for me to interview secretaries," he teases.

Jay reaches into her briefcase and takes out some papers. "I'm sure this is not the proper protocol for applying for a position, but I figured why not. Here is my résumé as well as my references. I have several years of secretarial experience."

"Oh," Dr. Cook says, clearly taken aback. But he accepts the papers and pulls out his glasses.

"Before you ask, the gap of unemployment is due to my past drug addiction," Jay says. "However, I recently celebrated my eighth year of sobriety."

"Wow. That's commendable, Mrs. Jackson."

Now Jay seems to be the one taken aback. "Really?"

"Yes," he says. "It shows your determination. That's a good character skill. I'm thirty years sober myself from alcoholism. Have to take it one day at a time. I can only imagine the type of willpower you must have. You should be proud of yourself."

From the looks of it, Jay never thought of it like that. I haven't either, honestly. I'm proud of her, but I always looked at it like she got off of drugs, and that was that. She used to say she went to rehab so she could fight her way back to me and Trey.

Dr. Cook makes it seem like she fights to stay, too.

He tucks her résumé and references inside his jacket pocket and holds his hand out to her. "I'll be in touch."

Jay looks dazed as she shakes his hand.

By the time we leave the band room, everyone's made their way outside. Aunt Gina, Aunt 'Chelle, Sonny, and Malik wait for us in the parking lot.

"Lord, if I get that job," Jay mutters. "Benefits, Jesus. Benefits!"

There are jobs, and there are jobs with benefits. Big difference. Whenever somebody in my family gets a job, the first question is, "Does it have benefits?"

Jay immediately tells Aunt 'Chelle and Aunt Gina what just went down. They're so happy that they suggest we go out to dinner for a precelebration, their treat. Nothing's guaranteed, but I'm pretty sure they just wanna get my mom's mind off all the other stuff.

I'm usually good with free food, but free food with my mom and her friends? I shake my head. "No thank you. I cannot go out to eat with you three."

Sonny busts out laughing, 'cause he knows why. Malik doesn't smirk or even look at me.

Jay sets her hand on her hip. "What's wrong with going out with us?"

"What's *not* wrong?" I say. "Y'all are the worst at restaurants." First off, anything I order, Jay has to have some of it, too, and before I know it most of my food is gone. Secondly, Aunt Gina loves to send stuff back to the kitchen until it's "right," and I wouldn't be surprised if they spit in our food. Third, my mom and my godmothers don't know how to leave. Their butts will be sitting there laughing and talking until the restaurant closes. Especially if it's one of those "bottomless drinks and appetizers" places.

"She's right," Sonny says. "Unless we have a table to ourselves, it's a no from me, too."

"Y'all hear this?" Jay asks the other two. "We carried these jokers, birthed them, and now they got the nerve to be ashamed of us."

Aunt Gina kisses her teeth. "Mm-hmm. Bet they won't be ashamed when we pay the bill."

Sonny grins. "Now that's a fact."

Aunt 'Chelle laughs. "Whatever. You three can have your li'l table to yourselves."

"Nah," says Malik. "Count me out."

He looks at me as he says it.

Malik kisses his mom's cheek, says something about hanging out with Shana, and walks away from us.

But it feels like he's walking away from me.

TWENTY-FIVE

Ten days after I sent my text, Aunt Pooh finally responds to me.

Meet me at the Maple after school

I almost walk out of Long Fiction class when I see it. After that, I swear the day seems to drag. The moment the last bell rings at the end of the day, I head straight for the school bus. When Mr. Watson pulls up at Maple Grove to drop off Curtis, I get off, too.

We cross the parking lot together. I can almost feel every single rock I step on. These fake Timbs are wearing out. Jay was up and about when I left this morning, and I have yet to talk to her about Supreme, so I couldn't wear the real ones. Hell, I still gotta break the news to Aunt Pooh.

"What you doing in the Maple?" Curtis asks. "You stalking me now, Princess?"

You know, there was a time his little jokes would've made me roll my eyes. They still do, but now I smirk. "Boy, nobody's stalking you. I'm here to see my aunt."

We dodge some shirtless guy who runs to catch a football sailing in the air. He's gotta be freezing.

Curtis stuffs his hands in his pockets. "I've been meaning to tell you, I went to see my mom this weekend."

"For real? How'd it go?"

"She was so happy she cried. I hadn't really thought of how much it hurt her when I was staying away. I thought I was helping. Kinda messed up that I was hurting her more than any of that prison shit."

"You didn't know," I say. "Besides, I'm sure she understood why it was hard for you."

"She actually did. I told her you convinced me to go. She said that you sound like a smart girl. She ain't lying about that."

"Wow, all of these compliments lately, from the same person who said my head was big enough. Why are you trying to make it bigger?"

"Whatever, Princess. For real though. Thank you," Curtis says.

"You're welcome." I punch his arm. "But that's for calling my head big."

"Was I lying?"

A gang of little kids bound toward us. Jojo pedals behind

them on his bike. Curtis goes, "Whoa!" and jumps out of their way just before they swarm me.

"Bri, can I get your autograph?" a little girl with a ponytail asks.

"Your song is my favorite!" a boy in a puffy coat adds.

They all want me to sign something or pose for a selfie.

"Y'all, stop being thirsty," Jojo says. "One at a time, people."

Curtis laughs as he walks away. "You hood famous, Princess."

Damn, I guess I am. I have to come up with an autograph on the spot. I've never signed anything other than school forms, and that's different. These kids are cool with my little scribbles.

"Bri, tell them me and you homies," Jojo says. "They don't believe me."

"We're homies," I say, signing my name for a little boy who's sucking his thumb. "Long as you've been going to school and staying out of trouble." I look up at him as I write.

"I been going to school!" he says. No mention of the trouble part.

"Me and my twin know all the words to your song!" this snaggle-toothed girl pipes up.

I scribble my name for her. "Oh, for real?"

"'Strapped like backpacks, I pull triggers,'" she and her sister squeak. "'All the clips on my hips change my figure.'"

I stop writing.

How old are they? Six? Seven?

"I told them you be blasting niggas, Bri," Jojo says. "Don't you?"

My stomach churns. "No, I don't, Jo—"

"Ay, ay, ay!" Aunt Pooh calls out as she comes over. She moves several of the kids out of her way. "Y'all, chill out. Give the superstar a break, a'ight?"

Aunt Pooh leads me toward the courtyard. I glance back at Jojo and his friends. I've got them rapping about guns and shit. Is that even okay?

Aunt Pooh hops up on the hood of Scrap's car. He's nowhere around. She pats the spot beside her. "You good?"

She's been MIA for over a week after vowing to go kill somebody. How does she think I am? "Where you been?"

"Look, that ain't your business."

"Are you kidding—I been texting you! You had me worried! You remember the last time I saw you?"

"Yeah."

"Did you—"

"Don't worry 'bout what I did. I ain't get the chain back, so it don't even matter."

Oh, shit. She did something. I fold my hands on top of my head. "Please don't tell me you killed—"

"Ain't nobody dead, Bri," she says.

"I'm supposed to feel better about that? What did you do?"

"The less you know, the better, a'ight!" she snaps.

Oh, God. Thing is, nobody has to be dead. Aunt Pooh just started something, regardless, and starting something in the Garden is never good.

Retaliation never ends around here. But lives do. Worst part? It's on me.

"Shit," I hiss.

"Bri, chill!" Aunt Pooh says. "I told you, ain't nobody dead."

"That won't make a difference! They could—"

"They ain't gon' do shit," Aunt Pooh claims.

"I shouldn't have called you. I don't want them coming after you."

"Look, I'm ready for whatever, whenever," she says. "I'm sorrier that I didn't get that chain back for you."

Once upon a time I was devastated to lose that thing, but now? It seems worthless. "I'd rather have you."

"Me." She says it almost mockingly, as if she's a joke. "Shit, I ain't gon' lie. You just gave me an excuse to go after them fools. I been wanting to do something to them."

"Because of Dad?"

Aunt Pooh nods. "Why you think I became a Garden Disciple in the first place? I wanted to go after whoever killed Law."

Add that to the list of things I didn't know. I hop up onto the hood beside her. "Really?"

It takes her a second to answer. She stares at this black car with tinted windows that cruises through the parking lot.

"Yeah," she finally says. "Law was my brother, my Yoda, or

whatever that li'l green dude's name is."

"You got it right." Impressively. I mean, damn, she knew the name *and* that he's green.

"Yeah, him," she says. "He looked out for me and genuinely cared about me, you know? When they killed him, it was one of the worst days of my life. Losing Momma and Daddy was bad enough. Then Jay got on that stuff not long after he died. Felt like I ain't have anybody."

"You had me and Trey."

"Nah. Your grandma and granddaddy had you and Trey," she says. "That grandma of yours is a trip. She ain't really want me coming around y'all. Can't blame her though. I wanted blood. I went to the GDs that used to hang with Law and told them I was down for whatever to get revenge. They told me I don't want that on me. But they let me join. If it wasn't for them, I wouldn't have had anybody."

"Well, you've got us now."

Her lips slowly turn up. "Corny ass. Getting all sentimental. You know you done pissed off a hell of a lot of people, right? That news report and that petition?" She laughs. "Goddamn, who knew a song could get folks that upset?"

I gotta tell her about Supreme. She may hate me, might cuss me out, but she has to know. "Hype invited me on his show to talk about it."

"Whaaaat?" she says, pulling her head back. "Li'l Bit going on the *Hot Hour*?"

"Yeah. Saturday morning."

"Yoooo. That's major! How'd that happen?"

Here we go. "Supreme set it up."

Her eyebrows meet. "Law's old manager?"

"Yeah. He, umm . . . he actually wants to be my manager."

I keep my eyes on my faux Timbs. I just have to tell her that I took Supreme up on his offer. Just spit it out like I'm in the middle of a freestyle in a battle.

Before I can say anything though, Aunt Pooh goes, "You took him up on it, didn't you?"

My entire face gets hot. "It's nothing against you, Aunt Pooh! I swear it's not. I still want you to be a part of all of this."

"Just not as your manager."

I swallow. "Yeah."

Aunt Pooh slowly lets out a sigh. "I get it. It's cool."

"Wait, what?"

"A'ight, maybe not *cool*, but I understand," she says. "I've got too much else going on to help you the way you really need."

Here's an idea: "You could just let that stuff go."

"I don't know enough about the music business either." She totally ignores what I said. "I've had folks hitting me up about the petition, and I ain't got a damn clue what to say or do. This could either make you sink or swim, you know? I don't wanna mess that up."

Aunt Pooh's not one to front, but maybe she fronts with me more than I realize. "You sure you okay with this?"

"I can help you out, even if I'm not your manager," she says. "I can be on your team. Help you put together songs. Make sure you ain't rapping stuff that makes white ladies shit themselves." She playfully ruffles my braids.

I snicker. "Whatever."

She holds her palm out. I slap it, but she pulls me across her lap and plants the longest, sloppiest kiss on my cheek, like she would do when I was little. I crack up. "You gotta come up with a title for me, superstar."

"Head Aunty in Charge."

"You know damn well Jay ain't gon' be cool with anybody else thinking they're in—"

Something catches her eye again. That same black car with tinted windows is back in the parking lot. The driver turns the engine off and the car sits there, facing us.

Aunt Pooh stares at it. "Bri, promise me something."

"What?" I say with my head still in her lap.

She won't look away from the car. "Promise you gon' get outta the Garden."

"Huh? What are you talking about?"

"Promise that you gon' do whatever you gotta do to make it. Promise like it's the last thing you'll ever promise me."

"Now look who's getting all sentimental," I tease.

"I'm serious! Promise!"

"I . . . I promise?" I somewhat say, somewhat ask. "What's got you talking like this?"

She makes me sit up and nudges me off the car. "Go home."

"What?"

"Go ho—"

Two black vans screech into the parking lot. Cops in SWAT gear rush out, guns pointed in every direction.

TWENTY-SIX

"Bri, go!" Aunt Pooh yells.

I'm stuck. The SWAT team swarms the projects, going after the Garden Disciples. All around, people run and scream. Parents dash for their kids or carry them as quickly as they can. Some kids are left crying by themselves.

Aunt Pooh drops to her knees with her hands behind her head. A SWAT team member rushes toward her, gun pointed.

Oh, God. "Aunty—"

"Go!" she yells again.

Somebody grabs my arm.

"C'mon!" Curtis says.

He pulls me with him. I try to look back for Aunt Pooh, but the stampede makes it impossible.

Along the way, something . . . weird happens with one of my shoes. Like it's off balance. It forces me to limp as I try to keep up with Curtis. He leads me to the apartment where he lives with his grandma. We don't stop until we get inside.

Curtis fastens every lock on the door. "Bri, you okay?"

"What the hell's happening?"

He lifts a blind to peek out. "Drug bust. I knew something was about to go down. That black car kept circling the parking lot. Looked like an undercover."

Drug bust?

Shit.

I rush over to the window and lift a blind myself. Curtis's grandma's apartment faces the courtyard, and I've got a clear view of everything. If Maple Grove was an ant bed, it's like somebody just stomped on it. SWAT team members knock down apartment doors, and Garden Disciples rush outside or get dragged out with guns pointed in their faces. A few brave ones make runs for it.

Aunt Pooh lies flat on the courtyard, her hands cuffed behind her back. A cop pats her down.

"Please, God," I pray. "Please, God."

God ignores me. The officer pulls a baggie from Aunt Pooh's back pocket. Suddenly, the sky is no longer our limit. That bag of cocaine is.

I back away from the window. "No, no, no . . ."

Curtis looks out, too. "Oh, shit."

For days, I thought I'd lost her, and I just got her back. Now . . .

There's suddenly an invisible hand gripping every single

muscle inside my chest. I gasp for air.

"Bri, Bri, Bri," Curtis says, taking my arms. He guides me toward the sofa and helps me sit down. "Bri, breathe."

It's impossible, like my body doesn't even know what breathing is, but it knows what crying is. Tears fall from my eyes. Sobs make me gasp harder, louder.

"Hey, hey," Curtis says. His eyes catch mine. "Breathe."

"Everybody . . ." I gulp for air. "Everybody leaves me."

I sound as small as I feel. This is my mom telling me Daddy left us to go to heaven. This is her backing out of the driveway, even as I scream for her not to leave me. Nobody ever realized they took part of me with them.

Curtis sits beside me. He hesitates at first, but he gently guides my head so it's resting on his shoulder. I let him.

"Yeah, people leave us," he says softly. "But it doesn't mean we alone."

All I can do is close my eyes. There's yelling and sirens outside. The cops are probably taking down every single Garden Disciple in Maple Grove.

Slowly, breathing becomes a habit again. "Thank you—" My nose is so stopped up, I sound funny. I sniff. "Thank you for getting me."

"It's all good," Curtis says. "I was watering my grandma's plants when I saw you and Pooh talking in the courtyard. Then the SWAT van rolled up. Knowing what I know 'bout Pooh, I knew you had to get up outta there."

I open my eyes. "You water your grandma's plants?"

"Yeah. Somebody gotta keep these things alive while she at work."

I sit up some more. There are potted plants and flowers all over the living room and kitchen. "Damn," I say. "You've got a lot of work."

He chuckles. "Yeah. Plus, she's got a couple on the stoop. I like helping her with them though. They easier to deal with than a dog or a little brother or sister." Curtis stands up. "You want some water or something?"

My throat is kinda dry. "Water would be good."

"No prob—" He frowns at my foot. "Yo, what's wrong with your shoe?"

"What?" I look down at them. One fake Timb is much shorter than the other. That's because the entire heel is missing.

My shoe literally came apart.

"Fuck!" I bury my face in my hands. "Fuck, fuck, fuck!"

At this point, this shit is laughable. Of all the days and times for my shoe to fall apart, it had to happen while my life is falling apart.

"Look, I got you, okay?" Curtis says. He unties his Nikes. He slides them off and holds them toward me. "Here."

He can't be for real. "Curtis, put your shoes back on."

Instead he goes down on one knee in front of me, puts his right sneaker on my right foot, and ties it super tight. He carefully removes my other Not-Timb, slips his left Nike on, and ties it too. When he's done, he straightens up.

"There," he says. "You got shoes."

"I can't keep your shoes, Curtis."

"You can at least wear them to go home," he says. "A'ight?"

Not like I have any other options. "All right."

"Good." He goes to the kitchen area. "You want ice in your water or nah?"

"No, thank you," I say. The yelling and shrieking has quieted down. I can't make myself look outside though.

Curtis brings me a tall glass of water. He sits beside me, wiggling his toes in his Spider-Man socks. There's a hell of a lot I don't know about him, and what I'm seeing doesn't match up with what I thought.

"Nice socks," I say.

He rolls his eyes. "Go ahead and clown me. I don't care. Peter Parker is that dude."

"He is." I sip my water. "That's why I wouldn't clown you. In fact, I think I have the same pair."

Curtis laughs. "For real?"

"Yep."

"That's cool," he says.

A loud clang comes from outside, like a large door closing on a vehicle. They must have loaded up all the drug dealers to take downtown.

"I'm sorry about your aunt," Curtis says.

He makes it sound like she's dead. Around here though, folks in jail get T-shirts in their honor just like folks in the grave. "Thank you."

We're quiet for a long while. I finish up the water and set the glass on his grandma's coffee table, beside an ashtray that's definitely been used. Unless it's for Curtis, which I doubt, Sister holier-than-thou Daniels smokes. Go figure.

"Thanks again for helping me."

"Don't mention it," he says. "But I wouldn't be against it if you decided to write a song about me as a token of your appreciation."

"Boy, bye. A shout-out? Maybe. An entire song? No."

"A shout-out?" he says. "C'mon, you gotta give me more than that. How about a verse?"

"Wow. A whole verse, huh?"

"Yep. Something like, 'Curtis is my homie, he gon' always know me, and when I'm making money, I'm gon' go buy him a pony. What!" He crosses his arms, B-boy style.

I bust out laughing. "You thought you could beat me in a battle, rhyming like that?"

"What? Girl, that's skill."

"No, that's a mess."

"Hold up, you can't call anybody a mess with how you're looking right now." He thumbs some of the wetness from my cheek away. "Getting your snot and tears all over my grandma's sofa."

His hand lingers. Slowly, it cups my cheek.

I get this pang in my stomach, like a little knot that's twisted up tight, and I think—well, hope—that I'm still breathing.

When he moves closer, I don't move away. I can't think; I can't breathe. I can only kiss him back.

Every single inch of me is aware of him, of the way his fingertips graze the back of my neck, the way his tongue perfectly tangles with mine. My heart races, and it somehow tells me I want more and to take my time all at once.

I wrap my arms around his neck and lean back on the couch, pulling him down with me. Touching him is a need. My fingers find his hair, coiled and soft, his back. Boy's got a donk that's meant for squeezing.

Curtis grins, his forehead against mine. "You like that, huh?"

"Mm-hmm."

"A'ight then. Let's see if you like this."

He kisses me again, and slowly, his hand travels under my sweatshirt and under my bra. He grazes a spot that makes me stop kissing him long enough to make a sound I've never made before. I feel it in more places than my chest.

"Shit, girl," he groans, and pulls back. He props himself up over me, out of breath. "You're killing me here."

I smirk. "*I'm* killing *you*?"

"Yeah." He kisses my nose. "I like it though."

He cups my cheek, leans down, and kisses me again, slow and steady. For a while, nothing exists beyond us and this kiss . . .

TWENTY-SEVEN

. . . Until Curtis's grandma comes home.

By then we're just watching TV. She still gives me a suspicious eye. Curtis asks to borrow her car so he can take me home. She gives him the keys and says, "We gon' have a li'l talk later, boy."

That talk's gonna find its way to my grandma.

The courtyard is deserted when we leave. The only signs that anything happened are the clusters of footprints all over the dirt. Scrap's car remains in its normal spot. It's weird that nobody's sitting on the hood of it.

Curtis drives his grandma's Chevy with one hand. The other hand holds mine. We don't really say much, but I don't think we have to. That kiss said more than words really could.

He pulls up in front of my house. I lean over and kiss him

again. It's the best way to slow down time. But I have to go inside, so I pull away. "I need to go talk to my mom about . . . my aunt."

I can barely say it to Curtis. How can I say it to Jay?

He gives my lips a feathery-soft peck. "It'll be okay."

Those are just words though. Reality is, I take off Curtis's shoes, put my raggedy ones back on, and go inside. Some song about how "Jesus will" plays on my mom's phone in the kitchen, and she hums along, not knowing that Jesus will have to perform a miracle when it comes to Aunt Pooh.

"Hey, Bookie," she says. She stands over a pot. "We're having spaghetti tonight."

My legs shake almost too much for me to stand. "Aunt Pooh."

"What about her?"

"She . . . she got arrested."

"Goddammit!" She holds her forehead and closes her eyes. "This girl. What she do this time? Get into a fight? Speeding? I told her all those traffic tickets would—"

"There was a drug bust," I murmur.

Jay opens her eyes. "What?"

My voice is thick. "There was a SWAT team, and they found coke on her."

My mom just stares at me. Suddenly, she picks up her phone. "God, no. Please, no."

She calls the police station. They can't provide any info yet.

She calls Lena, who's sobbing so hard I can hear her from across the room. She calls Trey, who's at work but says he'll go by the station on his way home. She calls Scrap. His phone goes to voice mail. I think they got him, too.

Jay goes to her room, closes the door, and stays there. I don't think I'm supposed to hear her crying, but it's the only thing I hear all night.

I can't stop her from crying. I can't save Aunt Pooh. And now with her gone and nobody else for the Crowns to target, I may not even be able to save myself.

I'm powerless.

Jay doesn't come out of her room the next day, or the next. When I get up Saturday morning, she's still in there. Trey's in his room, sleeping off a late-night shift. Supreme picks me up and takes me downtown for my interview with Hype.

Supreme runs his mouth the whole drive, but I barely hear him. My mom's sobs won't leave my ears. Besides, he's saying the same ol' shit. This is a major deal. I'm on my way. This interview will take me to a new level.

But it won't save Aunt Pooh.

Supreme must realize I'm not saying much because he glances away from the road long enough to sneak a look over at me. "You good, Li'l Law?"

"Don't call me that."

"Oh, you wanna stand on your own two, huh?" he teases.

Ain't shit funny. I've got no choice but to stand on my own two. Excuse me if I don't wanna wear the name of the person who's not here to carry all of this with me.

I don't even answer Supreme. I just stare out of the window.

Hot 105 is in one of the skyscrapers downtown. The station is just as legendary as the artists they have photographed on the walls. All around the reception area, there are framed pictures of the various DJs with hip-hop royalty they've interviewed over the years.

Hype's voice pours out of speakers around the reception area. He's live on the air in one of the studios. Jay used to have his show playing on her car stereo every Saturday morning when she'd pick me and Trey up. Whenever Hype played one of Dad's songs, she'd let the windows down and turn it all the way up. He'd sound so alive that I'd forget he was dead.

Hype's assistant leads me and Supreme to the studio. The red "live" light above the door means we have to wait outside at first. On the other side of a large window, Hype sits at a table that's crowded with computer monitors, microphones, and headphones. There's a guy in the studio with him pointing a camera in Hype's direction. A sign on the wall says, "*The Hot Hour.*"

"As always, we gotta pay some bills," Hype says over the speakers in the hallway. "But y'all stick around, because after the commercial break, I'm gonna be talking to one of the hottest young rappers in the country right now: Bri! We're gonna get the scoop on the controversy, her next moves, all of that. It's the *Hot Hour,* baby, on Hot 105!"

Hype takes off his headphones, and his assistant ushers us into the studio.

"The princess of the Garden!" Hype says. He gives me a half hug. "I still get chills thinking about your battle. No offense, 'Preme, but she killed your son. Straight up."

"I can't deny it," Supreme says. "Why you think I had to sign her myself?"

"Can't blame you," Hype says. "The song is dope, too. Of course, all the controversy ain't, but hey, at least they talking, right? I know my listeners wanna hear from you, Bri. We just ask that you keep the cussing to a minimum. Ain't nobody got time for FCC fees."

"We're live in one minute, Hype," the cameraman says.

Hype points me to a chair across from his where a mic and headphones await. "Have a seat, Bri," he says, and I do. "'Preme, you staying?"

"Nah, I'll be out there," Supreme says. He kneels beside my chair. "Look, he may try to push your buttons," he says, keeping his voice low. "That's Hype though. Don't let him rile you up too much. Just be yourself and say what you feel. All right?"

Say what I feel? He must not know how I'm feeling.

"We go live in five, Bri," Hype says. "Four . . ."

Supreme pats my shoulder and goes into the hall. I slip the headphones on.

Hype puts up three fingers.

Two.

One.

"Welcome back to the *Hot Hour*," he says into the mic. "Y'all, I got a very special guest in the house. If you know anything 'bout me, you know one of my favorite rappers of all time is Lawless, rest in peace to my brother. Today, I have the pleasure of having his baby girl in the studio. She's got one of the hottest songs out at the moment, "On the Come Up," and it's got a lot of folks talking. Of course, we had to bring her to the *Hot Hour*. So, Bri, welcome to the studio."

He plays an applause track.

"Thanks," I say into the mic.

"Y'all, I had a chance to hear Bri a while back at the Ring. That was your debut, right?"

"Yep."

"Y'all, she killed it," he says. "After the show is over, go on YouTube and pull up that battle. It'll blow you away. Bri was supposed to return to the Ring, but there was a little mishap a few weeks ago. We'll get into that later. Right now, let's talk about this song!" He smacks the table to prove his point. "'On the Come Up.' Y'all request it on the show all the time. The kids love it. A lot of us old heads enjoy it. But there's a petition to get it taken off Dat Cloud because some people say it led to a riot at a local school. Other people say it's antipolice, blah, blah, blah. As the artist behind the song, what do *you* have to say?"

Supreme said to say what I feel. Thing is, all I feel is pissed. "Screw them."

Hype chuckles. "No hesitation at all, huh?"

"Why should I hesitate? They didn't hesitate to come at me."

"Okay, okay," Hype says. "A lot of folks have been focusing on the violent nature of the lyrics. Do you think they encouraged those students at that school to act out violently?"

Is he serious? "Do you think half the songs you play encourage people to act out violently?"

"We're talking about your song and this situation though."

"Does it matter?" I say. "They were clearly upset about other stuff. A song didn't make them do anything. All these people are using me as a cop-out instead of asking what the real problems are."

"All these people who?" he actually asks.

"Bruh, the news!" I say. "The lady with the petition. She wrote an entire article about me, made me out to be the bad guy, and never wondered why the students were protesting in the first place. Lyrics didn't force anyone to do anything. The whole protest was about—"

"But c'mon," Hype cuts me off, "even you gotta admit that some of the lyrics are a bit much, baby girl. You talk about being strapped, you insinuate that you'll kill cops—"

Whoa, whoa, whoa. "I never insinuated anything about killing no damn cops."

"'If a cop come at me, I'll be lawless'?" he asks instead of says. "What's that supposed to mean?"

How the hell did he take that as me saying I'll kill anyone? "Bruh, it means that I'll be considered unruly, no matter what I do!" Goddamn, I really gotta break this down for him? "'Like my poppa, fear nada,' aka his last album, *Fear None*. 'Take solace in my hood going hard in my honor' means if something happens to me, the Garden will have my back. That's it. I never said anything about killing a cop."

"Okay, but you can see how some people took that the wrong way, right?"

"Hell no, I don't."

"Look, I'm not trying to come at you," Hype claims. "I love the song. I can't lie though, knowing that a sixteen-year-old girl is talking about being strapped and stuff like that, it caught me off guard."

Not that a sixteen-year-old rapped about it. But that a sixteen-year-old *girl* rapped about it. "Did it catch you off guard when my dad rapped about it at sixteen?"

"No."

"Why not?"

"Aw, c'mon, you know why," Hype says. "It's different."

"Different how? I know girls who were strapped at sixteen, seventeen, who had to do foul stuff just to survive."

And who got taken down by a SWAT team who didn't give a damn what their gender was.

"It's just different, li'l momma. I ain't make the rules," Hype says. "My thing is, are we really supposed to believe you out here popping on folks like that? C'mon, now. Who wrote those lines for you?"

What the hell? "The song isn't about 'popping' on anybody, and I wrote them."

"You wrote the whole song?" he says. "And the freestyles in the battle?"

Seriously, what the hell? "I wrote the song, and I came up with the freestyles on the spot just like you're supposed to do in a battle. What are you trying to say?"

"Chill, baby girl," Hype says. "Look, ain't nothing wrong with a ghostwriter, all right? My thing is, ghostwriters need to write authentically for the person. Ain't no way you out here strapped like backpacks."

You know what? Screw this. It doesn't matter what I say or do. Everybody will have their own idea of me and of that song, regardless. I snatch the headphones off. "I'm out."

"Whoa, we're not done, Li'l Law."

"My name is Bri!" Feels like every bone in my body yells that out.

"Okay, *Bri*. Look, it's all good," he says with a smirk. I wanna wipe it off his face, I swear. "We were having a good conversation. No need to get mad."

"You accused me of not writing my own shit! How the hell is that good?"

"You must not write your stuff if you getting this defensive."

The door flies open and Supreme rushes in. "Bri, calm down."

"It's all good, 'Preme," Hype says. "If she strapped like she said in the song, she'll handle me."

He plays a laugh track.

I almost jump over the table, but Supreme holds me back. "Fuck you!"

"Aww, see? This why they kicked you out of the Ring. Baby girl PMSing up in here." Hype plays a drum kick to cap off his "joke."

Supreme has to practically drag me out. We pass all these station workers in the hallway, and they stare and whisper as Hype makes another "joke" over the speakers. I have no problem whooping all of their asses.

Supreme gets me to the lobby. I snatch out of his grasp.

He chuckles. "Goddamn. What's got you riled up?"

Everything. I breathe hard and blink harder, but my eyes burn anyway. "Did you hear him?"

"I told you he would push your buttons. That's what Hype does." Supreme pats my cheek. "You're a goddamn genius, you know that? You did exactly what I told you all those weeks ago. I'm surprised you remembered."

I look at him as my breath finally catches up with my pounding heart. "What?"

"You played that ratchet hood rat role. You know how

much publicity you 'bout to get from this?"

It's like having a bucket of ice water thrown into my face.

Ratchet hood rat.

Thousands of people just heard me act like that. Millions more may see the video. They won't care that my life is a mess and I had every right to be mad. They'll just see an angry black girl from the ghetto, acting like they expected me to act.

Supreme laughs to himself. "You played the role," he says. "Goddamn, you played the role."

Problem is, I wasn't playing. That's what I've become.

TWENTY-EIGHT

I ask Supreme to take me to Sal's. I need my brother.

Supreme's phone blows up the whole way. He can't stay still for bouncing in his seat.

"Whooo!" He smacks the steering wheel like he's giving it a high five. "We 'bout to get paid, baby girl! I swear, this the best shit you could've done! We on our goddamn way!"

Ratchet hood rat. Three words, four syllables.

Everybody's gonna think I'm a hood rat, that's good at
being ratchet and blowing gaskets.

The Closed sign is on Big Sal's door when Supreme drops me off. It's still morning, and the shop doesn't open until noon. Sal spots me peeking in through the glass and lets me in the shop anyway. She tells me that Trey's in the back.

It's hard to say what Trey's position is at Sal's. Sometimes he waits tables, other times he oversees the orders in the kitchen. Today, he mops the kitchen floor.

Ms. Tique . . . I mean Kayla, watches nearby. She wears the hoop earrings like she wore in the Ring and a green apron. She's much smaller than she seemed in the Ring though—she doesn't even come to Trey's shoulder. I guess the mic makes her larger than life.

They're the only two in the kitchen. Usually, this place is bustling as employees toss pizza dough in the air, yell out orders, and slide pies into the oven. It's almost too quiet and still today. I guess everybody else hasn't come in yet. Leave it to Trey to show up early.

Trey wrings the mop in the bucket and starts rolling the bucket toward the storage room, but Kayla goes, "Uh-uhn. I know you're not leaving that floor looking like that."

"Like what?" he says.

"Like that." She points to a spot. "There's dirt on the floor, Trey."

He squints. "That li'l speck?"

Kayla takes the mop herself. "See, this is why you don't need to clean."

"Oh, I don't?"

"Nope!"

Trey smiles as he sneaks a quick peck to her lips. "But do I need to do that?"

"Hmmm . . ." She taps her chin. "The jury's still out."

Trey laughs and kisses her again.

I'm probably not supposed to see this, but I can't look away. Not on some creeper shit, but I haven't seen my brother this happy in a while. His eyes are bright, and his smile is so wide when he looks at her that it's contagious. Not saying he was depressed or anything these past few months, but compared to how he is right now, it's hard to say he's been happy.

Kayla looks away from him long enough to spot me in the doorway. "Trey."

He follows her gaze. The brightness leaves his eyes and his smile disappears. He focuses on mopping again. "What you doing here, Bri?"

I'm suddenly feeling like I shouldn't be here, and I've never felt like that around Trey. He's been my home when I wasn't sure what "home" was. "Can we talk?" I ask.

He won't look up from mopping. Kayla takes his arm to stop him. "Trey," she says. Firmly.

He looks at her. There's an unspoken conversation between them—it's all in their eyes. Trey sighs out of his nose.

Kayla stands on her tiptoes and kisses his cheek. "I'm gonna go see if Sal needs help up front."

She gives me this sad smile as she passes, like somebody does when you're in mourning.

What's that about? Aunt Pooh?

Trey mops, and it's like I'm invisible to him. Even as I inch closer, he doesn't look up.

"Is something wrong?" I ask. I'm almost afraid to know though. His response could turn my life even more upside down. "Is Jay—"

"Mom," he corrects, focused on the floor.

I don't know why that word won't come easily for me. "Is she okay?"

"She was in her room when I left."

"Oh." Messed up that I'm sorta relieved by that. "Any word on Aunt Pooh?"

"They're still processing her. What you want, Bri?"

What's that about? I've never had to explain why I wanted to see him before. "I just wanted to talk to you."

"You haven't done enough talking today?"

It's a verbal slap of the worst kind.

He heard the interview. Of the thousands of people who listened in, I never considered that one might be my brother. "Trey, I can explain."

He sets the mop in the bucket and looks at me. "Oh, so you have an explanation for acting a damn fool on the radio?"

"He pushed my buttons!"

"Didn't I tell you that you don't have to respond to everything? Huh, Bri?"

"I'm not gonna just take shit that's thrown at me!"

"You can speak up for yourself without acting like that!" he says. "First that Instagram video, now this? What the hell is wrong with you?"

I stare at this person who claims to be my brother. It looks like him, but it doesn't sound like him. "You're supposed to have my back," I say, just above a whisper. "Why are you so pissed at me?"

He damn near chucks the mop. "Because I'm busting my ass for you! I drag myself into this job for you! Work long hours to make sure you're good! And here you go, ruining any shot you have at making any goddamn thing of yourself by showing your ass every chance you get!"

"I'm just trying to save us!"

Somehow my voice is weak and loud all at once.

The fury leaves his eyes, and it's my big brother staring at me again. "Bri—"

"I'm tired, Trey." Tears prickle my eyes. "I'm tired of not knowing what's gonna happen next. I'm tired of being scared. I'm tired!"

There's a shuffling of feet, and two arms wrap around me tightly. I bury my face in Trey's shirt.

He rubs my back. "Let it out."

I scream until my throat is raw. I've lost Aunt Pooh. I may be losing my mom. I lost my cool so bad that I've lost more than I realize. *I'm* lost. I'm so lost that I'm exhausted from trying to find my way.

Trey leads me over to this little corner in the back of the kitchen that he calls his. Sometimes when I visit, I'll find him sitting on the floor over here, wedged between the refrigerator and storage-room door. He says it's the one place he can get away from the chaos.

Trey lowers himself to the floor and helps me sit down with him.

I rest my head in his lap. "I'm sorry I'm a burden."

"Burden?" Trey says. "Where you get that from?"

From our whole lives. When Jay first got sick, she would disappear into her room for days on end. Trey couldn't reach into all of the kitchen cabinets, but he always made sure I ate. He'd comb my hair and get me ready for preschool. He was ten. He didn't have to do any of that. Then when we moved in with Grandma and Granddaddy, he still took care of me, insisting that he read me stories every night and walk me to and from school every day. If I had a nightmare about those gunshots that took Dad, Trey would run into my room and comfort me until I fell asleep.

He gives up so much for me. The least I can do is make it, so he doesn't have to give up anything else. "You've always taken care of me," I say.

"Li'l Bit, I do that because I want to," Trey says. "A burden? Never. You're too much of a gift to me."

Gift. One word, one syllable. I don't know if it rhymes with anything because it's a word I never thought could be used when it comes to me.

Suddenly, it's as if a cage has been unlocked and all of these tears I've had stored up inside fall down my cheeks.

Trey brushes them away. "I wish you'd cry more."

I smirk. "Dr. Trey is back."

"I'm serious. Crying doesn't make you weak, Bri, and even if it did, there's nothing wrong with that. Admitting that you're weak is one of the strongest things you can do."

I turn and look up at him. "That sounds like something Yoda would say."

"Nah. Yoda would say, 'Weak, strength is admitting you are.'" He kisses my cheek with a loud, sloppy "Muah!"

I quickly wipe the spot. I *know* I felt some of his spit. "Ill! Getting your germs all on me."

"Just for that—" Trey kisses my cheek again, even louder, even sloppier. I squirm to get away, but yeah, I'm laughing, too.

He smiles at me. "I know you think I've done a lot for you, Li'l Bit, but you've done just as much for me. I think about everything we've been through, and if I'd gone through it by myself, I'd probably be where Pooh is right now."

Damn. Aunt Pooh did say she became a GD because she didn't have anyone. Now she's in a jail cell without anyone again. I never realized that Trey could've been like her, with a record instead of a diploma. I know there's so much else that made their lives turn out differently, but he makes it sound like the difference between them was me.

Maybe it's not on me to save Aunt Pooh. Maybe it's on Aunt Pooh to save herself for me.

Maybe it *was*. "She's not getting out for a long time, huh?" I ask.

"Probably not."

"What do we do?"

"Live," he says. "I mean, we're gonna support her through this, but you gotta remember that she made choices, Bri. She always knew there was a chance this would happen and did it anyway. This is on her. Period."

The kitchen door opens just barely, and Kayla peeks in. "Trey? Sorry to bother, but Sal needs your help with something up front."

I take that as my cue to sit up. Trey stands and gives me a hand up, too.

"No more radio interviews, all right?" he says. "Having one DJ on my list is enough."

"What list?"

"My ass-whooping list. If I see him in the streets, I'm whooping his ass."

I laugh as he kisses my cheek. Fact is, even when he's mad at me, even when he's so disappointed that he yells at me, my brother will always have my back.

TWENTY-NINE

Monday morning, I knock on my mom's bedroom door.

I've been up a while. Gotten dressed, had some cereal, and cleaned up my room a little. Jay hasn't come out of her bedroom yet.

The first two knocks don't get a response. I try again, and my heart knocks even harder against my chest. It takes two more tries before I hear the small "What is it?"

I slowly crack the door open. There's no smell. I know, that's a weird thing to look—well, *sniff*—for, but I still remember the odor that would come from her room when she first got sick. It was like rotten eggs and burning plastic mixed together. Crack reeks.

The room is covered in darkness—the lights are off, and the blinds and curtains are closed. But I can make out the lump beneath a mound of bedding that's my mom.

"I just wanted to say bye," I tell her. "The bus will be here soon."

"C'mere."

I inch over to the side of the bed. Jay's head pokes out from under the comforter. About half of her hair is protected by a silk bonnet. It partially slid off at some point, and she doesn't seem to care enough to fix it. Her eyes are puffy and pink, and there's balled-up tissues on the nightstand and scattered around her pillow.

She reaches up and runs her fingers through my baby hairs. "You're starting to outgrow these braids. I need to do some new ones soon. Did you eat?"

I nod. "You want anything?"

"No, but thank you, baby."

There's so much I wanna say but don't know how to say. I mean, how do you tell your mom that you're scared you're losing her again? How selfish is it to say, "I need you to be okay so that I'll be okay"?

Jay cups my cheek. "I'm okay."

I swear, moms are equipped with mind-reading abilities.

Jay sits up and pulls me closer. I sit on the edge of the bed. She wraps her arms around me from behind and kisses the back of my head, resting her chin on my shoulder.

"It's been a dark couple of days," she admits softly. "But I'm getting through it. Just needed some time. I'm thinking about going downtown to see Pooh tomorrow. You wanna come? We can go after your ACT prep."

I nod. "Any word from Dr. Cook yet?" It's been over a week since she gave him her résumé at the PTA meeting. I get it, that's not a long time, but days feel like years lately.

"No," Jay says, and sighs. "Those folks at the school district probably don't want a former drug addict working with them. It'll be okay. I gotta believe that."

"But will *you* be okay?"

I sound five. I *feel* five. I sat on her bed once back then, stared into red eyes hazy from drugs, and asked her that same question. A day or so later, she left me and Trey at our grandparents' house.

She stills when I ask it now. Several moments pass before she responds.

"I will be," she says. "I promise."

She kisses my temple to seal the deal.

My mom's up and getting dressed when I go outside and wait for the bus.

She's doing it for me, I know it. Making herself be strong so I won't be scared.

I sit on the curb, slip my headphones over my ears, and hit Shuffle on my phone. J. Cole's "Apparently" starts. I rap along as he talks about all the hell his mom went through. Then that part where he says he wants his dream to rescue him? I don't think I've ever repeated truer words. It's like he knew I'd be sitting on a curb in front of my house, listening to this song and needing it.

I used to say I wanted to do that for some kid. Have them listen to my music and feel every single word, as if I wrote it just for them. Lately, though, I just wanna make it.

The song stops as my ring tone goes off. Supreme's name appears on the screen.

"Li'l Law!" he says the second I answer. "I got big news."

"Another radio interview?" I'd rather eat all the leftovers in the world, and I hate leftovers.

"Bigger!" he says. "I got some execs that wanna meet you."

It's like I've suddenly broken into a sprint, that's how much my heart speeds up. I almost drop my phone. "Ex—" I can't even say it. "Execs? As in record execs?"

"Hell yes!" Supreme says. "This is it, baby girl! This is your chance!"

"Wait." I hold my forehead. This is too fast. "How—why—when—"

"When? This afternoon," he says. "Why? The interview! The song! How? They hit me up. Thing is, they wanna hear what else you can do. I know you don't have any other songs recorded, so I thought we could meet them in the studio, right? Let you record some shit while they're there. Then they can really see what you're capable of. A contract will be as good as ours!"

Ho. Ly. Shit. "You're serious?"

"As hell." He laughs. "I can pick you up after school and bring you to the studio. Sound good?"

I look back at my house. "It definitely does."

The moment I take my seat on the bus, I fish through my backpack for my notebook. I either need to write a new song or find a song that I've already written. One that's so dope, the record execs will lose their minds. I could go with "Unarmed and Dangerous" this time around, the song I wrote after that kid was killed. Or maybe I need another hype—high-energy song. Even in a different context, I refuse to use the word "hype" again.

I'm so busy flipping through pages that when somebody goes, "Hey," I jump.

Curtis smirks in the seat behind me. "What's got you all jittery, Princess?"

"Nothing. Just didn't notice you back there." That came out wrong. "Not that I wouldn't notice you. I just didn't notice you this time."

"I know what you meant." He's got this almost sly look in his eyes, like he gets whenever he tells one of his little jokes. This time, it's an inside joke between us. "So . . . how you been?"

"I'm fine."

I don't know what else to say. This is the part of relationships that I fail at. Okay, I don't even know if we have a relationship. I've actually never been in one. But it's like, what do you do after the kiss? What do you say? That's the part that trips me up.

Curtis moves to the spot beside me. "I've been thinking 'bout you. Been thinking 'bout that kiss, too."

"Oh." I glance down at my notebook. I should be searching for a song right now.

"I know, it's probably been all on your mind since it happened, huh?" he says. "I tend to have that effect."

I look up. "What?"

"Ay, I'm just saying, my kissing game? One hundred."

I bust out laughing. "You're so full of it."

"I got your attention though, *and* I got you smiling." He gently pokes one of my dimples. "That's a win to me. What's up with you this morning, Princess?"

"I've got some stuff going on with this rap thing," I say. "You heard my Hype interview, right?"

"*Everybody* heard your Hype interview. You really went in on dude."

I rest my head back. "Yeah. For somebody who was once invisible, I'm definitely making up for it now."

He frowns. "Invisible?"

"Curtis, you know damn well nobody at school noticed me until I got a little fame as a rapper."

He looks me up and down and licks his lips. "I can't speak for anyone else, but I definitely noticed you. Fact is, I've been wanting to talk to you for a minute, Princess. But you seemed so caught up in your boy Malik that I didn't think I had a shot."

"Wait, what?"

"I thought y'all were together," he says. "You acted like you couldn't hang out with anybody but him and Sonny."

"That's not true!"

"Yeah, it is. Name somebody else you hang out with."

Okay, there's nobody else. "I always figured nobody else wanted to hang out with me, to be honest," I admit.

"And I always figured you didn't wanna hang out with anybody else, to be honest."

Damn.

I mean, I don't know. I'm always weird about new people, I guess. The more people in your life, the more people who can leave your life, you know? I've lost enough as it is.

But right now, Curtis makes me wonder if I've been missing out.

"You know what? Fuck it," he says. "You wanna go out with me tomorrow afternoon for Valentine's Day?"

Oh, damn. I forgot that's tomorrow. Honestly, Valentine's Day is never on my radar. "Like out on a date?" I ask.

"Yeah. A date. You and me. We can do some romantic Valentine's shit."

"Um, wow. Well, one, I can't do tomorrow. I'm going to see my aunt. Two, I'm sure it will be *really* romantic considering how you just asked me out."

"What's wrong with how I asked you out?"

"Boy, you literally said 'fuck it.'"

"Goddamn, Princess? Can I get a break?"

"Um, no. Not if you're asking me out."

"What? You want me to make it a big deal?" he asks. "Because I can make it a big deal."

The bus stops in front of Sonny's and Malik's houses. They climb on board just as Curtis climbs onto our seat. Seriously, he stands on the seat.

"Brianna Middle-Name-Here-'Cause-I-Don't-Know-It Jackson," he says, loud enough for the whole bus to hear.

"Boy, get down from there!" Mr. Watson calls.

Curtis waves him off. "Bri, even though you busy tomorrow, will you go out with me on a date at some point so we can do some romantic shit?"

My face is so hot. Every eye on the bus watches us. Sonny wiggles his eyebrows. Malik's mouth is slightly open. Deon takes out his phone, talking about, "Do it for the 'Gram, Curtis!"

Oh my God. "Curtis, get down," I say through my teeth.

"C'mon, girl. Please?"

"Yes, now get down!"

"Ayyyy, she said yes!" he just has to announce, and a couple of people actually clap. Including Sonny. Curtis plops down next to me, grinning. "See? I told you I can do it big."

I roll my eyes. "You're so extra."

"You're still going out with me though."

Yes, I grin, too. No, I can't help it. No, I don't know what the hell is wrong with me.

And I think I'm okay with that.

The bus pulls up at Midtown. Curtis gets off with Deon, who's immediately like, "Bruh, teach me your ways!"

Ridiculous.

I slip my headphones on my ears and turn Cardi all the way up. I still gotta figure out what I'm doing at the studio. Plus, the music will keep me from Sonny's interrogation, because I can't answer him if I can't hear him. But as I hop off the bus, he's not waiting for me at the bottom of the steps. Shana is.

There's a clipboard tucked under her arm. Her mouth moves, but I can't hear her at first.

I turn my music down. "What?"

"Can we talk?" she asks, louder than she should.

"I can hear you now."

"Oh. You got a minute?"

A few feet away, Malik focuses on his phone a little too hard. He glances in our direction, but when our eyes meet, he quickly looks at his phone again.

He's still not talking to me. I'm really not in the mood for his girlfriend trying to patch things up between us. "What is it?" I ask her.

"The superintendent agreed to meet with the coalition today, after school," Shana says. "We hoped you would join us. He's meeting with us because of you, after all."

I slide my headphones down around my neck. "What makes you think that?"

"He said he talked to you."

"Oh." But he can't call my mom about a job.

"Yeah. And he said he saw your music video too, and it shed new light on the situation with Long and Tate. It looks like it's helping our cause. So, thank you."

Awkward silence rolls in. Fact is, one of the last conversations we had, I came this close to smacking Shana. Hard to forget that.

She clears her throat and holds up the clipboard. "We're taking this petition to the meeting, too. It asks him to remove the armed police officers as security. If we get enough signatures, hopefully he'll listen."

"Hopefully."

"Yeah," she says. "The meeting starts at four in the band—"

"I have other plans."

"Bri, look, if this is about me and you, let's squash whatever it is," Shana says. "We could really use you at this meeting. You have a voice that they'll listen to."

"I really do have something else planned."

"Oh."

The silence returns.

I take my pencil from behind my ear and motion to her clipboard. She holds it out, and I scribble my name on an available line. "Good luck with the meeting."

I lift my headphones over my ears and start for the steps.

"Hype is an asshole," Shana calls.

I turn back. "What?"

"He shouldn't have done you like that during your interview. A lot of people support you, too. I saw some pretty big names talking about it on Twitter."

I haven't looked at social media since all of this went down. There's only so much you can take being described as somebody you're not. "Thank you."

"No problem," she says. "We have your back, Bri."

We. That includes Malik. There was a time he would've told me that himself. He doesn't have my back that much if his girlfriend has to tell me for him.

I think I've lost him for good.

"Thank you," I mutter to Shana.

I turn around and hurry up the stairs before she or Malik can see how glossy my eyes get.

Doesn't matter that I may have gained Curtis or that I may be hours away from getting everything I want. I'm still losing Malik, and it still hurts.

THIRTY

The studio Supreme takes me to makes the one I first went to look like a dump.

It's in an old warehouse in Midtown-the-neighborhood. Not too far from my school, actually. A wrought-iron fence surrounds the parking lot, and Supreme has to let security know who we are before they let us through the gate.

Platinum and gold plaques line the walls of the reception area. All of the light fixtures look like real gold, and they've got one of the biggest fish tanks I've ever seen in my life, with tropical fish swimming around.

Supreme squeezes my shoulders. "You done made it, Li'l Law. This the big time!"

He's more chill as he tells the receptionist who we are and who we're here to see. I look around at the plaques. Legendary songs and albums have been recorded at this place. Aunt Pooh would lose her mind if she saw some of these.

It doesn't feel right, being here without her.

There's also the fact that I lied to my mom. I texted her and said I was staying after school to do some additional ACT prep. I'll tell her the truth soon as I go home. Because if this meeting goes like I hope it goes, I'm about to change our lives.

The receptionist leads us to a studio in the back. The whole way, I tug at my hoodie strings and wipe my palms along my jeans. They're sweaty as hell. My lunch churns in my stomach, too. I don't know if I wanna puke or run into that studio.

"Be cool," Supreme says to me under his breath. "Record the song like you'd normally do and everything will be fine, all right? Just follow my lead on the other stuff."

Other stuff? "What other stuff?"

He simply pats my back with a smile.

The receptionist opens the last door in the hallway, and I swear, I stop breathing. She opened the door to heaven.

Okay, that's a giant overstatement, but this is the closest I've ever been to those pearly gates. It's a studio. Not a nice setup in somebody's shed, but an actual, professional studio. There's a soundboard that has hundreds of buttons, gigantic speakers in the walls, a large window that reveals a recording booth on the other side. Not a mic in a corner, but a real recording booth with a real microphone.

An older white man in a polo shirt, jeans, and a baseball

cap meets Supreme at the doorway with a handshake. "Clarence! It's been a while!"

Clarence? Who the hell is Clarence?

"Hella long, James," Supreme says.

"Indeed," says the man who must be James. He turns to me and clasps my hand with both of his. "The superstar! James Irving, CEO of Vine Records. It's a pleasure to meet you, Bri."

Oh, shit. "I've heard of you."

He wraps his arm around my shoulder, pointing me out to this tatted Latino guy who sits at the soundboard and a white woman with a ponytail. "See? I like this one already. She's heard of me."

He chuckles. It's not until he does that Supreme and the other two laugh as well.

James makes himself comfortable on a leather sofa across the room. "This is my head of A&R, Liz." He points at the woman, who nods at me. "I gotta tell you, Bri. I'm so glad you agreed to let me see this studio session. So, so glad. You can learn a shit ton about an artist by watching how they work, you know? I've seen some goddamn geniuses in my day. Blows me away every fucking time, I swear."

He talks super fast. It's almost hard to keep up with him.

Supreme seems to keep up just fine. "Dawg, I'm telling you, you 'bout to witness some dope shit. Phenomenal even."

I look at him. Why is he talking like that?

"Oh, I believe it. We heard your interview, Bri," James goes on. "I already loved the song, but that? It sealed the goddamn deal for us, no bullshit. Only thing I like more than good rappers are good rappers who get people talking."

"Fa'sho," Supreme says for me. "We knew Hype was gon' push shorty's buttons from jump. I told her if she lost her shit, everybody would be talking, ya know?"

James chugs back some of his drink. "That's why you're a goddamn genius, Clarence. I still remember what you did with Lawless. God, that guy could've gone far. Such a tragedy, you know? I always tell folks, rap about that street shit but leave it in the streets. You can act like a fucking hoodlum and not be one."

Every inch of me has tensed up. "My dad wasn't a hoodlum."

The words come out so tight and cold that they silence the room.

Supreme tries to laugh again, but it's forced. He grabs my shoulder and squeezes it a little too hard. "Grief lingers, nah'mean?" he explains me to James.

I move my shoulder away. I don't need him to explain. I meant what I said.

But James takes his words as truth. "Understandably. Jesus, I can't imagine. Some of the bullshit you inner-city kids gotta deal with."

Or I'm just a daughter who doesn't let people disrespect her dad. What the hell?

There's a knock at the door, and the receptionist peeks in. "Mr. Irving, the other guest has arrived."

"Let him in!" James says, motioning her to do so. She opens the door all the way, and Dee-Nice steps into the studio.

He slaps palms with Supreme. He shakes James's hand. He shuffles a folder from under one arm to the other so that he can half-hug me. "Whaddup, baby girl? You ready to do this song?"

"Oh, yeah, she is," Supreme says.

Dee-Nice holds up the folder. "I got these bars ready."

So we're doing a song together. Okay, cool. "Damn, I'm slacking," I say. "I haven't decided what song I wanna do from my notebook. If y'all just give me about twenty minutes, I can write—"

Supreme laughs, and once again it brings on a chorus of laughter. "Nah, baby girl. Dee wrote your song for you."

Time out. Time. Out. "What?"

"I already heard the beat," Dee-Nice says. "Wrote it last night. Got your verses, the hook, everything."

"He let me hear it earlier," says Supreme. "I'm telling you, shit's straight fire."

James gives an excited clap. "Hell yes!"

Hold up, pause, back up, slow down, all of that. "I write my own stuff though."

"Nah," Supreme says, like I asked if he was cold or something. "Dee got you."

Did he not hear what I said? "But I got me."

Supreme laughs again, though this time it doesn't sound like he's amused. He seems to look around at everyone from behind those shades. "You hear this? She got her." He turns to me, and the laughter is gone. "Like I said, Dee got you."

Dee hands me the folder.

I open it. Instead of wildly scribbled rhymes all over a piece of notebook paper like I'd usually have, Dee has typed up an entire song. There are verses, a hook, and a bridge. He even wrote a damn intro, like I can't get in there and spontaneously say something.

What the hell?

But the lyrics? The lyrics are what really get me.

"'I pack gats the size of rats, and give fiends what they need,'" I mutter, and can't believe I'm saying this my own self. "'In the hood they call me PMS, I make chicks . . . bleed'?"

This has gotta be a joke.

"Fire, right?" Supreme says.

Like hell. For some reason, I think about those kids at Maple Grove. When they repeated "On the Come Up" back to me, I felt some kinda way. I knew what I meant with that song, but I don't know if they did.

The idea of those six-year-olds repeating that I make chicks bleed . . . it makes me feel sick. "I can't rap this."

Supreme gives another one of those unamused chuckles, and it leads to more chuckles.

"I told you, James, shorty got a mouth on her," he says.

"Aw, you know me, I love that sassy black-girl shit," says James.

The fuck? That word *sassy* has always rubbed me the wrong way for some reason, like *articulate*. "Sassy black girl" is ten times worse. "What the hell did you—"

"Y'all, give us a few minutes," says Supreme. He takes me by my shoulder and guides me out into the hall. The second we're out there though, I shake him off.

"Look, you can say what you want," I tell him straight up. "But I'm not about to rap something I didn't write, and I'm damn sure not about to rap something that's not me. I already got people thinking I'm a hood rat and a hoodlum. That song won't help!"

Slowly, Supreme lifts his sunglasses, and I can't lie, I don't know what to expect. I've never seen him without them. I've always wondered if he was scarred or had lost an eye or something. But deep-set brown eyes look back at me.

"Didn't I tell your ass to follow my lead?" he growls.

I step back. "But—"

He advances. "You're trying to ruin this shit before we get it?"

I may have backed up but I'm not backing down. "I can write a song myself. I don't need Dee to write shit for me. Hype already clowned me, saying I had a ghostwriter. I can't go and actually have one. That's phony as hell."

Supreme clenches his hands at his sides. "Baby girl"—he

says each word slowly, as if to make sure I hear him—"you're in the music business now. Keyword, *business*. This is about making money. That man in there"—he points toward the studio door—"got more cash at his disposal than he knows what to do with. We're about to damn near commit robbery and take as much of it as we can. You just gotta do this song."

I hear him, and I almost get it, but I shake my head. "That song isn't me. This ain't cool."

He slaps the back of one hand into the palm of the other. "Neither is being broke! Or food drives! What? You scared you won't look 'real' rapping this shit? I can get you some goons to roll with, baby girl. Make this shit look as real as possible. I did it for your daddy."

"What?"

"Law wasn't no damn gangster when I met him," Supreme says. "He was barely out of the church choir. Working some ol' raggedy-ass jobs to support your momma and your brother. *I'm the one* who told him he had to start rapping that street shit. *I'm the one* who told him to roll with them GDs to look authentic. But his ass took the shit seriously.

"You though"—he holds my cheeks between his hands—"you can be smarter than that. You just gotta remember to play the role, not become it. We can do everything Law and I didn't get a chance to do."

Granddaddy calls the eyes the windows to the soul, and I suddenly get that. Now that Supreme doesn't have his shades on, I can finally see what I am to him: a do-over of my dad.

I move away from him.

"I'm trying to help you, Li'l Law," he claims. "I'm your Moses, leading you to the promised land! Get out of your goddamn feelings and let's get this money."

Let's. We. Us. *I'm* the one going into that booth. *I'm* the one who people will see and talk about. Not him.

Yet I follow him back into the studio like the desperate idiot that I am.

Soundboard guy plays the beat, and Dee-Nice goes over the song with me so I can get the flow right. James watches and listens eagerly over on the sofa, elbowing Supreme at every other line I recite.

I go into the recording booth and slip the headphones over my ears.

Everyone watches me from the other side of the glass. There's excitement in their eyes. Supreme wears an eager grin. They're ready for me to perform.

I catch a glimpse of my reflection in the window.

When I was around eight, Grandma and Granddaddy took me and Trey to the zoo. There was this one family who ended up at every exhibit at the same time we did. The two kids would try to get the animals to do whatever they wanted. They'd tell them to make sounds or come closer to the glass, anything in hopes of getting a laugh. The animals wouldn't obey, of course, but I remember feeling so bad for them. It must've been awful to have people gawk at you and demand you entertain them how they see fit.

I'm suddenly in an exhibit, and there's a room full of people waiting for me to entertain them. I have to say what they want me to say. Be what they want me to be.

The worst part? I do it.

THIRTY-ONE

"You okay, Bookie?"

I look away from the window and over at my mom. "Why you ask?"

It's Tuesday, and she just picked me up from ACT prep to go see Aunt Pooh.

"Because that's my third time asking if you're okay, and this is only the first time you've heard me. You've been so quiet."

"Oh. Sorry."

"Nothing to apologize for. Something on your mind?"

More than I'd like. I recorded that song for Supreme and them. They loved it. I hated it. James still wasn't fully "sold" though. Said he wants to see me perform it and see how people react to it.

I really am just something to entertain them.

Supreme's all in though. Said he's gonna set it up so I can

premiere the song in a live performance at the Ring. He's booking it for next Thursday. James claims that if I knock it out of the park, a big contract is as good as mine.

It doesn't feel like it'll be mine though. Not when I'm saying somebody else's words and fitting somebody else's image just to get it.

I don't know how to tell Jay about it. It could go two ways—she'll either A, be pissed that I've kept all this from her, or B, be ready to handle Supreme. Of course, because I'm still a minor, I can't sign anything without her permission. But I got myself into this, and I gotta figure it out.

I sit up some more. "It's nothing. Just school stuff."

"Well, whatever it is, you can tell me. You know I always got you."

"I know," I say. "I got you too."

We pull into the parking lot of this tall brick building that seems like it's been around since before my grandparents were born. It would look like a regular building, honestly, but there's a barbed-wire fence around the back.

We leave our phones, watches, and anything else that could set off the metal detector in the car. Jay only takes her keys and ID. This is the routine we've always followed whenever we've visited Aunt Pooh in jail. It helps us see her quicker.

There's a guy sitting on the curb near the entrance. His head rests between his knees, making it hard to see his face. But his hair is half braided, half Afro. If I didn't know any better . . .

"Scrap?" I say.

He looks up. It's Scrap, all right.

"Boy." Jay outstretches her arms. Scrap walks into them. "I thought they got you, too."

"Nah. I wasn't there when it happened. But everybody else . . ."

Is locked up. Word is, most of the Maple Grove Garden Disciples got busted.

Jay frames his face with her hands like he's a little boy. I guess when you've known someone their entire life, you can still see them that way. Pooh and Scrap have been running together since diaper days. "Well, I'm glad you're okay. You're here to see P, huh?"

"Yeah. She asked me to come when y'all came. Hope that's all right."

"Of course it is. You're family." Jay takes his hand. "C'mon."

Scrap follows her inside. Something's off about him. I can't put my finger on it. He doesn't walk, he marches. His jaw ticks; his face is tight. It's like he's a bubble—one wrong move and he'll burst at any second.

Pink and red streamers and a little Valentine's Day banner decorate the sign-in desk, but if you're coming in here to visit somebody, it's hard to celebrate any holiday.

Curtis brought me a little bouquet of candy bars to school today. I gotta admit, it did make the day a little better. Boy's got more game than I thought.

Jay gives the lady at the sign-in desk Aunt Pooh's real name—Katricia Bordeaux. It's always weird hearing it. She's been Pooh my whole life. We fill out paperwork and go through security before we're led to this small gray room. There are no windows, so no sunlight. Just stark bright lights that you see long after closing your eyes. A guard tells us to sit at the table and wait.

Scrap drums the table the whole time. After about twenty minutes, one of the guards brings Aunt Pooh in.

Jay hugs her the moment she can. Aunt Pooh and Scrap do their little handshake. Then Aunt Pooh looks at me.

I didn't know that I'd wanna cry when I'd see her, but I swear I almost do. She holds her arms out, and I let her wrap me up in the biggest, tightest hug I didn't know I needed.

She kisses the side of my head. "Missed you, Li'l Bit."

"I missed you, too," I murmur into her shoulder.

The four of us sit at the table. Aunt Pooh has to sit across from us though. Jail rules. It's supposed to be so we won't slip her any contraband, but it always feels like they're saying she's diseased or something. Jail seems isolating as hell, even when people visit you.

"I talked to your attorney this morning," says Jay. "It's one of those court-appointed ones. He thinks they'll have you arraigned early next week."

"Good," says Aunt Pooh. "Sooner I can get outta here, sooner me and Bri can get our come up." She holds her palm out to me across the table with a grin. I slap it. "I heard about your interview. I promise, I can handle that fool for you once I'm out. No question."

Jay glances back and forth between us. "What interview? What fool?"

This definitely isn't how I wanted her to find out. My leg suddenly won't stay still.

"The DJ Hype interview, you know?" Pooh says.

Jay turns all the way toward me. "No. I don't know."

I stare straight ahead. If you look an angry black momma in her eyes, there's a chance you will turn into a pillar of salt on the spot, like ol' girl in the Bible.

"Yeah, Bri went on his show," Aunt Pooh snitches. "He riled her up apparently. Accused her of not writing her shit, all kinds of nonsense. I heard you went straight off, Bri." Aunt Pooh laughs into her fist. "Got folks in here even talking."

I can *feel* Jay's glare. It's bad. Oh, it's bad. I stare at the wall. Somebody carved "D wuz here" into the cinder block, and I don't know what's worse—the fact that they were bragging about being here or that they can't spell "was."

"Didn't I tell you to lay low, Bri?" Jay says.

"It's all good, Jayda," Aunt Pooh says. "Don't blame her. This on Hype." She looks at Scrap. "How that other thing going?"

"They eating this shit up," he bites out. "We gotta handle them."

"Handle who?" I ask.

"That's what I wanna know," Jay adds.

"It's them Crown bitches," Scrap hisses. "They think it's funny that most of the Maple Grove GDs got taken down. Now they moving in our territory and shit. Even bragging about how they took Law's chain from Bri. Flaunting it around."

"Aww, hell nah," Aunt Pooh says.

The same words go through my head, but for an entirely different reason. Once again, this is not how I wanted my mom to find out.

She turns to me. "How in the world did they get your dad's chain?"

It's a question, not an accusation, but honestly, it should be an accusation. I should've done more to keep that safety net for us. I swallow. "They robbed me. I swear, I didn't wanna give it up, but—"

"*Robbed?*" she shrieks. "Oh my God, Brianna! Why didn't you tell me?"

"Oh, don't worry. I already sent a message to bitch-ass that did it. Just didn't get the chain back," Aunt Pooh says. "We working on that though." She eyes Scrap, and he nods.

Jay looks from him to her. "What?"

"I got some new li'l homies running with me now," says Scrap. "They down for whatever. Bri just gotta give the word."

"Facts," says Aunt Pooh, slapping his palm.

It feels like a boulder just dropped into my stomach. "It's on me to give the word?"

"They took it from you," Aunt Pooh says. "I mean, hell yeah, we down for whatever to get one over on them fools, but this your call ultimately."

How the hell do I suddenly have an entire gang at my disposal?

Jay closes her eyes and puts her hands up. "Wait. Are y'all saying what I think y'all are saying?"

"It's war," Aunt Pooh says, as if it's nothing. "Word is some of them snitched on us in the first place. That's why the cops was watching. Now they trying to move in on our shit, clowning us, and got the nerve to brag about robbing my niece? Nah. It's whatever now."

We've started a gang war. People may lose their lives because of us. Shit, what if it comes back at me?

I don't know how long it's quiet, but it is for a while. Jay stares at Aunt Pooh with her mouth slightly open.

"Wow," she says. "Wow, wow, wow."

"Jay, you gotta understand," says Aunt Pooh. "This 'bout respect! We can't let them fools think they won."

My mom's eyes glisten. "They haven't won. But you're so lost that you've lost."

"What?"

"You're in jail, Katricia," Jay says. "*Jail!* Yet you're sitting here plotting some of that same street mess that landed you here in the first place. You don't care that this has been hell for your family. You aren't showing any remorse. You're plotting!"

"Jayda, they took Law's chain," Aunt Pooh says. "They bragging about pointing a gun in your baby's face! They laughing about me being in here. I'm supposed to let that go?"

"Yes!" Jay says. "I don't give a damn about that chain! Bri is okay, and that's all that matters to me."

"This bigger than that though," Scrap says. "We can't let them get away with this shit."

"Actually, you can." Jay looks at Aunt Pooh again. "You know what? I'm starting to realize that maybe you need to stay in here."

"What? You not gon' bail me out?"

"With what?" Jay bellows. "What, you got some money stashed somewhere? Huh? Please tell me if you do. Maybe I can use it to pay some of my goddamn bills!"

"Look, I got it all figured out, a'ight? You can get a loan. Use that to pay my bail and pay for a better attorney who will clear me of these charges. I'll pay you back—"

"By doing the same stuff that put you in here in the first place!" Jay yells. She puts her hands together and holds them at her mouth. "I've cried over you," she says thickly. "But I don't think you've cried over yourself, and that's the problem."

"Jay, c'mon, please?" Her voice cracks. "If they get me for this, I'm going to prison! I can't go to prison!"

"I don't want you to go," Jay says. "I don't want you in the system, Katricia. Hell, I've been telling you for *years* that it's built to keep you in it. But you gotta get the streets out of you somehow. Maybe this is it." She stands and holds her hand out to me. "C'mon, Brianna."

"Bri," Aunt Pooh pleads. "Bri, c'mon. Tell her I'm gon' change."

I can't say what I don't know.

"Brianna, let's go," Jay repeats.

"Bri, tell her!"

"Stop using my child as your cover! It's not on her to fix you, Katricia! It's on you!"

Aunt Pooh's jaw hardens. She straightens up, lifts her chin, and narrows her eyes. "So it's like that? You left me to fend for myself when you got hooked on that shit, and now you leaving me to fend for myself again, huh?"

It's a punch in my gut, and she's not even talking about me. "How can you say that? This isn't on—"

Jay puts her hand up to cut me off. She looks solely at Pooh. "You know what? I'm so sorry for abandoning you. It's one of the biggest mistakes of my life. But there's only so long you can blame what you've been through for what you do. At some point, you gotta blame yourself."

She grabs my hand and takes me with her. I look back at Aunt Pooh. Her face is hard, but her lips tremble. I've got a feeling it's the last time I'll see her for a long time.

The clouds seem darker than they were when we first got here. Or I'm just imagining it. There's no way the sky is mourning my aunt, too.

In the driver's seat, Jay wipes her eyes. Her tears started the moment we walked out of the building.

I bite my lip. "You're really not gonna try to bail her out?"

"I'm not getting a loan to pay her bail when we have bills, Bri, and I'm especially not doing that for somebody who's just gonna be up to the same ol' mess in no time."

"She can change though," I damn near plead. "I know she can."

"I know it, too, Bri, but *she's* gotta know it. *She* has to decide that enough is enough. We can't do it for her."

"What if she never gets there?"

Jay holds her hand out. I put mine in it. "You have to prepare yourself for that possibility, baby."

I don't like it, I don't like it, I don't like it. "I don't wanna lose her," I croak.

"I don't either," she says roughly. "God knows, I don't. We can love her with everything in us, but it doesn't matter if she doesn't love herself. She's sitting in there more worried about a chain than about her own well-being."

I stare down at my chest where the pendant used to be. "I'm sorry they took it."

"You don't need to apologize for that, baby," Jay says. "But girl, what in the world is going on with you? First it was the song, and I found out about that from a *TV report*. Now this chain and the Hype interview? What else are you hiding, Brianna? Huh?"

There is a superpower that black mommas possess—they

can somehow go from being gentle to firm in a matter of seconds. Hell, sometimes in the same sentence.

My mouth is dry all of a sudden. "I . . . "

"What. Else?"

I stare at my Timbs. "Supreme."

"What about Supreme? And those shoes didn't give birth to you. Look at me when I'm talking to you."

I make my eyes meet hers. "He's got a big record deal in the works for me."

"Whoa, whoa, whoa. Why would *he* have a record deal for *you*? He's not your manager."

"But he is. I hired him."

"Oh, *you* hired him," she says with this fake lightness that scares me. "My bad, I must've missed the memo that you grown. Last time I checked, you were sixteen years old, Brianna. Six. Teen!"

"I was gonna tell you, I swear! I was just trying to get everything into place first. This was my way of saving us."

"It's not on you to save us!" She closes her eyes. "God, I'm not doing my job."

Oh, crap. I never meant for her to blame herself. "It's not like that."

"It must be. For you to be out here, pulling stunts like this to help us, that means I'm not doing enough."

"But you are." My voice cracks. "You and Trey try so hard. I just wanted to make things easier. But I'm making it worse for myself. People are saying all kinds of stuff about me after that interview."

Jay takes a deep breath. "Hype got you, huh?" She's gentle again.

"Unfortunately. I acted a fool. Supreme's eating it up though. The record exec, too. They think it's great that people think I'm a 'ratchet hood rat.' Supreme calls it a 'role.'"

"I'm not surprised. Supreme's always been money hungry. That's where he and your daddy clashed. Let me guess, he baited you, didn't he? Threw something expensive at you so you'd wanna hire him."

I stare at the boots. "Yep. He bought me these Timbs."

"Wait, those aren't the boots I bought you from the swap meet?"

"No. Those came apart."

"What? Why didn't you tell me?"

I fumble with my fingers. "Because I didn't want you to feel bad. Like you probably do right now."

She sighs. "Lord. You should've told me, Bri. You should've told me all of this. I could've kept you out of so much mess. Instead, you lied to me."

"Wait, I didn't lie."

"Omitting the truth is lying, Bri," she says. "Plus, at some point, you flat-out lied. You've been sneaking around to meet with Supreme. That requires a lie."

Damn, she's right. "I'm sorry."

Jay kisses her teeth. "Oh, I'm sure you are. Especially since this is about to come to a halt. All of this li'l rap stuff of yours? It's over."

"What? No! This could be my shot at making it."

"Didn't you just say that people are making assumptions about you?" she asks. "You wanna keep going, knowing that?"

"I just wanna make it!"

I'm loud, I'm rough. But I'm also desperate.

Feels like hours pass as my mom quietly stares at me.

"Brianna," she says, "do you know what your aunt's biggest problem is?"

I look at the jailhouse. That's kinda obvious at the moment. "She's locked up."

"No. That's not even her biggest problem," says Jay. "Pooh doesn't know who she is, and by not knowing who she is, she doesn't know her worth. So, who are you?"

"What?"

"Who are you?" she repeats. "Of the millions and billions of people in the world, you're the only person who can answer that. Not people online or at your school. I can't even answer that. I can say who *I think* you are." She cups my cheek. "And I think you're brilliant, talented, courageous, beautiful. You're my miracle. But you're the only one who can say who you are with authority. So, who are you?"

"I'm . . ."

I can't find the words.

My mom leans over and kisses my forehead. "Work on figuring it out. I think it'll give you more answers than you realize."

She cranks up the Jeep. Before she can back out of the parking spot, her phone rings.

"Baby, get that for me, please?"

"Okay," I say, and fish through her purse. It takes a second—my mom keeps her purse full of "just in case" stuff, like Kleenex, gum, a pocketknife. She's ready for whatever.

I grab her phone, but I don't recognize the number. "I don't know who this is."

"Answer it like you've got some sense then."

I roll my eyes. I know what she means—talk all "proper," but damn, act "like I have some sense" makes it seem as if I have none. "Hello?"

"Hi. Is Mrs. Jayda Jackson available?" a man asks.

That voice is familiar. I think. It could be a bill collector for all I know, and they always get the dial tone. "May I ask who's calling?"

"Yes, this is Superintendent Cook."

The phone falls from my hand.

"Brianna!" Jay scolds through her teeth. "I know damn well you didn't drop my phone! Give it here!"

I scoop it up from the floor.

She snatches it. "Hello? Who is this?"

Dr. Cook responds, and the car slightly swerves. She almost dropped the phone, too.

"I'm so sorry, Dr. Cook," Jay says, and cuts me a glare. "My daughter can be reckless."

Why she gotta throw me under the bus though?

Dr. Cook starts talking, and my mom pulls over to the side of the road. I can't make out what he's saying for the life of me. Jay just goes, "Uh-huh, yes, sir," over and over again.

"Well?" I whisper, but she swats in my direction to shut me up.

After an eternity she says, "Thank you so much, sir. I will see you next week."

My eyes widen. The moment she hangs up, I'm like, "You got the job?"

"An interview. But it's an interview with a background check and fingerprints."

I'm missing something here. "What's so good about that?"

"It means that they are seriously considering hiring me," she says.

"So you . . ." This feels so surreal that it's hard to speak. "You may have a job?"

"Nothing's guaranteed, but based on what Dr. Cook just said"—she smiles—"I may have a job."

THIRTY-TWO

Saturday morning, I get a weird text from Sonny.

Meet me at Oak Park ASAP.

Oak Park is a couple of blocks away from my grandparents' house. Trey used to take me there almost every weekend when I was younger. It's where I saw Jay strung out that time.

It's also where Sonny spray-painted his rainbow fist piece.

It's on the side of the restrooms near the empty community pool. Granddaddy says the city used to open it up every summer. They've never done that in my lifetime.

I look around twice as I cross the park. I've still got the Crowns to think about. I've been ducking and hiding any time I spot a gray car in the neighborhood.

Sonny's and Malik's bikes are propped up against the back of the restroom wall. Should've known Malik would be here, too. Sonny paces in the dirt so much, a small dust tornado is swirling near his feet. Malik says something, but it doesn't slow Sonny down.

I hop off my bike and walk it over to them. "Hey, what's up?"

"He's on his way," Sonny says.

"Who?"

"Rapid! Why else would I have y'all meet me here?"

"Oh. I thought you needed my help hiding a body or something."

Sonny's lips thin. "And *I'm* the disturbing one?"

Malik glances at his phone. "What time did he say he'd be here?"

Sonny takes a peek at his phone, too. "Ten on the dot. He told me to look out for a black Benz."

"Damn, a Benz?" I say. "At sixteen? Somebody's got mon-ey." I rub my fingers together.

"Or he's really a fifty-year-old man," Malik just has to add.

The horror that appears on Sonny's face. "Not funny!"

Malik and I snicker. This is the closest we've come to speaking to each other in a while.

"My bad, my bad," Malik says, and takes Sonny's shoulder. "Look, Son', this is gonna work out, all right? You gotta believe that. If this guy isn't who he says he is, it's his loss. Not yours. Okay?"

Sonny slowly exhales. "Okay."

"Good." Malik straightens out Sonny's collar. He wore one

of his nice polo shirts today. I run my fingers along his curls to fix them. "No matter what happens, we're here," Malik reminds him.

"One hundred percent," I add.

Sonny smiles. "I'm glad y'all came—"

A black Mercedes turns into the parking lot.

"Take y'all asses and hide!" Sonny switches on us with the quickness.

I look him up and down. "Excuse you?"

"Hide!" He turns us both toward a tree. "I don't want him knowing I didn't trust him enough to not bring backup."

"But you didn't trust him enough," Malik says.

"Not the point! Go!"

We stumble behind a large oak tree that's big enough to hide us both. A car door closes. I peer around the tree trunk.

A brown-skinned boy crosses the park. His short hair has zigzags cut into it, and a cross pendant dangles from his neck.

It's Miles. Supreme's son-the-rapper-with-that-annoying-song Miles. "Holy shit," I mutter.

"Holy shit," Malik echoes me.

I can see the "Holy shit" all over Sonny's face, too. Miles holds the back of his neck and looks at Sonny sheepishly.

"I definitely wasn't expecting this," Malik says.

I guess he's talking to me again. "Yeah. Me either."

"What do you think they're saying?"

I tilt my head. Sonny's eyes are super wide. Like a cartoon's. I smirk. I don't know what Sonny's *saying*, but he's definitely thinking, "What the hell?"

"Ha! Probably right." Malik says in his best Sonny voice, "'Have I really been talking to a guy who thinks *swagerific* is a word?'"

I laugh. "'Am I gonna have to tell him that I hate his song?'" My imitation of Sonny is not as good as Malik's, but it makes him chuckle. "I don't know if this is gonna go well."

Or maybe it will. They're smiling as they look into each other's eyes.

"Oh, wow," says Malik.

"I still got hands ready though if Miles hurts him somehow," I say.

"For real," Malik agrees. "I've missed you, Breezy."

I turn around.

"As a friend," he clarifies. "I miss talking to you."

"And whose fault is it that we haven't been talking?"

"Um, yours," he says.

My mouth drops. "How?"

"Bri, c'mon, you gotta know why I was pissed at you. The night of the robbery, you were more concerned about that chain than about me, your friend who got a black eye. I was supposed to be cool with that? Then you basically asked me to lie to my mom so you and Pooh could do some dirt."

Okay, yeah. He has a point. "I just wanted the chain back, Malik. It was my family's safety net. I figured we could pawn it if things got worse."

"See, that's the problem. Lately, you only care about money.

Money isn't everything, Bri."

"That's so easy for you to say. I know your mom works hard and that y'all aren't rich, but you've got it better than me. We didn't have lights for a while, Malik. We've barely had food some days. You aren't worried about stuff like that. I am. My freaking shoes fell apart, bruh. You're standing here in Jordans."

He glances down at his kicks and bites his lip. "Yeah. I guess I understand."

"No, you don't," I say. "It's okay that you don't. I'm *glad* you don't. But I need you to try to."

"It's been rough, huh?"

I swallow. "Real."

Silence.

"I'm sorry I haven't been there for you," he says. "I'm also sorry for making a move on you. It was foul, for a lot of reasons."

I nod. "It was."

"Wow, no 'Don't be so hard on yourself, Malik'?"

"Hell no. It was a fuckboy move."

"Typical Bri." Malik stuffs his hands in his pockets. "Things are so different than they used to be. *We're* different. Hard to figure all of this out sometimes, you know? But do you think we can figure out how to be different and still be friends?"

I'd like to say that ten, twenty, thirty years from now, me, Sonny, and Malik will be as tight as we've always been, but that could be a lie. We're changing in different ways, and we'll keep changing.

Yet I'd like to think that we care enough to get to know

whoever we become. Hey, maybe someday Malik and I will have something beyond friendship. Right now, I simply want my friend back.

"Yeah," I tell him. "I think we can still be friends."

He smiles. "Good. Because when you get that Grammy, I expect to get a shout-out along with an invitation to all of the after-parties."

I roll my eyes. "Opportunist."

He hooks his arm around my neck. "Nah. Just one of your biggest cheerleaders."

Sonny and Miles make their way over to us. They're so close that their hands brush.

"Guys, this is Miles, without a *z*," Sonny says. "Miles, this is Malik and Bri, my best friends slash potential bodyguards. You've met Bri though."

"Yeah, when you said that bullshit about her dad in the Ring," Malik points out.

Oh, we're definitely good again, because here Malik is, going in on somebody on my behalf. I missed having him in my corner.

Miles shifts his weight from foot to foot. "My bad. I apologized to Bri, if that helps. I was only saying what my dad wanted me to say."

Sonny cocks his eyebrows. "Your dad *wanted* you to be an asshole?"

"Basically. It's part of who Milez with a *z* is. But that's his creation. It's not me."

Not surprised. Supreme seems to be all about creating people. "Does he know you're—"

"Gay? Yeah. He knows. He chooses to ignore it."

Malik tilts his head, and, because he's Malik, he goes for it. "Your dad makes you pretend to be straight?"

"Malik!" I hiss. Good lord. "You can't ask people stuff like that!"

"Why not? He hinted at it!"

"That wasn't a hint. He does make me pretend to be straight," Miles says. "Milez with a *z* is supposed to be the teen heartthrob all the girls love, and one of Dad's next cash cows."

He looks at me as he says it. I'm the other one.

"Nobody can know that Miles with an *s* hates rapping, prefers photography, and is completely, one hundred percent gay."

"Why'd you show up here then?" Sonny asks him.

Miles twists his foot behind him. "Because. For once, I decided to do what *I* wanna do. I wanted to finally meet the guy who keeps me up every night, talking about everything and nothing, who makes me smile a hell of a lot, even though I didn't know how cute he was until now."

Sonny blushes so hard. "Oh."

"I'm done being who my dad wants me to be," Miles says. "It's not worth it."

Does he mean what I think he means? "You're giving up your rap career?"

Miles slowly nods. "Yeah. I am. Besides, is it really mine if I'm not being myself?"

THIRTY-THREE

I'm still thinking about what Miles said yesterday when we arrive at Christ Temple.

I guess the prospect of a job gave my mom the courage to come today and face the gossip. This is the first Sunday we've been here in a while, and the only thing church folks love more than talking about people is talking about people who haven't been to church.

Whatever.

Trey holds Kayla's hand as he follows me and Jay across the gravel parking lot next to the church. Earlier, he introduced Kayla to Jay as his girlfriend. They must be pretty serious if he invited her to church: church-where-everybody-is-gonna-talk-about-him-bringing-a-girl-to-church. That's major.

Seems like half the congregation fills the foyer. Jay wears a bigger smile than usual as we make our rounds, greeting folks.

It's an unspoken rule that when you've been gone, you have to speak to everybody. Well, my mom and my brother do. I stand here, trying to keep my facial expressions in check.

Pastor Eldridge's wife hugs us and says that we've been gone so long, she almost forgot what we look like. I only side-eye her a little bit. Sister Barnes tries me though. Jay tells her good morning, and Sister Barnes responds with, "Y'all been too busy for the Lord?"

I open my mouth, but before I can tell her to kiss our asses, Jay moves close to me. So close that nobody notices how hard she pinches my arm.

"Brianna, why don't you go have a seat," she tells me, which is mom-at-church speak for "Girl, you better go somewhere before I whoop your behind."

I'd much rather sit in the corner anyway. I plop down in one of the high-back chairs under the portrait of Pastor Eldridge. On one hand, I don't get why my mom is taking all of this shade from people. But on the other, she must be in a really good headspace if she's willing to take it.

Sister Daniels comes into the foyer, in a floral dress with a matching hat that's big enough to block the sun. Curtis holds the door open for her.

I sit up a little. My edges? Laid and slayed. Jay French-braided my hair last night, and I put my silk bonnet on extra tight to keep everything in check. This dress and these wedge heels? Super cute. But the way Curtis's eyes light up when he sees me, I don't think I needed any of it.

He moves around people and makes his way over to me, giving quick "hellos" and polite nods along the way.

"Hey, Bri," he says, the smile all on his face and in his voice.

Here I go, cheesing. "Hey."

Curtis sits on the arm of the chair and checks me out. "I know I ain't supposed to cuss in church, but damn, girl, you looking kinda fine today."

"You're not so bad yourself," I say. Most Sundays, he shows up in a polo and dress pants. Today, he put on a suit and tie.

Curtis adjusts the tie a bit. "Thanks. I was scared I was gon' look like I should be giving the sermon. Glad you like it, since I did this for you."

"You don't need to."

"Oh, so I'm sexy without it?" Curtis wiggles his eyebrows.

I laugh. "Bye, Curtis."

"You can't admit it, don't be scared," he says. "So, this date of ours. We never figured out the details. I was thinking we could leave campus one day this week and go somewhere around Midtown for lunch."

I get this weird feeling that somebody's watching us. I glance around.

Somebody's watching all right. My mom and my brother are near the sanctuary door, paying more attention to us than to Pastor Eldridge. They both look amused.

Lord. I can hear them now. Jay's gonna try to get all in my

business, and Trey's gonna mess with me worse than Sonny.

But you know what? I don't care. "Lunch sounds good," I tell Curtis.

"Tomorrow works for you?"

"Yep."

"First time I'll actually look forward to a Monday." Curtis leans over and kisses my cheek, so close to my lips that I almost wish he would've kissed them. "Later, Princess."

I go over to my mom, Trey, and Kayla, and this grin seems stuck on my face.

"Ooooh, Bri got a boyfriend," Trey teases. "Ooooh!"

"Shut up," I say. But boyfriend? I wouldn't say he's my boyfriend. Yet I wouldn't have a problem with him having that title.

Jesus, my face is starting to hurt from smiling so hard.

Jay goes, "Mm," which in black momma speak could mean a number of things. "I just wanna know how long that's been going on, and do we need to have a refresher course on the birds and the bees?"

"Really?" I groan.

"Yes, ma'am. I'm too young to be a grandma. Ain't nobody got time for that."

Okay, Sweet Brown.

We get our usual pew near the back of the sanctuary. Grandma and Granddaddy come up the center aisle together. His silver tie matches her hat. He carries a stack of empty gold plates. It's their Sunday to staff the communion table, which means they gotta go get the crackers and grape juice.

"All right now, y'all," Granddaddy says. He gives Jay a kiss and gets his sugar from me. "Who is this beautiful young lady with y'all today?"

"Grandma and Granddaddy, this is Kayla, my girlfriend," Trey says. "Kayla, these are my grandparents."

Kayla shakes their hands. Oh, yeah, this is really serious if he's introducing her to our grandparents. "Nice meeting you, Mr. and Mrs. Jackson. I've heard a lot about you."

"I hope it's all good," Grandma says.

"Of course, Grandma," Trey says, a little too brightly. He's lying.

"We still set for after church, Jayda?" Granddaddy asks.

"Yes, sir, we are."

"What's after church?" Trey asks.

"We're having a family dinner," Grandma says. She looks at my mom. "All of us."

Hold up. She's not glaring at Jay. In fact, Grandma has been over here more than a minute and hasn't made one snide remark about her yet. Then, on top of that, my mom is invited to *family* dinner, as in, Grandma considers her part of the family?

Oh, God. "Somebody's dying! Who's dying? Granddaddy, it's your diabetes, ain't it?"

"What?" Granddaddy says. "Li'l Bit, I swear, you jump to conclusions so fast, you gon' pull a muscle. Ain't nobody dying. We just gon' have dinner. Kayla, you invited, too. I gotta tell you, I make some of the best blackberry cobbler you gon' ever have in your life. Bring your appetite now."

"See y'all later," Grandma says, and she and Granddaddy walk off. She didn't even ask me and Trey to sit with her today.

I turn to my mom. I'm so confused. "What's going on?"

The band begins an upbeat song, and the choir marches down the aisles, swaying their arms and clapping to the beat.

"We'll talk later, baby," Jay claims. She stands and claps along with them.

I still haven't gotten any answers when we pull into my grandparents' driveway.

Grandma and Granddaddy live in "that house" in the Garden. The one that almost looks too nice to be in the hood. It's brick with an iron fence surrounding it. There's a second story and an expanded den that my grandparents added back when my dad was a kid. Grandma keeps the front yard looking nice. They've got a small fountain for birds and enough flowers to give a botanical garden a run for its money.

I can't help the feeling of déjà vu that hits me. Jay once pulled into this driveway and left me and Trey here when things got tough. They're not nearly as tough now, but I'm not sure I like this. "What's going on?" I ask.

Jay puts her Jeep in park. It's just me and her. Trey and Kayla went to the store in his car. Grandma asked him to pick up some buttermilk and cornmeal for the cornbread. "Like your grandparents said, we're gonna have dinner and talk about some things."

"What kinda things?"

"It's good stuff, I promise."

I nod. I hate that that five-year-old is still inside of me, and I hate that she's freaking out right now. I mean, I know my mom isn't about to leave me here again, but that fear. It's deep, but it's there, like it's part of my DNA.

Jay stares at the house, lightly tapping the steering wheel. "Every time I pull in this driveway, I can't help but think about the day I left you and Trey here. I don't think I've ever gotten your screams for me out of my ears."

I didn't know that. "Really?"

"Yeah," she says softly. "Hardest day of my life. Even harder than the day we lost your daddy. I couldn't control his death. No decision I made could've changed that. But *I* decided to do drugs, *I* decided to bring you and Trey here. I knew that the moment I pulled out of this driveway, it would change everything. Knew it. Did it anyway."

I can't find any words.

Jay takes a deep breath. "I know I've told you a million times, but I'm sorry, baby. I'll always regret putting you through that. I'm sorry that you still have nightmares about it."

I look at her. "What?"

"You talk in your sleep, Bri. That's why I check on you so much at night."

It's the secret I planned to die with, I swear. I never even wanted her to know that I remember that day. I blink fast. "I didn't mean for you to find—"

"Hey." She lifts my chin. "It's okay. I also know that it's hard for you to trust that I won't end up on drugs again. I get it. But I hope you know that every single day, my goal is to be here for you."

I knew it was a daily fight for her to stay clean. I just didn't realize I was the reason she fights.

We're quiet for a while. My mom strokes my cheek.

"I love you," she says.

There's a lot I don't know and may never know. I don't know why she chose drugs over me and Trey. I don't know if five-year-old Bri will ever stop being afraid. I don't know if Jay'll stay clean for the rest of her life. But I know that she loves me.

"I love you too . . . Mom."

One word, one syllable. All of my life it's been synonymous with Jay but for years it hasn't been easy to say. I guess I gotta work on it, like I've gotta work on trusting that I won't lose her again.

Her eyes glisten. She must have noticed that I rarely call her that, too. She frames my face and kisses my forehead. "C'mon. Let's go inside and pray your grandma hasn't decided to slip some poison on my plate."

Granddaddy lets us in. I don't think my grandparents have changed anything in their house since Trey and I moved out.

There's a painting of President Obama on the living room wall (the *only* president, according to Granddaddy), right between Dr. King and a portrait of my grandparents on their wedding day. There's this portrait of Grandma in a feathered boa and a diamond bracelet. (I've never asked and don't wanna know.) Next to it, there's a painting of a much younger Granddaddy in his navy uniform. There are pictures of me, Dad, and Trey all over the house. Wallet-size photos of my grandparents' nieces and nephews line the shelf in the hallway, along with the little baby Jesus and praying-hands statues that Grandma collects.

Granddaddy goes to the backyard to work on this old pickup truck he's been restoring since I was a kid. Grandma's in the kitchen. She's changed into one of her favorite muumuus and already has a couple of pots and pans on the stovetop.

"You need help with anything, Mrs. Jackson?" J—Mom—asks.

"Yeah. Hand me that seasoning salt out the cabinet. You think you can get them greens going for me?"

Who is this alien, and what has it done with my grandmother? See, Grandma never lets anyone cook in her kitchen. Nev-er. For her to let my mom help out with dinner . . .

This is the goddamn *Twilight Zone*. I swear it is.

Meanwhile, I'm only allowed to sit and watch. Grandma says I "ain't got a lick of patience," therefore I "ain't touching one pot or pan in her kitchen."

Trey and Kayla show up. Trey goes out back to help

Granddaddy. I honestly don't think they do a thing to that truck. They just go out there to talk about stuff they don't want us to hear. Kayla asks if she can help with dinner. Grandma gives her this sugary sweet smile and says, "That's all right, baby. Just sit your pretty self down."

Translation: Girl, I don't know you well enough to let you in my kitchen like that.

Grandma tells Kayla all about her recipes though. It only takes Kayla saying, "This already smells divine, Mrs. Jackson," and Grandma's head practically doubles in size. When she starts telling Kayla how to make cornbread, that's when I slip out. Nothing makes me hungrier than people talking about food, and my stomach is already growling like it belongs in a cage.

I go upstairs. Whenever I spend holidays with my grandparents, I stay in my old bedroom.

Just like the house, my room hasn't changed at all. I think Grandma expected me to come back someday, and for things to be the way they used to be, right down to me being the Tweety Bird–loving eleven-year-old who cried when she had to leave.

I throw myself onto the bed. It's always weird being here, can't lie. It's like stepping into a time machine or something. Not just because of the Tweety shrine but all of the memories made in this room. Sonny, Malik, and I spent so much time in here. It's where Trey introduced me to Uno. Granddaddy played dolls with me in here.

My mom isn't part of any of those memories though.

There's a knock at the door, and my mom peeks in. Trey's behind her. "Hey. Okay if we come in?" she asks.

I sit up. "Yeah, sure—"

"I ain't gotta ask to come in this room," Trey says, and lets himself in. Then he has the nerve to plop onto my bed.

"Um, excuse you? This is still my room."

"Wow," my mom says, looking around. "Tweety, huh?"

She's never been in here before. Back when she only had me and Trey on weekends, she'd only get as far as the driveway. Grandma wouldn't let her come inside.

Mom moves around my room. She picks up one of my stuffed Tweety Birds. "I hadn't realized I hadn't been in here before. Wait, I take that back. I was definitely in here when it was your daddy's room."

"Wait, you saying that you two had sex in the room that ended up being Bri's room?" Trey asks.

There goes my appetite. "Ill!"

"Trey, stop!" says Mom. "They probably changed the bed."

Oh my God, she just confirmed that they did have sex in here. Trey falls onto the bed, screaming laughing. "Bri got the sex room!"

I punch him. "Shut up!"

"Cut it out, y'all," says Mom. "I need to talk to you about something."

"Hold up—first things first," Trey says, sitting up. "What's up with you and Grandma?"

"What you mean?"

"Y'all been here, what?" Trey glances at his watch. "An hour now, and nobody's argued yet. I haven't even heard any snide remarks."

"Fact," I say. "Y'all have been lacking shade like a sunny day."

Oh, God. I sound like Granddaddy.

"Your grandmother and I had a discussion," J—Mom—claims. "That's all."

"That's *all*?" says Trey. "Any discussion between you two is monumental. When did this happen?"

"The other day," Jay says. "We talked for a few hours. Hashed out a lot of things, even stuff from way back when."

"Did Jesus moderate it?" I ask. "'Cause that's the only way I see this working."

Trey goes, "Haaaa!"

Mom kisses her teeth. "Anyway! I'm not gonna act like we're best friends, hell no. That woman still knows how to work my nerves. But we realized that we love you two and want what's best for you. We're willing to set our differences aside in the name of that."

Trey picks up his phone. "Ah. That explains it. I just got a notification that it's below zero in hell."

I snort.

"Whatever, boy," says Mom. "We also came to a decision. Your grandparents offered that all three of us stay here until we get on our feet. I accepted."

"Whoa. Really?" I say.

"Hold up, hold up," Trey says. "We're moving in here?"

Wow. For once, I'm finding out when he finds out.

"Look, something may or may not come from my interview with Dr. Cook, but either way this will take some pressure off," Mom says. "I told your grandparents I'd help with household expenses, but this would mean a lot less bills to worry about. Besides, we've been trying to play catch-up on rent so long that it's almost impossible to catch up at this point."

"But I've got us," Trey claims.

"*I've* got us," she says. "I appreciate all you're doing to keep us afloat, baby, I really do, but this is honestly for the best. This way, I can go back to school and finish up. Once I do get a job, I can save up for a place. It also means you can go to grad school."

He immediately shakes his head. "No. Absolutely not."

"Why not?" I ask.

"The school is three hours away, Bri."

"If this is about Kayla, if she really cares about you, she'll be fine with that, baby," Mom says. "Heck, she better be."

"It's not just her. I can't leave you and Li'l Bit."

"Why not?" Mom asks.

"Because."

"Because you think you have to take care of us," Mom finishes for him. "And you don't. The only person you have to take care of is yourself."

Trey slowly lets out a breath. "I don't know about this."

Mom comes over and lifts his chin. "You gotta go after your dream, baby."

I get an ache in my chest. That's the exact opposite of what she told me in the car when she said I couldn't rap anymore. I mean, I get it. I've messed up big-time. But what makes Trey's dreams more important than mine?

"You'll never know what you could become if you stay here," she goes on, and I stare at the rug. "I gotta be able to brag about my son, the doctor. They won't be able to tell me a damn thing then."

Trey laughs. "You're gonna brag to everybody, huh?"

"Every damn body." She laughs, too. "But first, you gotta go to grad school and get that master's. Then that doctorate. You can't stay here to do either."

Trey groans and tiredly wipes his face. "That's more student loans and more school."

"But it's worth it," Mom says. "It's your dream."

He slowly nods and looks over at me. I try to keep my eyes on my Tweety rug. Don't know if I should smile for him or cry for myself.

"Ma," Trey says. "You gotta let Bri go after her dreams, too."

"What are you talking about?"

"You told her she can't rap anymore. You're not even letting her perform at the Ring."

"Trey, you know damn well why I'm not. You've seen the mess she's gotten herself into. Then Supreme wants her out here, acting a fool. *I'd* be a fool to let that happen. What? So she can end up like your daddy?"

I look up. "I'm not him."

Three words. I've thought them plenty of times. Honestly, people act like I'm my dad more than I'm myself. I've got his dimples, his smile, his temper, his stubbornness, his rap skills. Hell, I got his room. But I'm not him. Period.

"Bri, we already discussed this."

"Discussed? You dictated to me. You wanna talk to Trey about pursuing his dream, but I can't pursue mine?"

"Trey's dream won't get him killed!"

"Mine won't either because I'm smarter than that!"

She puts her hands at her mouth, like she's praying for the Lord to keep her from hurting me. "Brianna—"

"I don't like what Supreme wants me to do," I admit. I swear, I hate that damn song. "But this is the only thing I'm really good at. It's all I wanna do. Can't I at least see if I can make it?"

She stares at the ceiling for the longest.

"Ma, look," says Trey. "I don't like it either, I don't. But this sounds like a big opportunity."

"Yeah, to make Supreme rich," she says.

"We can figure out what to do with him and all this image stuff later," Trey says. "But damn. Do you really want Bri to spend the rest of her life wondering what could've happened?"

Her foot taps the floor. She wraps her arms around herself. "Your daddy—"

"Made bad decisions," Trey says. "And yeah, Bri has, too—"

Was that even necessary to point out?

"But I believe that she's smarter than that," he says. "Don't you?"

"I know she is."

"Can you act like it then?" I ask, and my voice is super soft. "It's not like anybody else does."

This look of surprise quickly appears in my mom's eyes. Slowly, it's replaced by sadness and, soon, realization. She closes her eyes and takes a deep breath. "Fine. Bri, if you wanna perform at the Ring, you can. But if you go out there, acting a damn fool, best believe I will snatch your soul from your body."

Oh, I definitely believe it. "Yes, ma'am."

"Good," she says. "After this li'l performance, Supreme ain't gonna be your manager anymore. Hell, I'll do it before I let him."

Oh, dear God. "Um . . . yeah. Sure."

"Hey! Dinner ready, and I'm hungry," Granddaddy calls from downstairs. "So bring y'all asses on!"

"Sit your behind down somewhere and hush!" Grandma says.

"Ah, the sweet sound of dysfunction," Trey says as he leaves my room. "We'll have to deal with that all the time now."

"Lord, help us," Mom adds, following him out.

I stay back and glance around. Like I said, I have a lot of good memories in this room. But I also woke up here a lot of nights, screaming for my mom not to leave me. See, the one thing good memories and bad memories have in common is that they both stay with you. I guess that's why I've never known how to feel about this place. Or about my mom, even.

And you know what? Maybe that's okay. Maybe we'll be okay.

Maybe *I'll* be okay.

All six of us sit at the dining room table and pass platters and bowls around. Grandma has gotten all in Kayla's business while Trey was upstairs and gives us the 411. Kayla is a straight-up saint because she lets her.

"She say she got two brothers. One older and one around your age, Brianna," Grandma says. "Her momma is a teacher at some private school, and her daddy is an electrician. Senior, I got his card. He can fix that light on the back porch for us."

"Ain't no man coming in my house fixing nothing," Granddaddy says. "I got it."

Grandma goes, "Mm-hmm. That's why it's been flickering

forever. Trey, you found a smart girl here. She got a high GPA. Studying marketing and even pursuing a music career on the side."

"Look at that," Mom says. "It's possible to go college *and* rap."

I don't even justify that with a glance.

"It's hard juggling it all," Kayla admits. "I work to not only pay my bills but to fund my music projects. I'm independent."

"An independent woman!" Granddaddy grins as he opens his can of soda. "Go 'head, then!"

"Granddaddy, she means independent music-wise," says Trey. "Not that she's not independent overall, but she doesn't have a record label behind her."

"Like Junior before he passed—Brianna, put some more greens on your plate!" Grandma snips.

"Oh my God," I say under my breath. I swear, I'll never eat enough vegetables to meet this woman's quota. Besides, as many ham hocks as she's got in these greens, it's hard to say they're vegetables anymore.

"Aww, leave my Li'l Bit alone," Granddaddy says. He presses his greasy lips against my cheek. "She a carnivore like her granddaddy."

"No, she stubborn like her granddaddy, that's all that is," Grandma says.

"He's not the only stubborn one," I mumble.

"Heh-heh-heh!" Granddaddy chuckles and puts his fist

out to me. I bump it. "My girl!"

I laugh as he kisses my cheek again. Not long ago, my mom asked me who I am. I'm starting to think I know.

You see, I'm headstrong (and petty) like Grandma.

I'm creative like Granddaddy. If that's what you can call what he is, but yeah, I'm that.

I speak my mind like Mom. I might be as strong as her, too.

I care so much that it hurts. Like Trey.

I'm like my dad in a lot of ways, even if I'm not him.

And although Kayla isn't family (yet), maybe she's a glimpse at who I could be.

If I'm nothing else, I'm them, and they're me.

That's more than enough.

THIRTY-FOUR

On Thursday night, Trey chaperones me to the Ring.

Mom asked him to go. She refused to come along herself. She said she might hurt Supreme, and that wouldn't help me at all. Plus, according to her, "We only need one family member in jail."

Yeah, I'm going for it. Things may be looking up, but who's to say they won't fall apart again? What I look like, giving up this chance?

Trey lets all the windows in his Honda down and blasts "On the Come Up" on high as we roll through the Garden. There's a chill in the air just like there was when Aunt Pooh took me weeks ago. The combination of the cold and the warmth from Trey's heater is just as A-1 tonight as it was then.

"'You can't stop me, dun-dun-dun-dun,'" Trey tries to rap

along. "'You can't stop me, nope, nope. Dun-dun-dun-dun, get done up.'"

The rap gene clearly skipped him. Clearly.

Sonny and Malik snicker in the backseat. "Yas, kill it, boo," Sonny eggs him on. "Kill it!"

"Get it, Trey!" says Malik.

I glare back at them. I swear to God, if they don't stop encouraging this, I will murder them.

"I got bars, son!" Trey says. "Bars! Deadass."

Oh my God, since when did he become a New Yorker? I tug my hoodie over my eyes. He's trying to amp me up, I get that, but this? This is the hottest of hot messes.

It's totally something Aunt Pooh would do though. Except she'd get the lyrics right.

It's weird going to the Ring without her. Actually, it's weird that she's not around, period. This isn't like when she'd disappear and I'd worry about where she was. Somehow knowing where she is feels worse. If she were here, she'd tell me to shake it off and keep it moving. That's what I'm trying to do. That's what I *gotta* do if I wanna kill this performance and get this record deal.

Trey stops his poor attempt at rapping when we pull into the Ring. Tonight, the marquee sign lets everyone know that there will be "a special performance by the Garden's own Bri!"

"Damn. We're hanging with a celebrity, huh?" Malik teases from the backseat.

"Ha! I'm only hood famous. I'm glad y'all came."

"We couldn't miss this," Sonny says. "You know we've always got your back."

"Yeah, I know." I know that even if I don't know anything else about our friendship.

The "let out" in the parking lot is already happening. Music blasts around us, folks show off their cars. I get shouts and nods along the way. One guy tells me, "Keep reppin' the Garden, Bri!"

"All day!" I call back. "East side!"

That gets me even more love.

Another thing I am? The Garden. And the Garden is me. I'm forever good with that.

"Hey, Bri!" a squeaky voice calls.

I turn around. Jojo pedals over on that dirt bike of his. The beads on his braids clink against each other.

What in the world? "What you doing out here?" I ask him.

He skids to a stop just in front of me. This child loves to give me heart attacks. "I came to see you perform."

"By yourself?" Trey asks.

Jojo stares at the ground as he rolls his front wheel back and forth a bit. "I ain't by myself. I'm with y'all."

"Jojo, you don't need to be out alone at night."

"I wanted to see you do your new song. I bet that sh—thing—is dope!"

I sigh. "Jojo."

He puts his hands together. "Pleeeease."

This child. But the truth is, it's better if he's with us than if he's by himself. "Okay, fine," I say, and he pumps his fist. "But we're taking you straight home afterward, Jojo. I'm not even playing."

"And you're gonna give me your momma's number so I can call her," Trey adds. "Somebody needs to know where you at."

Jojo climbs off his bike. "Man, y'all worried for nothing! I go where I wanna go."

Trey hooks an arm around his neck. "Then we need to find out why that's so."

Jojo puffs up his chest. "I'm almost grown."

The four of us bust out laughing.

"Sweetie, your voice still squeaks," Sonny says. "Stop playing yourself."

My phone buzzes in my pocket as we head for the building. It's Curtis. I've officially gone off the deep end. After our date on Monday, I put the heart-eyes emoji next to his name in my contacts. I mean, the boy brought me flowers and a Storm comic, and since we didn't have time to stay for dessert at the restaurant, he brought me a small pack of Chips Ahoy! to eat on the way back to school. He earned those heart eyes. He just sent a couple of texts to guarantee that he keeps them.

Do your thing tonight, Princess.

Wish I could be there.

I probably couldn't pay attention to your song tho

I'd be staring at you too hard

Corny? Yes. But it gets a smile out of me. Before I can respond, though, he adds:

I'd be staring at that ass too but you know I probably ain't supposed to admit that.

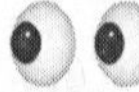

I smirk.

Why you admitting it now then?

His answer?

Cause I bet it made you smile

Just for that, I'm adding a second heart-eyes emoji to his name.

We skip the line like I usually do. I get shoulder slaps, dap, and nods along the way. I really do feel like the princess of the Garden.

But there's a gang of guys in gray who look at me like I'm anything but a princess.

About five or six Crowns are in the line. One notices me and nudges another one, and soon all of them are staring hard. I swallow and look straight ahead. It's kinda like how it is with dogs—you can't let them see your fear or otherwise you're screwed.

Trey touches my shoulder. He knows what happened. "Just keep going," he whispers.

"Look who's back," Reggie the stocky bouncer says when we get to the doors. "Heard you're gonna put on a show for us tonight."

"That's the plan," I say.

"Still carrying the torch for Law, huh?" says Frank, the taller one, as he waves the metal detector wand around us.

"Nah. Got my own torch. I think that's what my dad would want."

Frank nods. "You probably right about that."

Reggie motions us through and points at my *Black Panther* hoodie. "Wakanda forever." He crosses his arms over his chest.

Look at him, actually getting a catchphrase right.

Frank and Reggie let Jojo leave his bike with them. We're about to head inside when a deep voice says, "How the fuck they skipping the line?"

I don't even have to look. I know it's a Crown. They're probably itching for a reason to start some shit.

"Man, chill," says Frank. "Li'l Law performing tonight."

"I don't give a damn what that bitch doing," says a Crown in a gray beanie. "They can take their asses to the back."

"Hold up now," says Trey. "Who—"

Jojo advances on the Crown. "Who the fuck you think you talking to?"

I grab his collar before he can get any closer. "Jojo, no!"

"Man, sit your li'l ass down!" says the Crown in the beanie. He eyes me. "See, we thought we had put you in your place for that shit you rapped, but apparently not. Your aunty should've shot to kill when she had the chance. Now she just done gave you problems."

At this point, I don't know how I'm standing.

"Try it if you want!" says Jojo. "We'll mess you up!"

The Crowns bust out laughing.

I feel sick though. This little boy is serious.

Malik grabs Jojo's arm. "C'mon," he says, and pulls Jojo with him. He and Sonny walk in, glancing back at the Crowns.

Trey's right by my side, staring every single one of them down. He leads me inside.

Every inch of me is tense until the doors of the boxing gym close behind us.

Trey takes a deep breath too. "You okay?" he asks.

No, but I nod because I'm supposed to.

"Look, we can go home, all right?" he says. "This ain't worth all that."

"I'm good."

He sighs. "Bri—"

"They stopped Dad, Trey. I can't let them stop me, too."

He wants to argue. I see it in his eyes.

"Look, they can't do anything in here tonight," I say. "Reggie and Frank don't let weapons come through the doors. I gotta go after this."

He bites his lip. "And then what? This ain't gonna just go away, Bri."

"I'll figure something out," I say. "But please? I gotta stay."

He lets out a heavy sigh. "All right. It's your call."

He holds his fist out to me. I bump it.

I don't know how any of those people in line will get in—this place is already super packed. I'm talking wall-to-wall. That dumbass Hype plays some Lil Wayne over all the chatter.

It takes me a second to spot Supreme. He's over near the boxing ring itself. I throw up my hand to get his attention. He notices and makes his way over.

"You good with this, too?" Trey whispers.

He may have taken Mom's place so she wouldn't jump Supreme, but I'm sure Trey's not too fond of him either. "You good" really means, "You want me to check this guy or nah?"

"I'm good with that, too." I say.

"The superstar is here!" Supreme announces. I let him give me a quick hug. "And I see you brought your li'l crew with you, huh? Trey, boy, I ain't seen you since you were about as little as this one here." He reaches to ruffle Jojo's hair.

Jojo dodges his hand. "I ain't little!"

Supreme chuckles. "My bad, man. My bad."

"So you're Supreme?" Sonny says.

His eyes are almost narrowed at Miles's dad. I can tell it's taking a lot for him to not say what's on his mind. But from what Sonny told me, Miles isn't ready to tell his dad about them.

"The one and only," Supreme says, and turns to me. "I got James a front row seat. I also got you a li'l greenroom in the back so you can make your grand entrance later."

"We'll come back with you," Malik says, eyeing him. He's not too crazy about Supreme either.

"Y'all go ahead. I'm gonna take this li'l wanna-be gangsta to find a good spot," Trey says. "C'mon, Jojo. We need to have a li'l chat. How to not show your ass, one-oh-one."

I watch them until they disappear into the crowd.

Supreme grasps my shoulder. "You ready to get this contract?"

I thought I was. But like Aunt Pooh would say, I gotta shake it off. I swallow. "Yeah. Let's do it."

Malik, Sonny, and I follow Supreme to the back. The hallway walls are covered in posters of hip-hop legends. It's like they watch every single step that I take.

Supreme takes me to the "greenroom" — it used to be a storage room. It's tiny, with just a few chairs and a refrigerator, but it's a quiet place away from the chaos.

Supreme leaves so I can get in my zone. Plus, he wants to go keep James company out front.

I lower myself into one of the chairs. Sonny and Malik take the other two. I suck in a deep breath and let it out.

"I'm sorry about the Crowns," Malik says.

"This is on me and Aunt Pooh."

"All this over some lyrics?" Sonny asks.

I nod.

"That's bullshit," says Sonny.

"Jojo was ready to go to war for you though," Malik says with a smirk.

Sonny laughs. "Like he was actually gonna do something." He helps himself to some chips from the snack basket on the coffee table. "I know you're not taking that li'l boy seriously, Bri."

"Right. We used to pretend to be 'gangster' when we were younger, too," Malik adds.

We did go through a phase. I saw Aunt Pooh throw up Garden Disciple signs so much that I figured I could, too. Even drew the GD symbol in my notebooks.

But I wasn't going around telling people I'd mess them up.

There's a knock at the door.

"Come in," Sonny calls with a mouth full of chips.

Scrap, of all people, peeks into the greenroom. "Ay, Bri? You got a minute?"

I straighten up. "Yeah. What you doing here?"

Scrap gives Malik and Sonny quick nods. "Had to come see my new favorite rapper perform. Plus, your boy is the reason you here tonight, you know?"

I raise my eyebrows. "Nah, I don't know."

"I'm the one told you to make a banger!" Scrap says. "I told you it had to be catchy, too. I know, I know. I'm a genius, right?"

On what planet? "Umm . . . yeah. Sure."

"Just give me my shout-out onstage and we good," he claims. "I got somebody who wanna holla at you."

He hands me his phone.

There is no way this is who I think it is. "Hello?"

"Now, see, I ain't been gone long, and you already ain't sounding like yourself," Aunt Pooh says. "How you gon' be a superstar tonight, sounding all soft and shit?"

"Shut up." I laugh, and she joins in. I almost forgot what her laugh sounds like. "Damn. I miss you."

"I miss you too," she says. "Ay, look, I ain't got a lot of time, but I had to talk to you. Scrap told me you performing tonight. Go in there and kill it, a'ight? If you choke again, I'm gon' bust outta here just to whoop your ass. On my momma."

That's her way of saying, "I love you." I don't tell her about the Crowns. She doesn't need that on her right now. "Don't worry. I've got this."

"You know I may be getting out sooner than later, right?" she says. "My attorney thinks he can get me the minimum. Especially since I ain't got no violent offenses."

That they know about. But hey, I'll take it. "That's dope."

Supreme comes back. He seems to stare at Scrap. Scrap gives him an up-and-down like, "*We got a problem?*"

Supreme turns to me and points to his watch.

"I gotta go," I tell Aunt Pooh.

"A'ight. Go kill it," Aunt Pooh says. "Sky's still the limit, superstar."

"We'll see them chumps on top," I finish for her. "I love you."

"Sentimental ass, I love you, too. Now go do your thing."

My eyes prickle as I pass Scrap his phone. “Thank you,” I tell him.

“Don’t mention it,” he says. “Go kill it. For Pooh.”

Malik, Sonny, and I follow Supreme into the hallway. Supreme wraps an arm around me and pulls me close into his side.

“Look at you, hanging with GDs,” he whispers. “Trying to make it look authentic like I suggested, huh?”

I move away from him. “Nah, I don’t do that.”

We step into the gym and a rush of sound and lights hit us. There’s barely room to move in here, yet somehow the crowd clears a path for us. Supreme leads me toward the boxing ring. Like outside in the line, people give me palm slaps or pat my back along the way. Anything to touch me, as if it’s their way of wishing me luck.

“All right, y’all. She got her start right here in the Ring,” Hype says to the crowd as I make my way over. “Ever since, she’s been on the come up, pun intended.”

He’s so much cornier than I realized.

“Here to perform her new single, give it up for Bri, y’all!”

I hold my fist out to Sonny and Malik. They knock theirs against it, we give each other dap, and chunk the deuces. We’re still the Unholy Trinity.

“Bam!” we say.

“Don’t choke this time,” Sonny adds. “I don’t wanna have to disown you.”

I purse my lips. He cheeses.

Supreme lifts the ropes so I can climb into the Ring and hands me a mic. The spotlight hits me, just like it did all those weeks ago. The screams are deafening.

I squint and look around the crowd. My brother, Jojo, and Kayla are right beside the Ring. Sonny and Malik join them. James and Supreme are next to them. Scrap's found a spot not too far away. A ways back behind him, something glistens.

A mouth full of silver teeth smiles at me. The Crown in a gray beanie holds my dad's pendant and makes a kissy-face at me. His friends smirk and snicker.

Scrap follows my gaze. I don't hear him, but I read his lips. *"Aw, hell nah."*

He catches my eyes and silently asks a deadly question: *"Want me to handle that?"*

"Sooo . . . you not gon' introduce yourself or nothing?" Hype asks. I forgot he was here. Shit, I forgot where I was. "Don't tell me you're about to choke again. Gotta call you Lady Chokes-a-Lot."

He plays a drum kick. Who the hell told this guy he was funny?

The Crown holds the chain up higher for me to see. His friends crack up.

Scrap once again silently asks, "*Want me to handle that?*"

"Y'all wanna hear this song, right?" Hype calls to the crowd. The answer is yeah. "Let's get it, then!"

The beat starts.

I'm supposed to go right into the hook and then do the

verses Dee-Nice wrote. Supreme and James watch me with amused expressions, and it's as if I'm their pet, about to perform a trick.

Pet. Rhymes with met, let, get. Set.

Sets. Gang sets, like the Crowns staring me down and the Maple Grove GDs that Scrap claims. Jojo wants to be just like them. I do this song, I may give him more ammunition. I'll also be doing exactly what Hype accused me of—saying words that aren't my own.

Own. Clone.

For the longest, people acted like I was my dad's clone. Supreme acts like I'm a puppet, too. But my brother called me a gift. My mom calls me her miracle. If I'm nothing else, I'm her daughter, and I'm Trey's sister.

Sister. A lot of words can rhyme with that if delivered a certain way. Even something like "mirror."

Mirror. Maybe that's what I am to Jojo.

He's got a distorted picture though. He took my words the wrong way, just like Emily, and just like the Crowns. They're all mistaken.

Mistaken. Awaken.

Maybe it's time to wake everybody up.

"Stop the music," I say into the mic.

The beat goes off. There are whispers and murmurs.

Supreme frowns. I hear James ask, "What the hell's going on?"

I ignore them both. "I was supposed to come up here and

do this new song, but I'd rather do something from my heart. Is that okay with y'all?"

The answer is hell yes, that's how loud they cheer.

"Uh-oh, we 'bout to get a freestyle!" Hype says. "You need a beat?"

"No thanks, ass-wipe Hype."

Everybody laughs at that.

I close my eyes. There's plenty of words waiting inside me. Words I hope Jojo hears and understands.

I lift the mic and let them pour out.

I refuse to be their laugh, I refuse to be their pet,
I refuse to be the reason some kid now claims a set.
I refuse to stand up here and say words that aren't my own.
Refuse to be a puppet, refuse to be a clone.
You see, I'm somebody's daughter, I'm somebody's sister,
I'm somebody's hope. And I'm somebody's mirror.
I'm a genius, I'm a star, call me all of the above,
But you'll never call me sellout, and you'll never call me thug.
In the Garden kids are starving, hearts are hardened, beg my pardon,
But fuck the system. Your assumptions? They just show just where your heart is.

You see, they figure I'm a nigga that's gon' rap 'bout
pulling triggers,
Just to make their pockets bigger while the world
yells I'm a sinner.
Here's the kicker, they get richer, only if we take that
picture
As the truth, and as us. It's not just rap, this shit is
bigger.
But they blame hip-hop. Yet we just speak on what we
see.
But I'm gon' speak on what I see and never claim it to
be me.
When I say I'm a queen, it means my crown cannot be
taken
That's nothing against your set, and I'm sorry that
you're mistaken.
Retaliation's segregation of our hood, so please
awaken.
You'll never silence me and you'll never kill my dream,
Just recognize when you say brilliant that you're also
saying Bri.
I'm not for sale.

There's an explosion of cheers.

"Bri! Bri! Bri!" they chant, and my name rocks the room. "Bri! Bri! Bri!"

Who's not chanting? The Crowns. Supreme and James don't either. James makes his way to the door, shaking his head. Supreme rushes after him. He looks back at me, and though I can't see his eyes, I can read his expression easily: We're done.

I lower the mic to my side. When I was little, I used to stand in front of mirrors with hairbrushes and imagine crowds chanting my name. Yet I don't think I could've ever imagined *this*. This feeling. See, for the first time in my life, I know I'm exactly where I'm supposed to be. I'm doing what I'm supposed to do. Hell, what I was made to do. The crowd could be silent and I'd still know that.

When Aunt Pooh introduced me to hip-hop, Nas told me the world was mine, and I believed it could be. Now, standing here on this stage, I know it is.

EPILOGUE

All of the words on the page have blurred together, I swear. I glance at my phone. "How long have we been at this?"

Curtis looks at his phone, too. "Only two hours, Princess."

"Only?" I groan. Our ACT prep books and laptops are spread out around us on my bedroom floor. We're taking another practice test tomorrow—the real exam is a little over a month away. Curtis comes over a lot so we can study together. I think I'm ready, even though our studying usually turns into something else.

That's exactly why I say, "We need to take a break."

"Oh, for real?"

"For real," I say.

"Let me guess—you wanna do this instead?"

He's all grins as he steals a quick kiss. One kiss becomes

two, two become three, and three become making out on the floor of my Tweety shrine of a bedroom. My mom, Trey, and I have been living with my grandparents for less than a week now, and I haven't had time to redecorate.

"Hey, hey!" Trey calls from the doorway. Curtis and I separate so fast. "That ain't no damn studying!"

I roll onto my back and groan. "Right now, I actually look forward to the day you go off to grad school."

"Unfortunately for you, you stuck with me for a couple more months," he says, and looks at Curtis. "Bruh, you better watch yourself. I will drive three hours to whoop some ass."

Curtis innocently puts his hands up. "My bad."

"Uh-huh," Trey says. "I'm watching, Curtis."

I sigh. "Don't you need to go pick up Jojo?"

Trey's taking Jojo to a Markham State basketball game. Jojo's been geeking out about it all week like it's an NBA game. Poor baby, he doesn't realize Markham can't play worth shit.

"I'm going." He kicks my door. "But keep this damn door open, too. Ain't nobody got time to be called 'Uncle Trey.' I oughta tell Granddaddy y'all up in there, passing cooties."

He goes off down the hall. Curtis waits a few seconds before he leans over and kisses me. "Cooties, huh?"

But there we go, getting interrupted again. My mom loudly clears her throat. "That ain't studying."

"That's what I said," Trey calls from wherever he is.

Curtis gets this ridiculously cute sheepish look about him

and oh my God, I almost can't deal. "Sorry, Mrs. Jackson."

She kisses her teeth. "Mm-hmm. Bri, which one do you prefer?"

She holds up two outfits. One's a navy pencil skirt with matching blazer that Aunt Gina bought for her. The other is a gray suit that Aunt 'Chelle bought.

"They look so much alike—does it matter?"

"Yes, it matters," she says. "I gotta look right for my first day."

She starts at the school district on Monday as Dr. Cook's secretary. One of the first things he wants her to do? Schedule monthly meetings with the Midtown Black and Latinx Coalition so he can make sure things are going smoothly. The other order of business? Look into a new security firm for the district.

"What, you're not gonna go with the one Grandma bought you?" I ask.

Mom's lips thin. Grandma bought her a floral print suit. It's loud. It's bold. It'll blind you if you stare at it too long.

"I'm saving that for church," she lies. "C'mon now. Help me choose."

"The navy," I say. "It says, 'I wanna be here, I mean business, but I still got some style, and I may cut you if you cross me.'"

She snaps her fingers and points at me. "That's what I'm talking about. Thank you, baby. Y'all can get back to studying . . . *studying!*" she adds with raised eyebrows. "Curtis, you're welcome to stay for dinner. I'm making gumbo."

Yes, Grandma is actually letting her cook in her kitchen. No, I don't know where the aliens put my real grandma or if we'll ever get her back.

"Thank you, Mrs. Jackson," Curtis tells my mom.

My phone buzzes on the floor, and Sonny's smiling face appears on my screen. I hit the speaker button. "What's up, Sonny Bunny," I tease.

"Shut up, Bookie."

"Hey, Bri," Miles calls from the background.

"Hey, Miles."

"Y'all better have some adult supervision over there, I know that!" Mom hollers.

"Chill, Aunty Jay. Nothing's happening," Sonny says. "Bri, you need to get on Twitter. Something huge just happened."

"Huh?" I say.

"I'm serious, Bri. Get on Twitter."

Curtis grabs his phone. I type in the address on my laptop. "What for?" I ask.

"You won't believe who posted your freestyle from the other night," he says.

"What are you—"

My notifications are at 99+, like Twitter can't keep up anymore. There's one tweet that people keep liking and retweeting. I click it and stare at it. Then I stare at the profile pic and name, too.

Mom comes over and stares at it with me.

"Oh my God," she says.

"'This girl is the future of hip-hop.'" Curtis reads the tweet aloud. "'@LawlessBri, we gotta do a song together. Let's make it happen!'"

It was tweeted by . . .

Oh my God.

"Goddamn, Princess," Curtis says. "That's some life-changing shit—stuff."

Mom still side-eyes him. "Bri, you wanna do it, baby?"

I stare at the tweet. This is major. It could be the shot I need.

"Yeah," I say, and look at my mom. "Long as I can do it my way."

ACKNOWLEDGMENTS

Like last time, this will probably sound like a rapper's acceptance speech, but hey, for this book, it should, right? I first have to thank my Lord and Savior, Jesus Christ. It has been quite a journey, and I wouldn't have made it this far without you. Thank you for carrying me and keeping me. Whatever you want to continue to do through me, I'm yours.

To my incredible, amazing, phenomenal editor Donna Bray. There aren't enough adjectives in the English language to describe someone as awesome as you. This wasn't an easy journey, and I wouldn't have survived it without you. Thank you for being there every step of the way and for believing in me as much as you do. Also, thank you for being so patient haha. We got it done!

Brooks Sherman, aka the best literary agent an author could hope for. Thank you for keeping me going and for always having my back. Even more so, thank you for knowing I would get here with this book, even when I didn't know that I would. I'm eternally grateful to call you my agent and my friend.

Mary Pender-Coplan, you are an angel, a lifesaver, and I still don't know what I did to deserve to have such an incredible film agent. From the bottom of my heart, thank you. Thank you, Akhil Hegde, for being an amazing assistant angel, and Nancy Taylor, the former assistant angel. Thank you to everyone at UTA.

To every single person at Balzer + Bray/HarperCollins. I feel like the luckiest author in the world with you all on my side. Your love, your support, and your hard work do not go unnoticed. I can never thank you enough. Special thanks to Suzanne Murphy, Alessandra Balzer, Olivia Russo, Tiara Kittrell, Alison Donalty, Jenna Stempel-Lobell, Anjola Coker, Nellie Kurtzman, Bess Braswell, Ebony LaDelle, Patty Rosati, Rebecca McGuire, Josh Weiss, Mark Rifkin, Dana Hayward, Emily Rader, Ronnie Ambrose, Erica Ferguson, Megan Gendell, Andrea Pappenheimer, Kerry Moynagh, Kathy Faber, and Jen Wygand.

My incredible UK publishing family at Walker Books, aka my cheerleaders across the pond, especially Annalie Grainger and Rosi Crawley. Thank you for always giving me a home away from home.

My international publishers, thank you for taking a chance on me and my stories.

To my Janklow & Nesbit family, thank you for all of the love and support. Special thanks to Wendi Gu. Thank you also to Stephanie Koven and everyone at Cullen Stanley International.

Molly Ker Hawn, the fact that you introduced me to roasted beets was enough to get you my eternal gratitude, but thank you for your love, support, and for being just an all-around badass.

Marina Addison, I seriously don't know what I'd do without you as my assistant. Thanks for putting up with all of the chaos.

David Lavin, Charles Yao, and everyone at the Lavin Agency, thank you for believing in me, supporting me, and investing in me.

To the homies: Becky Albertalli, Adam Silvera, Nic Stone, Justin Reynolds, Dhonielle Clayton, Sabaa Tahir, Julie Murphy, Rose Brock, Tiffany Jackson, Ashley Woodfolk, Jason Reynolds, Sarah Cannon, Dede Nesbitt, Leatrice McKinney, Camryn Garrett, Adrianne Russell, Cara Davis, Justina Ireland, Heidi Heilig, Kosoko Jackson, Zoraida Córdova, Nicola Yoon, Ellen Oh. Every single one of you played a role in this book's birth, simply by being there. Thank you.

To my THUG movie family—George, Marcia, and Chase Tillman, Shamell Bell, Bob Teitel, Marty Bowen, Wyck Godfrey, Tim Bourne, John Fischer, Jay Marcus, Isaac Klausner, Elizabeth Gabler, Erin Siminoff, Molly Saffron, everyone at Temple Hill, State Street, and Fox 2000, and the entire cast and crew, thank you all for making one of my dreams come true. Amandla, thank you for being the best Starr I could've asked for and most of all for being you. I'm honored to call you my little sis. Common, thank you for the inspiration and the encouragement.

To all of my family and friends, thank you for knowing that I'm still Angie. Please don't be upset that your name isn't here. There are way too many of you to list but know that I appreciate and love you.

To my mom, Julia. Thank you for being who you are and for always making sure I know who I am. I love you.

To hip-hop. Thank you for being my voice, for giving me a voice, and for showing me myself. The world criticizes you often, and sometimes rightfully so. Hell, sometimes, I'm one of your biggest critics. But I do it from a place of love. I've seen what you're capable of—you can, you will, and you have changed the world. I'll never give up on you. I'll always have your back. Keep sparking brains and making noise.

And finally, to those roses in concrete in the real Gardens of the world—even when they doubt you, even when they try to silence you, never be quiet. They can't stop you, so get your come up.

EXCLUSIVE COLLECTOR'S EDITION BONUS MATERIAL

Angie "Young Short-A" Thomas, age 15

Dear Reader,

I'll be honest with you—*On the Come Up* was a hard book to write.

It's a known fact in publishing that the second book is the hardest book for an author to pen. Ask any of your favorite authors and there is a big chance they struggled the most with their second book baby. For one, there's the pressure that comes with suddenly being a published author—your hobby is now your career. Secondly, there's the pressure and expectations we place on ourselves. So many of you connected with *The Hate U Give* in one way or another, and I wanted all of you to have a similar experience with *On the Come Up*. But I have to admit, reader, the best thing I could've done was to stop thinking about you as I wrote this book.

Instead, I thought of sixteen-year-old Angie.

At sixteen years old, I was a dreamer. A big one. I think I spent most of my time thinking about what the future could be. It was the best way to escape the world around me, where poverty seemed to reign supreme. I wanted to make myself heard in a world that often ignored young people like me, and I thought the only way anyone would listen was through hip-hop. At a young age, I picked up a microphone and wrote rhymes. I mimicked my favorite MCs and went through one bad stage name after another, from Li'l Trouble to Young Short-A. (Don't ask.) By the time I hit sixteen, I had recorded a mixtape, done radio interviews, had my first public performance, and had been in a hip-hop magazine.

But I hadn't made it.

"Making it" was my ultimate goal. For me that meant having enough money to provide for my family or at least get us out of our impoverished neighborhood. Maybe, just maybe, I could buy a pair of Timberland boots and not depend on secondhand clothes from a local church to get me through winter.

Clearly, young Angie and Bri have a lot in common.

I was Bri, but so many of you are Bri, too. You want to make it; you want to change your circumstances. And in a world that often tells you you're either too much or not enough, it's easy to give up. While I thought a lot of young Angie when writing this book, I once again started to think of you too, and my mission became clear:

I want this book to inspire you to keep going.

Through Bri's journey, my hope is that you decide that your dreams are worth fighting for. *You're* worth fighting for. No matter how hard things may get, no matter what gets in your way, like Bri you will decide that failure isn't an option. Will you have your obstacles along the way? Absolutely. But hopefully, you will also have your Sonnys, Maliks, Treys, and Jays to be there through it all. If you don't, I hope you'll find comfort in them in these pages.

No one can stop you on the come up, dreamer.

No one can stop you.

Keep going.

Love,

Angie Thomas

YOU

CAN'T

Stop Me,

NOPE,

NOPE.

EXCLUSIVE DELETED SCENES FROM

ON THE COME UP

After three hours on the road (not including the four times we pulled over so Granddaddy could use the bathroom in the back—he says his bladder is weaker than watered-down whiskey), we pull into the stadium parking lot. It's packed like it's game day. My grandparents and I have attended almost every Markham State home football game since Trey was a freshman. Trey didn't play, he was a drum major, but the band is just as important as the football team at HBCUs. Some people only go to games for the halftime shows. Shoot, we did.

Granddaddy parks way in the back like he'd do if we were tailgating. "Text Niecey to see if she got us some seats."

"Okay," I say, and take out my phone. Grandma hasn't mastered texting, and Granddaddy hates texting as much as he hates people confusing the Temptations with the Four Tops.

Aunt Niecey texts back and tells me what section she's in.

Between the crowd and the massiveness of the stadium, it takes us a while to find her.

The moment she sees me, she comes at me with open arms.

"Hey, Li'l Bit." Her hugs are always extra tight and extra long whenever I see her. She's a flight attendant, so it's not nearly enough. "You okay?"

"Yeah," I mumble into her shoulder. She pulls back and stares at me. Now *that's* who I look like, if you ask me. Most people say I look like my dad, but he and Aunt Niecey could've been twins if she wasn't five years younger.

"You're sure?" she says.

I nod. She's an expert at knowing when I'm lying, but she's gonna have to accept this one for now.

"All right. I just got done texting your momma back. She's on her way from the motel."

We haven't been sitting down for long when Jay makes her way up the stairs toward us. Aunt Niecey meets her with a hug, too.

"You okay, girl?" she says.

"I'm making it," Jay says. "The real question is how are you? You're the one who helped Trey pack up this week."

"Tired," Aunt Niecey says. "That boy know he got a lot of stuff."

"Thank you for helping him. I hate I couldn't get off to help him myself."

Aunt Niecey waves her off. "No problem, girl. That's what family's for—Momma, don't say a word."

Grandma sure did open her mouth, most likely to say something extremely petty, but she snaps it shut.

Jay sits on the other side of me, placing me between her and Grandma.

The symbolism.

But Aunt Niecey got us some good seats. The sun isn't glaring on us, and we're facing the stage. We're not too far back either—the chairs on the football field don't look extremely tiny. May even be able to spot Trey.

Granddaddy passes some programs down to us. A couple of the pages are covered with photographs of the graduating class. I find one of Trey in his uniform, leading the four other drum majors, and one of him in a tux with a crown on his head. He was named Mr. Markham State last year at homecoming.

He made a cool-ass life for himself here, only to have to go back to the Garden.

It's so messed up.

"They got over eight hundred folks graduating this year," says Granddaddy. "It's gon' be a while before he walk across the stage and we can get out of here."

"Daddy, you're not leaving right after Trey gets his diploma, are you?" Aunt Niecey asks.

"Hell yeah, I am. You seen all them cars in that parking lot? It's gon' be hell getting out of here. Y'all can deal with that if y'all want."

The graduates march in. It's impossible to make out faces

from up here, but that's where the JumboTron comes in handy. Seems like they've shown just about half the graduating class when finally my brother appears.

"Trey!" Jay shouts.

He smiles on the screen, his dimples showing like he heard her. She does have a loud mouth, so it's possible.

"Why he got all that hair on his face?" Grandma asks about his new beard and mustache.

"He a grown man," Granddaddy says with a grin. "That's what we do."

"But it makes him look old," says Grandma.

"It makes me *feel* old." Aunt Niecey laughs. "Jay, I remember when you were pregnant with that boy."

"Girl, who you telling?" Jay chuckles. "Feet swollen all the damn time, back hurting, but I was cute." She goes quiet, then says softly, "Law would be so proud of him."

Granddaddy takes a deep breath. Grandma blinks fast. Aunt Niecey rests her head on Granddaddy's shoulder.

Grief hasn't left my family. It hides in the shadows, waiting for moments to hit.

I wish whoever pulled that trigger and killed him had to deal with this.

Grief is forced to hide again about two hours later when my brother's name is called and he walks across the stage. We cheer and clap. On the JumboTron Trey wears the widest grin.

We end up staying for the entire ceremony, and Granddaddy's chin ends up on his chest. He snores, and drool dribbles down his chin. Aunt Niecey has to shake him a couple of times when it's time to leave.

We maneuver through all the people to the football field, and the crowd is even thicker down here. I don't know how we're gonna find Trey. After a few minutes of searching, someone says, "Is that them dysfunctional Jacksons?"

I turn around.

"Trey!" I run to him like I'm a little kid, and he catches me in a hug.

"Li'l Bit!" he says. Trey was the first person in the family to call me that. Word is he didn't get why everybody was fawning over me when our parents brought me home, because I was just a "li'l bit, not a lot." It stuck.

He lets me go. We bump fists, give each other dap, and chunk the deuces.

"Bam!" we say.

"Gotta catch 'em all, huh?" He tugs at my bucket hat. It's got Pokémon all over it. Got it for a steal at the swap meet. "May have to borrow that one."

"Trey!" Grandma says. I move, and she kisses his cheek, leaving a pink lipstick mark.

"My man!" Granddaddy slaps his palm and pulls him into a half hug. "Magna cum laude! Sophisticated with it, boy."

"You know how I do," Trey says as he hugs Aunt Niecey with one arm.

Jay has kinda been standing back this whole time.

Trey's eyes meet hers. "Hey, Ma," he says, a small smile on his lips.

Jay moves forward and hugs him, wrapping her arms around his neck. Trey smiles even wider over her shoulder.

"I'm so proud of you." She frames his face. "My baby boy. All grown up."

I look at some random family crowded around a graduate. Jay and Trey . . . it's different with them. Sometimes it seems like there's a wall between me and Jay. With them, there is no wall. Ever. I'm not jealous or anything. Okay, maybe a little bit, but I think what hurts the most is not knowing why there's one between us.

I don't get it.

Aunt Niecey wraps her arm around my shoulder and mouths, *I love you*.

I love you too, I mouth back. I think my aunt is telepathic.

"Y'all ready to go eat?" Granddaddy pats his belly. "My stomach 'bout to start rumbling loud enough for everybody in this stadium to hear."

"Yeah, I got us a reservation at a place not too far from here," says Aunt Niecey.

"Oh, damn. I'm sorry, y'all," Trey says. "I already got plans. Me and some of the homies hanging out. You know, one last turn up." He does the dab.

Jay pats his face. "That's fine, baby. Have fun with your friends."

"You oughta take your sister with you," Grandma says. "Be good for her to hang out with some mature young folks. Maybe y'all can give her advice about college."

Oh God. She did not. There is nothing worse than an adult assuming that your life is so basic that they have to make plans on your behalf.

"Uhh . . . Bri can't go where we're going, Grandma," he says.

Grandma puts her hand on her hip. "And where exactly are y'all going?"

"Grown-folk places," Granddaddy says, and gives a *heh-heh-heh* chuckle.

"For real," Trey says, and they slap palms. "I definitely can't be hanging out with Bri tonight."

"Ouch," I say. "You didn't have to say it like that."

"Bri, you know what I mean."

"I don't know anything. Just like I didn't know that you'll be working at Sal's."

I don't mean to catch an attitude, it's just happening. And it possibly makes me a shitty sister, but it is what it is.

Trey sighs. "We'll talk later, okay?" He kisses Jay's cheek, Grandma's cheek, Aunt Niecey's cheek, and slaps palms with Granddaddy. He holds his fists toward me.

I just look at them at first.

"Damn, it's like that?" he says.

No. That's a whole new level of shitty that I don't think I'm capable of achieving. We bump fists, give each other dap, and chunk the deuces.

"Bam," we say.

Trey kisses my forehead. "I'll see you tomorrow."

And he leaves.

Michael Jackson wakes me up.

Let me clarify—the deceased King of Pop is not standing next to me, saying "Hee-hee" and doing leg kicks. His song "Don't Stop 'Til You Get Enough" plays loudly from somewhere nearby. So loud that I'm ready to cuss.

Floral curtains hang from the window above me, and there's red-oak wood everywhere. It takes a few seconds to realize I'm on the couch-turned-bed in my grandparents' RV. They move around in the "bedroom" in the back as Granddaddy fusses about music playing so damn loud so damn early.

Mike's coming from outside. I lift the window blinds. Don't know what the hell I was thinking. The sun practically murders my eyesight. I have to squint to see anything at all.

We're at a campsite. There are tons of trees, a lake not too far away, Trey, and his old Honda Civic. A U-Haul trailer is attached to his car, and boxes are stacked on the back seat. Michael Jackson blasts from the car stereo as Trey pops his crotch and lip-synchs along.

"There she is!" He points at me in the window. He bites his lip, does the MJ kick, and ends with a "Hee-hee!"

I go outside, arms folded to make it clear that I'm not falling for this nonsense. Whenever I was upset when I was younger,

Trey would do his best MJ impersonation to cheer me up. And let me be clear—his best impersonation was pretty awful, but it was so bad that I'd have no choice but to laugh.

I'm not five. I'm sixteen now. Two years shy of eighteen, four years shy of twenty. This shouldn't work on me like it did way back when, and I'm slightly offended he thinks it will.

But it *is* hard not to laugh.

"C'mon, girl!" he says, and tries to moonwalk in the dirt. His moonwalk always looks like it'll turn into a moon-trip. "Come dance with your brother."

"You look a mess."

"Just like your hair." He does another kick.

I touch my head. My hair is all over the place, but that's not the point. "You know how early it is?"

"Never too early for MJ. Hee-hee!"

Jesus. "If this is your way of making up for not telling me—"

"Come dance with your brother, girl." He does the "Thriller" shoulder shimmy.

"You couldn't even text me and tell me? And then you threw shade at me yesterday like I'm some basic-ass thot and not your sister."

"If you don't dance with me, I'll start singing."

Oh God. No. "Trey—"

"At least forgive me? Or I'll bust out with some off-key notes, I swear."

I purse my lips.

"Whoooo! Touch meeeeee—"

"Okay, okay!" I say. "I forgive you! Damn."

He leans into the car and turns the music off. "Good. 'Cause this music ain't helping my headache." He comes over and hugs me. "How you doing?"

"Fine," I mutter into his shirt. An odor invades my nostrils, and I push away so damn fast. "Dang, did you shower? You're musty as hell."

Trey sniffs under his own arm. Now that I think about it, he looks kinda rough this morning. His face is extra bristly, and there are bags under his eyes. His hair hasn't been brushed, his shirt is wrinkled, and he *clearly* hasn't showered in twenty-four hours. At least.

"Damn," he says. "Didn't know I was that bad."

"I think the word you're looking for is 'rancid'."

"Just for that." He has the audacity, the *audacity*, to pull me to him and put his musty underarms all over me and in my face.

"Nooooo!" I shout, as the germaphobe in me freaks the hell out. "Stoooop!"

Trey finally lets me go. He grins. "Now we smell alike."

I could murder him and think nothing of it. "Asshole."

Grandma comes out of the RV, pulling her robe together. "What's all this racket out here?"

Trey kisses her cheek. "Morning, beautiful."

She side-eyes him, but she's smiling as she smacks his chest. "Suck up all you want. Your granddaddy was ready to beat your behind for waking us up with that music."

"I still might," Granddaddy grumbles, coming down the RV steps. "And didn't I tell you not to pull that U-Haul with your car? You gon' mess up your transmission, boy."

"I was trying to save my amazing, wonderful grandparents some time," Trey says. "Instead of you bringing the RV all the way to my apartment, I figured I'd bring my trailer to you. Plus, I'm ready to hit the road with my Li'l Bit."

He is laying it on so damn thick. "Who said I'm riding back with you?" I ask.

"You did last night," Grandma says, 'cause I did. "Girl, stop acting stubborn. Just like your daddy."

Therefore just like her, but anyway.

"C'mon, Bri," Trey says. "I got snacks for days and the ultimate MJ playlist. How can you turn that down?"

Damn, he's going for low blows. He knows how much I love Michael. It started when I saw a YouTube video of the first time Mike performed "Billie Jean." I was six, and Michael was magic. The way he moved effortlessly. The way the crowd responded to every kick, every step. It didn't hurt that he had my last name. I loved him like I knew him.

I watched that performance until I learned every move. My grandparents played "Billie Jean" at family gatherings, and I put on a show. Cookouts, Sunday dinners, repasts, didn't matter. Everybody got a kick out of it, and I got a kick out of their reactions.

Yeah, dude had his problems—some stuff I won't even try to figure out—but his talent remained. No matter what, he was always Michael Fucking Jackson.

I wanna be like that. Wait, not exactly like that, no shade to Mike, but one day I want people to look at me and say, "Despite the fact this girl lost her father to gang violence, had a drug addict for a mom, and is technically a ghetto statistic, she's Brianna Fucking Jackson, and she's done some amazing shit."

Anyway, I can't turn down Michael Fucking Jackson. "All right, fine," I tell Trey. "I'll ride with your musty butt."

"Thank you, madam. But do something with that head before you get in my car. I ain't hitting the road with Medusa."

"I'll do something with my hair if you do something with your funk."

"Oooh!" he says. "Testy this morning."

It takes us a while to hit the road. I shower and get dressed, and Granddaddy tells Trey he needs to shower too 'cause he "smell like a goat's ass on a Friday night." How Granddaddy knows what a goat's ass smells like I don't know, and what a Friday night's gotta do with it I have no clue, but I believe him.

Trey and Granddaddy hook the U-Haul up to the RV, then Grandma tries to get us to eat the eggs, bacon, and toast she whips up. It's usually not in a Jackson's DNA to turn down food, but Trey acts like even the smell of it is getting to him. He throws some Advil back instead.

The funk, the rolled-out-of-bed look, the headache, the nerve to turn down food—my brother *clearly* has a hangover.

He's hiding it pretty well. I mean, when we finally get on the road, he blasts "Smooth Criminal" on high and sings it with me at the top of his lungs, and I know it's probably killing him to hear all that noise. That's true dedication to playing it off.

Neither of us knows exactly what Mike is saying in "Smooth Criminal" (like most people), so basically we sing what we think he's singing. We do know the "Annie, are you okay" part. I sing that, and Trey, in a high voice, ad-libs "No!" each time. "Smooth Criminal," the remix.

When "Man in the Mirror" comes on, Trey turns it down.

"All right," he says. "Time for me to face the man in my mirror and apologize to you."

"Soooo corny."

He laughs and pushes my shoulder. "I'm trying, okay? But for real, I'm sorry that I didn't tell you about my job. That was foul."

I nod. "It was."

"You're not gonna let up, are you?"

"Nope."

Trey shakes his head. "Petty Betty. But honestly, it was hard to talk to you, Bri. I was ashamed."

"Of what?"

"Here I am, fresh outta college, and I not only gotta move back home, I gotta make pizzas for a living," he says. "That's not an easy thing to deal with, you know? Shit makes you feel about this big." He barely holds his fingers apart. "And you've always looked up to me. I didn't want you to be disappointed. I'm already disappointed in myself."

Damn.

Guess who feels like shit personified?

That'd be me.

"You don't have to be ashamed. It's fine," I say. "Scratch that—not exactly fine, 'cause the situation is messed up, but it's not your fault."

"I guess. But hey, we're gonna make the best out of this."

"Even if we got evicted again?"

Trey nods slowly. "Yeah. Ma told me earlier. How you feeling about all of that?"

I rest my head back. Telling him I'm fine won't cut it. There's a reason my brother majored in psychology—he's always in somebody's business about their feelings. Now he has a degree to certify his nosiness. "I don't know," I tell him. "I know it could be a lot worse. . . ."

"It's messed up," he says.

"Yeah. Jay was already struggling to make things work, Trey," I whisper. "It'll only be worse now."

"We'll make it," he says. "Ma's working, and although it's

not the best job, I'll be bringing a check in too. Don't worry, all right? Your almighty, all-knowing big bro is coming to the rescue."

I snort. "I didn't know I had another big brother."

Trey laughs. "You're such a hater! But I promise, it'll be fine. Okay?" He holds his fist toward me.

I bump it. That's Trey. The fixer. Things can never go wrong on his watch.

He shouldn't have to fix this. He shouldn't even have to come back to Garden Heights. At Markham State he was literally king. Graduated with honors. Worked his ass off to get there in the first place, only to have to come back to the hood.

It's bullshit.

The kinda bullshit I now plan on avoiding too. "I got in the Ring," I tell him.

"Whaaat?" he says, and holds his palm toward me. I give him a high five. "That's what I'm talking 'bout! Congrats, Li'l Bit."

"Thanks. If I keep at it, maybe I can get a record deal. That'll change our—"

"Whoa." He looks over at me. "You're joking, right?"

"Why would I be joking?"

"A record deal? Really, Bri?" He kinda laughs.

"Yeah . . ." I trail off, waiting for the punch line. I feel sick all of a sudden. It's like he's saying it's funny that I think I'm good enough to get a deal.

"Hey, I'm not saying you're not good," he says, as if he read my mind. "You're damn good. A beast, in fact. But I thought you only rapped for fun?"

"I mean, I used to. But did you hear about Dee-Nice? I think he went to Midtown with you. He just signed a million-dollar deal. A million dollars, Trey!"

"He's the exception, not the rule. Look, I'm not trying to be a pessimist here—"

"You're not?"

"Hear me out, Bri. That rap stuff, it seems all glitz and glamour, but the industry is no joke. Nothing is guaranteed. Look at Pops."

"He's a legend."

"Yeah, a legend who got caught up in some gang shit, and left us with much of nothing."

He's not even talking about me, and I still feel the sting of that.

"Then you got damn near a million folks in the Garden alone who claim they're rappers," he says, "like that's the only thing black people can do. Entertain. Yeah, you're good at it, but you're also smart, Bri. Endless possibilities ahead of you. Why sell yourself short with some rap shit?"

Because it seems like the only thing that'll get me out of the Garden.

THIS WILL Change your LIFE with A FEW Lines.

I GET ON
the MIC
'Cause
IT'S
MY LIFE.

AN *ON THE COME UP* PLAYLIST

1. "Rapper's Delight" by Sugarhill Gang (1979)

This song is the genesis of hip-hop, so it's only right that I include it. "Rapper's Delight" introduced the world to hip-hop and to the art of rapping. Originally, I planned to name every chapter after an iconic hip-hop song, so, naturally, this would've been the first chapter.

2. "The Message" by Grandmaster Flash and the Furious Five (1982)

Another old school classic, "The Message" is considered to be the first socially conscious hip-hop song—Kendrick Lamar couldn't do what he does now if it weren't for Grandmaster Flash and the Furious Five. Although it was first recorded back in the '80s, the message (pun intended) is still relevant. So many of Bri's experiences are described in the song, especially in the last verse.

3. "U.N.I.T.Y." by Queen Latifah (1993)

All hail the queen! Queen Latifah is one of my personal heroes.

As a kid, it was incredible to see a Black woman not only holding her own in hip-hop but doing it her way. "U.N.I.T.Y." is one of the most empowering songs that exists in hip-hop. Of course, it's an anthem for Bri.

4. "I Used to Love H.E.R." by Common (1994)

This is probably one of the most important songs for *On the Come Up*—it IS *On the Come Up*. In this classic track, Common personifies hip-hop by describing her as a young lady trying to find her way. That's exactly who Bri is, so in turn, Bri is a personification of hip-hop. Reread the book with that in mind.

5. "Sky's the Limit" by the Notorious B.I.G. (1997)

Yes, I am a 2Pac fan, and yes, I like Biggie's music, too. It's not a crime; I swear it's not. "Sky's the Limit" influenced *On the Come Up* in a lot of ways; for one, the phrase is Bri and Pooh's motto. But the song itself is all about finding a way to make it despite your circumstances. That's Bri to a T.

6. "Sojourner" by Rapsody (2018)

Stop whatever you're doing and go add Rapsody to your playlist RIGHT NOW. Her latest album, *Eve*, is a masterpiece from beginning to end. This song is just one of many that displays her brilliance. If Bri were real, she would strive to be as dope as Rapsody.

7. "Juicy" by the Notorious B.I.G. (1994)

Yes, there's another Biggie song on this list. "Juicy" is the ultimate theme song for anyone trying to get their come up.

8. "Alright" by Kendrick Lamar (2015)

This song is essential to both *On the Come Up* and *The Hate U Give*—I think it would be an anthem for Bri and Starr. It's all about fighting against difficult circumstances, and that's something both girls can connect with.

9. "Did It On 'Em" by Nicki Minaj (2010)

I could see Bri channeling her inner Nicki as she gears up to record "On the Come Up," and she would use this song to do it. It would also speak to her later on as she deals with the backlash. She did it on 'em.

10. "Apparently" by J. Cole (2014)

This song would definitely speak to Bri. In the hook, J. Cole talks about wanting his dreams to rescue him, and that's Bri 100%. The first verse is dedicated to his mom, and he apologizes for not being there for her enough. Considering Bri's complicated relationship with Jay, it would strike a chord.

ROYALTY in my BLOOD, DIDN'T Choose IT.

MY TOP 5 MCS

1. 2Pac

Anyone who knows me knows that I'm a huge 2Pac fan, so this is a no-brainer. You can find a 2Pac song for every mood and every occasion. On top of that, he was revolutionary beyond the mic. I can only imagine what he would be doing if he were alive now—it would've shaken the world, for sure. This is why, in my eyes, he will always be the GOAT—Greatest of All Time.

2. Notorious B.I.G.

Like I said—yes, I like both 2Pac and Biggie. Even to this day, Biggie is the undisputed King of New York. There's no other rapper with a flow like his—it was effortless. His wordplay was legendary.

3. Lauryn Hill

With one album, Lauryn Hill created a masterpiece. She is truly one of the best lyricists to ever touch a mic, and although *The Miseducation of Lauryn Hill* is over twenty years old, it somehow sounds as if it were made yesterday—it's timeless.

4. André 3000

As a southerner, I will always include André 3000 of Outkast on my top MC lists. Always. He showed the world that southern rappers could hold their own, too.

5. Nas

Nas's first album, *Illmatic*, is arguably the greatest hip-hop album ever recorded. He more than earned a spot on this list.

That

FLOW

THOUGH!

ANGIE'S NOTES ON BRI'S BATTLE RAP

I underline all rhymes in order to craft the flow. This includes internal rhymes (IR). They're just as important as end rhymes and add variety.

My apologies, see, I forgot my manners. — start with a word that's easy to rhyme with
I get on the mic 'cause it's my life. You show off for girls and cameras.
You a pop star, not a rapper. A Vanilla Ice or a Hammer.
Y'all hear this crap he dumping out? Somebody get him a Pamper.
And a crown for me. The best have heard about me.
You can only spell brilliant by first spelling Bri. — No matter what, this line was a must
You see, naturally, I do my shit with perfection.
Better call a bodyguard, cause you gon' need some protection,
And on this here election, the people crown a new leader. — I wrote this post 2016 election
You didn't see this coming, and your ghostwriters didn't either. → IR
I came here to ether. I'm sorry to do this to you. — Ether is the greatest diss song ever
This is no longer a battle, it's your funeral, boo. I'm murdering you.
On my corner they call me coroner, I'm warning ya. — Another IR. Say each syllable in coroner for it to pack a punch
Tell the truth, this dude is borin' ya.
You confused like a foreigner, I'll explain with ease:
You're just a casualty in the reality of the madness of Bri.
No fallacies, I spit maladies, causin' fatalities,
And do it casually, damaging rappers without bandaging.
Imagining managing my own label, my own salary.
And actually, factually, there's no MC that's as bad as me. — Phrases can rhyme too

Big Pun inspired this flow, too. R.I.P.

Milez? That's cute. But it don't make me cower.
I move at light speed, you stuck at per hour. — this was a must, too. I had to play with his name
You spit like a lisp. I spit like a high power.
Bri's the future, and you Today like Matt Lauer.
You coward. But you're a G? It ain't convincing to me. — Another IR
You talk about your clothes, about your shopping sprees.
You talk about your Glock, about your i-c-e.
But in this here ring, they all talking 'bout me,
Bri!

(Left margin: Internal Rhyme (IR); Not a rhyme but using 2 one-syllable words makes the flow smoother)

I always wanted to end with Bri's name. Names are powerful, and for a girl who feels powerless, it's important that she remind people of hers.

AN EXCLUSIVE SNEAK PEEK FROM

CONCRETE ROSE

CHAPTER ONE

It was only one time. Not just that, but it was the only time I ever slipped up. Ever. Unless God got some vendetta against me, ain't no way.

Maybe he do got something against me. It seem like it sometimes.

To be real, I ain't wanna go through all this, but Ma think it's best we find out the truth now instead of later. She right by my side in the waiting room. Her leg won't stay still, like she wanna get up and run out this clinic, away from this. Away from me. But she never run from me. Go off on me? Hell yeah. She do that all the time. But she never run.

I wanna run. For real, I wanna run. But in seventeen years, Maverick Carter ain't ran from shit, so I stay in my seat.

The free clinic is real busy for a Thursday morning. Everybody in the Garden would rather come here than go to the ER at County. Folks who go to County rarely go home. Some man on crutches talk loud as hell on the pay phone. I think he want all of us to hear that he need a ride home. Somehow the old lady in the wheelchair next to us ain't woke up 'cause of his loud ass. A girl around my age chase this snot-nosed kid and call after him in Spanish.

Depending on what this DNA test says, that might be me in two years, chasing my son.

Ma glance at her watch, this gold joint with diamonds that Pops gave her before the Feds took him down. "Maverick, what time did she say she was coming?"

"She didn't. I ain't heard from her since the other day."

Ma pinch the space between her eyes. "Lord. We gon' have our hands full with this girl."

Ma always talks to God. It's usually, "Lord, this boy getting on my last nerve," or "Lord, keep me from hurting this boy." Guess it's nice she talking to him 'bout somebody else for once.

Let her tell it, I got her aging early from stress. She keep her hair cut shorter than mine and got a couple of grays she shouldn't have at thirty-eight. Her brown eyes got dark circles under them. But all that ain't my fault. It's from them long hours she work. Ma check people into a hotel during the day and clean offices at night. I tell her all the time, "I'm gon' take care of you one day." She smile and say, "Take care of yourself, Maverick. That's all I need."

For weeks it's been, "Take care of your son." She convinced I'm his daddy.

"Why we doing this?" I mumble. "He ain't mine."

"You don't know that. Don't tell me it was only one time. All it takes is once."

"But he King's baby, Ma. They named him after King."

"Yeah, but who does he look like?"

She got me there. When King Jr. was born three months ago, he ain't really look like anybody. All newborns look like aliens if you ask me. After a couple of weeks, he got the same dark complexion as me, the same wide eyes as me, same nose, lips, thick eyebrows. King was nowhere to be found. The baby don't even look like Iesha.

How I possibly get my best friend's girlfriend pregnant? First off, King don't claim Iesha. They mess around, but King say they just homies. Iesha wanna be his girl though.

About a year ago, I was over at King's crib, stressed out. Lisa had broke up with me after her brother said he saw me with another girl. A straight-up lie—it was really my cousin, Dre, he saw—but Lisa believed it. I went to King's house to clear my head. King told Iesha to hook me up, and she do whatever he say. King meant one thing, but it led to another, and here I am at the free clinic, waiting for DNA test results.

Messed up, I know.

My beeper go off. Dre's number pop up on the screen, but I slide it back in my pocket. I'll have to hit him up later.

Ma watch me with a smile. "You think you something 'cause you got a pager now, huh?"

I laugh. "Nah, Ma. Never that."

"I'm proud of you for getting that job, Maverick. How's it been at the warehouse?"

"Good," I lie.

"They're willing to work with your school schedule?"

Summer vacation end in 'bout two weeks. "Yes, ma'am."

"Good. Long as they know your education is the most important thing."

They don't know. They don't know me. Ma think I got a part-time job at UPS. She can't know what I really do to afford this pager, my clothes, and sneakers. She'd kick me out.

Ms. Robinson come in the clinic in her McDonald's uniform. She hold the door open for somebody. "Bring your ass in here, girl!"

Iesha walk in, rolling her eyes. She got a car seat in her hand and a baby bag on her shoulder. It's hot as hell today, and she wearing a tank top with these tight booty shorts that's hitting in all the right places. But I can't be looking at her like that. One, me and Lisa back together, and I wanna keep it that way, and two, what's in them shorts put me in this position in the first place.

Li'l man is knocked out in the car seat. He got his fist against his head and his eyebrows all wrinkled up, like he thinking 'bout something deep in his dreams.

I always notice stuff like that 'bout him. I don't think that make me his daddy.

"Hey, Faye," Ms. Robinson says to Ma. "Sorry we late."

Ma goes, "Mmmhmm." It ain't approval or judgment.

Then she look at me, like she expect me to do something.

"Oh, my bad." I give Iesha my seat. I forget to be a gentleman sometimes.

Iesha set the car seat on the floor in front of her. All of a sudden, Ma is starstruck.

"Aww, look at that li'l man," she says in that voice she only use on babies. "He knocked out, huh?"

"Finally," says Iesha. "Kept me up all night."

"Ain't like you had nowhere to go," Ms. Robinson snips. "Miss I-skip-summer-school-to-chase-some-boy."

"Oh my God," Iesha groans.

"He'll sleep through the night before you know it," Ma says. She tryna keep them from arguing. "Maverick didn't sleep through the night until he was about five months old. It was like he needed to know what was going on all the time."

"He the exact same way," Ms. Robinson says.

That don't make him mine.

"How Adonis doing, Faye?" Ms. Robinson asks.

"Making it. Tryna keep this one in check." She point at me.

My pops been in prison since I was eight. He call Ma every week, but I don't talk to him anymore. He always try to be on some father shit, telling me what to do. Nah, man. When you locked up, you lose that "daddy" power. For real.

"Tell him we're praying for him," Ms. Robinson says. "Neighborhood ain't the same without Big Don."

Ma's eyes get all dim. "Definitely ain't."

I hate that she still get sad over him just like I hate that she gotta work hard 'cause he messed up. I hate that she still love him. He don't deserve it. I told her that once, and she was like, "Do you deserve everything you get, Maverick?" I couldn't answer that.

Li'l man whine in the car seat.

Iesha sighs. "What now?"

I know she tired, but damn. "He probably want his pacifier, Iesha. Chill."

She put it in his mouth, and like I thought, he good.

I study Iesha real hard. She got circles under her eyes that's darker than Ma's. "King been helping you any?"

"No," her momma says for her. "He claims since the baby may not be his, he has no reason to help."

But he named the baby after him. How he gon' leave Iesha hanging like that?

Me and King ain't really talked 'bout all this since the baby started looking like me. He said, "Shit happens" and left it at that. But that's King. He say the same thing 'bout his parents getting murdered when he was twelve and 'bout the stuff he went through with all them foster parents he had. Shit happens.

We cool, far as I can tell.

"It's fine," Iesha claims.

"No, it's not," Ma says. "This is a lot for anyone to handle on their own, let alone a seventeen-year-old. You're a baby, baby."

"No, she ain't," Ms. Robinson says. "She wanna act grown, she can deal with this like she grown."

Iesha blink real fast.

I bend down in front of her. Did I ask for this? Nah. But she didn't either. "Look, if he is mine, you won't be doing this by yourself."

Five seconds ago, baby girl looked like she was 'bout to cry. Now she smirk at me. "Oh, word? Your girlfriend gon' be cool with that?"

I've tried not to think 'bout that a lot. Real talk, I don't know how Lisa gon' react. I haven't told her 'bout any of this. Not 'bout me and Iesha messing around that one time, not 'bout the baby. I figured if he wasn't mine, she didn't need to know. But if he is . . .

"Don't worry 'bout her," I tell Iesha.

"I ain't worried. But you should be. Her stuck-up ass gon' drop you when she find out."

"Ay, don't talk 'bout her like that!"

She roll her eyes. "Whatever. All them girls around school who drool over you, and you go for the bougie Catholic school girl. It's all good though. My baby ain't yours. Soon as I leave here, I'm taking him to his real daddy, and we gon' be a family."

"Oh, your li'l fast ass is more than welcome to go," Ms. Robinson says. "I got enough to worry about with your brothers and sisters. I don't need to deal with you."

"Whatever," Iesha says. "King gon' take care of me and my baby. Watch."

"Iesha Robinson!" the nurse calls.

All four of us look toward the desk.

This is it.

"Go on," Ms. Robinson tells Iesha.

Iesha sigh outta her nose as she get up. "This so stupid."

"What's stupid is that two boys could be the damn daddy!" her momma calls after her. "That's what's stupid!"

Now, straight up, me and Ma can get into it. But in public like this? Man, nah.

Iesha open the envelope as she come back over. She take the papers out and shove them into her momma's hands. "See? Told you!"

She ain't even looked at them.

Ms. Robinson read the results. By that smug look she get, I already know what they say.

"Congratulations, Maverick," she says, staring at her daughter. "You're a father."

Shit.

"Jesus." Ma hold her forehead. She been saying that he mine but saying it and knowing it two different things.

Iesha snatch the papers. She look them over, and her face fall. "Shit, no!"

Damn, it's like that? "What you mad for?" I ask.

"This supposed to be King's baby! I don't wanna deal with your ass!"

"I don't wanna deal with your ass either!"

"Maverick!" Ma snaps.

My son cry in the car seat.

Ma cut me a hard glare before she pick him up. "What's wrong, Man-Man? Huh?" she ask as she rub his back. She don't have to know you long to give you a nickname. Ma sniff near his butt, and her nose wrinkle. "Oh, I know what's wrong. Where are his diapers?"

"In the baby bag," Iesha mumbles.

"Grab the bag, Maverick," Ma says. "We'll handle this."

All of a sudden, I got a son and he got a dirty diaper. "I don't know how to change a diaper, Ma."

"Then it's time for you to learn. C'mon."

I follow her, but Ma don't go to the men's room. Nah, she walk right into the women's room and act like I'm supposed to follow her in there. Hell nah.

She come back to the door. "Boy, c'mon."

"I can't go in there!"

"Ain't nobody in here, and you're not doing anything perverted. Until they put changing tables in the men's restroom, come on."

Damn, this ain't cool, but I follow her in. Li'l man cry his head off. I get why. That diaper stank.

Ma hand him to me and search the diaper bag. "They sure got a lot of clothes in here. Let's see if she's got some changing pads. If she doesn't, I'll pick some—never mind, she does." Ma put one on the table. "All right, lay him down."

"What if he fall off?"

"He won't. There you go," she says as I lay him down. "Now you gotta unbutton his—"

I miss the rest. I'm staring at him.

Before when I'd look at him, I was in awe that he existed,

and that I possibly had something to do with it. Now I look at him and he mine, no question 'bout it.

Worst part? I'm his.

I didn't know what to feel earlier. Or maybe I felt everything I'm feeling right now and them papers made it clearer.

I'm scared.

I messed up.

I'm not eighteen yet. I only been seventeen for a month, and now I gotta take care of another person.

He need me.

He depending on me.

He gon' call me "Daddy."

"Maverick?"

Ma's hand on my shoulder. My eyes meet hers.

"You got this," she says. "I got you."

I doubt she only mean the diaper. "A'ight."

I change my first diaper with her help. This nurse come in and see us struggling—it's been a while since Ma did this—and she give us some tips, too.

Li'l man is clean, but he still fussy. I hold him against my shoulder and bounce him a bit.

"It's a'ight, man. We good."

Guess that's all he need to know, 'cause he calm down.

Ma grab his bag for me, and we head to the waiting room. My son's car seat is on the floor, and the DNA papers lie inside of it, but Ms. Robinson is gone.

So is Iesha.